Jackie Ball • Mollie Rose • Natalia

GOLDIE VANCE ™

Larceny in La La Land

BOOM!
BOX ™

GOLDIE

Ross Richie CEO & Founder
Joy Huffman CFO
Matt Gagnon Editor-in-Chief
Filip Sablik President, Publishing & Marketing
Stephen Christy President, Development
Lance Kreiter Vice President, Licensing & Merchandising
Arune Singh Vice President, Marketing
Bryce Carlson Vice President, Editorial & Creative Strategy
Kate Henning Director, Operations
Spencer Simpson Director, Sales
Scott Newman Manager, Production Design
Elyse Strandberg Manager, Finance
Sierra Hahn Executive Editor
Jeanine Schaefer Executive Editor
Dafna Pleban Senior Editor

Shannon Watters Senior Editor
Eric Harburn Senior Editor
Matthew Levine Editor
Sophie Philips-Roberts Associate Editor
Amanda LaFranco Associate Editor
Jonathan Manning Associate Editor
Gavin Gronenthal Assistant Editor
Gwen Waller Assistant Editor
Allyson Gronowitz Assistant Editor
Ramiro Portnoy Assistant Editor
Shelby Netschke Editorial Assistant
Michelle Ankley Design Coordinator
Marie Krupina Production Designer
Grace Park Production Designer
Chelsea Roberts Production Designer

Samantha Knapp Production Design Assistant
José Meza Live Events Lead
Stephanie Hocutt Digital Marketing Lead
Esther Kim Marketing Coordinator
Cat O'Grady Digital Marketing Coordinator
Breanna Sarpy Live Events Coordinator
Amanda Lawson Marketing Assistant
Holly Aitchison Digital Sales Coordinator
Morgan Perry Retail Sales Coordinator
Megan Christopher Operations Coordinator
Rodrigo Hernandez Operations Coordinator
Zipporah Smith Operations Assistant
Jason Lee Senior Accountant
Sabrina Lesin Accounting Assistant

BOOM! BOX™

GOLDIE VANCE: LARCENY IN LA LA LAND Volume Five, July 2020. Published by BOOM! Box, a division of Boom Entertainment, Inc. Goldie Vance is ™ & © 2020 Hope Larson & Brittney Williams. All rights reserved. BOOM! Box™ and the BOOM! Box logo are trademarks of Boom Entertainment, Inc., registered in various countries and categories. All characters, events, and institutions depicted herein are fictional. Any similarity between any of the names, characters, persons, events, and/or institutions in this publication to actual names, characters, and persons, whether living or dead, events, and/or institutions is unintended and purely coincidental. BOOM! Box does not read or accept unsolicited submissions of ideas, stories, or artwork.

BOOM! Studios, 5670 Wilshire Boulevard, Suite 400, Los Angeles, CA 90036-5679. Printed in China. First Printing.

ISBN: 978-1-68415-544-6, eISBN: 978-1-64144-710-2

VANCE™

created by **Hope Larson** & **Brittney Williams**

written by
Jackie Ball

illustrated by
Mollie Rose
with additional inks by **Lea Caballero**

colors by
Natalia Nesterenko

letters by
Jim Campbell

cover by
Brittney Williams

designers
**Jillian Crab
& Chelsea Roberts**

associate editor
Sophie Philips-Roberts

editor
Shannon Watters

chapter
SEVENTEEN

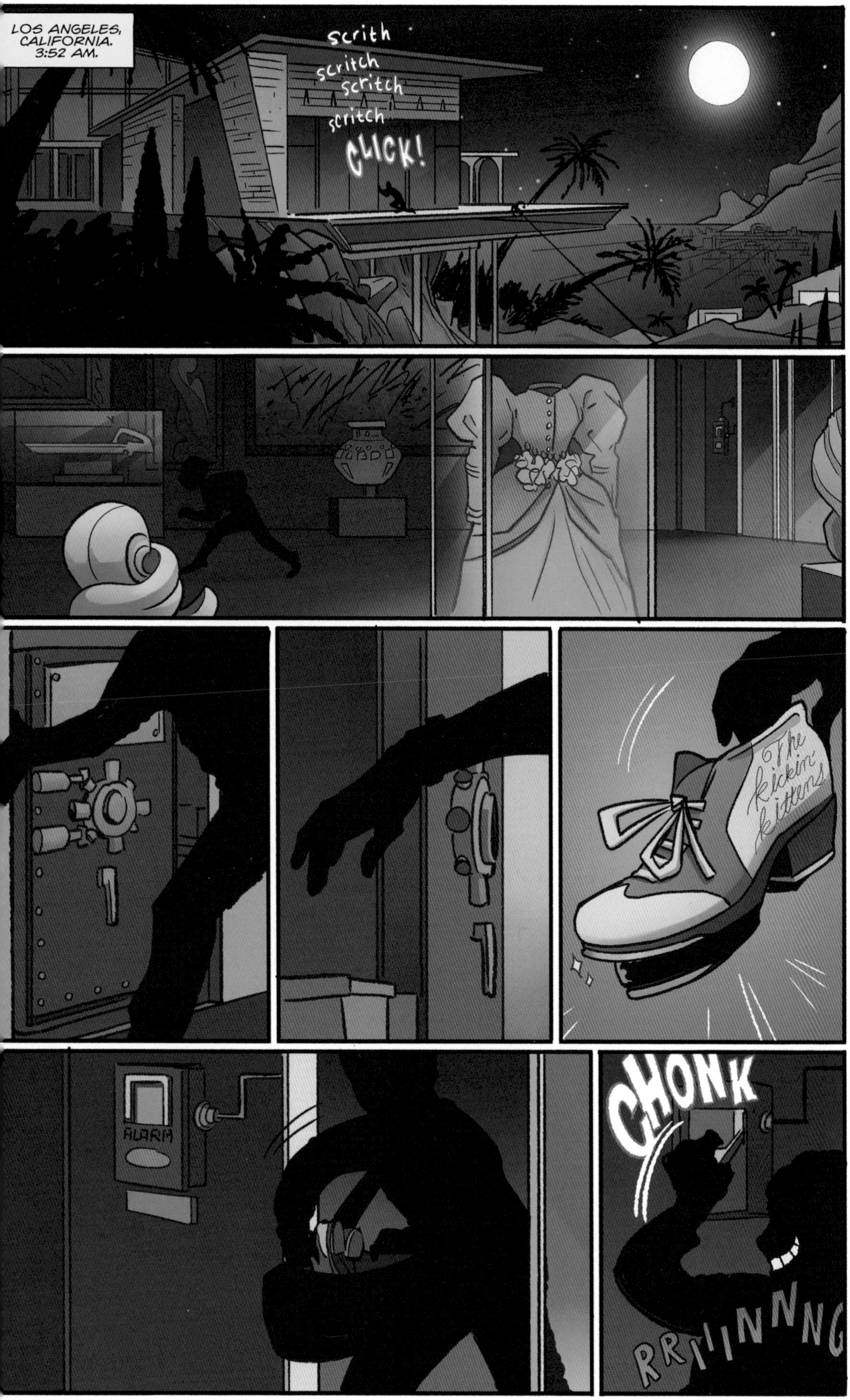
LOS ANGELES, CALIFORNIA. 3:52 AM.
scrith
scritch
scritch
scritch
CLICK!
The kickin' kittens
ALARM
CHONK
RRIIINNNG

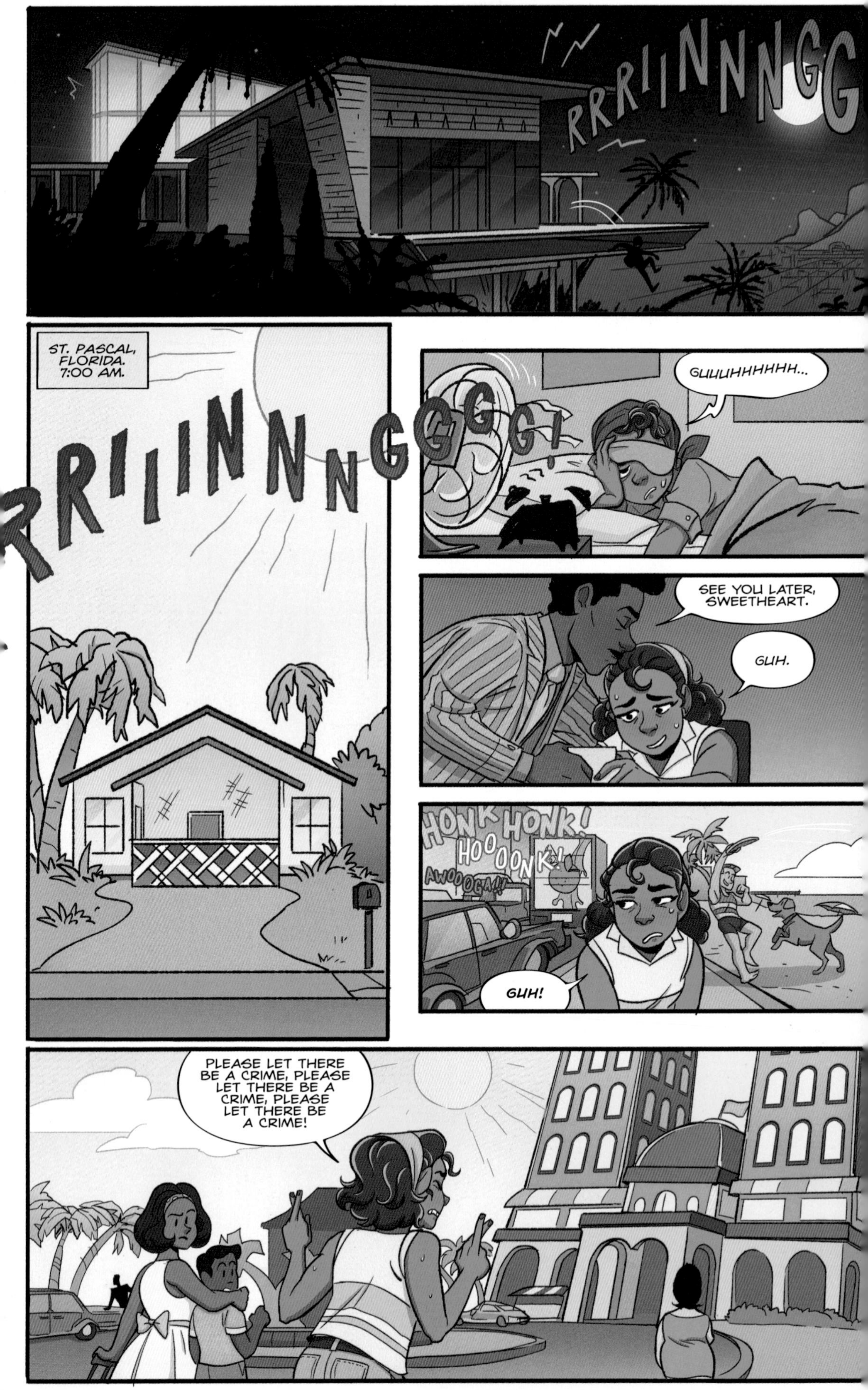

RRRIINNNGG
ST. PASCAL, FLORIDA. 7:00 AM.
RRIIINNNGGG!
GUUUHHHHHH...
SEE YOU LATER, SWEETHEART.
GUH.
HONK HONK!
HOOOONK!
AWOOOGA!!
GUH!
PLEASE LET THERE BE A CRIME, PLEASE LET THERE BE A CRIME, PLEASE LET THERE BE A CRIME!

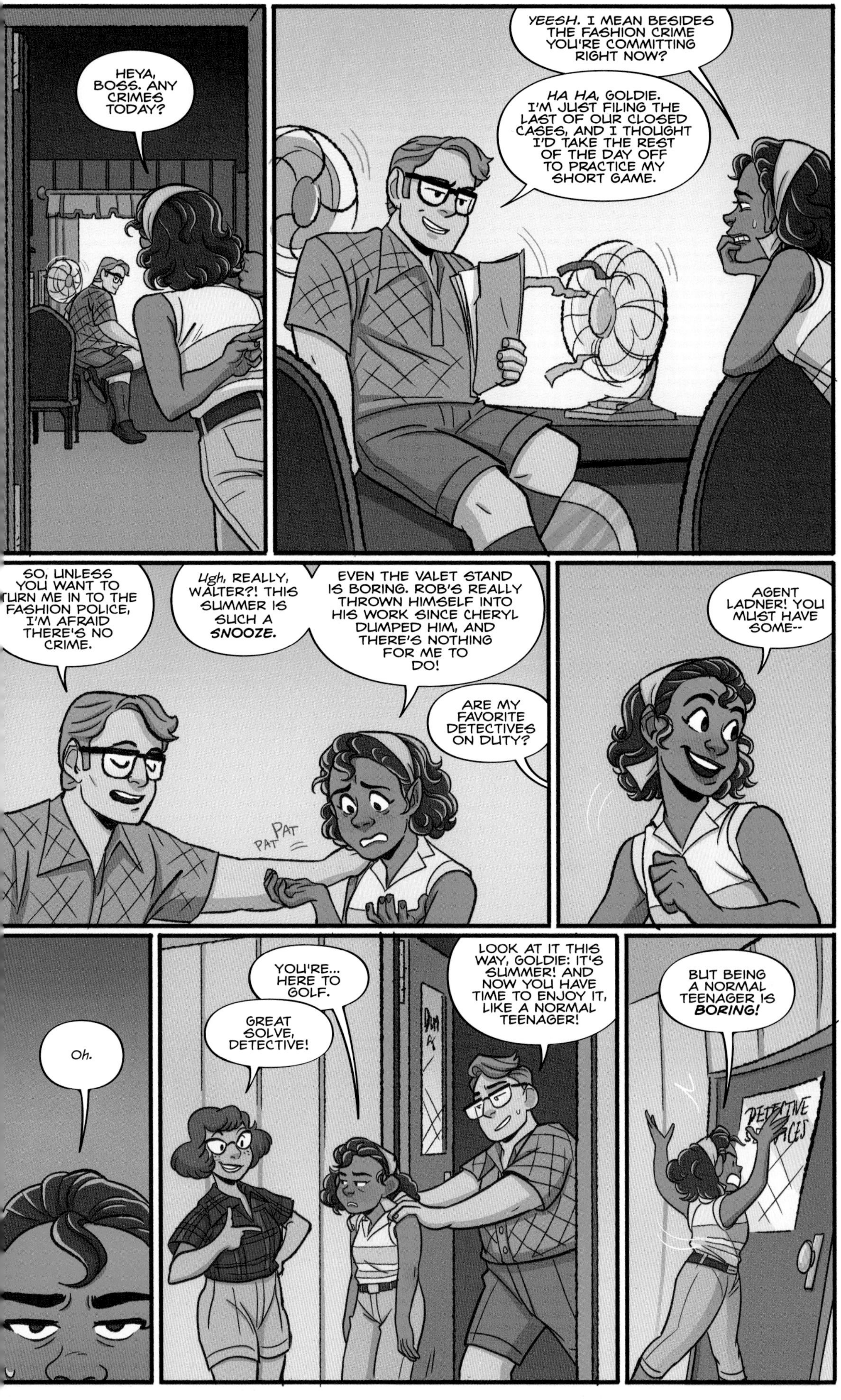
HEYA, BOSS. ANY CRIMES TODAY?
YEESH. I MEAN BESIDES THE FASHION CRIME YOU'RE COMMITTING RIGHT NOW?
HA HA, GOLDIE. I'M JUST FILING THE LAST OF OUR CLOSED CASES, AND I THOUGHT I'D TAKE THE REST OF THE DAY OFF TO PRACTICE MY SHORT GAME.
SO, UNLESS YOU WANT TO TURN ME IN TO THE FASHION POLICE, I'M AFRAID THERE'S NO CRIME.
Ugh, REALLY, WALTER?! THIS SUMMER IS SUCH A SNOOZE.
EVEN THE VALET STAND IS BORING. ROB'S REALLY THROWN HIMSELF INTO HIS WORK SINCE CHERYL DUMPED HIM, AND THERE'S NOTHING FOR ME TO DO!
PAT PAT
ARE MY FAVORITE DETECTIVES ON DUTY?
AGENT LADNER! YOU MUST HAVE SOME--
Oh.
YOU'RE... HERE TO GOLF.
GREAT SOLVE, DETECTIVE!
LOOK AT IT THIS WAY, GOLDIE: IT'S SUMMER! AND NOW YOU HAVE TIME TO ENJOY IT, LIKE A NORMAL TEENAGER!
BUT BEING A NORMAL TEENAGER IS BORING!

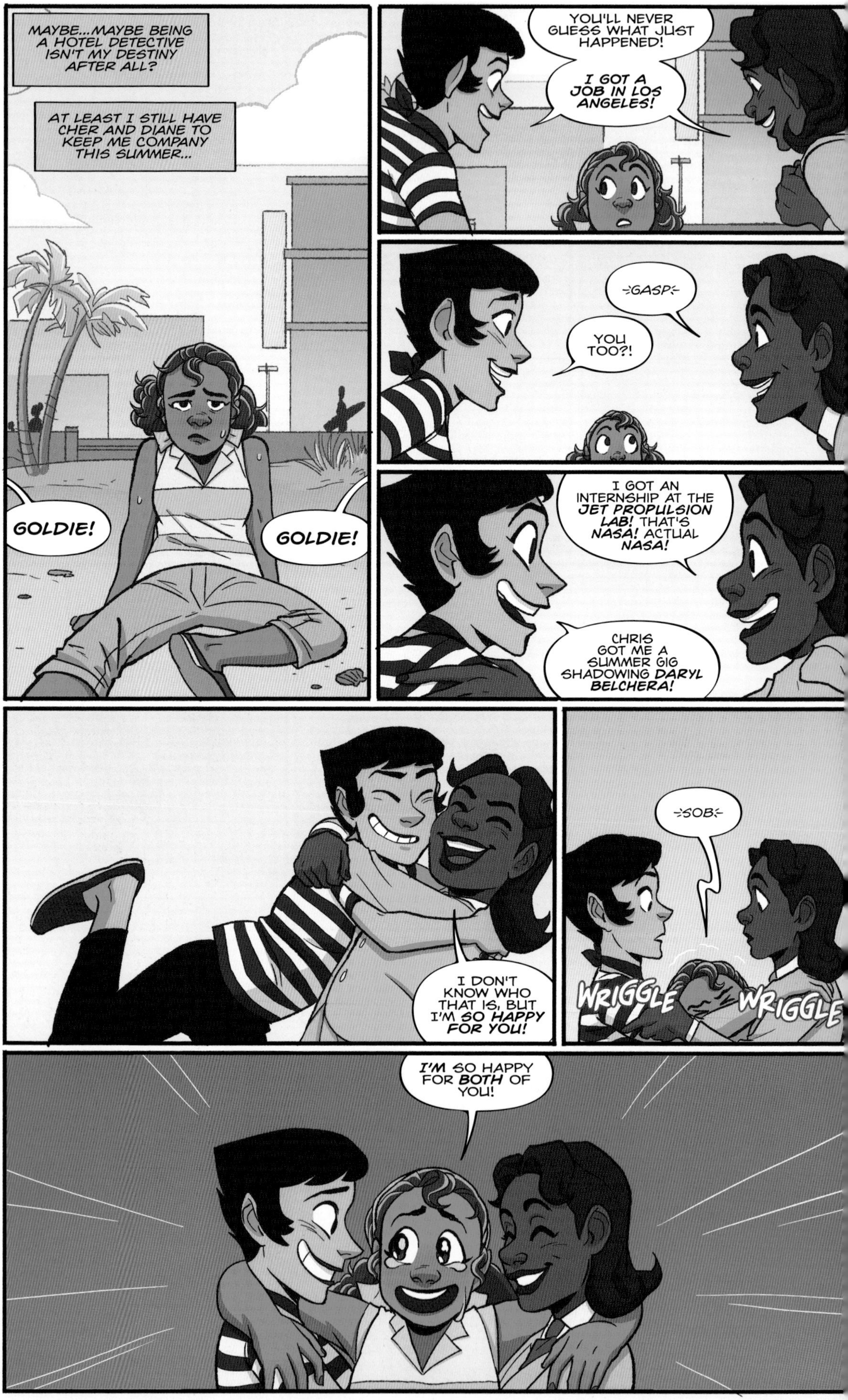
MAYBE...MAYBE BEING A HOTEL DETECTIVE ISN'T MY DESTINY AFTER ALL?
AT LEAST I STILL HAVE CHER AND DIANE TO KEEP ME COMPANY THIS SUMMER...
GOLDIE!
GOLDIE!
YOU'LL NEVER GUESS WHAT JUST HAPPENED!
I GOT A JOB IN LOS ANGELES!
GASP
YOU TOO?!
I GOT AN INTERNSHIP AT THE JET PROPULSION LAB! THAT'S NASA! ACTUAL NASA!
CHRIS GOT ME A SUMMER GIG SHADOWING DARYL BELCHERA!
I DON'T KNOW WHO THAT IS, BUT I'M SO HAPPY FOR YOU!
SOB
WRIGGLE
WRIGGLE
I'M SO HAPPY FOR BOTH OF YOU!

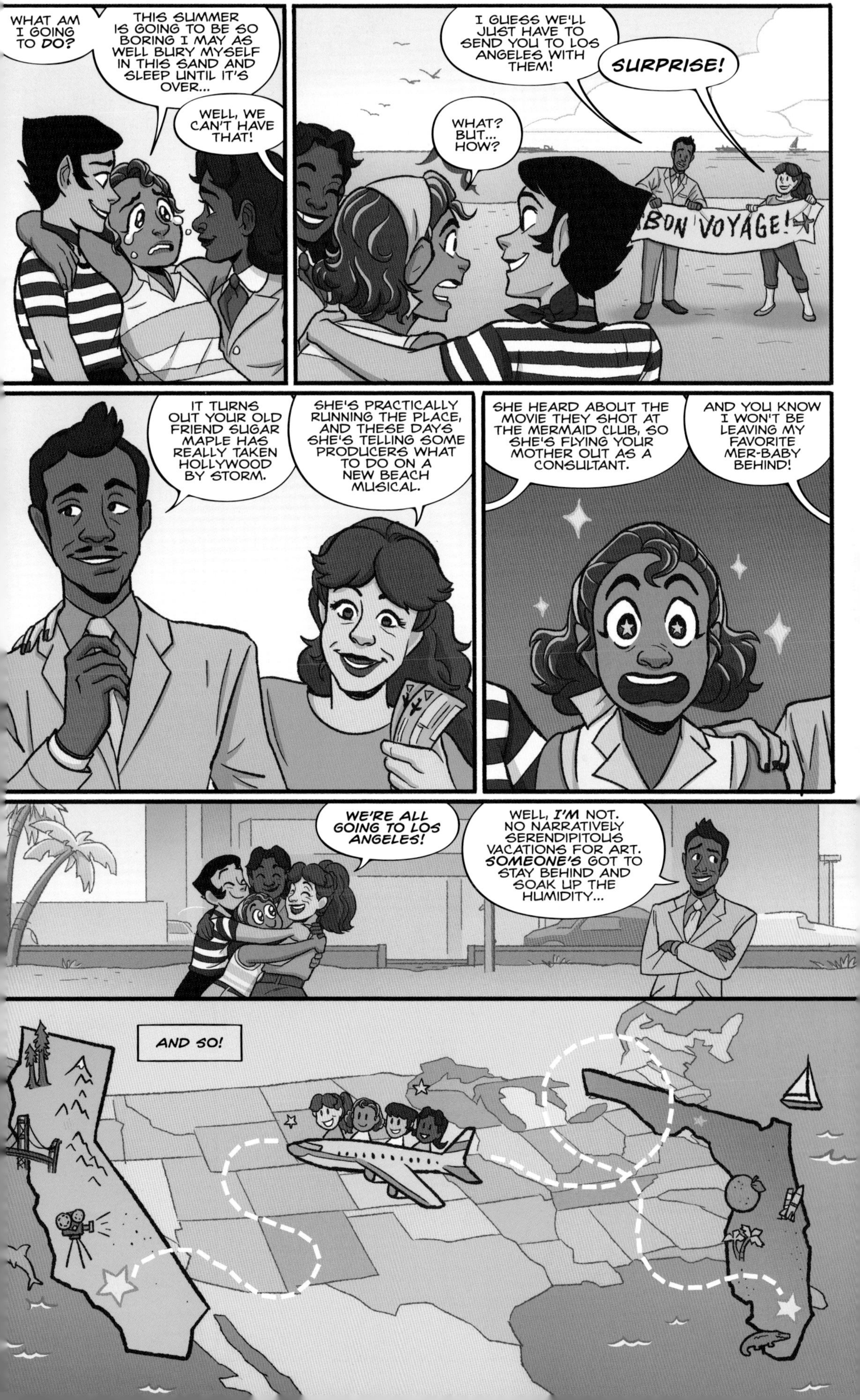

WHAT AM I GOING TO DO?
THIS SUMMER IS GOING TO BE SO BORING I MAY AS WELL BURY MYSELF IN THIS SAND AND SLEEP UNTIL IT'S OVER...
WELL, WE CAN'T HAVE THAT!
I GUESS WE'LL JUST HAVE TO SEND YOU TO LOS ANGELES WITH THEM!
SURPRISE!
WHAT? BUT... HOW?
BON VOYAGE!
IT TURNS OUT YOUR OLD FRIEND SUGAR MAPLE HAS REALLY TAKEN HOLLYWOOD BY STORM.
SHE'S PRACTICALLY RUNNING THE PLACE, AND THESE DAYS SHE'S TELLING SOME PRODUCERS WHAT TO DO ON A NEW BEACH MUSICAL.
SHE HEARD ABOUT THE MOVIE THEY SHOT AT THE MERMAID CLUB, SO SHE'S FLYING YOUR MOTHER OUT AS A CONSULTANT.
AND YOU KNOW I WON'T BE LEAVING MY FAVORITE MER-BABY BEHIND!
WE'RE ALL GOING TO LOS ANGELES!
WELL, I'M NOT. NO NARRATIVELY SERENDIPITOUS VACATIONS FOR ART. SOMEONE'S GOT TO STAY BEHIND AND SOAK UP THE HUMIDITY...
AND SO!

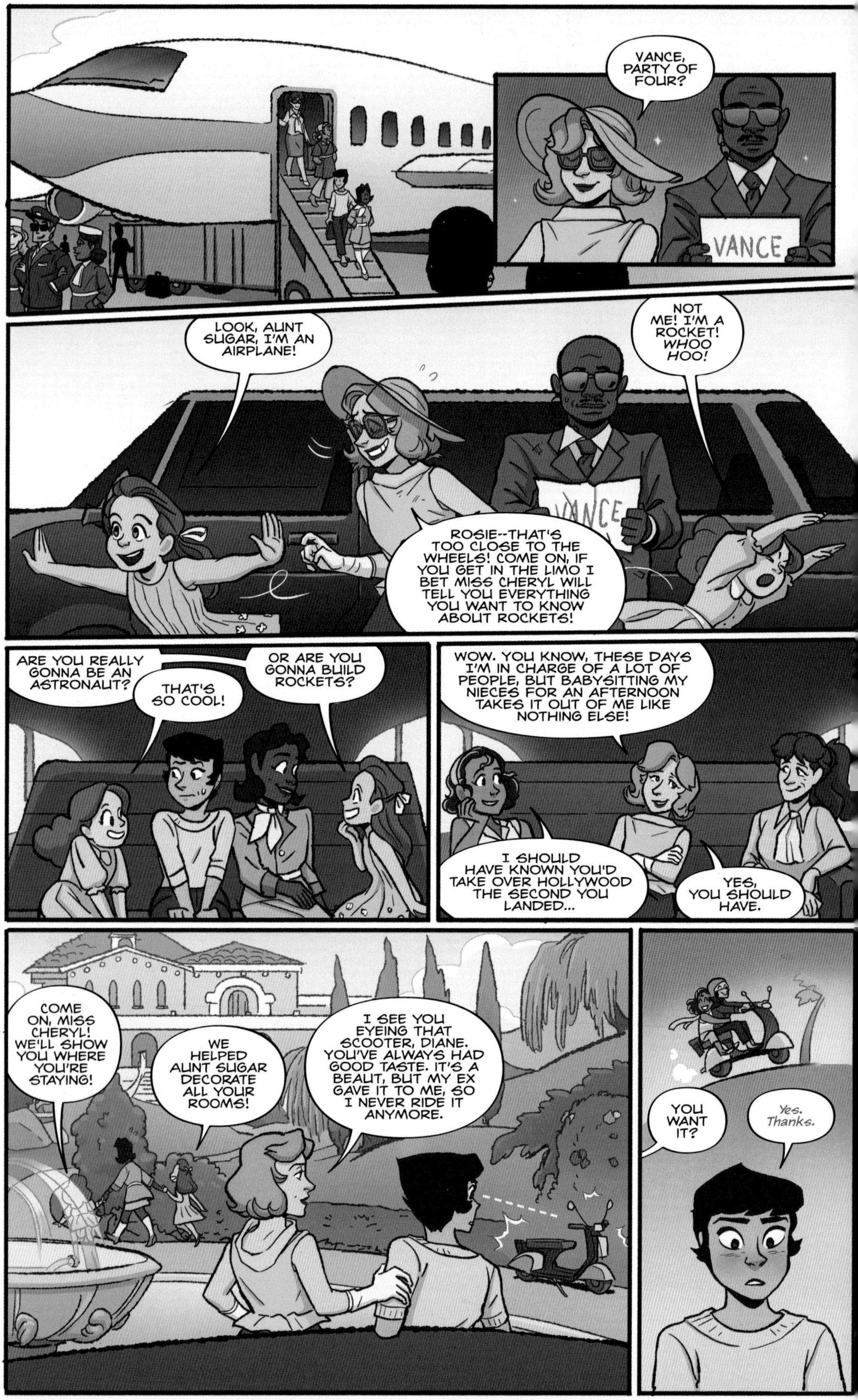
VANCE, PARTY OF FOUR?
VANCE
LOOK, AUNT SUGAR, I'M AN AIRPLANE!
NOT ME! I'M A ROCKET! WHOO HOO!
ROSIE--THAT'S TOO CLOSE TO THE WHEELS! COME ON, IF YOU GET IN THE LIMO I BET MISS CHERYL WILL TELL YOU EVERYTHING YOU WANT TO KNOW ABOUT ROCKETS!
ARE YOU REALLY GONNA BE AN ASTRONAUT?
THAT'S SO COOL!
OR ARE YOU GONNA BUILD ROCKETS?
WOW. YOU KNOW, THESE DAYS I'M IN CHARGE OF A LOT OF PEOPLE, BUT BABYSITTING MY NIECES FOR AN AFTERNOON TAKES IT OUT OF ME LIKE NOTHING ELSE!
I SHOULD HAVE KNOWN YOU'D TAKE OVER HOLLYWOOD THE SECOND YOU LANDED...
YES, YOU SHOULD HAVE.
COME ON, MISS CHERYL! WE'LL SHOW YOU WHERE YOU'RE STAYING!
WE HELPED AUNT SUGAR DECORATE ALL YOUR ROOMS!
I SEE YOU EYEING THAT SCOOTER, DIANE. YOU'VE ALWAYS HAD GOOD TASTE. IT'S A BEAUT, BUT MY EX GAVE IT TO ME, SO I NEVER RIDE IT ANYMORE.
YOU WANT IT?
Yes. Thanks.

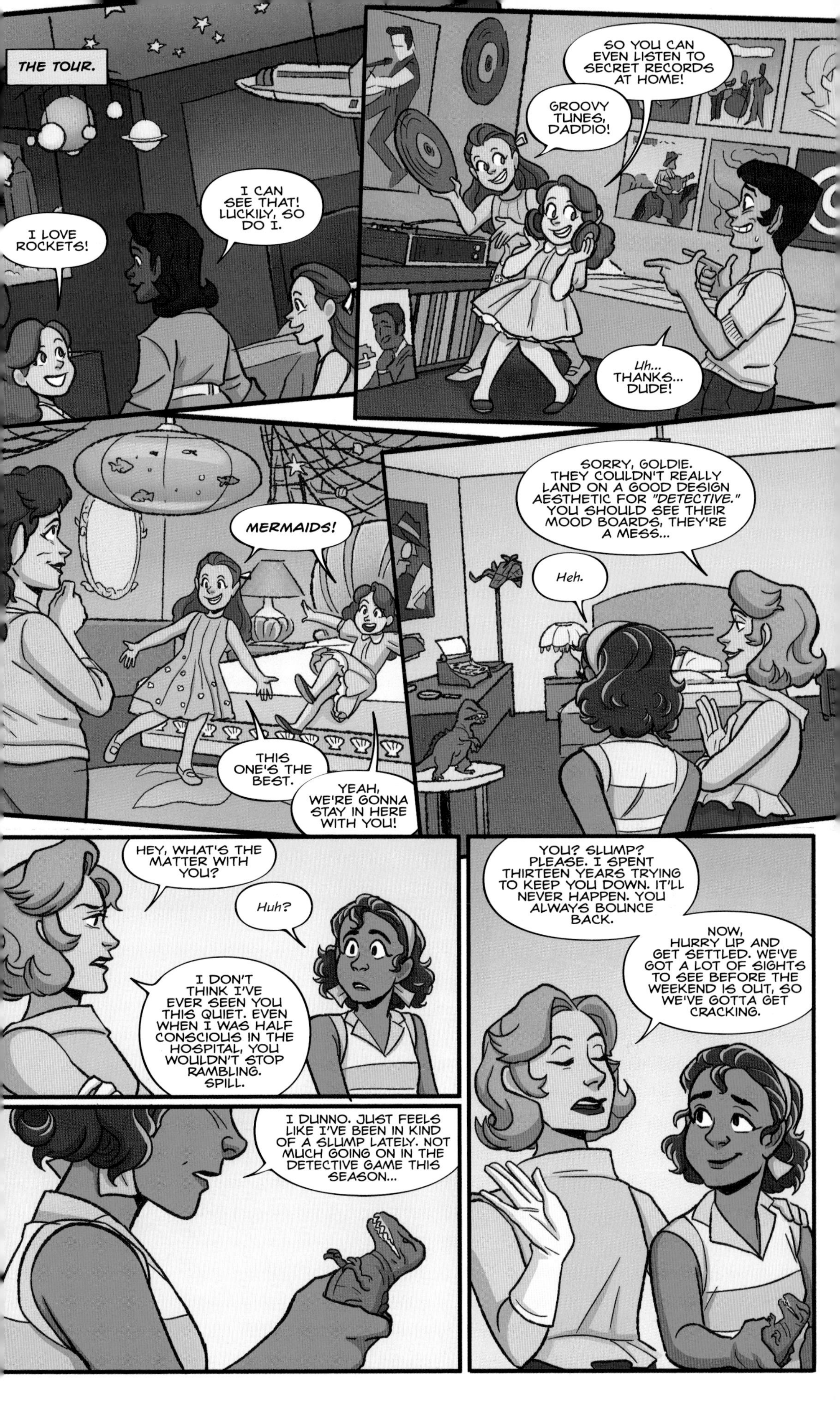
THE TOUR.
I LOVE ROCKETS!
I CAN SEE THAT! LUCKILY, SO DO I.
SO YOU CAN EVEN LISTEN TO SECRET RECORDS AT HOME!
GROOVY TUNES, DADDIO!
Uh... THANKS... DUDE!
MERMAIDS!
THIS ONE'S THE BEST.
YEAH, WE'RE GONNA STAY IN HERE WITH YOU!
SORRY, GOLDIE. THEY COULDN'T REALLY LAND ON A GOOD DESIGN AESTHETIC FOR "DETECTIVE." YOU SHOULD SEE THEIR MOOD BOARDS, THEY'RE A MESS...
Heh.
HEY, WHAT'S THE MATTER WITH YOU?
Huh?
I DON'T THINK I'VE EVER SEEN YOU THIS QUIET. EVEN WHEN I WAS HALF CONSCIOUS IN THE HOSPITAL, YOU WOULDN'T STOP RAMBLING. SPILL.
I DUNNO. JUST FEELS LIKE I'VE BEEN IN KIND OF A SLUMP LATELY. NOT MUCH GOING ON IN THE DETECTIVE GAME THIS SEASON...
YOU? SLUMP? PLEASE. I SPENT THIRTEEN YEARS TRYING TO KEEP YOU DOWN. IT'LL NEVER HAPPEN. YOU ALWAYS BOUNCE BACK.
NOW, HURRY UP AND GET SETTLED. WE'VE GOT A LOT OF SIGHTS TO SEE BEFORE THE WEEKEND IS OUT, SO WE'VE GOTTA GET CRACKING.

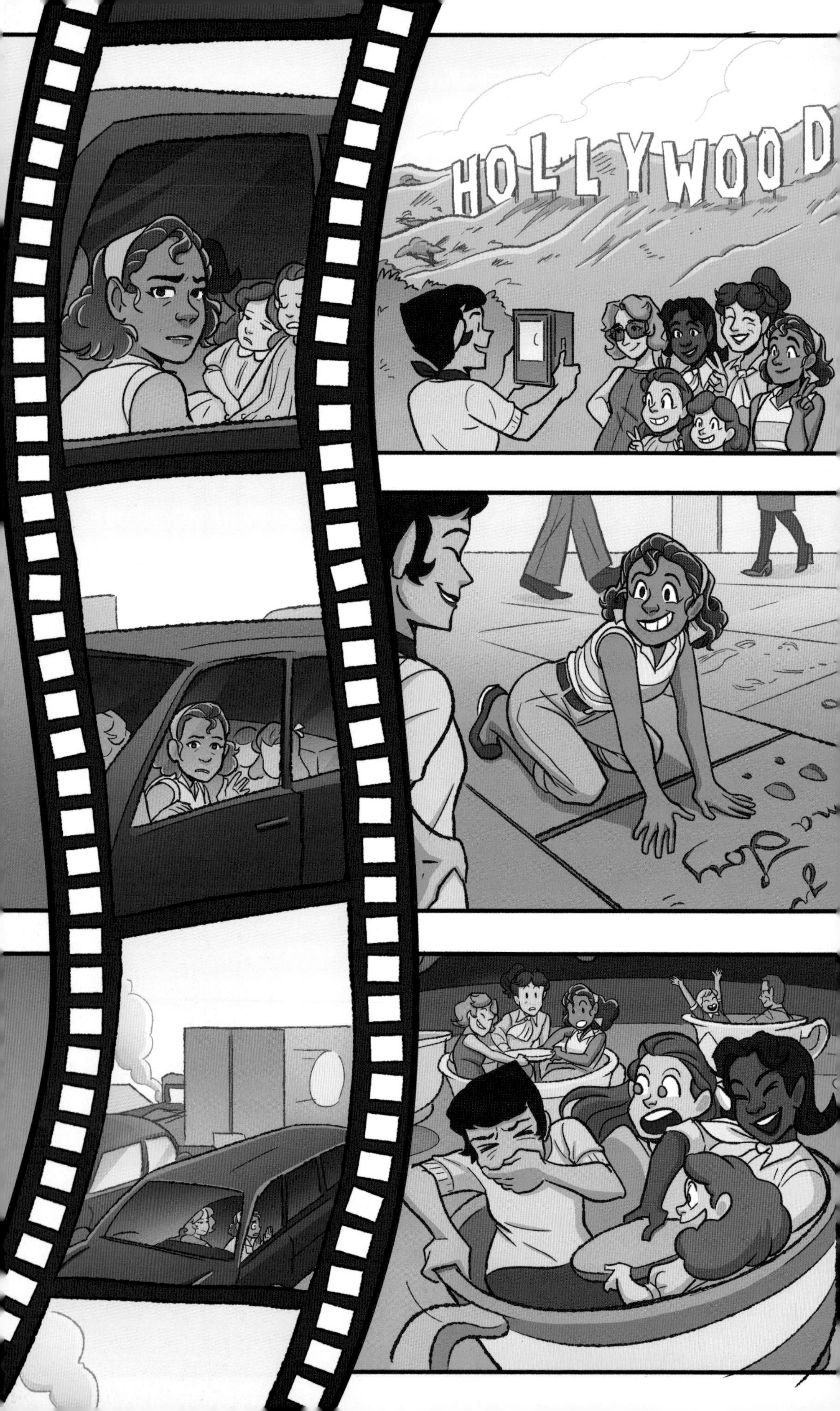
HOLLYWOOD

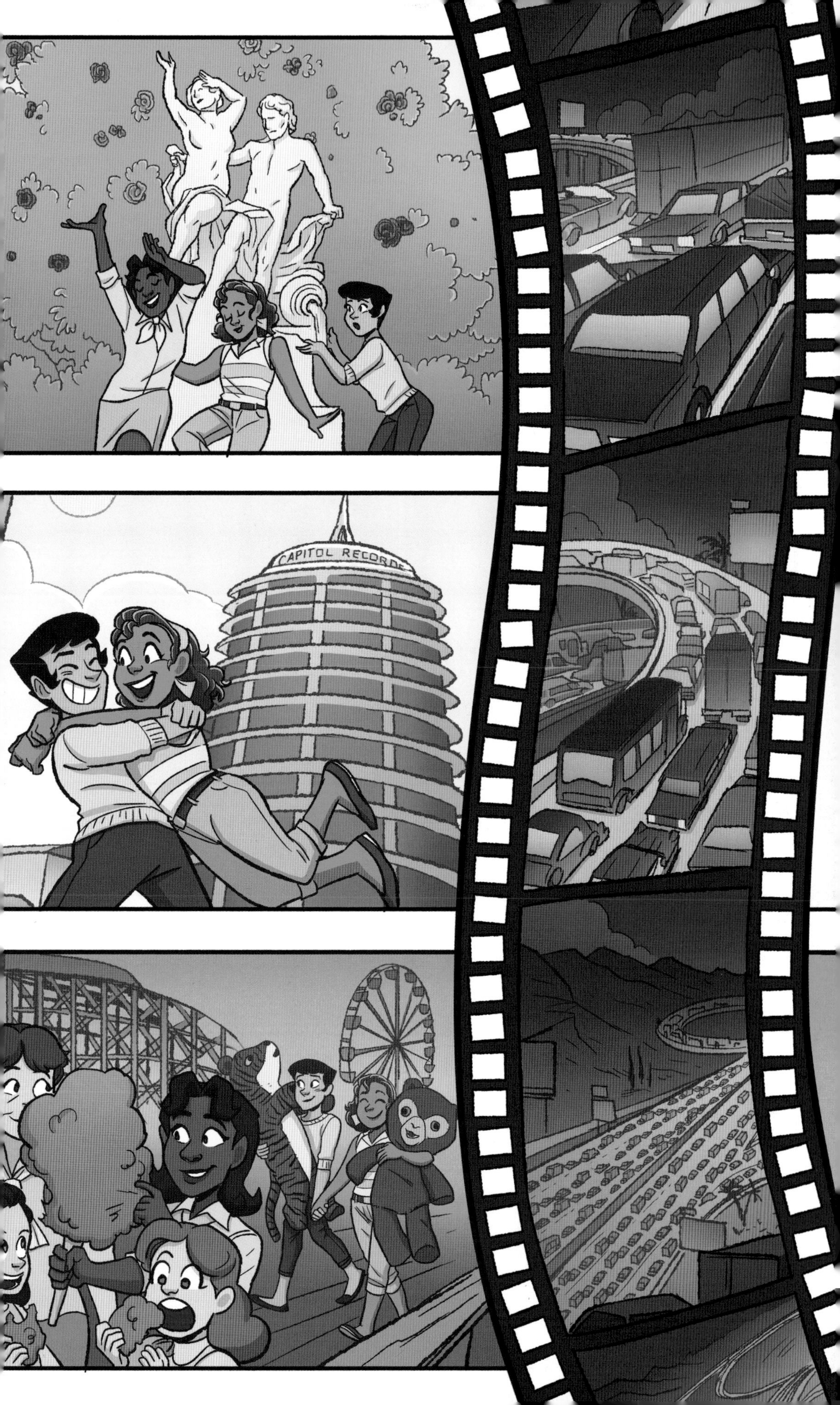
CAPITOL RECORDS

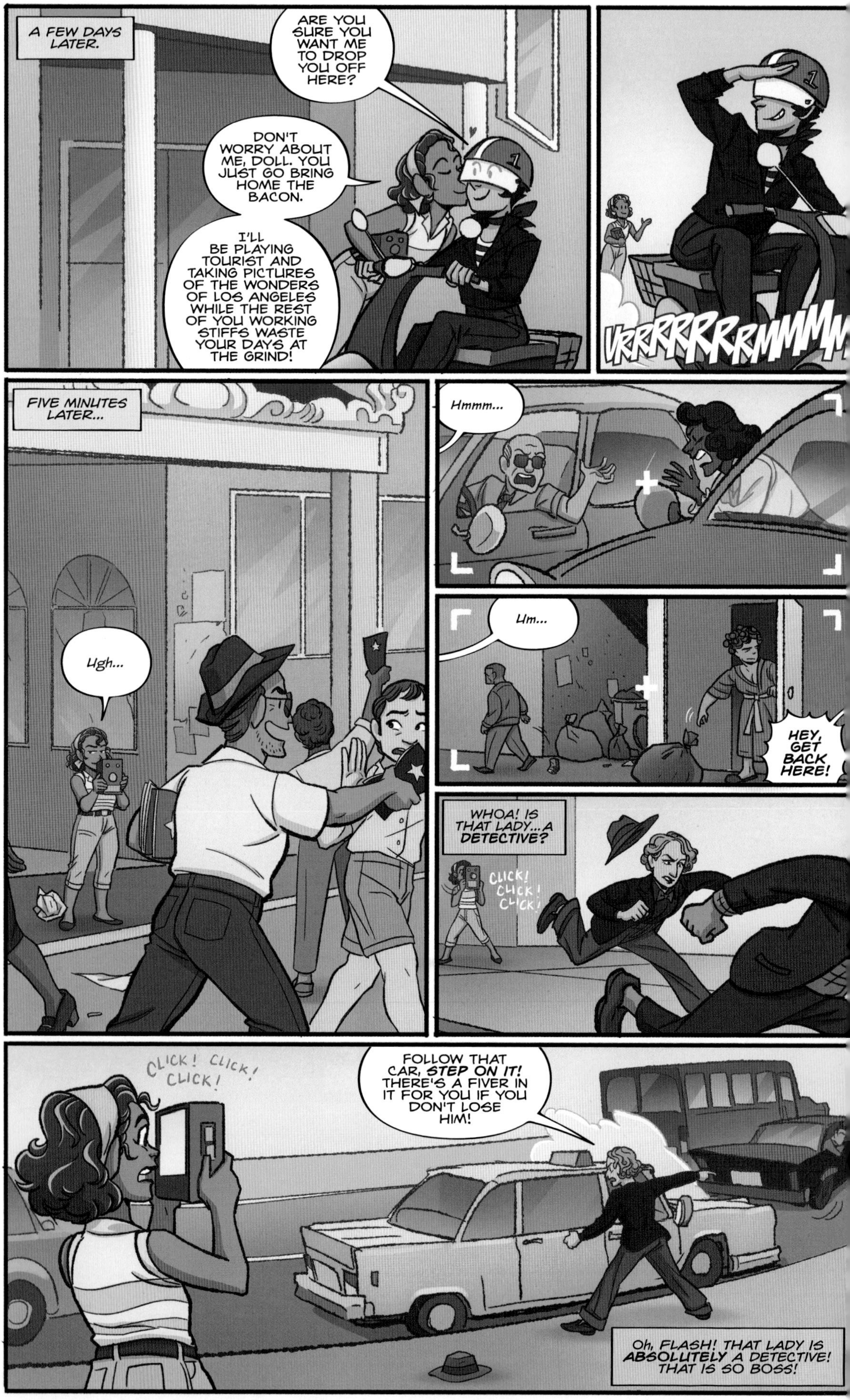
A FEW DAYS LATER.
ARE YOU SURE YOU WANT ME TO DROP YOU OFF HERE?
DON'T WORRY ABOUT ME, DOLL. YOU JUST GO BRING HOME THE BACON.
I'LL BE PLAYING TOURIST AND TAKING PICTURES OF THE WONDERS OF LOS ANGELES WHILE THE REST OF YOU WORKING STIFFS WASTE YOUR DAYS AT THE GRIND!
VRRRRRRRMMMM
FIVE MINUTES LATER...
Ugh...
Hmmm...
Um...
HEY, GET BACK HERE!
WHOA! IS THAT LADY...A DETECTIVE?
CLICK! CLICK! CLICK!
CLICK! CLICK! CLICK!
FOLLOW THAT CAR, STEP ON IT! THERE'S A FIVER IN IT FOR YOU IF YOU DON'T LOSE HIM!
Oh, FLASH! THAT LADY IS ABSOLUTELY A DETECTIVE! THAT IS SO BOSS!

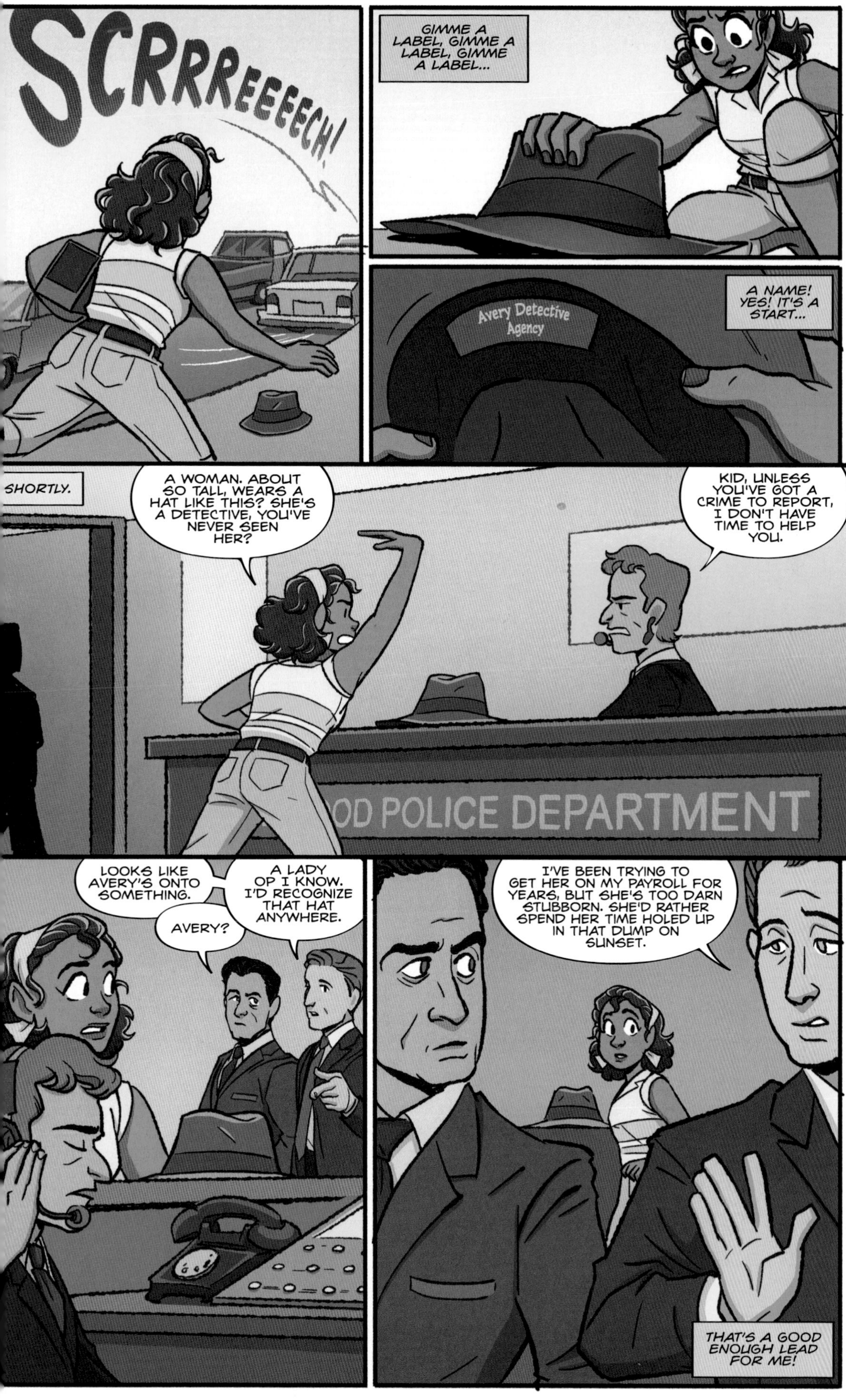
SCRRREEEEECH!
GIMME A LABEL, GIMME A LABEL, GIMME A LABEL...
Avery Detective Agency
A NAME! YES! IT'S A START...
SHORTLY.
A WOMAN. ABOUT SO TALL, WEARS A HAT LIKE THIS? SHE'S A DETECTIVE, YOU'VE NEVER SEEN HER?
KID, UNLESS YOU'VE GOT A CRIME TO REPORT, I DON'T HAVE TIME TO HELP YOU.
OD POLICE DEPARTMENT
LOOKS LIKE AVERY'S ONTO SOMETHING.
AVERY?
A LADY OP I KNOW. I'D RECOGNIZE THAT HAT ANYWHERE.
I'VE BEEN TRYING TO GET HER ON MY PAYROLL FOR YEARS, BUT SHE'S TOO DARN STUBBORN. SHE'D RATHER SPEND HER TIME HOLED UP IN THAT DUMP ON SUNSET.
THAT'S A GOOD ENOUGH LEAD FOR ME!

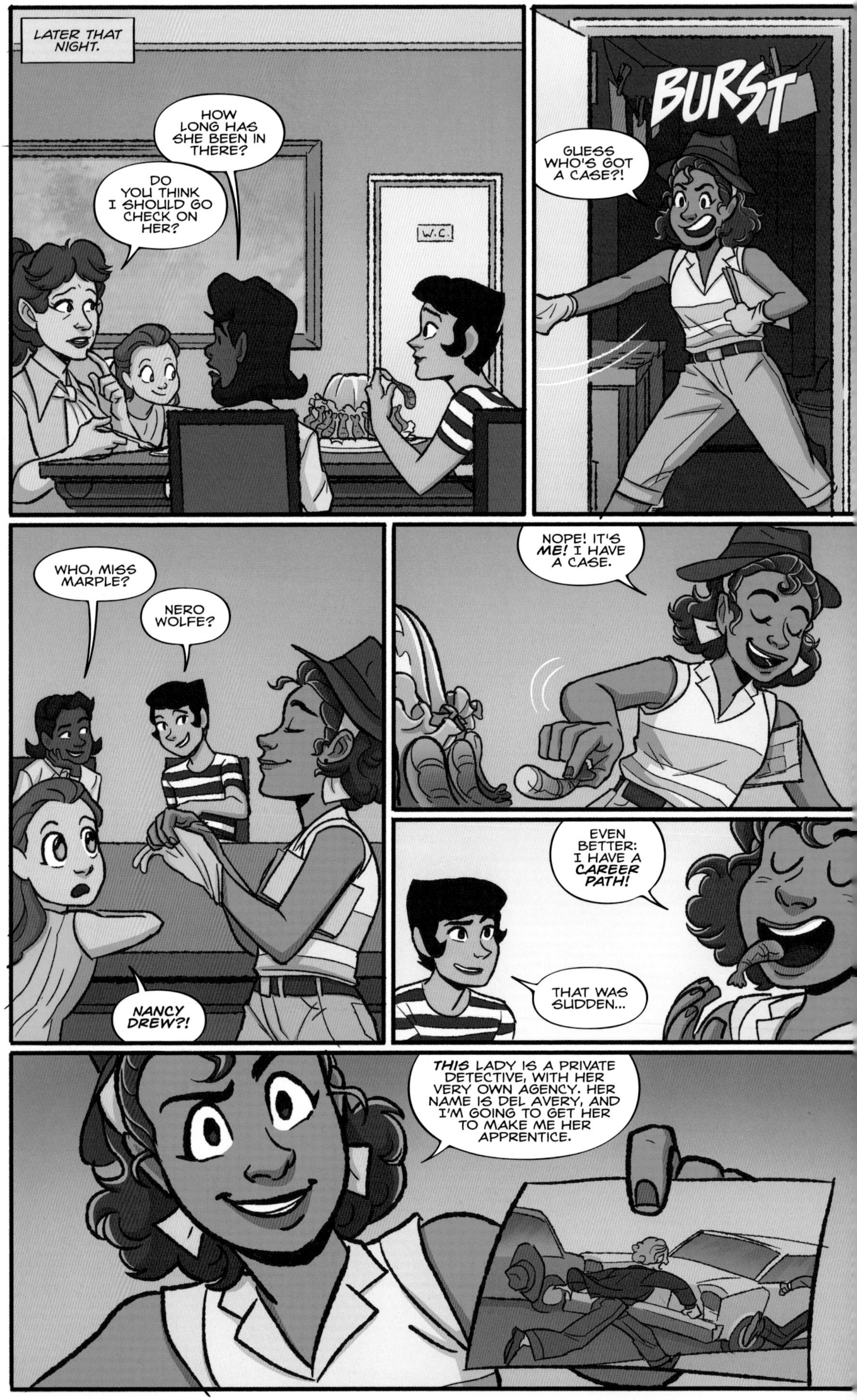

LATER THAT NIGHT.
DO YOU THINK I SHOULD GO CHECK ON HER?
HOW LONG HAS SHE BEEN IN THERE?
W.C.
BURST
GUESS WHO'S GOT A CASE?!
WHO, MISS MARPLE?
NERO WOLFE?
NANCY DREW?!
NOPE! IT'S ME! I HAVE A CASE.
EVEN BETTER: I HAVE A CAREER PATH!
THAT WAS SUDDEN...
THIS LADY IS A PRIVATE DETECTIVE, WITH HER VERY OWN AGENCY. HER NAME IS DEL AVERY, AND I'M GOING TO GET HER TO MAKE ME HER APPRENTICE.

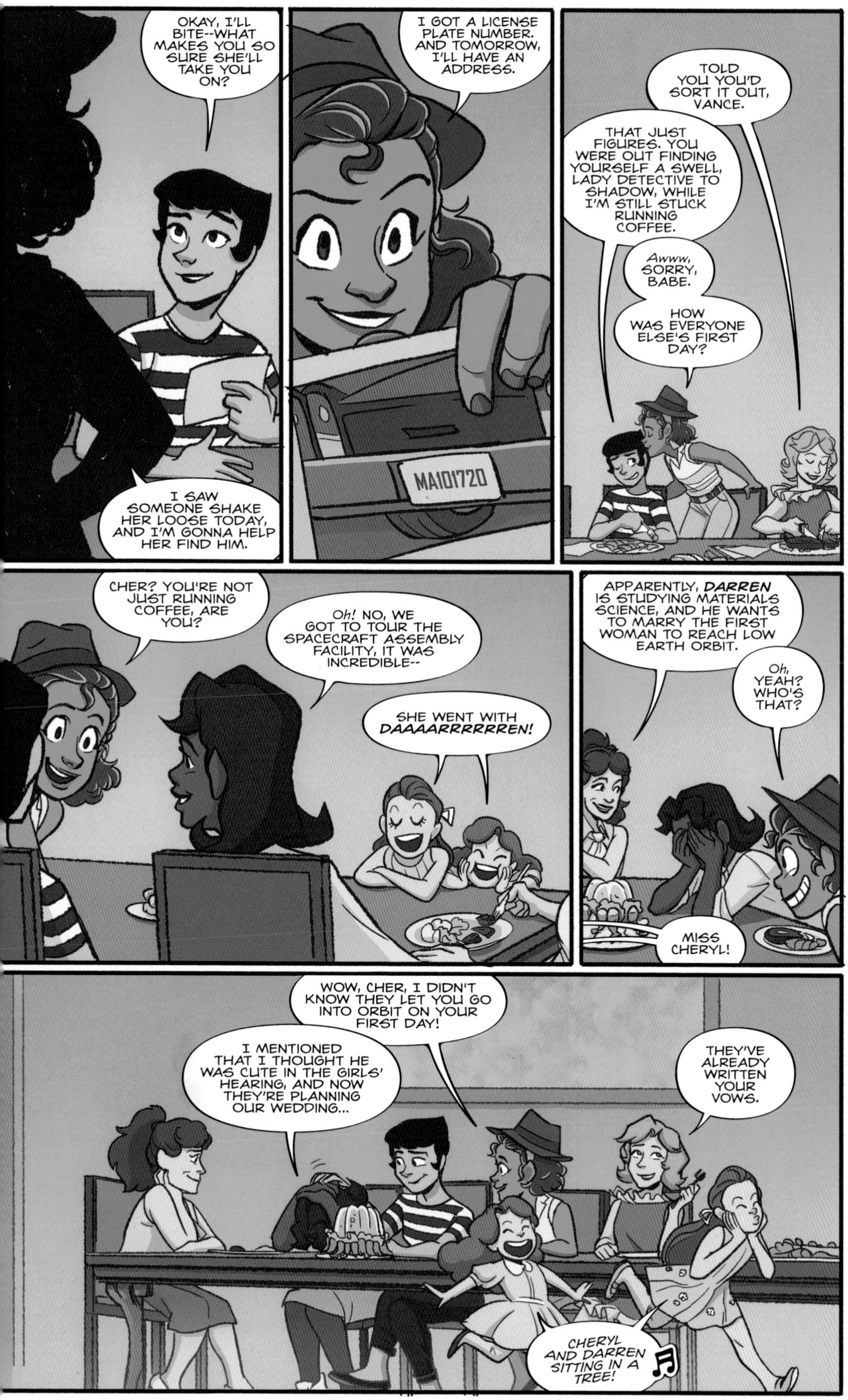
OKAY, I'LL BITE--WHAT MAKES YOU SO SURE SHE'LL TAKE YOU ON?
I SAW SOMEONE SHAKE HER LOOSE TODAY, AND I'M GONNA HELP HER FIND HIM.
I GOT A LICENSE PLATE NUMBER. AND TOMORROW, I'LL HAVE AN ADDRESS.
MA101720
TOLD YOU YOU'D SORT IT OUT, VANCE.
THAT JUST FIGURES. YOU WERE OUT FINDING YOURSELF A SWELL, LADY DETECTIVE TO SHADOW, WHILE I'M STILL STUCK RUNNING COFFEE.
Awww, SORRY, BABE.
HOW WAS EVERYONE ELSE'S FIRST DAY?
CHER? YOU'RE NOT JUST RUNNING COFFEE, ARE YOU?
Oh! NO, WE GOT TO TOUR THE SPACECRAFT ASSEMBLY FACILITY, IT WAS INCREDIBLE--
SHE WENT WITH ***DAAAARRRRRREN!***
APPARENTLY, ***DARREN*** IS STUDYING MATERIALS SCIENCE, AND HE WANTS TO MARRY THE FIRST WOMAN TO REACH LOW EARTH ORBIT.
Oh, YEAH? WHO'S THAT?
MISS CHERYL!
WOW, CHER, I DIDN'T KNOW THEY LET YOU GO INTO ORBIT ON YOUR FIRST DAY!
I MENTIONED THAT I THOUGHT HE WAS CUTE IN THE GIRLS' HEARING, AND NOW THEY'RE PLANNING OUR WEDDING...
THEY'VE ALREADY WRITTEN YOUR VOWS.
CHERYL AND DARREN SITTING IN A TREE!

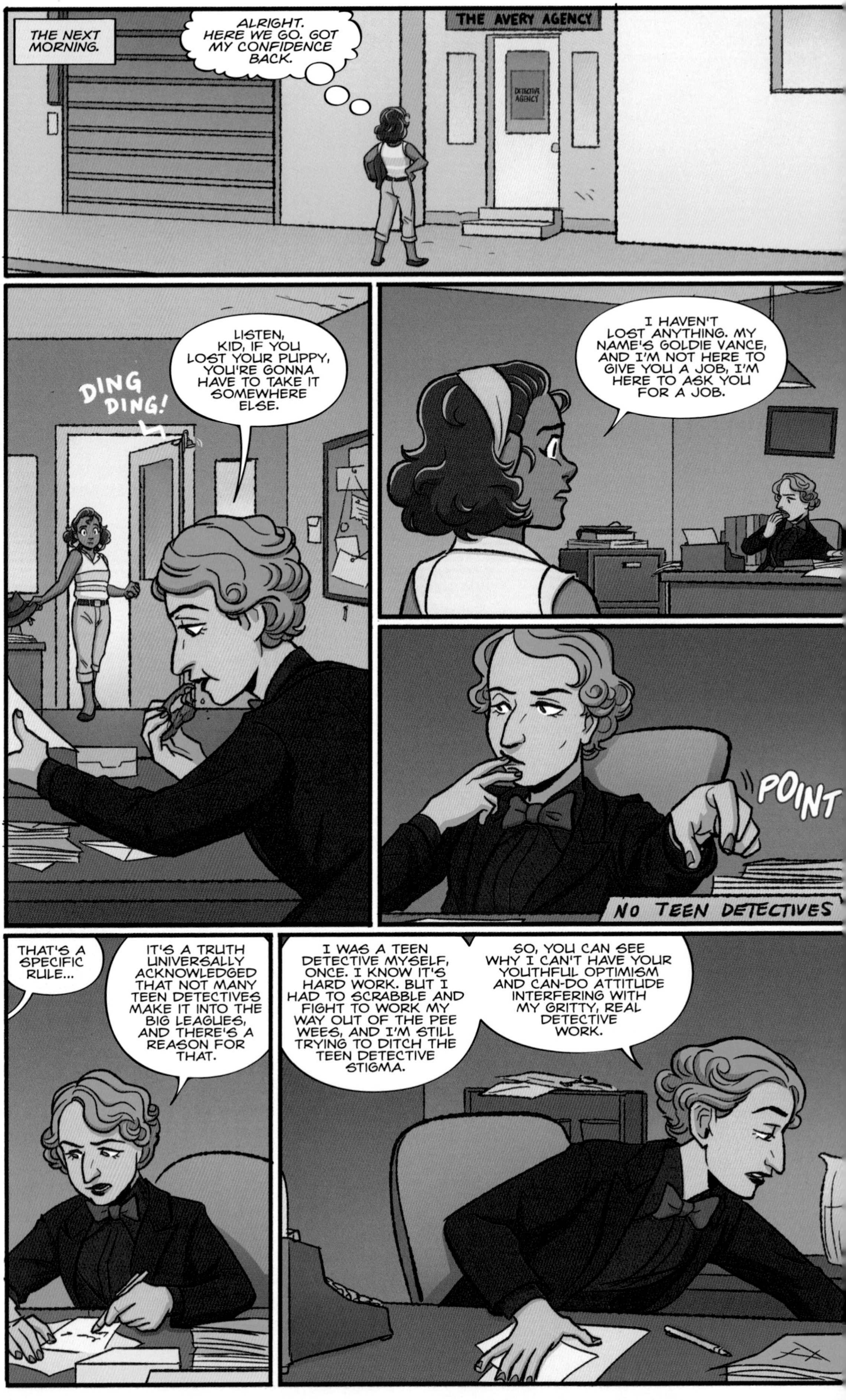
THE NEXT MORNING.
ALRIGHT. HERE WE GO. GOT MY CONFIDENCE BACK.
THE AVERY AGENCY
DETECTIVE AGENCY
DING DING!
LISTEN, KID, IF YOU LOST YOUR PUPPY, YOU'RE GONNA HAVE TO TAKE IT SOMEWHERE ELSE.
I HAVEN'T LOST ANYTHING. MY NAME'S GOLDIE VANCE, AND I'M NOT HERE TO GIVE YOU A JOB, I'M HERE TO ASK YOU FOR A JOB.
POINT
NO TEEN DETECTIVES
THAT'S A SPECIFIC RULE...
IT'S A TRUTH UNIVERSALLY ACKNOWLEDGED THAT NOT MANY TEEN DETECTIVES MAKE IT INTO THE BIG LEAGUES, AND THERE'S A REASON FOR THAT.
I WAS A TEEN DETECTIVE MYSELF, ONCE. I KNOW IT'S HARD WORK. BUT I HAD TO SCRABBLE AND FIGHT TO WORK MY WAY OUT OF THE PEE WEES, AND I'M STILL TRYING TO DITCH THE TEEN DETECTIVE STIGMA.
SO, YOU CAN SEE WHY I CAN'T HAVE YOUR YOUTHFUL OPTIMISM AND CAN-DO ATTITUDE INTERFERING WITH MY GRITTY, REAL DETECTIVE WORK.

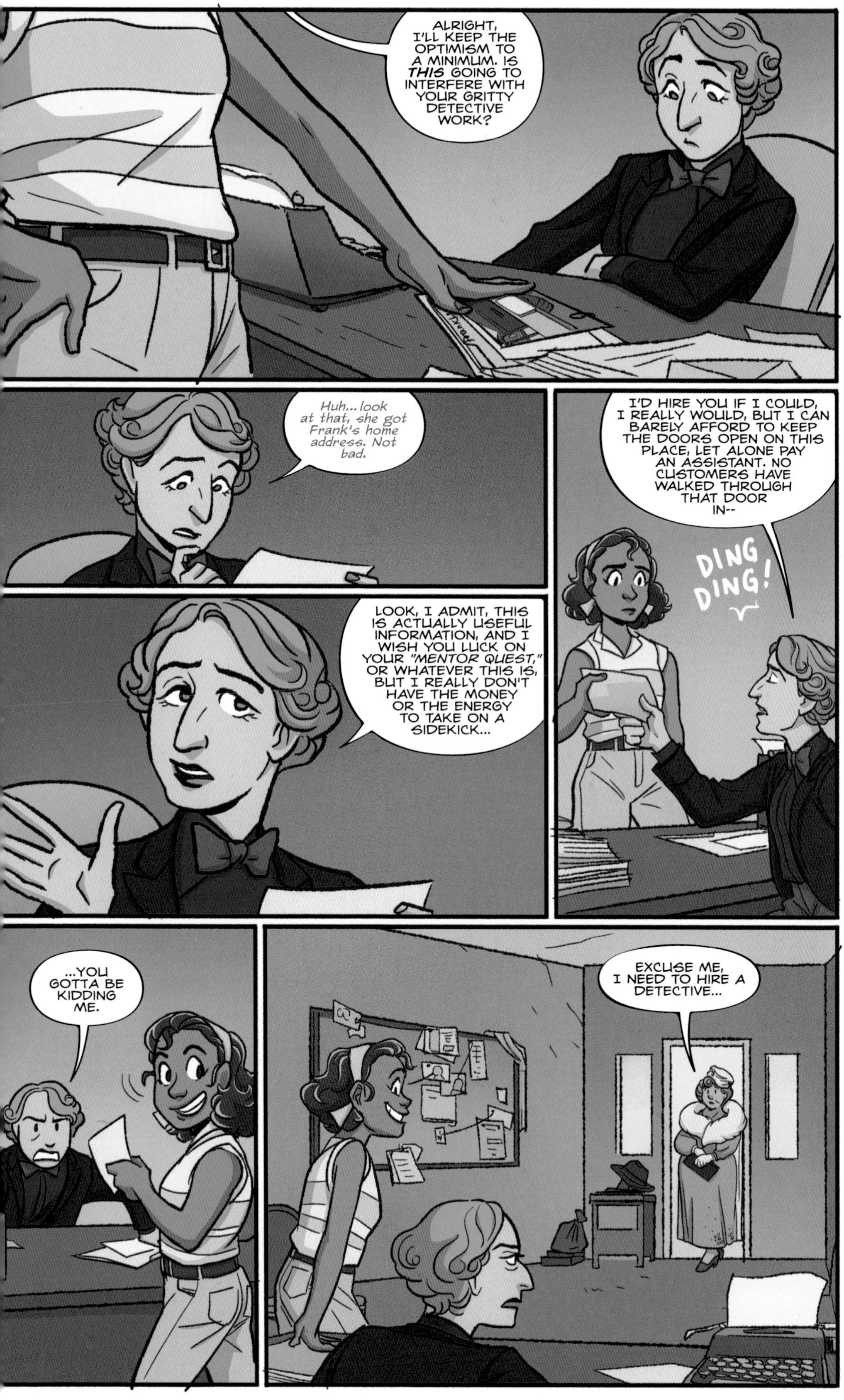
ALRIGHT, I'LL KEEP THE OPTIMISM TO A MINIMUM. IS THIS GOING TO INTERFERE WITH YOUR GRITTY DETECTIVE WORK?
Huh... look at that, she got Frank's home address. Not bad.
LOOK, I ADMIT, THIS IS ACTUALLY USEFUL INFORMATION, AND I WISH YOU LUCK ON YOUR "MENTOR QUEST," OR WHATEVER THIS IS, BUT I REALLY DON'T HAVE THE MONEY OR THE ENERGY TO TAKE ON A SIDEKICK...
I'D HIRE YOU IF I COULD, I REALLY WOULD, BUT I CAN BARELY AFFORD TO KEEP THE DOORS OPEN ON THIS PLACE, LET ALONE PAY AN ASSISTANT. NO CUSTOMERS HAVE WALKED THROUGH THAT DOOR IN--
DING DING!
...YOU GOTTA BE KIDDING ME.
EXCUSE ME, I NEED TO HIRE A DETECTIVE...

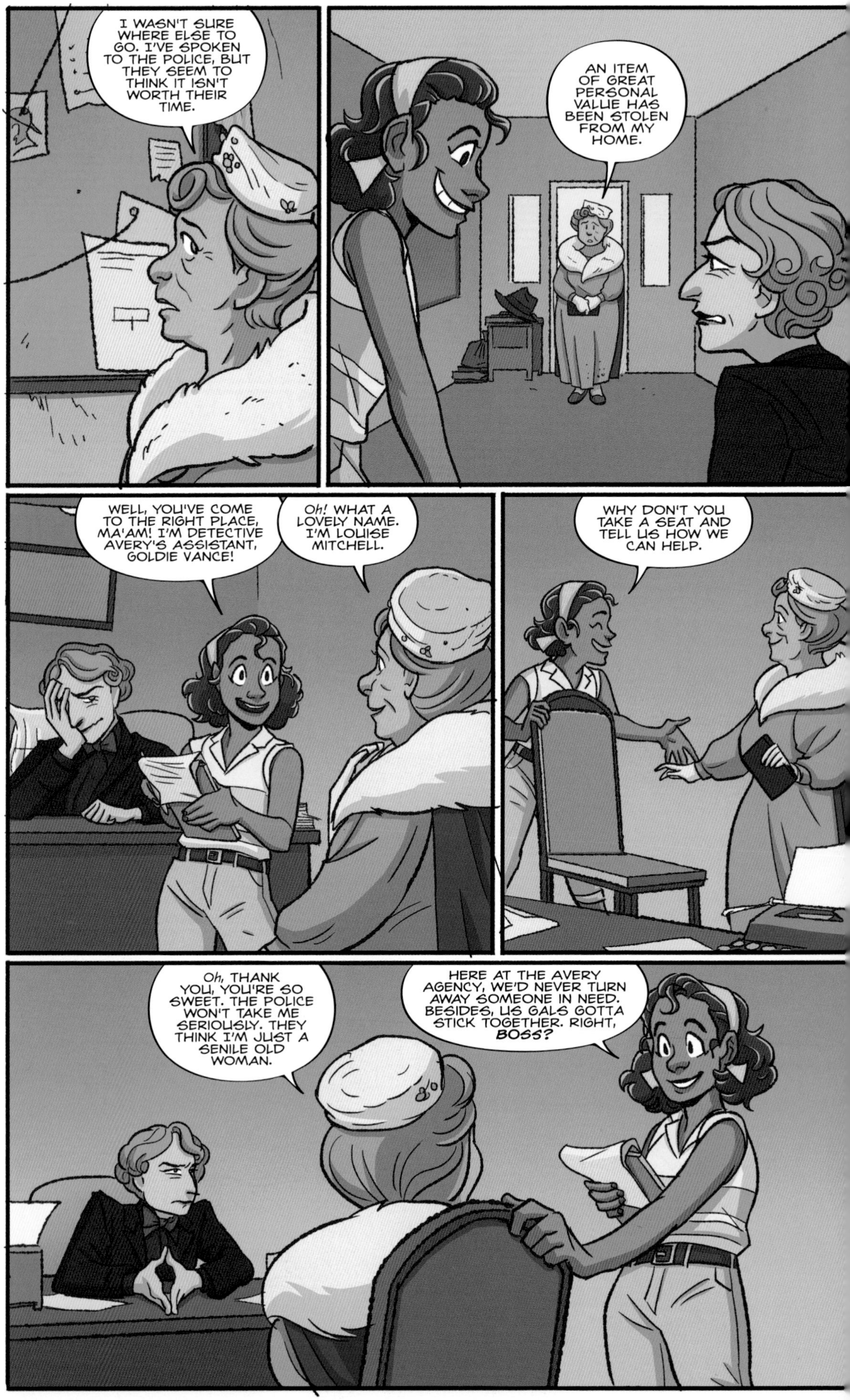
I WASN'T SURE WHERE ELSE TO GO. I'VE SPOKEN TO THE POLICE, BUT THEY SEEM TO THINK IT ISN'T WORTH THEIR TIME.
AN ITEM OF GREAT PERSONAL VALUE HAS BEEN STOLEN FROM MY HOME.
WELL, YOU'VE COME TO THE RIGHT PLACE, MA'AM! I'M DETECTIVE AVERY'S ASSISTANT, GOLDIE VANCE!
Oh! WHAT A LOVELY NAME. I'M LOUISE MITCHELL.
WHY DON'T YOU TAKE A SEAT AND TELL US HOW WE CAN HELP.
Oh, THANK YOU, YOU'RE SO SWEET. THE POLICE WON'T TAKE ME SERIOUSLY. THEY THINK I'M JUST A SENILE OLD WOMAN.
HERE AT THE AVERY AGENCY, WE'D NEVER TURN AWAY SOMEONE IN NEED. BESIDES, US GALS GOTTA STICK TOGETHER. RIGHT, ***BOSS?***

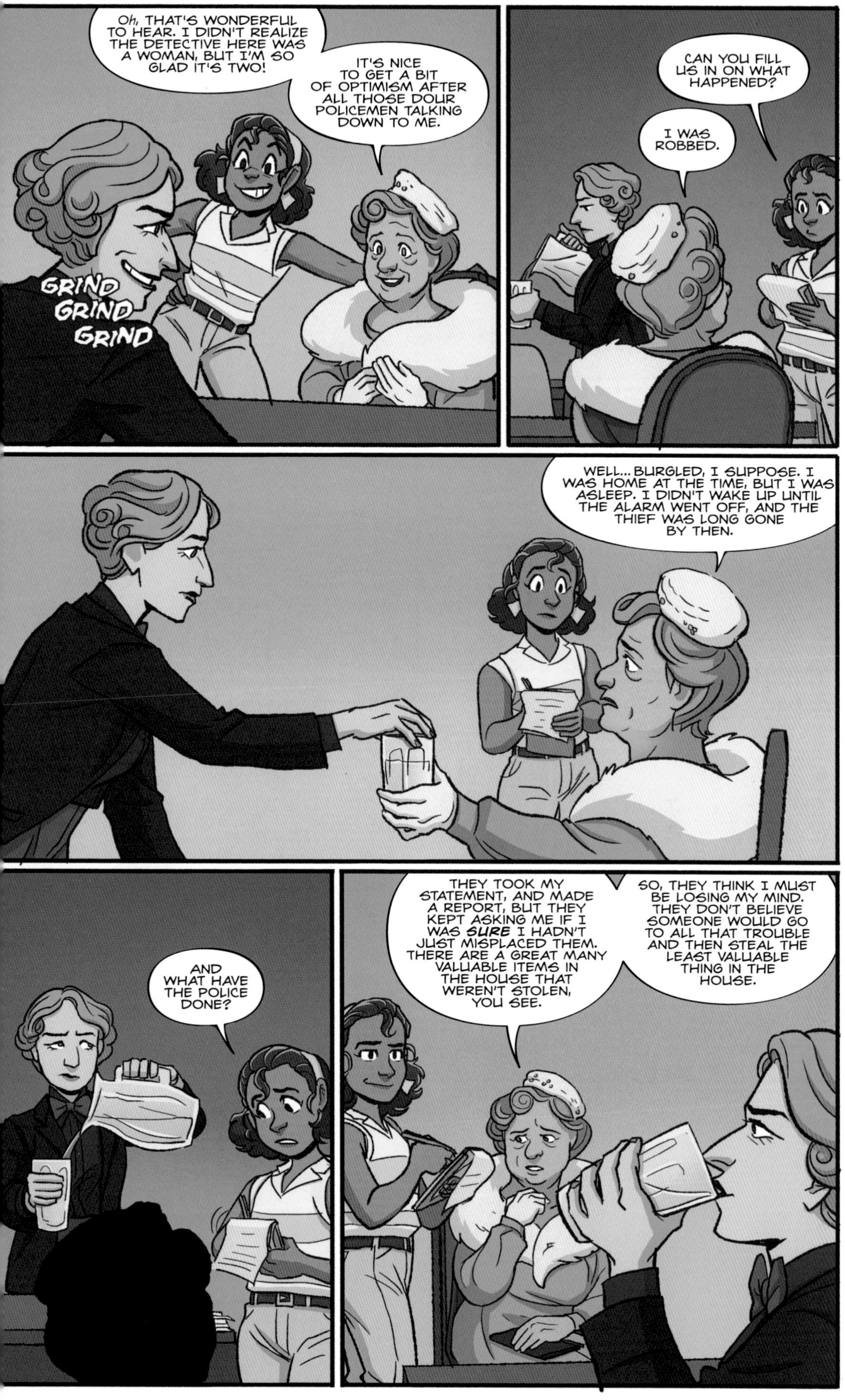

Oh, THAT'S WONDERFUL TO HEAR. I DIDN'T REALIZE THE DETECTIVE HERE WAS A WOMAN, BUT I'M SO GLAD IT'S TWO!
IT'S NICE TO GET A BIT OF OPTIMISM AFTER ALL THOSE DOUR POLICEMEN TALKING DOWN TO ME.
GRIND
GRIND
GRIND
CAN YOU FILL US IN ON WHAT HAPPENED?
I WAS ROBBED.
WELL... BURGLED, I SUPPOSE. I WAS HOME AT THE TIME, BUT I WAS ASLEEP. I DIDN'T WAKE UP UNTIL THE ALARM WENT OFF, AND THE THIEF WAS LONG GONE BY THEN.
AND WHAT HAVE THE POLICE DONE?
THEY TOOK MY STATEMENT, AND MADE A REPORT, BUT THEY KEPT ASKING ME IF I WAS SURE I HADN'T JUST MISPLACED THEM. THERE ARE A GREAT MANY VALUABLE ITEMS IN THE HOUSE THAT WEREN'T STOLEN, YOU SEE.
SO, THEY THINK I MUST BE LOSING MY MIND. THEY DON'T BELIEVE SOMEONE WOULD GO TO ALL THAT TROUBLE AND THEN STEAL THE LEAST VALUABLE THING IN THE HOUSE.

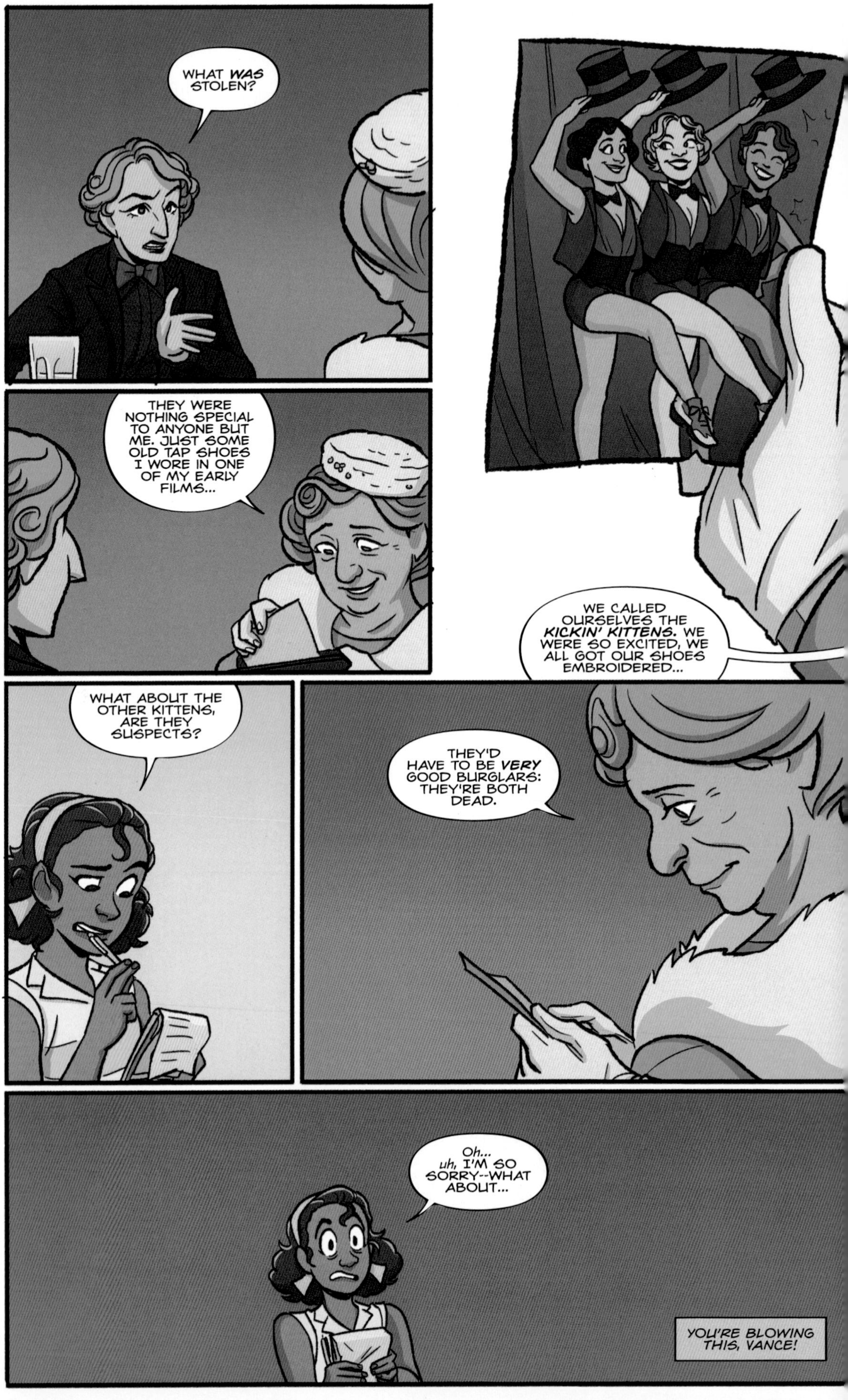
WHAT *WAS* STOLEN?
THEY WERE NOTHING SPECIAL TO ANYONE BUT ME. JUST SOME OLD TAP SHOES I WORE IN ONE OF MY EARLY FILMS...
WE CALLED OURSELVES THE *KICKIN' KITTENS.* WE WERE SO EXCITED, WE ALL GOT OUR SHOES EMBROIDERED...
WHAT ABOUT THE OTHER KITTENS, ARE THEY SUSPECTS?
THEY'D HAVE TO BE *VERY* GOOD BURGLARS: THEY'RE BOTH DEAD.
Oh... uh, I'M SO SORRY--WHAT ABOUT...
YOU'RE BLOWING THIS, VANCE!

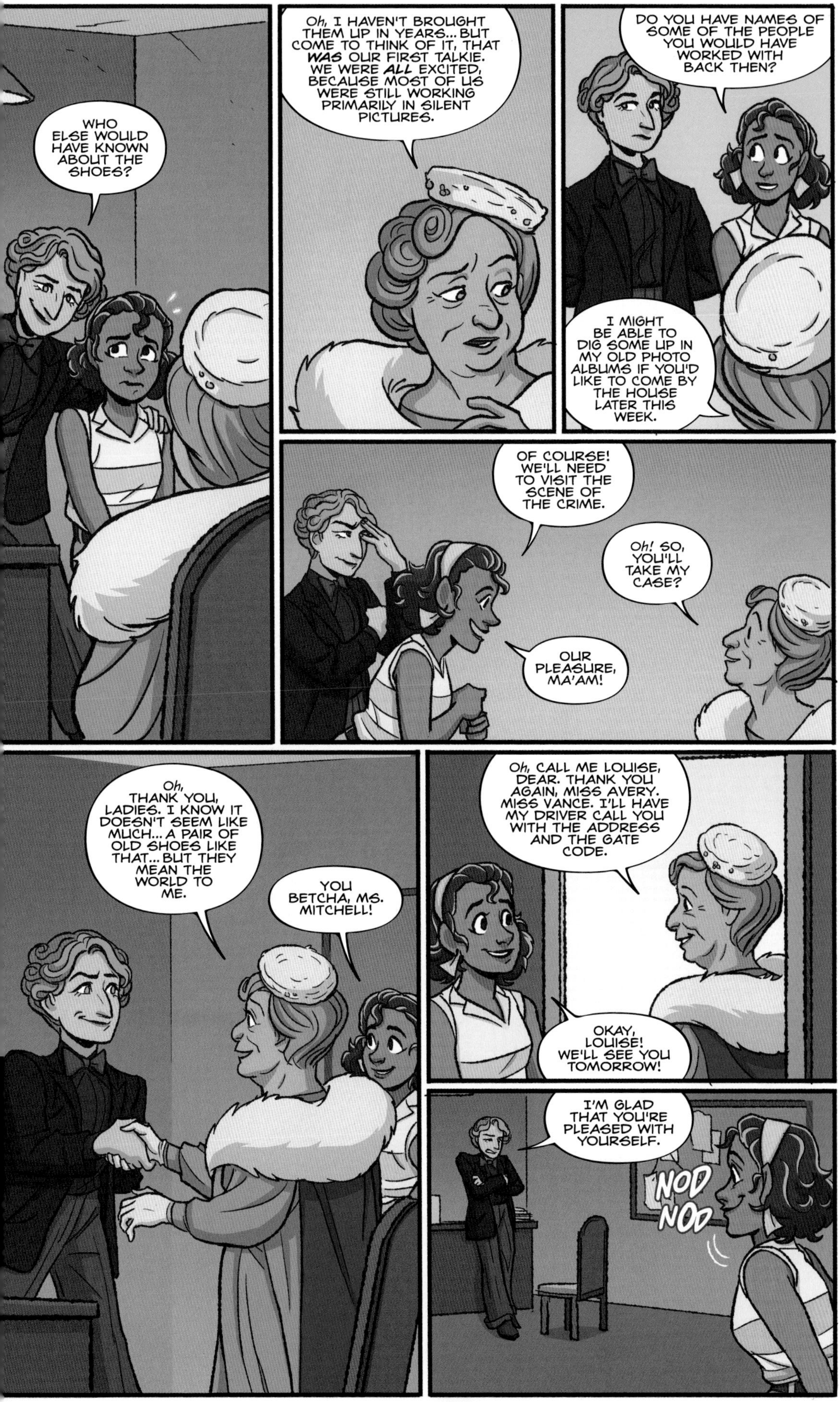
WHO ELSE WOULD HAVE KNOWN ABOUT THE SHOES?
Oh, I HAVEN'T BROUGHT THEM UP IN YEARS... BUT COME TO THINK OF IT, THAT ***WAS*** OUR FIRST TALKIE. WE WERE ***ALL*** EXCITED, BECAUSE MOST OF US WERE STILL WORKING PRIMARILY IN SILENT PICTURES.
DO YOU HAVE NAMES OF SOME OF THE PEOPLE YOU WOULD HAVE WORKED WITH BACK THEN?
I MIGHT BE ABLE TO DIG SOME UP IN MY OLD PHOTO ALBUMS IF YOU'D LIKE TO COME BY THE HOUSE LATER THIS WEEK.
OF COURSE! WE'LL NEED TO VISIT THE SCENE OF THE CRIME.
Oh! SO, YOU'LL TAKE MY CASE?
OUR PLEASURE, MA'AM!
Oh, THANK YOU, LADIES. I KNOW IT DOESN'T SEEM LIKE MUCH... A PAIR OF OLD SHOES LIKE THAT... BUT THEY MEAN THE WORLD TO ME.
YOU BETCHA, MS. MITCHELL!
Oh, CALL ME LOUISE, DEAR. THANK YOU AGAIN, MISS AVERY. MISS VANCE. I'LL HAVE MY DRIVER CALL YOU WITH THE ADDRESS AND THE GATE CODE.
OKAY, LOUISE! WE'LL SEE YOU TOMORROW!
I'M GLAD THAT YOU'RE PLEASED WITH YOURSELF.
NOD NOD

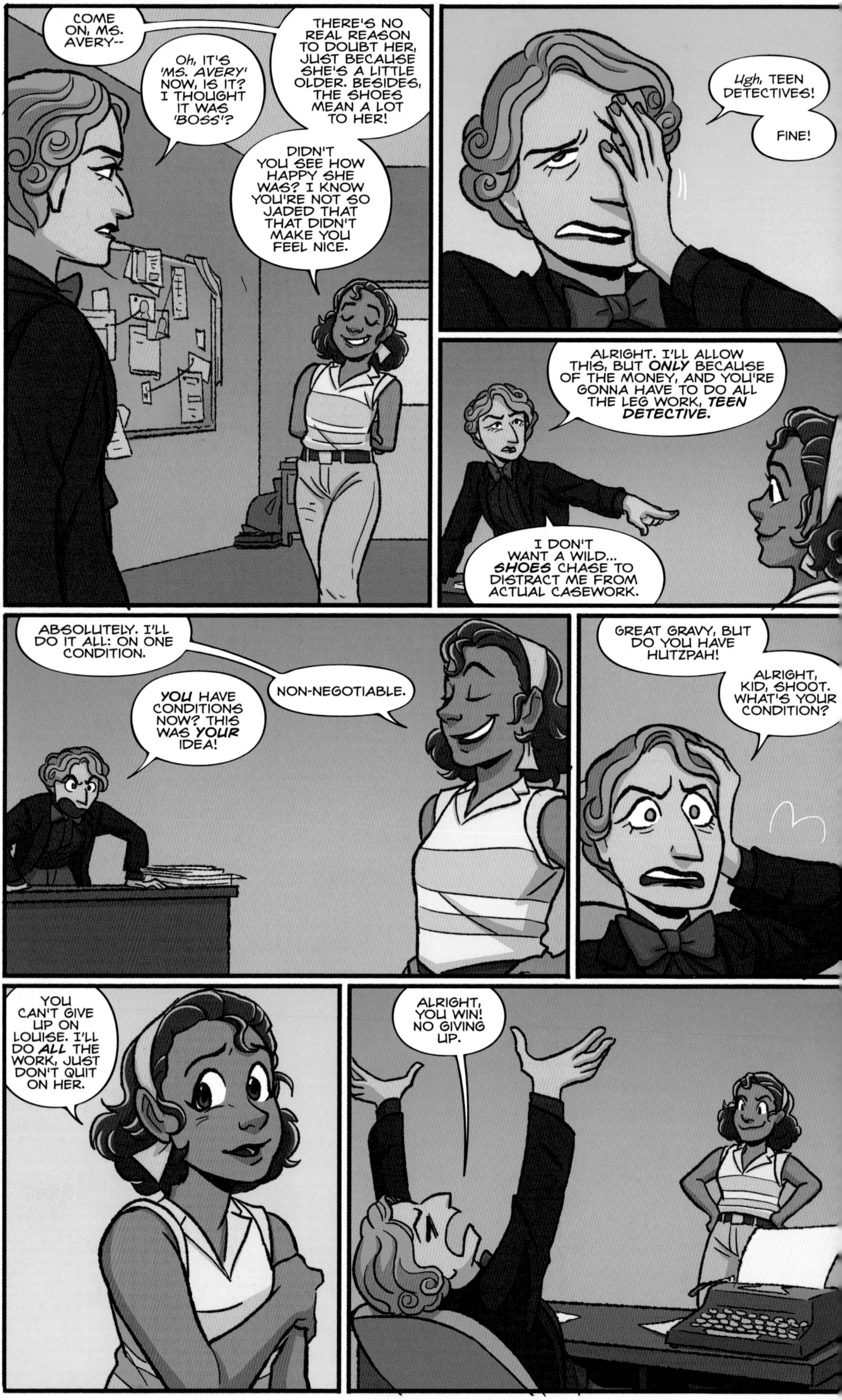
COME ON, MS. AVERY--
Oh, IT'S 'MS. AVERY' NOW, IS IT? I THOUGHT IT WAS 'BOSS'?
THERE'S NO REAL REASON TO DOUBT HER, JUST BECAUSE SHE'S A LITTLE OLDER. BESIDES, THE SHOES MEAN A LOT TO HER!
DIDN'T YOU SEE HOW HAPPY SHE WAS? I KNOW YOU'RE NOT SO JADED THAT THAT DIDN'T MAKE YOU FEEL NICE.
Ugh, TEEN DETECTIVES!
FINE!
ALRIGHT. I'LL ALLOW THIS, BUT ONLY BECAUSE OF THE MONEY, AND YOU'RE GONNA HAVE TO DO ALL THE LEG WORK, TEEN DETECTIVE.
I DON'T WANT A WILD... SHOES CHASE TO DISTRACT ME FROM ACTUAL CASEWORK.
ABSOLUTELY. I'LL DO IT ALL: ON ONE CONDITION.
YOU HAVE CONDITIONS NOW? THIS WAS YOUR IDEA!
NON-NEGOTIABLE.
GREAT GRAVY, BUT DO YOU HAVE HUTZPAH!
ALRIGHT, KID, SHOOT. WHAT'S YOUR CONDITION?
YOU CAN'T GIVE UP ON LOUISE. I'LL DO ALL THE WORK, JUST DON'T QUIT ON HER.
ALRIGHT, YOU WIN! NO GIVING UP.

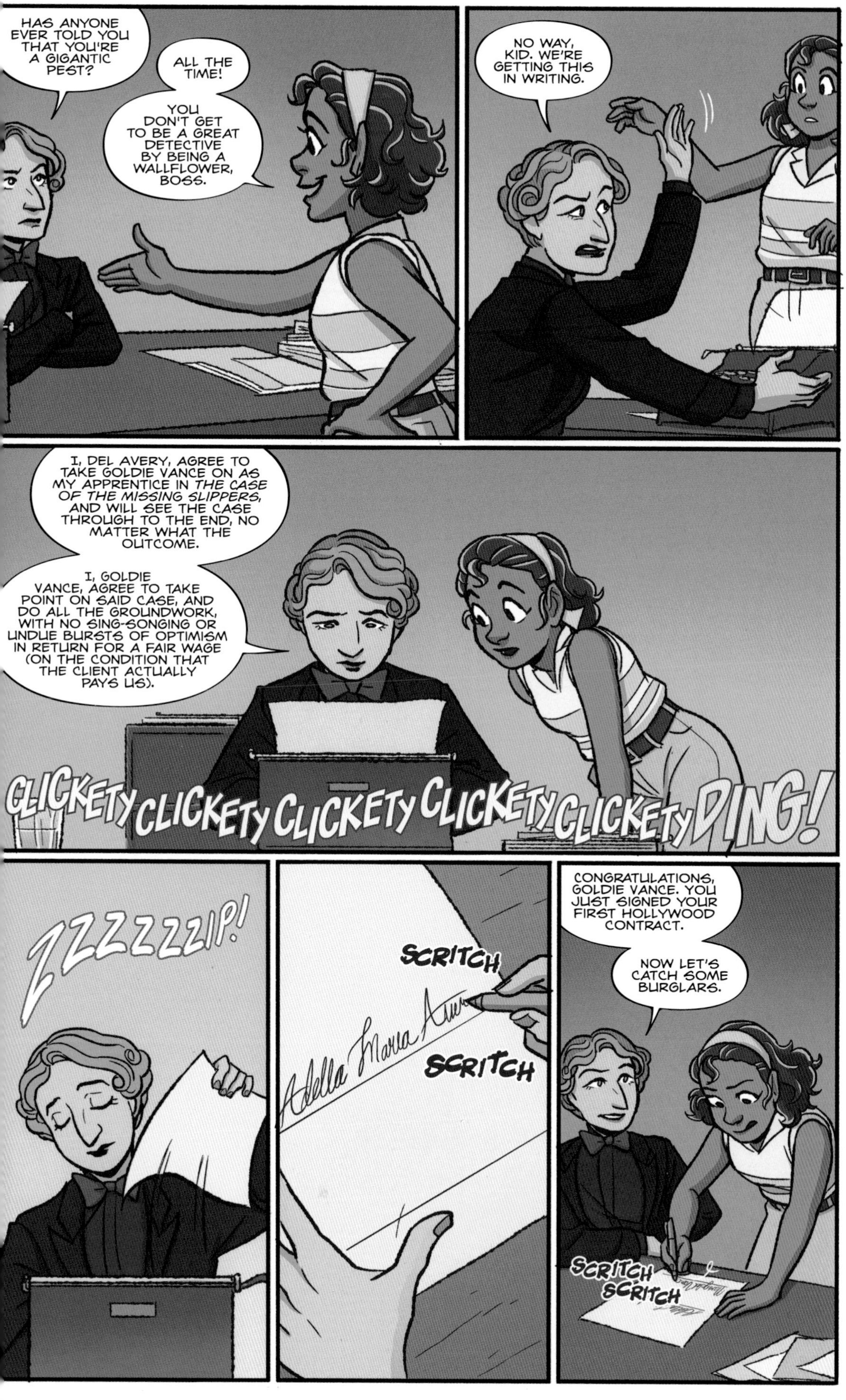
HAS ANYONE EVER TOLD YOU THAT YOU'RE A GIGANTIC PEST?
ALL THE TIME!
YOU DON'T GET TO BE A GREAT DETECTIVE BY BEING A WALLFLOWER, BOSS.
NO WAY, KID. WE'RE GETTING THIS IN WRITING.
I, DEL AVERY, AGREE TO TAKE GOLDIE VANCE ON AS MY APPRENTICE IN *THE CASE OF THE MISSING SLIPPERS*, AND WILL SEE THE CASE THROUGH TO THE END, NO MATTER WHAT THE OUTCOME.
I, GOLDIE VANCE, AGREE TO TAKE POINT ON SAID CASE, AND DO ALL THE GROUNDWORK, WITH NO SING-SONGING OR UNDUE BURSTS OF OPTIMISM IN RETURN FOR A FAIR WAGE (ON THE CONDITION THAT THE CLIENT ACTUALLY PAYS US).
CLICKETY CLICKETY CLICKETY CLICKETY CLICKETY DING!
ZZZZZZZIP!
SCRITCH
Adella Maria Aver
SCRITCH
CONGRATULATIONS, GOLDIE VANCE. YOU JUST SIGNED YOUR FIRST HOLLYWOOD CONTRACT.
NOW LET'S CATCH SOME BURGLARS.
SCRITCH SCRITCH

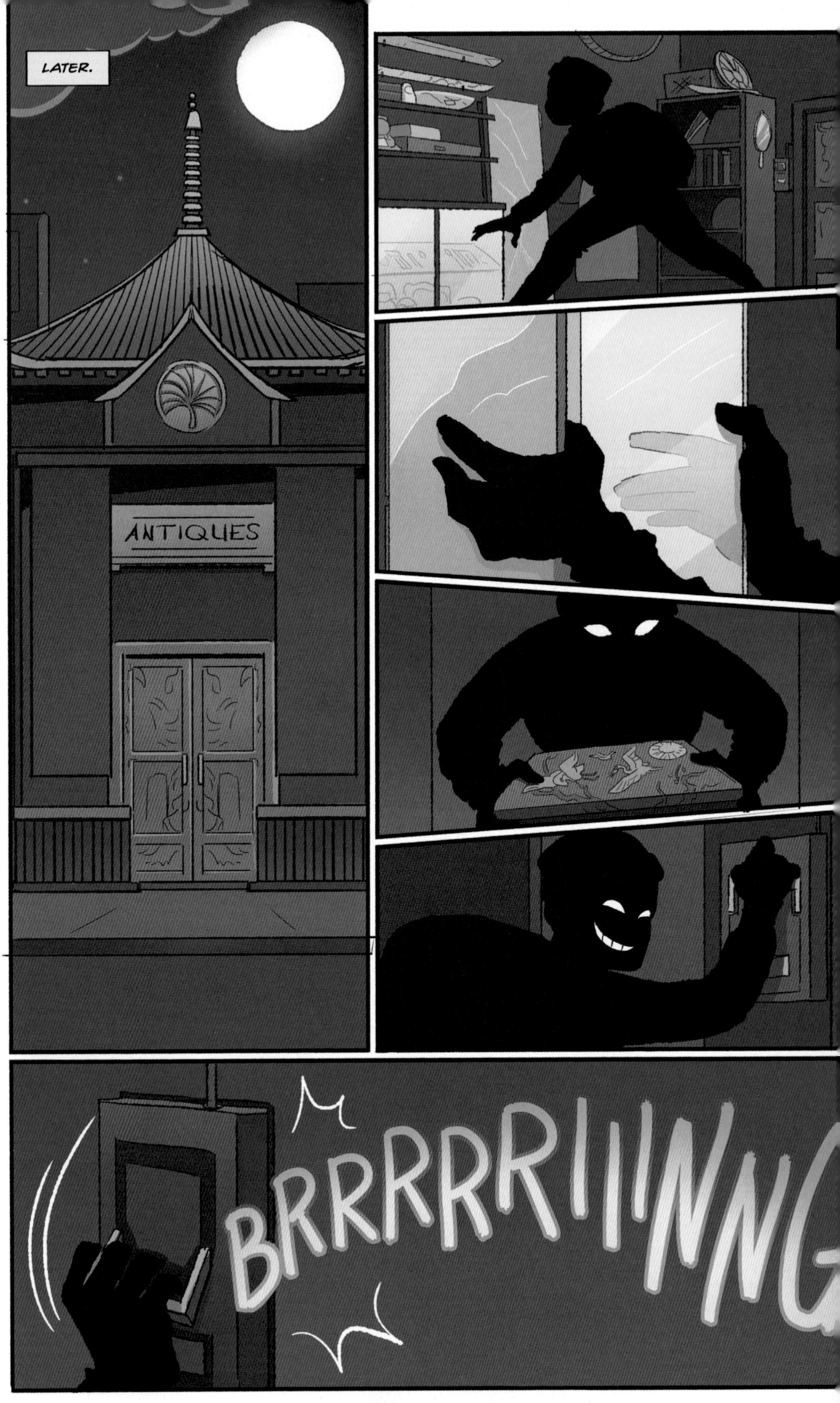
LATER.
ANTIQUES
BRRRRRRIIINNG

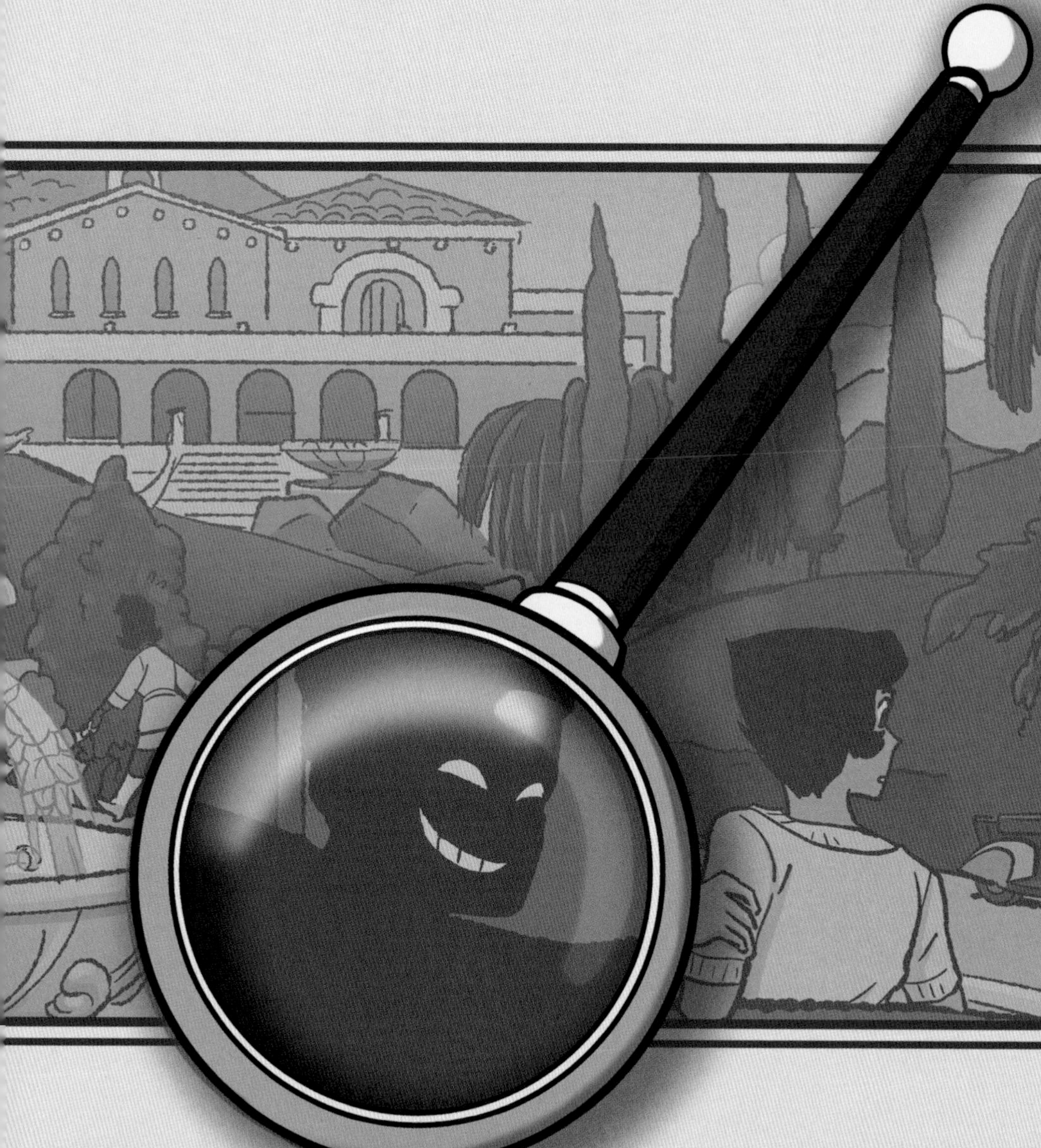

chapter
EIGHTEEN

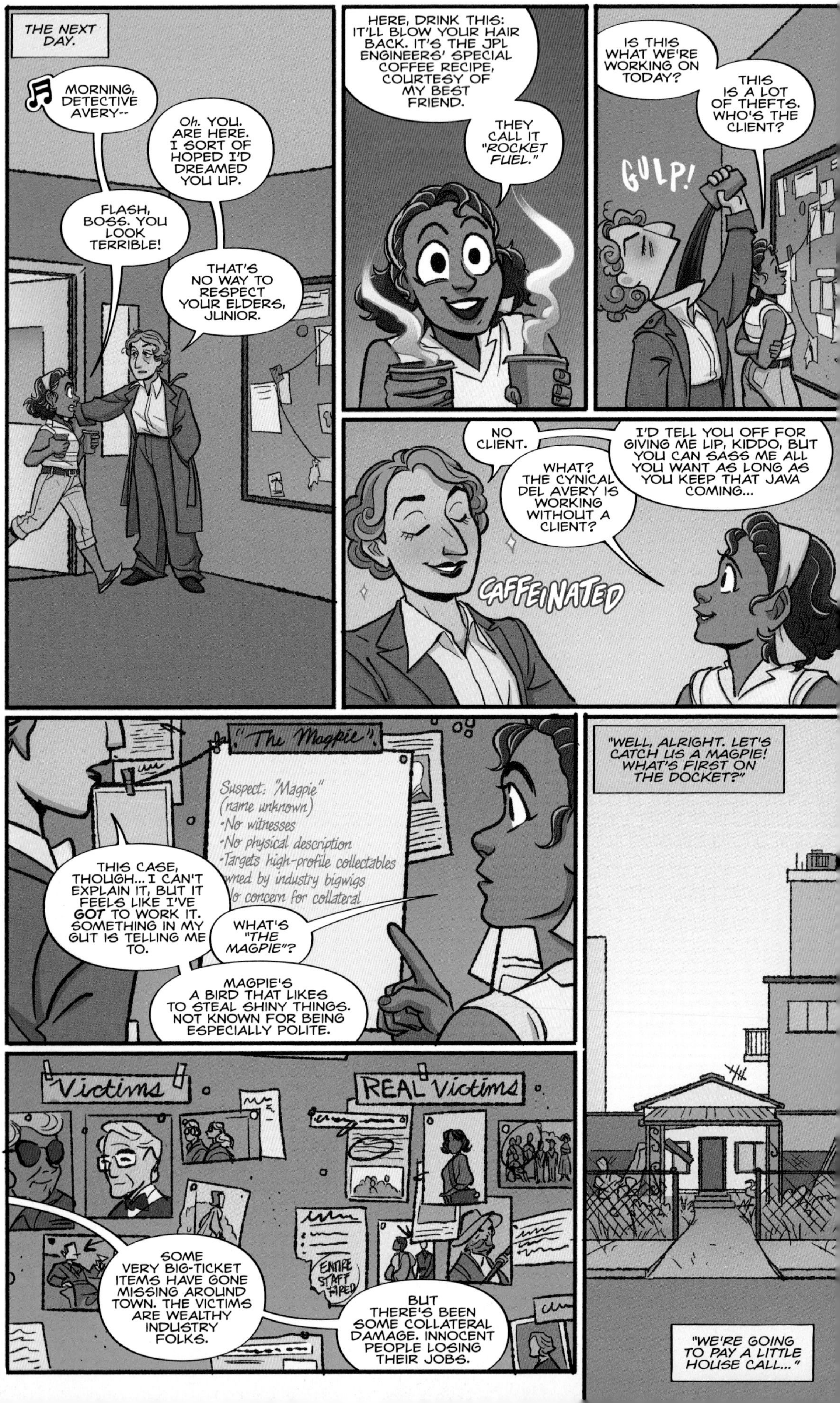
THE NEXT DAY.
MORNING, DETECTIVE AVERY--
Oh. YOU. ARE HERE. I SORT OF HOPED I'D DREAMED YOU UP.
FLASH, BOSS. YOU LOOK TERRIBLE!
THAT'S NO WAY TO RESPECT YOUR ELDERS, JUNIOR.
HERE, DRINK THIS: IT'LL BLOW YOUR HAIR BACK. IT'S THE JPL ENGINEERS' SPECIAL COFFEE RECIPE, COURTESY OF MY BEST FRIEND.
THEY CALL IT "ROCKET FUEL."
IS THIS WHAT WE'RE WORKING ON TODAY?
THIS IS A LOT OF THEFTS. WHO'S THE CLIENT?
GULP!
NO CLIENT.
WHAT? THE CYNICAL DEL AVERY IS WORKING WITHOUT A CLIENT?
I'D TELL YOU OFF FOR GIVING ME LIP, KIDDO, BUT YOU CAN SASS ME ALL YOU WANT AS LONG AS YOU KEEP THAT JAVA COMING...
CAFFEINATED
"The Magpie"
Suspect: "Magpie"
(name unknown)
-No witnesses
-No physical description
-Targets high-profile collectables
wned by industry bigwigs
lo concern for collateral
THIS CASE, THOUGH... I CAN'T EXPLAIN IT, BUT IT FEELS LIKE I'VE GOT TO WORK IT. SOMETHING IN MY GUT IS TELLING ME TO.
WHAT'S "THE MAGPIE"?
MAGPIE'S A BIRD THAT LIKES TO STEAL SHINY THINGS. NOT KNOWN FOR BEING ESPECIALLY POLITE.
Victims
REAL Victims
ENTIRE STAFF FIRED
SOME VERY BIG-TICKET ITEMS HAVE GONE MISSING AROUND TOWN. THE VICTIMS ARE WEALTHY INDUSTRY FOLKS.
BUT THERE'S BEEN SOME COLLATERAL DAMAGE. INNOCENT PEOPLE LOSING THEIR JOBS.
"WELL, ALRIGHT. LET'S CATCH US A MAGPIE! WHAT'S FIRST ON THE DOCKET?"
"WE'RE GOING TO PAY A LITTLE HOUSE CALL..."

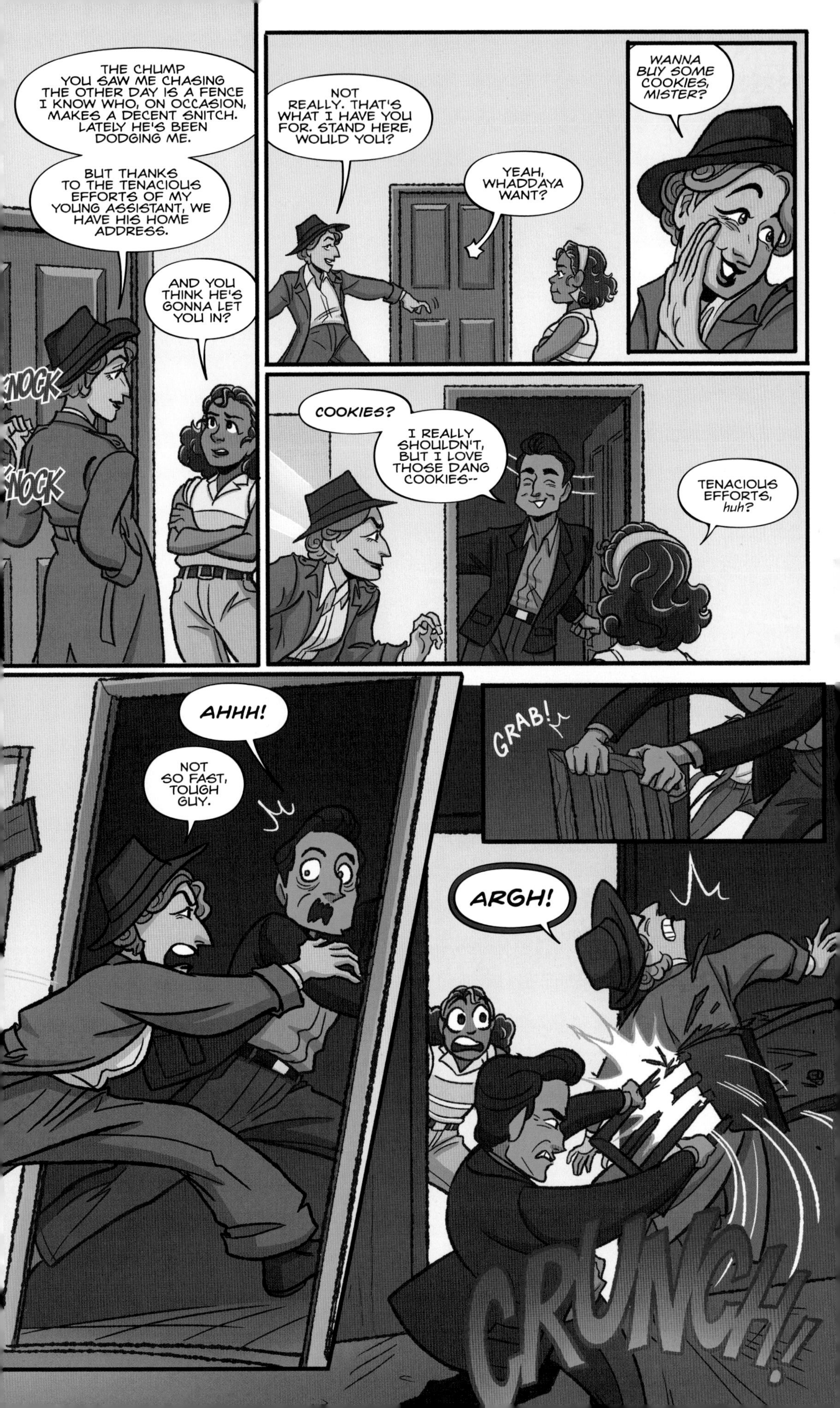
THE CHUMP YOU SAW ME CHASING THE OTHER DAY IS A FENCE I KNOW WHO, ON OCCASION, MAKES A DECENT SNITCH. LATELY HE'S BEEN DODGING ME.
BUT THANKS TO THE TENACIOUS EFFORTS OF MY YOUNG ASSISTANT, WE HAVE HIS HOME ADDRESS.
KNOCK
KNOCK
AND YOU THINK HE'S GONNA LET YOU IN?
NOT REALLY. THAT'S WHAT I HAVE YOU FOR. STAND HERE, WOULD YOU?
YEAH, WHADDAYA WANT?
WANNA BUY SOME COOKIES, MISTER?
COOKIES?
I REALLY SHOULDN'T, BUT I LOVE THOSE DANG COOKIES--
TENACIOUS EFFORTS, *huh?*
AHHH!
NOT SO FAST, TOUGH GUY.
GRAB!
ARGH!
CRUNCH!!

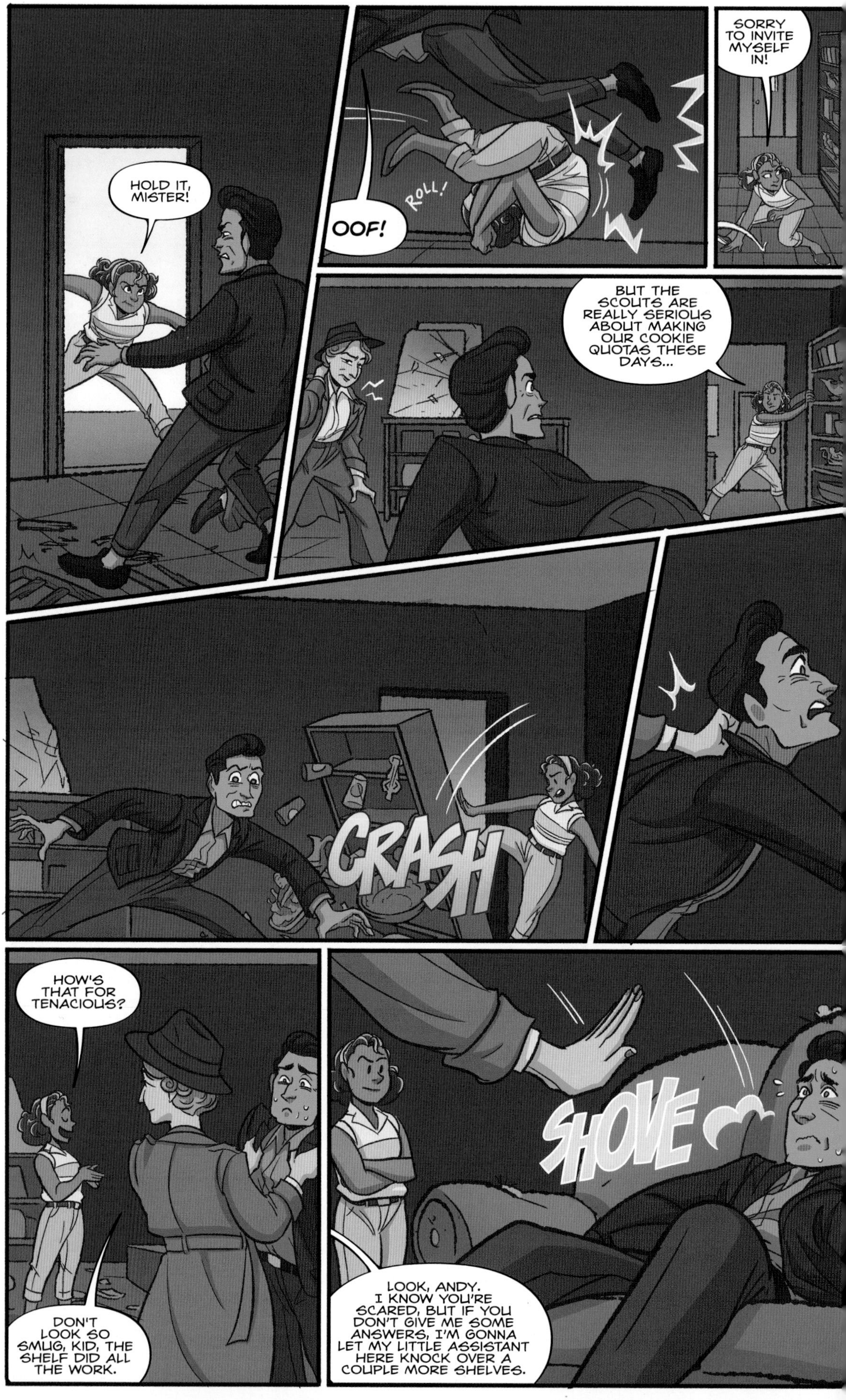
HOLD IT, MISTER!
OOF!
ROLL!
SORRY TO INVITE MYSELF IN!
BUT THE SCOUTS ARE REALLY SERIOUS ABOUT MAKING OUR COOKIE QUOTAS THESE DAYS...
CRASH
HOW'S THAT FOR TENACIOUS?
DON'T LOOK SO SMUG, KID, THE SHELF DID ALL THE WORK.
SHOVE
LOOK, ANDY. I KNOW YOU'RE SCARED, BUT IF YOU DON'T GIVE ME SOME ANSWERS, I'M GONNA LET MY LITTLE ASSISTANT HERE KNOCK OVER A COUPLE MORE SHELVES.

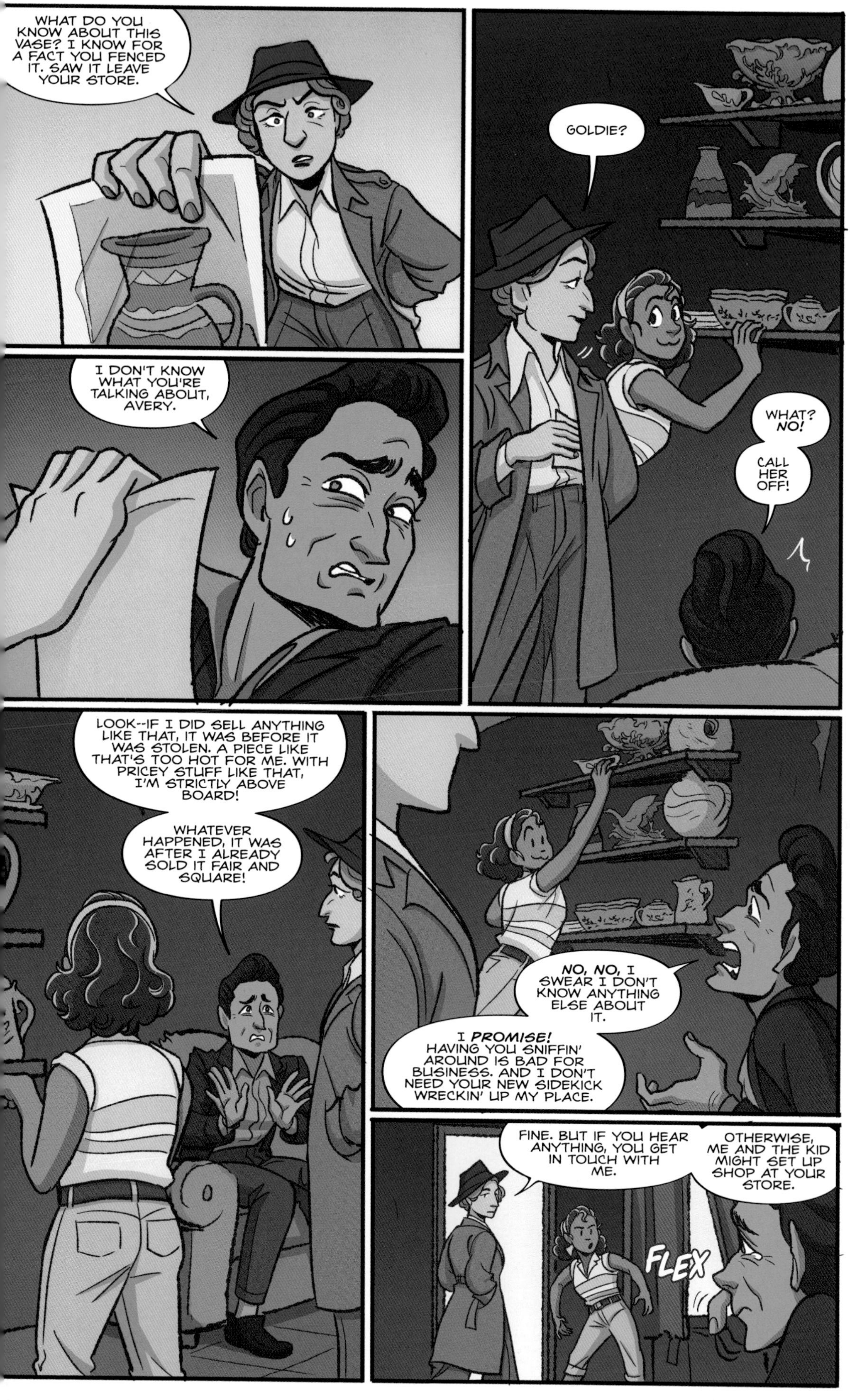
WHAT DO YOU KNOW ABOUT THIS VASE? I KNOW FOR A FACT YOU FENCED IT. SAW IT LEAVE YOUR STORE.
I DON'T KNOW WHAT YOU'RE TALKING ABOUT, AVERY.
GOLDIE?
WHAT? NO!
CALL HER OFF!
LOOK--IF I DID SELL ANYTHING LIKE THAT, IT WAS BEFORE IT WAS STOLEN. A PIECE LIKE THAT'S TOO HOT FOR ME. WITH PRICEY STUFF LIKE THAT, I'M STRICTLY ABOVE BOARD!
WHATEVER HAPPENED, IT WAS AFTER I ALREADY SOLD IT FAIR AND SQUARE!
NO, NO, I SWEAR I DON'T KNOW ANYTHING ELSE ABOUT IT.
I PROMISE! HAVING YOU SNIFFIN' AROUND IS BAD FOR BUSINESS. AND I DON'T NEED YOUR NEW SIDEKICK WRECKIN' UP MY PLACE.
FINE. BUT IF YOU HEAR ANYTHING, YOU GET IN TOUCH WITH ME.
OTHERWISE, ME AND THE KID MIGHT SET UP SHOP AT YOUR STORE.
FLEX

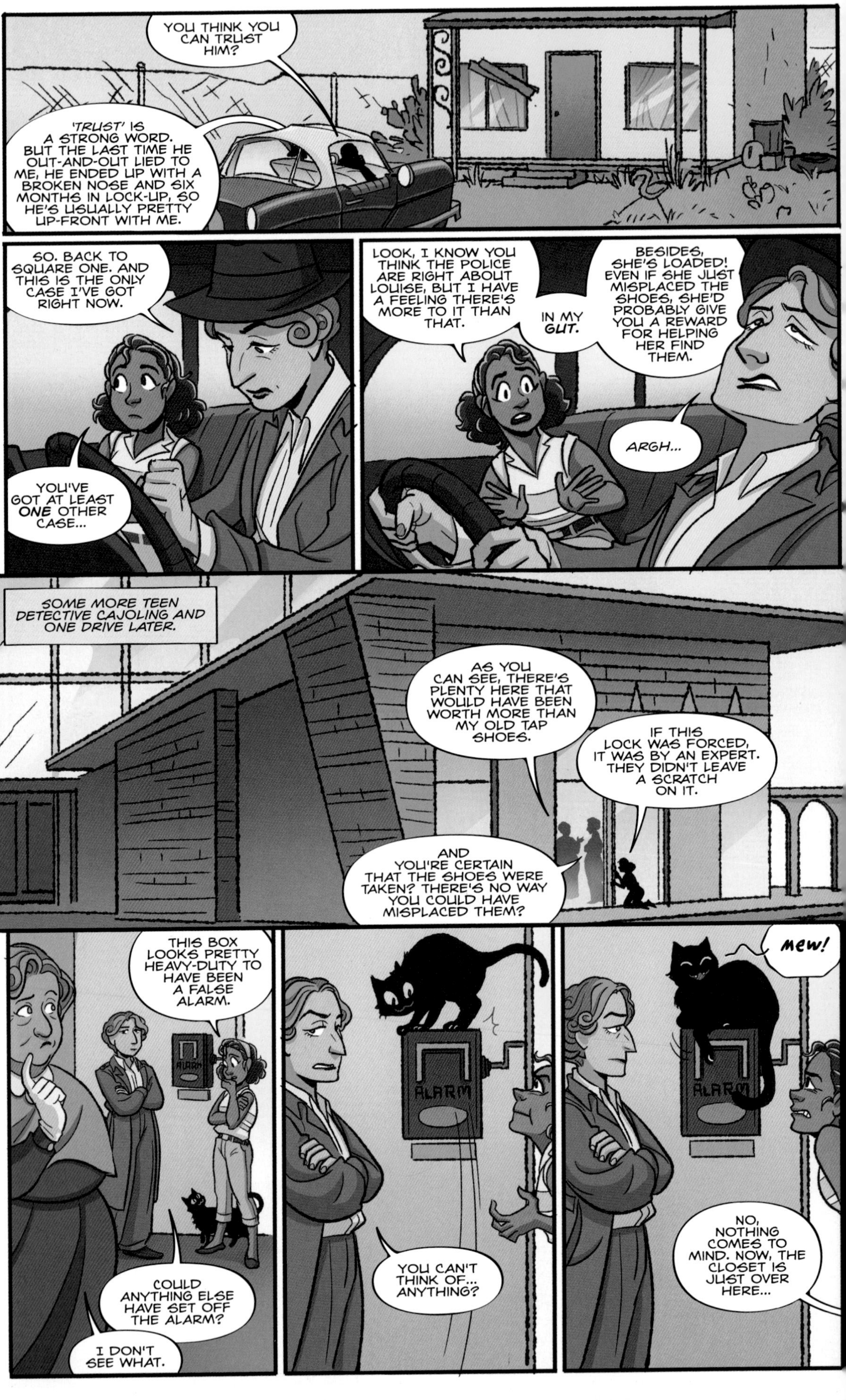

YOU THINK YOU CAN TRUST HIM?
'TRUST' IS A STRONG WORD. BUT THE LAST TIME HE OUT-AND-OUT LIED TO ME, HE ENDED UP WITH A BROKEN NOSE AND SIX MONTHS IN LOCK-UP, SO HE'S USUALLY PRETTY UP-FRONT WITH ME.
SO. BACK TO SQUARE ONE. AND THIS IS THE ONLY CASE I'VE GOT RIGHT NOW.
YOU'VE GOT AT LEAST ONE OTHER CASE...
LOOK, I KNOW YOU THINK THE POLICE ARE RIGHT ABOUT LOUISE, BUT I HAVE A FEELING THERE'S MORE TO IT THAN THAT.
IN MY GUT.
BESIDES, SHE'S LOADED! EVEN IF SHE JUST MISPLACED THE SHOES, SHE'D PROBABLY GIVE YOU A REWARD FOR HELPING HER FIND THEM.
ARGH...
SOME MORE TEEN DETECTIVE CAJOLING AND ONE DRIVE LATER.
AS YOU CAN SEE, THERE'S PLENTY HERE THAT WOULD HAVE BEEN WORTH MORE THAN MY OLD TAP SHOES.
IF THIS LOCK WAS FORCED, IT WAS BY AN EXPERT. THEY DIDN'T LEAVE A SCRATCH ON IT.
AND YOU'RE CERTAIN THAT THE SHOES WERE TAKEN? THERE'S NO WAY YOU COULD HAVE MISPLACED THEM?
THIS BOX LOOKS PRETTY HEAVY-DUTY TO HAVE BEEN A FALSE ALARM.
ALARM
COULD ANYTHING ELSE HAVE SET OFF THE ALARM?
I DON'T SEE WHAT.
ALARM
YOU CAN'T THINK OF... ANYTHING?
MEW!
ALARM
NO, NOTHING COMES TO MIND. NOW, THE CLOSET IS JUST OVER HERE...

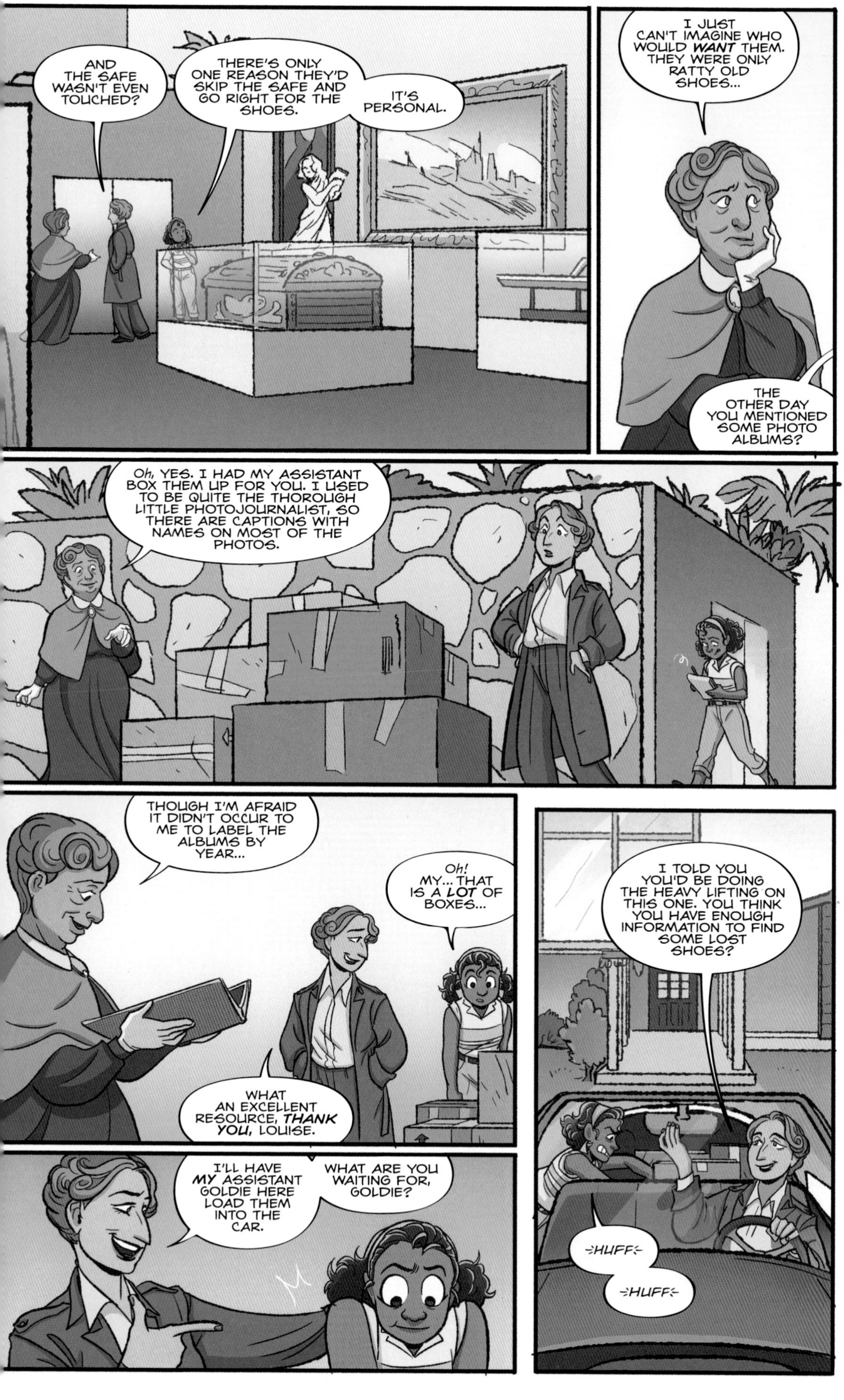
AND THE SAFE WASN'T EVEN TOUCHED?
THERE'S ONLY ONE REASON THEY'D SKIP THE SAFE AND GO RIGHT FOR THE SHOES.
IT'S PERSONAL.
I JUST CAN'T IMAGINE WHO WOULD *WANT* THEM. THEY WERE ONLY RATTY OLD SHOES...
THE OTHER DAY YOU MENTIONED SOME PHOTO ALBUMS?
Oh, YES. I HAD MY ASSISTANT BOX THEM UP FOR YOU. I USED TO BE QUITE THE THOROUGH LITTLE PHOTOJOURNALIST, SO THERE ARE CAPTIONS WITH NAMES ON MOST OF THE PHOTOS.
THOUGH I'M AFRAID IT DIDN'T OCCUR TO ME TO LABEL THE ALBUMS BY YEAR...
Oh! MY... THAT IS A ***LOT*** OF BOXES...
WHAT AN EXCELLENT RESOURCE, ***THANK YOU,*** LOUISE.
I'LL HAVE ***MY*** ASSISTANT GOLDIE HERE LOAD THEM INTO THE CAR.
WHAT ARE YOU WAITING FOR, GOLDIE?
I TOLD YOU YOU'D BE DOING THE HEAVY LIFTING ON THIS ONE. YOU THINK YOU HAVE ENOUGH INFORMATION TO FIND SOME LOST SHOES?
HUFF
HUFF

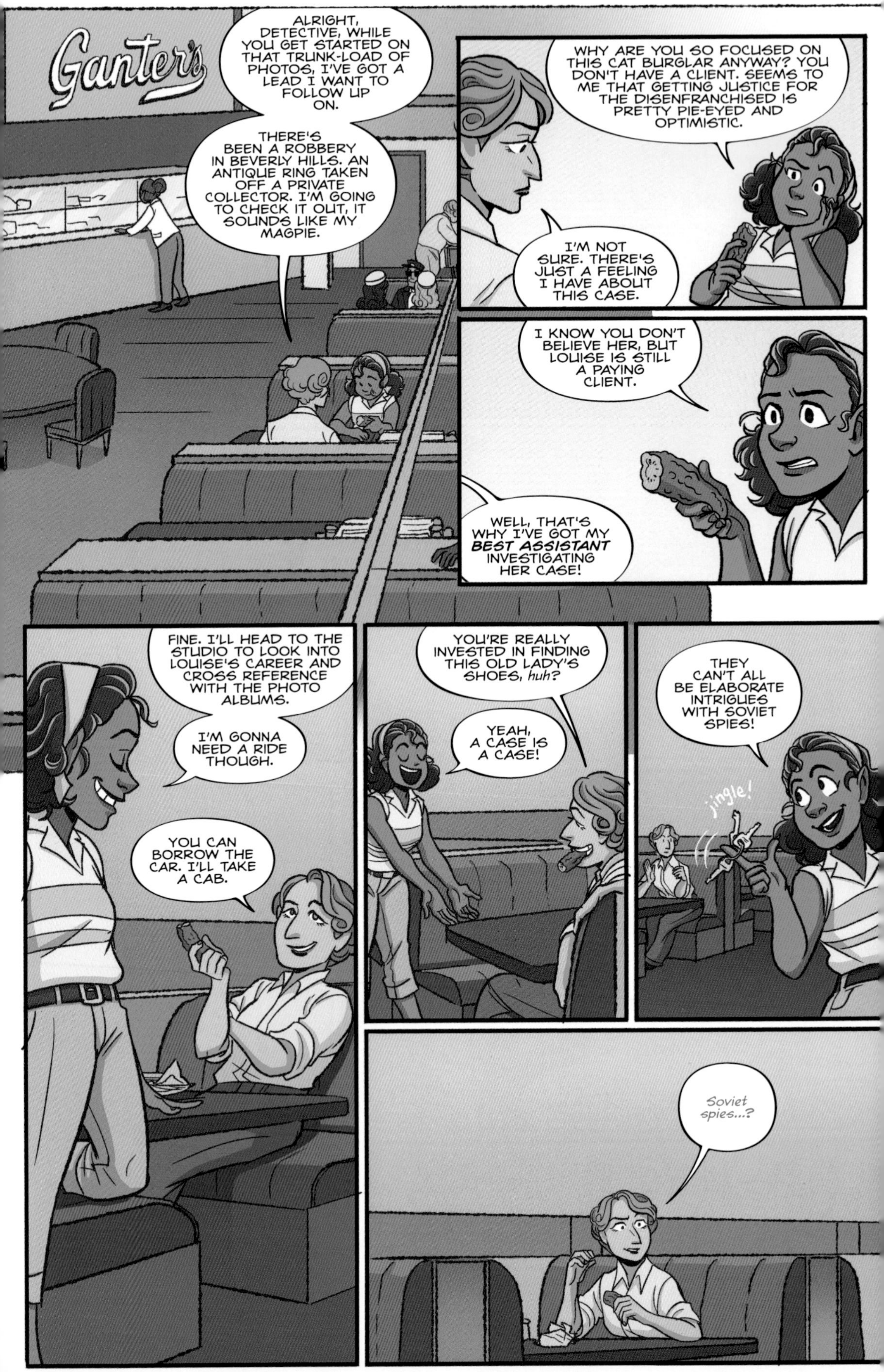
Ganter's
ALRIGHT, DETECTIVE, WHILE YOU GET STARTED ON THAT TRUNK-LOAD OF PHOTOS, I'VE GOT A LEAD I WANT TO FOLLOW UP ON.
THERE'S BEEN A ROBBERY IN BEVERLY HILLS. AN ANTIQUE RING TAKEN OFF A PRIVATE COLLECTOR. I'M GOING TO CHECK IT OUT, IT SOUNDS LIKE MY MAGPIE.
WHY ARE YOU SO FOCUSED ON THIS CAT BURGLAR ANYWAY? YOU DON'T HAVE A CLIENT. SEEMS TO ME THAT GETTING JUSTICE FOR THE DISENFRANCHISED IS PRETTY PIE-EYED AND OPTIMISTIC.
I'M NOT SURE. THERE'S JUST A FEELING I HAVE ABOUT THIS CASE.
I KNOW YOU DON'T BELIEVE HER, BUT LOUISE IS STILL A PAYING CLIENT.
WELL, THAT'S WHY I'VE GOT MY **BEST ASSISTANT** INVESTIGATING HER CASE!
FINE. I'LL HEAD TO THE STUDIO TO LOOK INTO LOUISE'S CAREER AND CROSS REFERENCE WITH THE PHOTO ALBUMS.
I'M GONNA NEED A RIDE THOUGH.
YOU CAN BORROW THE CAR. I'LL TAKE A CAB.
YOU'RE REALLY INVESTED IN FINDING THIS OLD LADY'S SHOES, *huh*?
YEAH, A CASE IS A CASE!
THEY CAN'T ALL BE ELABORATE INTRIGUES WITH SOVIET SPIES!
jingle!
Soviet spies...?

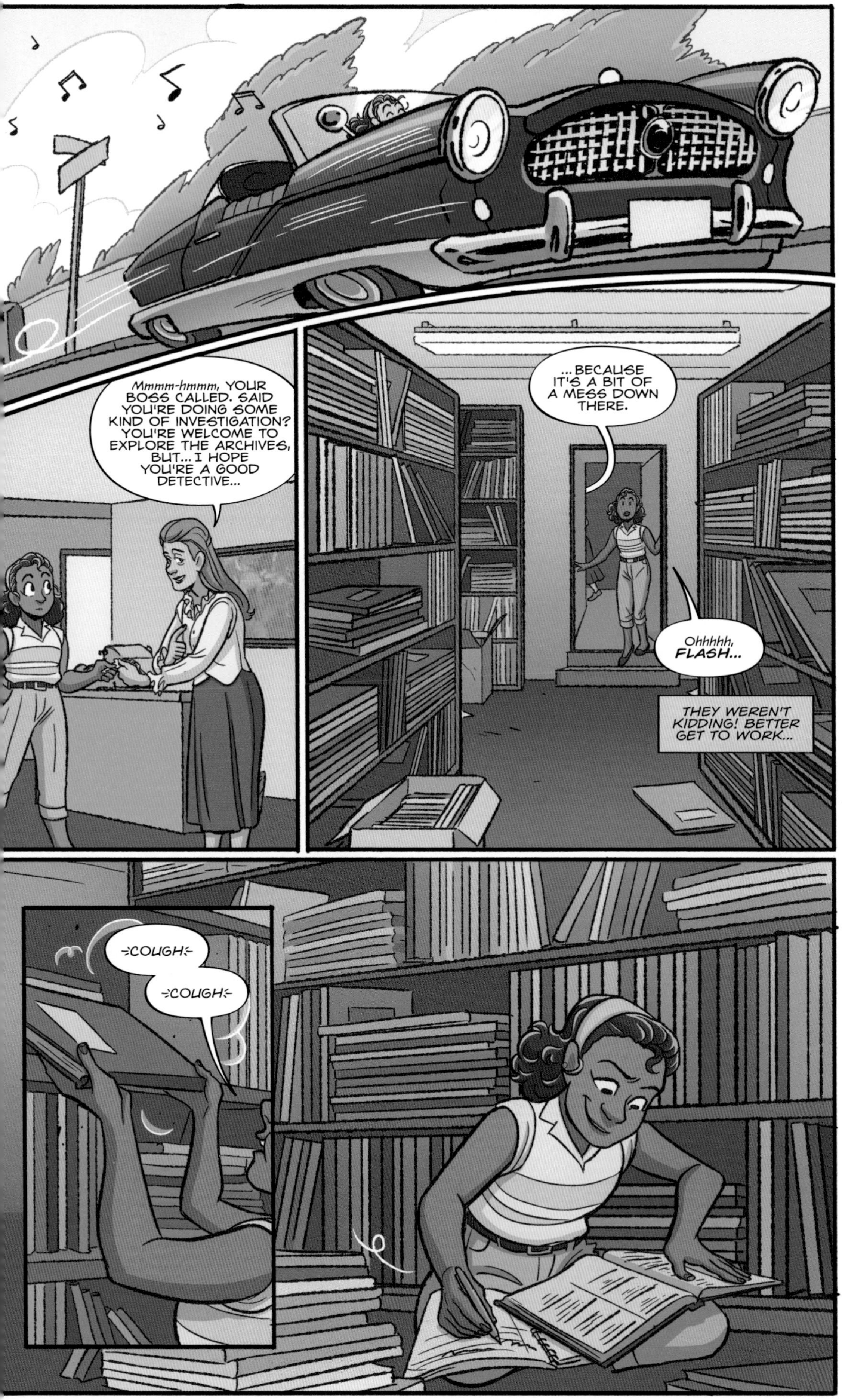
Mmmm-hmmm, YOUR BOSS CALLED. SAID YOU'RE DOING SOME KIND OF INVESTIGATION? YOU'RE WELCOME TO EXPLORE THE ARCHIVES, BUT... I HOPE YOU'RE A GOOD DETECTIVE...
...BECAUSE IT'S A BIT OF A MESS DOWN THERE.
Ohhhhh, FLASH...
THEY WEREN'T KIDDING! BETTER GET TO WORK...
=COUGH=
=COUGH=

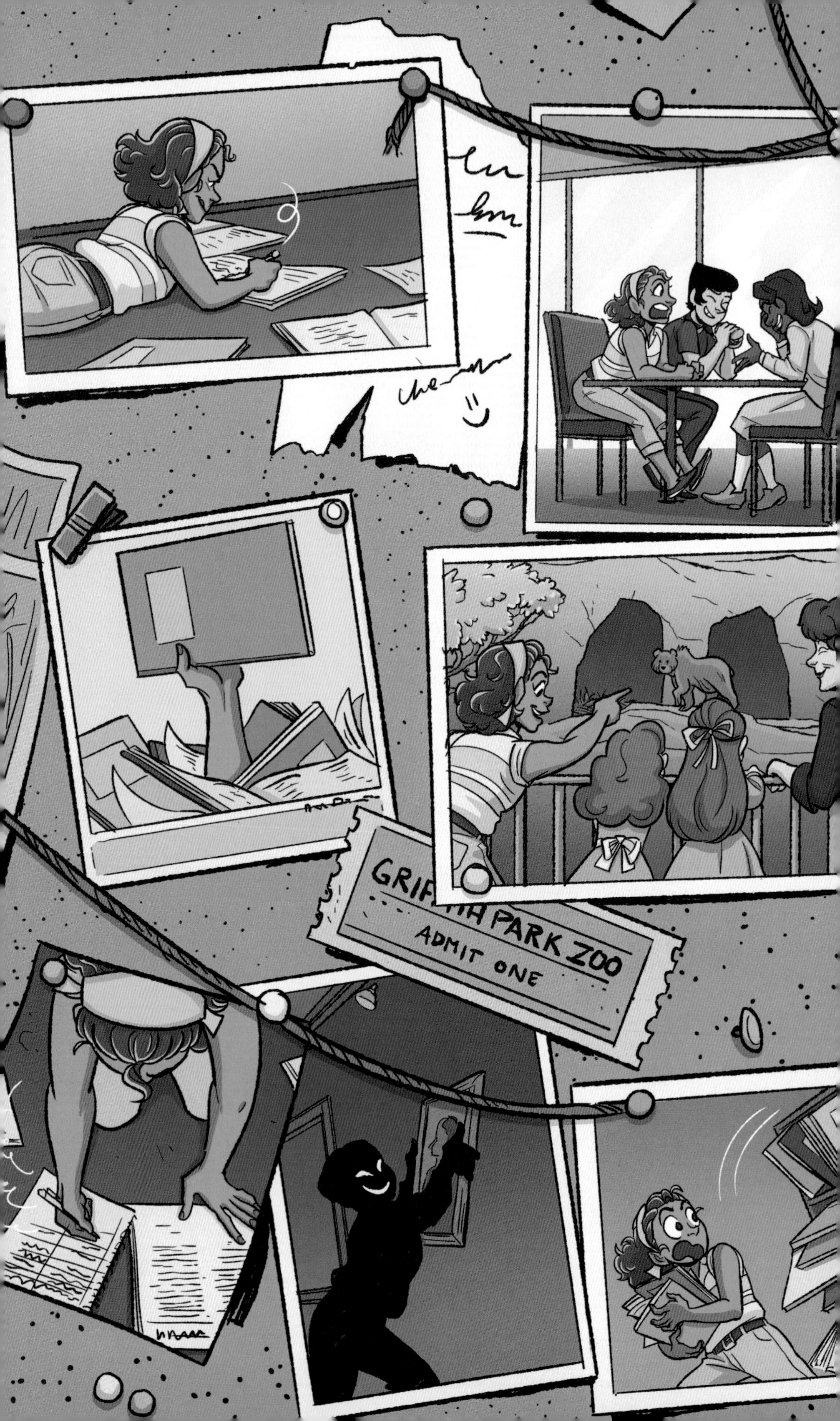
GRIFFITH PARK ZOO
ADMIT ONE

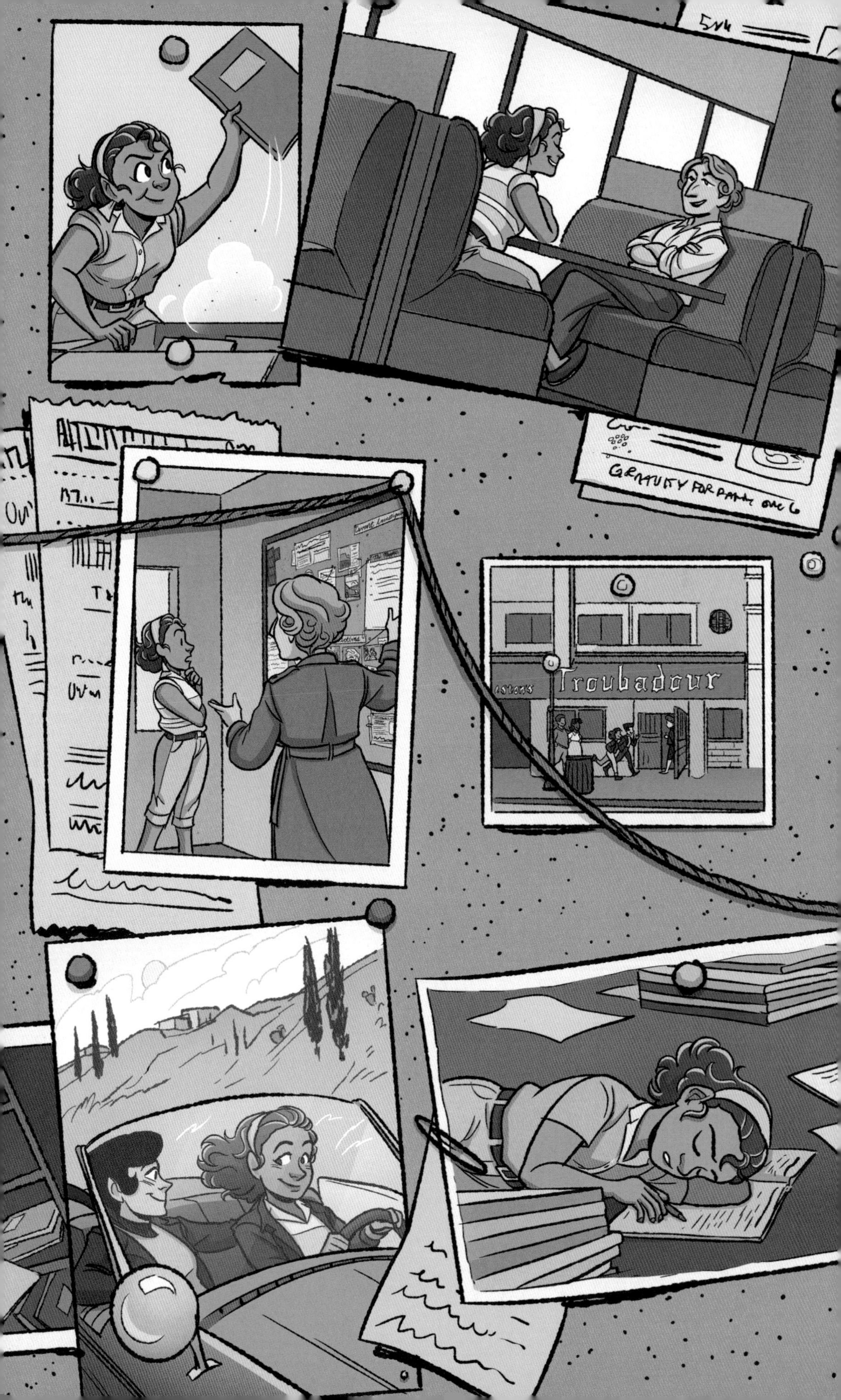
Troubadour

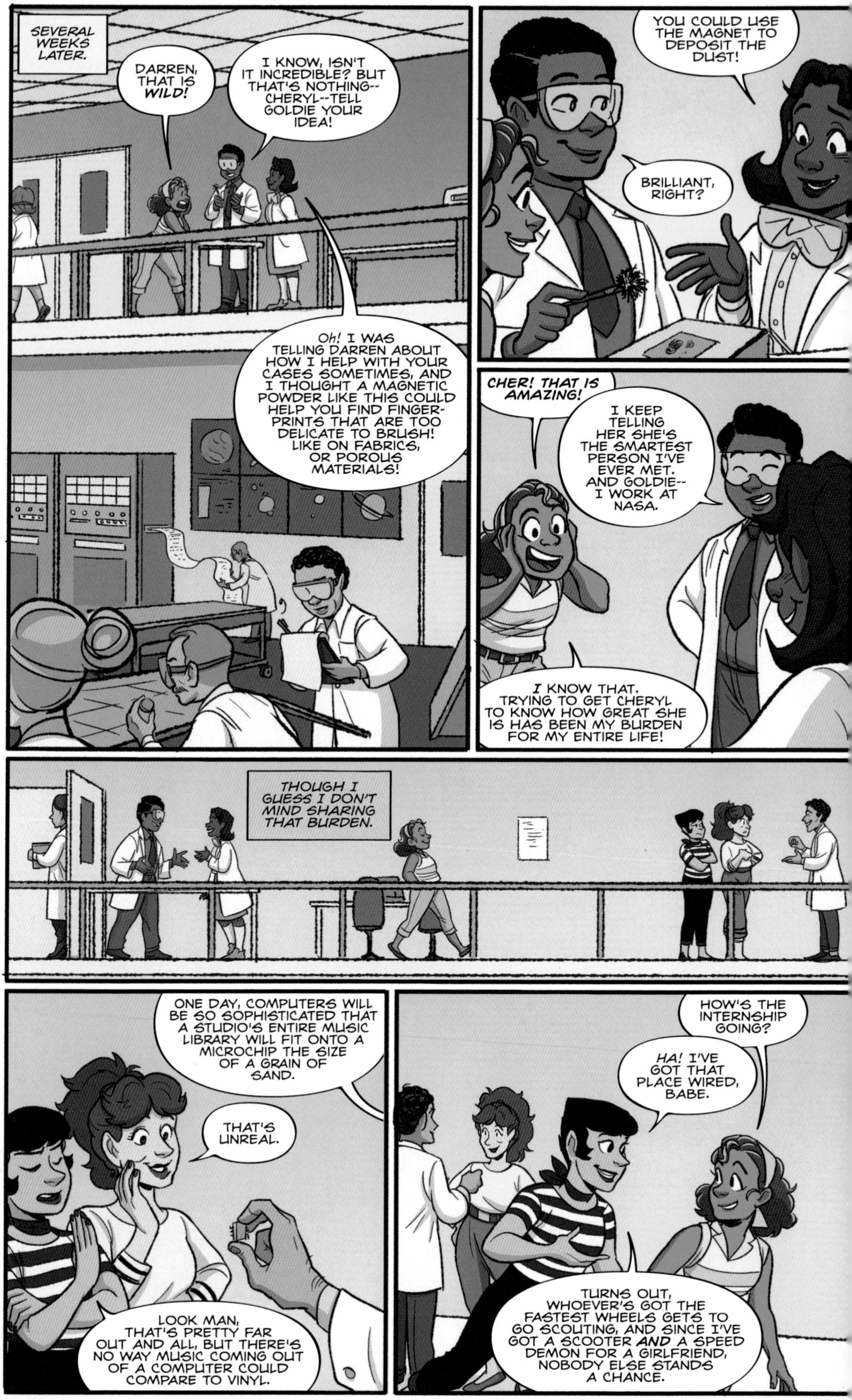

SEVERAL WEEKS LATER.
DARREN, THAT IS *WILD!*
I KNOW, ISN'T IT INCREDIBLE? BUT THAT'S NOTHING-- CHERYL--TELL GOLDIE YOUR IDEA!
Oh! I WAS TELLING DARREN ABOUT HOW I HELP WITH YOUR CASES SOMETIMES, AND I THOUGHT A MAGNETIC POWDER LIKE THIS COULD HELP YOU FIND FINGER-PRINTS THAT ARE TOO DELICATE TO BRUSH! LIKE ON FABRICS, OR POROUS MATERIALS!
YOU COULD USE THE MAGNET TO DEPOSIT THE DUST!
BRILLIANT, RIGHT?
CHER! THAT IS AMAZING!
I KEEP TELLING HER SHE'S THE SMARTEST PERSON I'VE EVER MET. AND GOLDIE-- I WORK AT NASA.
I KNOW THAT. TRYING TO GET CHERYL TO KNOW HOW GREAT SHE IS HAS BEEN MY BURDEN FOR MY ENTIRE LIFE!
THOUGH I GUESS I DON'T MIND SHARING THAT BURDEN.
ONE DAY, COMPUTERS WILL BE SO SOPHISTICATED THAT A STUDIO'S ENTIRE MUSIC LIBRARY WILL FIT ONTO A MICROCHIP THE SIZE OF A GRAIN OF SAND.
THAT'S UNREAL.
LOOK MAN, THAT'S PRETTY FAR OUT AND ALL, BUT THERE'S NO WAY MUSIC COMING OUT OF A COMPUTER COULD COMPARE TO VINYL.
HOW'S THE INTERNSHIP GOING?
HA! I'VE GOT THAT PLACE WIRED, BABE.
TURNS OUT, WHOEVER'S GOT THE FASTEST WHEELS GETS TO GO SCOUTING, AND SINCE I'VE GOT A SCOOTER *AND* A SPEED DEMON FOR A GIRLFRIEND, NOBODY ELSE STANDS A CHANCE.

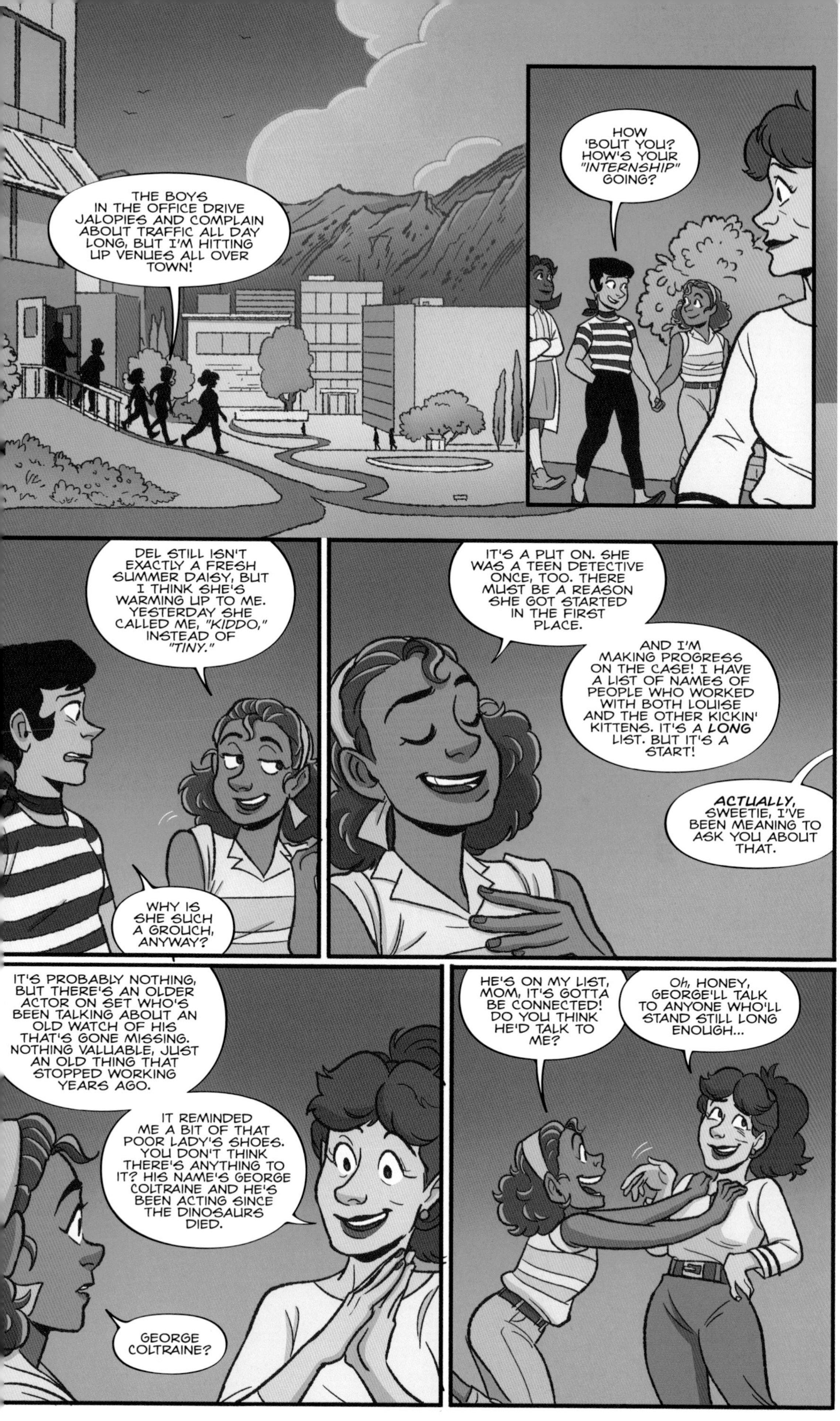
THE BOYS IN THE OFFICE DRIVE JALOPIES AND COMPLAIN ABOUT TRAFFIC ALL DAY LONG, BUT I'M HITTING UP VENUES ALL OVER TOWN!
HOW 'BOUT YOU? HOW'S YOUR "INTERNSHIP" GOING?
DEL STILL ISN'T EXACTLY A FRESH SUMMER DAISY, BUT I THINK SHE'S WARMING UP TO ME. YESTERDAY SHE CALLED ME, "KIDDO," INSTEAD OF "TINY."
WHY IS SHE SUCH A GROUCH, ANYWAY?
IT'S A PUT ON. SHE WAS A TEEN DETECTIVE ONCE, TOO. THERE MUST BE A REASON SHE GOT STARTED IN THE FIRST PLACE.
AND I'M MAKING PROGRESS ON THE CASE! I HAVE A LIST OF NAMES OF PEOPLE WHO WORKED WITH BOTH LOUISE AND THE OTHER KICKIN' KITTENS. IT'S A LONG LIST. BUT IT'S A START!
ACTUALLY, SWEETIE, I'VE BEEN MEANING TO ASK YOU ABOUT THAT.
IT'S PROBABLY NOTHING, BUT THERE'S AN OLDER ACTOR ON SET WHO'S BEEN TALKING ABOUT AN OLD WATCH OF HIS THAT'S GONE MISSING. NOTHING VALUABLE, JUST AN OLD THING THAT STOPPED WORKING YEARS AGO.
IT REMINDED ME A BIT OF THAT POOR LADY'S SHOES. YOU DON'T THINK THERE'S ANYTHING TO IT? HIS NAME'S GEORGE COLTRAINE AND HE'S BEEN ACTING SINCE THE DINOSAURS DIED.
GEORGE COLTRAINE?
HE'S ON MY LIST, MOM, IT'S GOTTA BE CONNECTED! DO YOU THINK HE'D TALK TO ME?
Oh, HONEY, GEORGE'LL TALK TO ANYONE WHO'LL STAND STILL LONG ENOUGH...

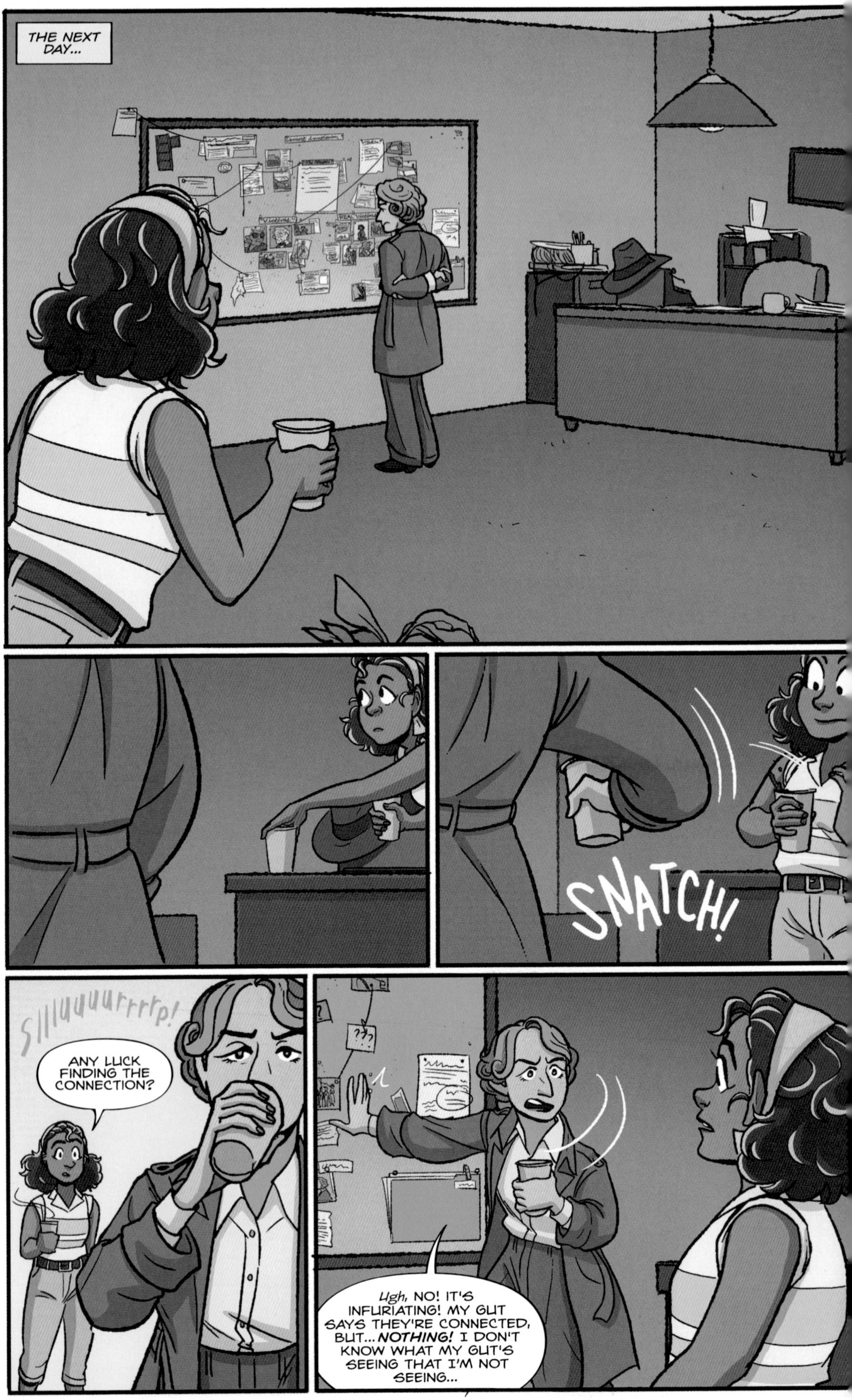
THE NEXT DAY...
SNATCH!
Sllluuuurrrrp!
ANY LUCK FINDING THE CONNECTION?
Ugh, NO! IT'S INFURIATING! MY GUT SAYS THEY'RE CONNECTED, BUT... NOTHING! I DON'T KNOW WHAT MY GUT'S SEEING THAT I'M NOT SEEING...

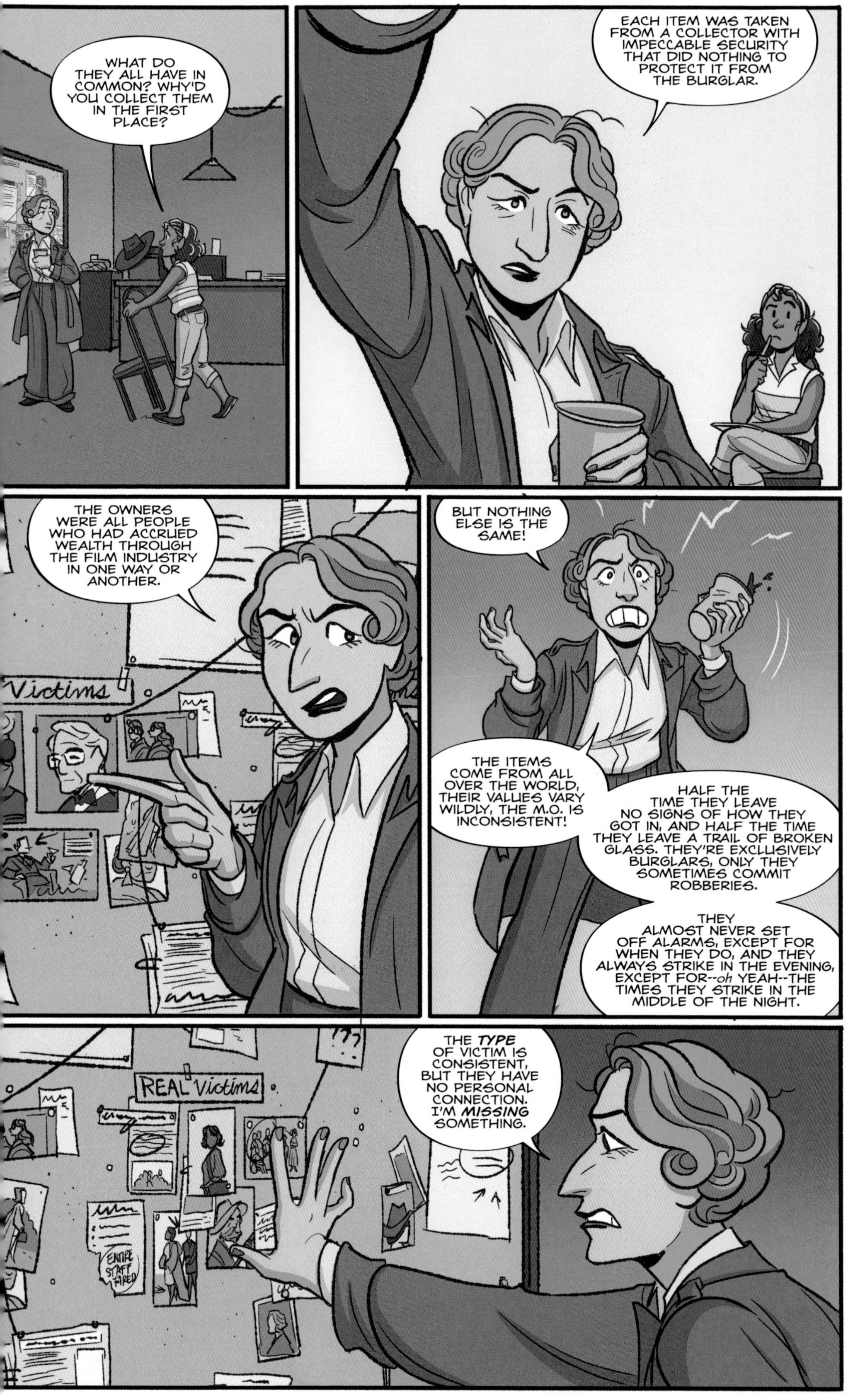
WHAT DO THEY ALL HAVE IN COMMON? WHY'D YOU COLLECT THEM IN THE FIRST PLACE?
EACH ITEM WAS TAKEN FROM A COLLECTOR WITH IMPECCABLE SECURITY THAT DID NOTHING TO PROTECT IT FROM THE BURGLAR.
THE OWNERS WERE ALL PEOPLE WHO HAD ACCRUED WEALTH THROUGH THE FILM INDUSTRY IN ONE WAY OR ANOTHER.
Victims
BUT NOTHING ELSE IS THE SAME!
THE ITEMS COME FROM ALL OVER THE WORLD, THEIR VALUES VARY WILDLY, THE M.O. IS INCONSISTENT!
HALF THE TIME THEY LEAVE NO SIGNS OF HOW THEY GOT IN, AND HALF THE TIME THEY LEAVE A TRAIL OF BROKEN GLASS. THEY'RE EXCLUSIVELY BURGLARS, ONLY THEY SOMETIMES COMMIT ROBBERIES.
THEY ALMOST NEVER SET OFF ALARMS, EXCEPT FOR WHEN THEY DO, AND THEY ALWAYS STRIKE IN THE EVENING, EXCEPT FOR--oh YEAH--THE TIMES THEY STRIKE IN THE MIDDLE OF THE NIGHT.
REAL Victims
???
ENTIRE STAFF FIRED
THE TYPE OF VICTIM IS CONSISTENT, BUT THEY HAVE NO PERSONAL CONNECTION. I'M MISSING SOMETHING.

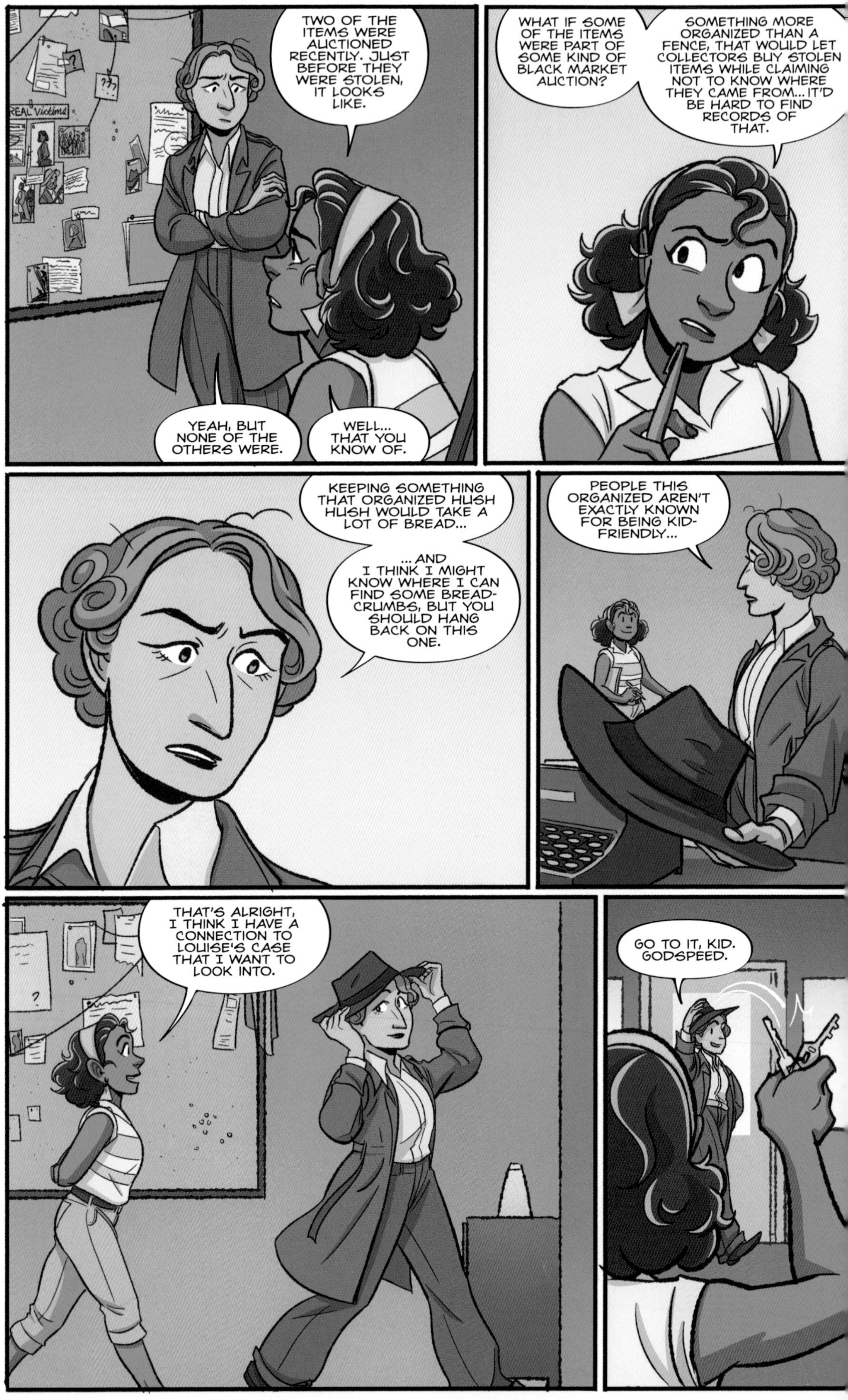

REAL Victims
TWO OF THE ITEMS WERE AUCTIONED RECENTLY. JUST BEFORE THEY WERE STOLEN, IT LOOKS LIKE.
YEAH, BUT NONE OF THE OTHERS WERE.
WELL... THAT YOU KNOW OF.
WHAT IF SOME OF THE ITEMS WERE PART OF SOME KIND OF BLACK MARKET AUCTION?
SOMETHING MORE ORGANIZED THAN A FENCE, THAT WOULD LET COLLECTORS BUY STOLEN ITEMS WHILE CLAIMING NOT TO KNOW WHERE THEY CAME FROM... IT'D BE HARD TO FIND RECORDS OF THAT.
KEEPING SOMETHING THAT ORGANIZED HUSH HUSH WOULD TAKE A LOT OF BREAD...
...AND I THINK I MIGHT KNOW WHERE I CAN FIND SOME BREAD-CRUMBS, BUT YOU SHOULD HANG BACK ON THIS ONE.
PEOPLE THIS ORGANIZED AREN'T EXACTLY KNOWN FOR BEING KID-FRIENDLY...
THAT'S ALRIGHT, I THINK I HAVE A CONNECTION TO LOUISE'S CASE THAT I WANT TO LOOK INTO.
GO TO IT, KID. GODSPEED.

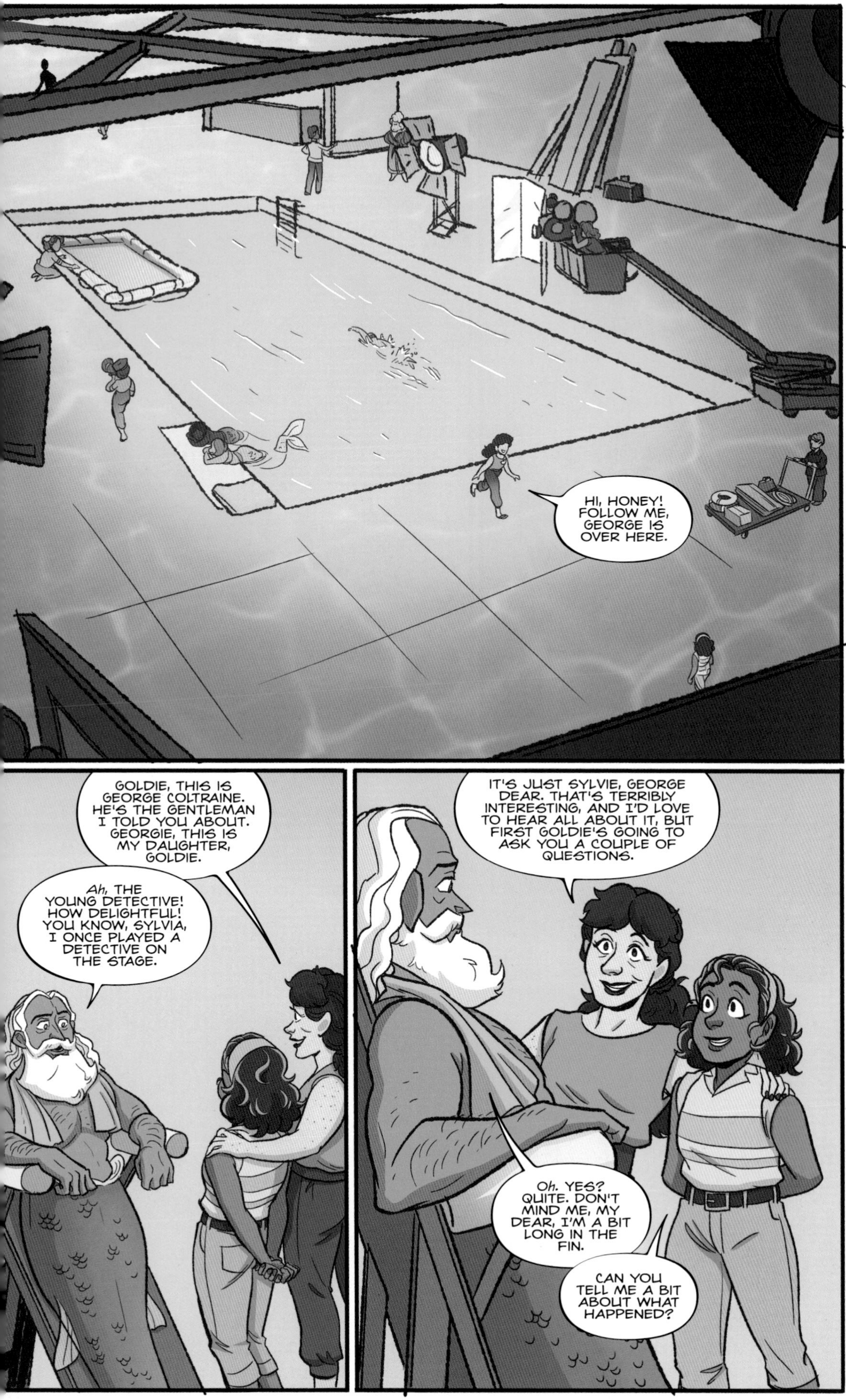
HI, HONEY! FOLLOW ME, GEORGE IS OVER HERE.
GOLDIE, THIS IS GEORGE COLTRAINE. HE'S THE GENTLEMAN I TOLD YOU ABOUT. GEORGIE, THIS IS MY DAUGHTER, GOLDIE.
Ah, THE YOUNG DETECTIVE! HOW DELIGHTFUL! YOU KNOW, SYLVIA, I ONCE PLAYED A DETECTIVE ON THE STAGE.
IT'S JUST SYLVIE, GEORGE DEAR. THAT'S TERRIBLY INTERESTING, AND I'D LOVE TO HEAR ALL ABOUT IT, BUT FIRST GOLDIE'S GOING TO ASK YOU A COUPLE OF QUESTIONS.
Oh. YES? QUITE. DON'T MIND ME, MY DEAR, I'M A BIT LONG IN THE FIN.
CAN YOU TELL ME A BIT ABOUT WHAT HAPPENED?

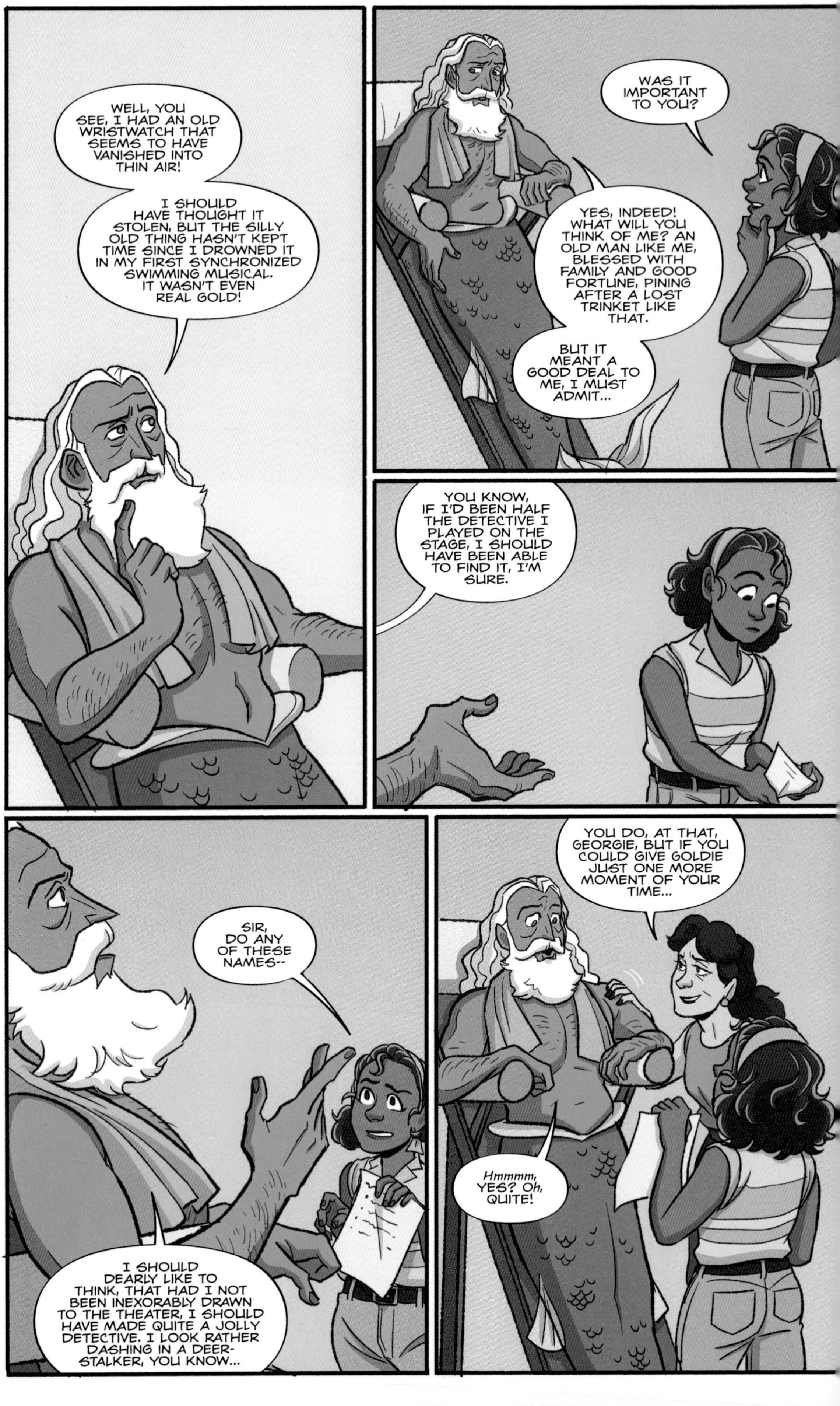

WELL, YOU SEE, I HAD AN OLD WRISTWATCH THAT SEEMS TO HAVE VANISHED INTO THIN AIR!
I SHOULD HAVE THOUGHT IT STOLEN, BUT THE SILLY OLD THING HASN'T KEPT TIME SINCE I DROWNED IT IN MY FIRST SYNCHRONIZED SWIMMING MUSICAL. IT WASN'T EVEN REAL GOLD!
WAS IT IMPORTANT TO YOU?
YES, INDEED! WHAT WILL YOU THINK OF ME? AN OLD MAN LIKE ME, BLESSED WITH FAMILY AND GOOD FORTUNE, PINING AFTER A LOST TRINKET LIKE THAT.
BUT IT MEANT A GOOD DEAL TO ME, I MUST ADMIT...
YOU KNOW, IF I'D BEEN HALF THE DETECTIVE I PLAYED ON THE STAGE, I SHOULD HAVE BEEN ABLE TO FIND IT, I'M SURE.
SIR, DO ANY OF THESE NAMES--
I SHOULD DEARLY LIKE TO THINK, THAT HAD I NOT BEEN INEXORABLY DRAWN TO THE THEATER, I SHOULD HAVE MADE QUITE A JOLLY DETECTIVE. I LOOK RATHER DASHING IN A DEER-STALKER, YOU KNOW...
YOU DO, AT THAT, GEORGIE, BUT IF YOU COULD GIVE GOLDIE JUST ONE MORE MOMENT OF YOUR TIME...
Hmmmm, YES? *Oh,* QUITE!

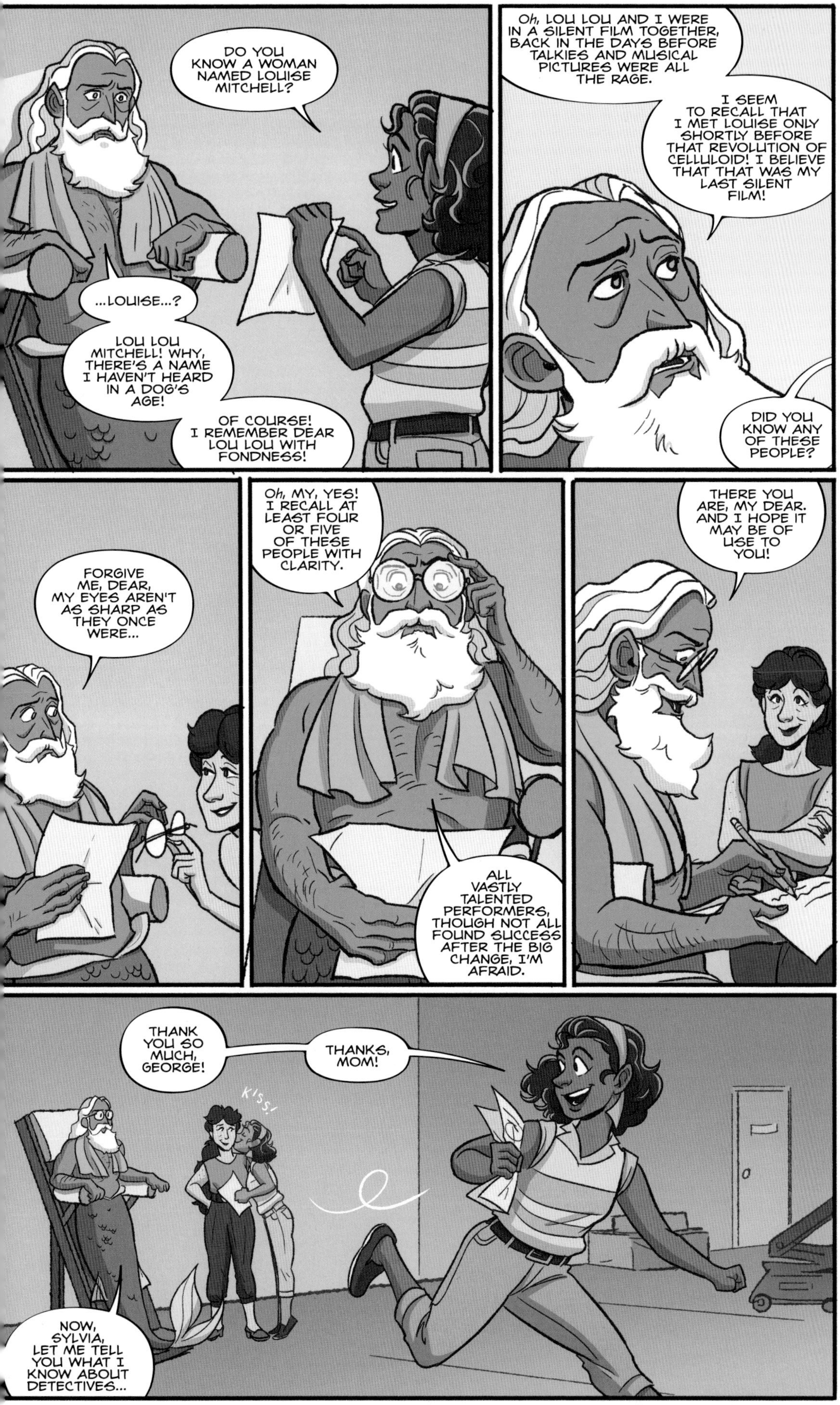
DO YOU KNOW A WOMAN NAMED LOUISE MITCHELL?
...LOUISE...?
LOU LOU MITCHELL! WHY, THERE'S A NAME I HAVEN'T HEARD IN A DOG'S AGE!
OF COURSE! I REMEMBER DEAR LOU LOU WITH FONDNESS!
Oh, LOU LOU AND I WERE IN A SILENT FILM TOGETHER, BACK IN THE DAYS BEFORE TALKIES AND MUSICAL PICTURES WERE ALL THE RAGE.
I SEEM TO RECALL THAT I MET LOUISE ONLY SHORTLY BEFORE THAT REVOLUTION OF CELLULOID! I BELIEVE THAT THAT WAS MY LAST SILENT FILM!
DID YOU KNOW ANY OF THESE PEOPLE?
FORGIVE ME, DEAR, MY EYES AREN'T AS SHARP AS THEY ONCE WERE...
Oh, MY, YES! I RECALL AT LEAST FOUR OR FIVE OF THESE PEOPLE WITH CLARITY.
ALL VASTLY TALENTED PERFORMERS, THOUGH NOT ALL FOUND SUCCESS AFTER THE BIG CHANGE, I'M AFRAID.
THERE YOU ARE, MY DEAR. AND I HOPE IT MAY BE OF USE TO YOU!
THANK YOU SO MUCH, GEORGE!
THANKS, MOM!
KISS!
NOW, SYLVIA, LET ME TELL YOU WHAT I KNOW ABOUT DETECTIVES...

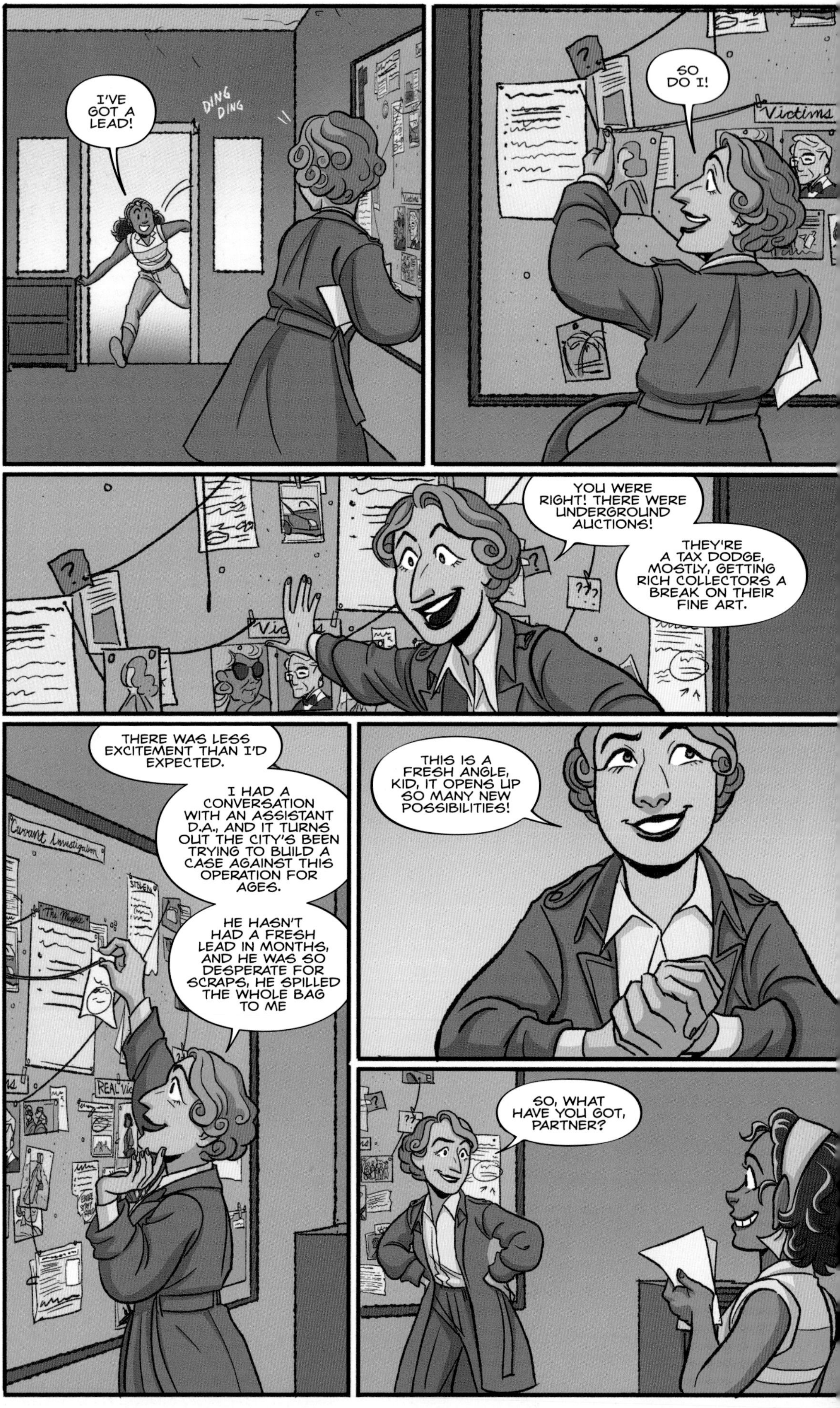
I'VE GOT A LEAD!
DING DING
SO DO I!
Victims
YOU WERE RIGHT! THERE WERE UNDERGROUND AUCTIONS!
THEY'RE A TAX DODGE, MOSTLY, GETTING RICH COLLECTORS A BREAK ON THEIR FINE ART.
THERE WAS LESS EXCITEMENT THAN I'D EXPECTED.
I HAD A CONVERSATION WITH AN ASSISTANT D.A., AND IT TURNS OUT THE CITY'S BEEN TRYING TO BUILD A CASE AGAINST THIS OPERATION FOR AGES.
HE HASN'T HAD A FRESH LEAD IN MONTHS, AND HE WAS SO DESPERATE FOR SCRAPS, HE SPILLED THE WHOLE BAG TO ME
Current Investigation
THIS IS A FRESH ANGLE, KID, IT OPENS UP SO MANY NEW POSSIBILITIES!
SO, WHAT HAVE YOU GOT, PARTNER?

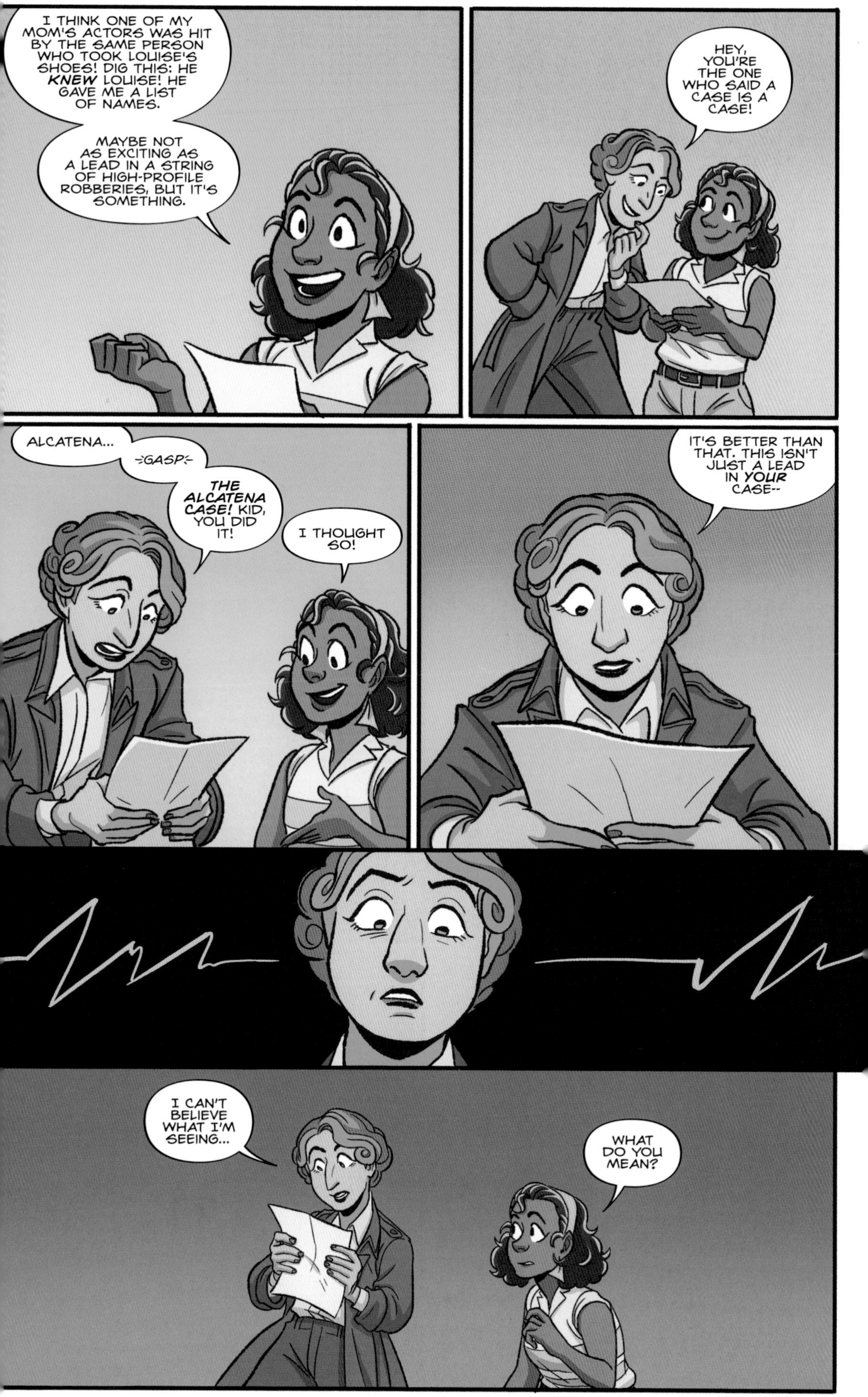
I THINK ONE OF MY MOM'S ACTORS WAS HIT BY THE SAME PERSON WHO TOOK LOUISE'S SHOES! DIG THIS: HE *KNEW* LOUISE! HE GAVE ME A LIST OF NAMES.
MAYBE NOT AS EXCITING AS A LEAD IN A STRING OF HIGH-PROFILE ROBBERIES, BUT IT'S SOMETHING.
HEY, YOU'RE THE ONE WHO SAID A CASE IS A CASE!
ALCATENA...
-GASP-
THE ALCATENA CASE! KID, YOU DID IT!
I THOUGHT SO!
IT'S BETTER THAN THAT. THIS ISN'T JUST A LEAD IN *YOUR* CASE--
I CAN'T BELIEVE WHAT I'M SEEING...
WHAT DO YOU MEAN?

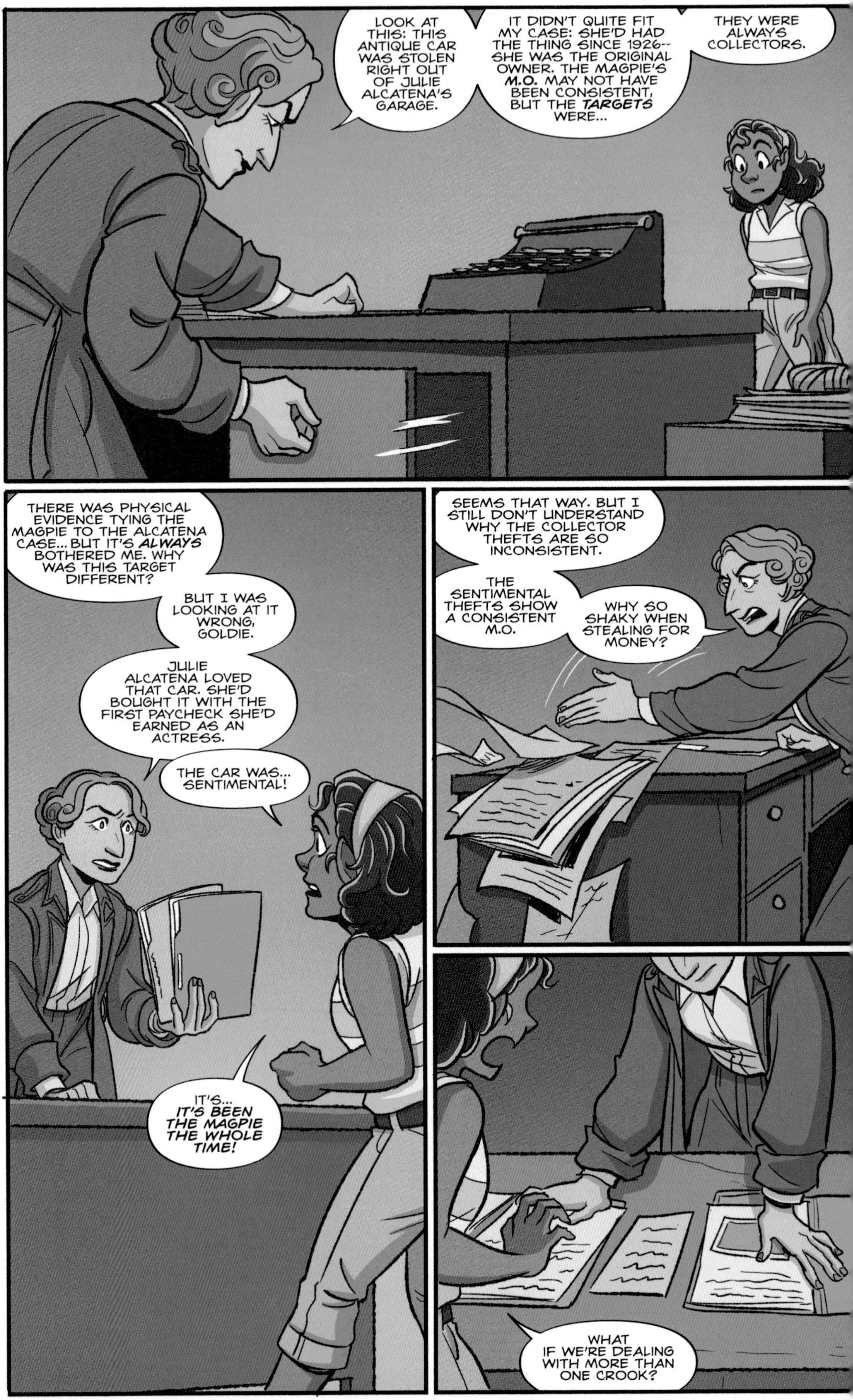
LOOK AT THIS: THIS ANTIQUE CAR WAS STOLEN RIGHT OUT OF JULIE ALCATENA'S GARAGE.
IT DIDN'T QUITE FIT MY CASE: SHE'D HAD THE THING SINCE 1926-- SHE WAS THE ORIGINAL OWNER. THE MAGPIE'S M.O. MAY NOT HAVE BEEN CONSISTENT, BUT THE TARGETS WERE...
THEY WERE ALWAYS COLLECTORS.
THERE WAS PHYSICAL EVIDENCE TYING THE MAGPIE TO THE ALCATENA CASE...BUT IT'S ALWAYS BOTHERED ME. WHY WAS THIS TARGET DIFFERENT?
BUT I WAS LOOKING AT IT WRONG, GOLDIE.
JULIE ALCATENA LOVED THAT CAR. SHE'D BOUGHT IT WITH THE FIRST PAYCHECK SHE'D EARNED AS AN ACTRESS.
THE CAR WAS... SENTIMENTAL!
IT'S... IT'S BEEN THE MAGPIE THE WHOLE TIME!
SEEMS THAT WAY. BUT I STILL DON'T UNDERSTAND WHY THE COLLECTOR THEFTS ARE SO INCONSISTENT.
THE SENTIMENTAL THEFTS SHOW A CONSISTENT M.O.
WHY SO SHAKY WHEN STEALING FOR MONEY?
WHAT IF WE'RE DEALING WITH MORE THAN ONE CROOK?

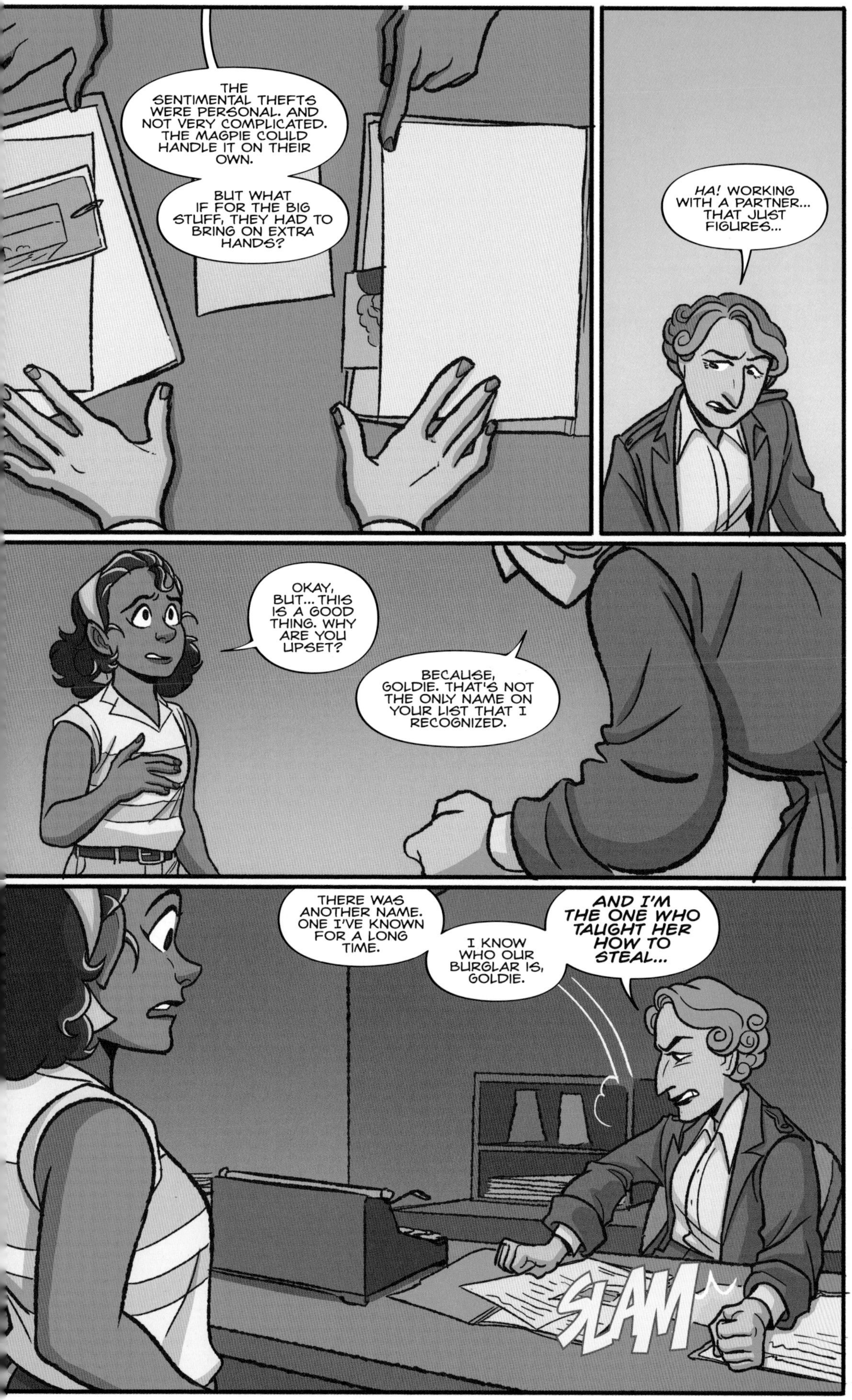
THE SENTIMENTAL THEFTS WERE PERSONAL. AND NOT VERY COMPLICATED. THE MAGPIE COULD HANDLE IT ON THEIR OWN.
BUT WHAT IF FOR THE BIG STUFF, THEY HAD TO BRING ON EXTRA HANDS?
HA! WORKING WITH A PARTNER... THAT JUST FIGURES...
OKAY, BUT... THIS IS A GOOD THING. WHY ARE YOU UPSET?
BECAUSE, GOLDIE. THAT'S NOT THE ONLY NAME ON YOUR LIST THAT I RECOGNIZED.
THERE WAS ANOTHER NAME. ONE I'VE KNOWN FOR A LONG TIME.
I KNOW WHO OUR BURGLAR IS, GOLDIE.
AND I'M THE ONE WHO TAUGHT HER HOW TO STEAL...
SLAM

chapter
NINETEEN

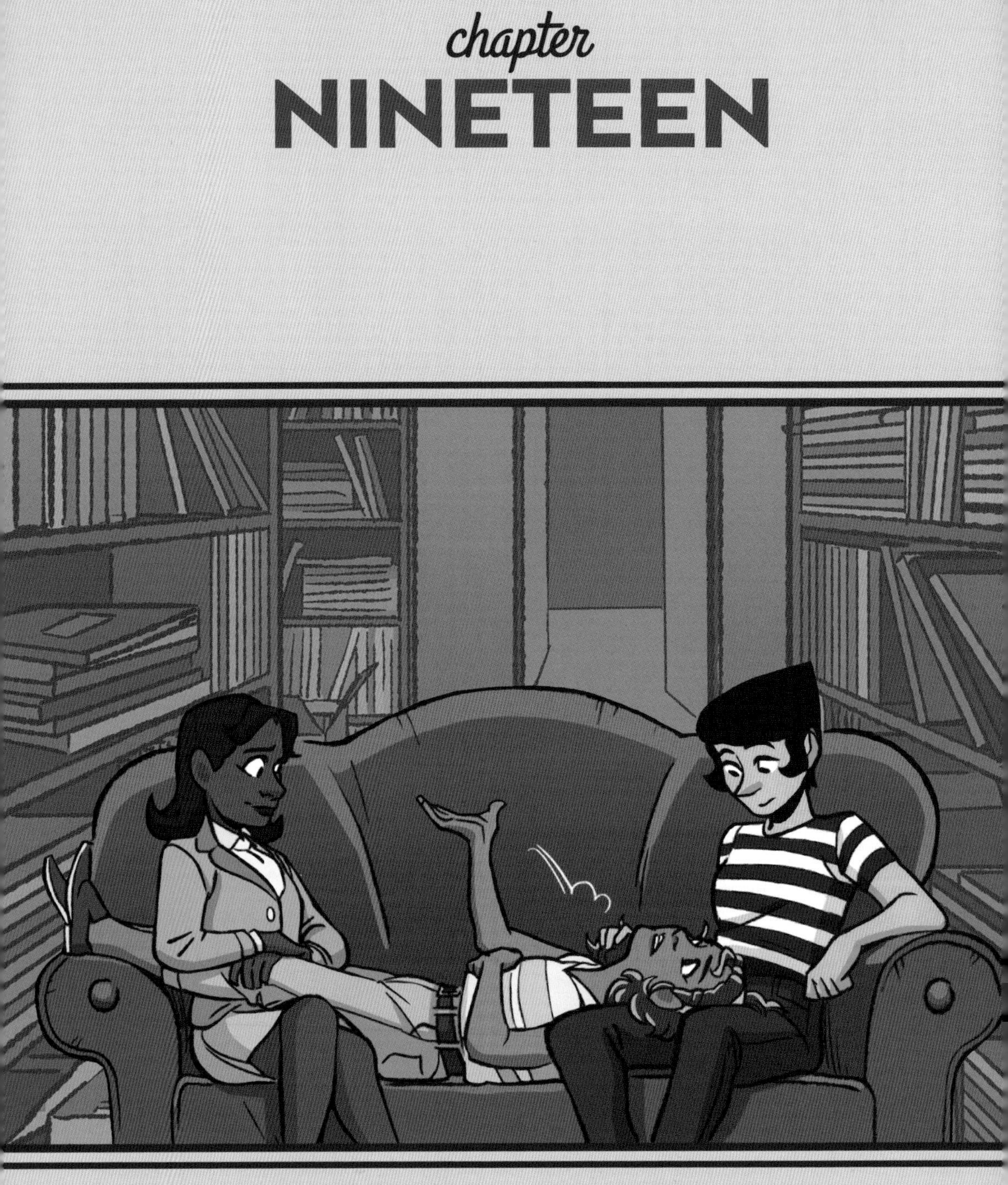

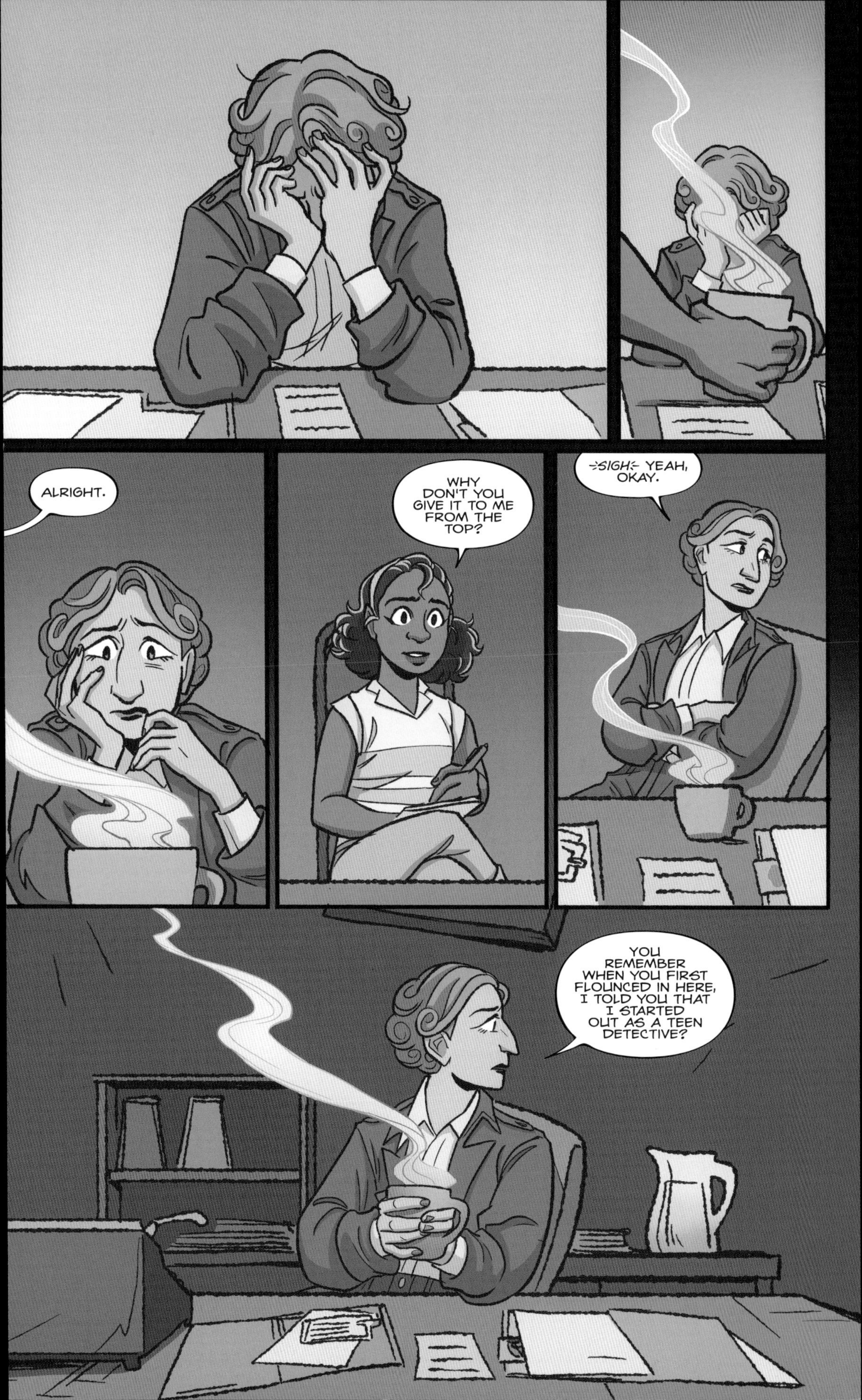
ALRIGHT.
WHY DON'T YOU GIVE IT TO ME FROM THE TOP?
-SIGH- YEAH, OKAY.
YOU REMEMBER WHEN YOU FIRST FLOUNCED IN HERE, I TOLD YOU THAT I STARTED OUT AS A TEEN DETECTIVE?

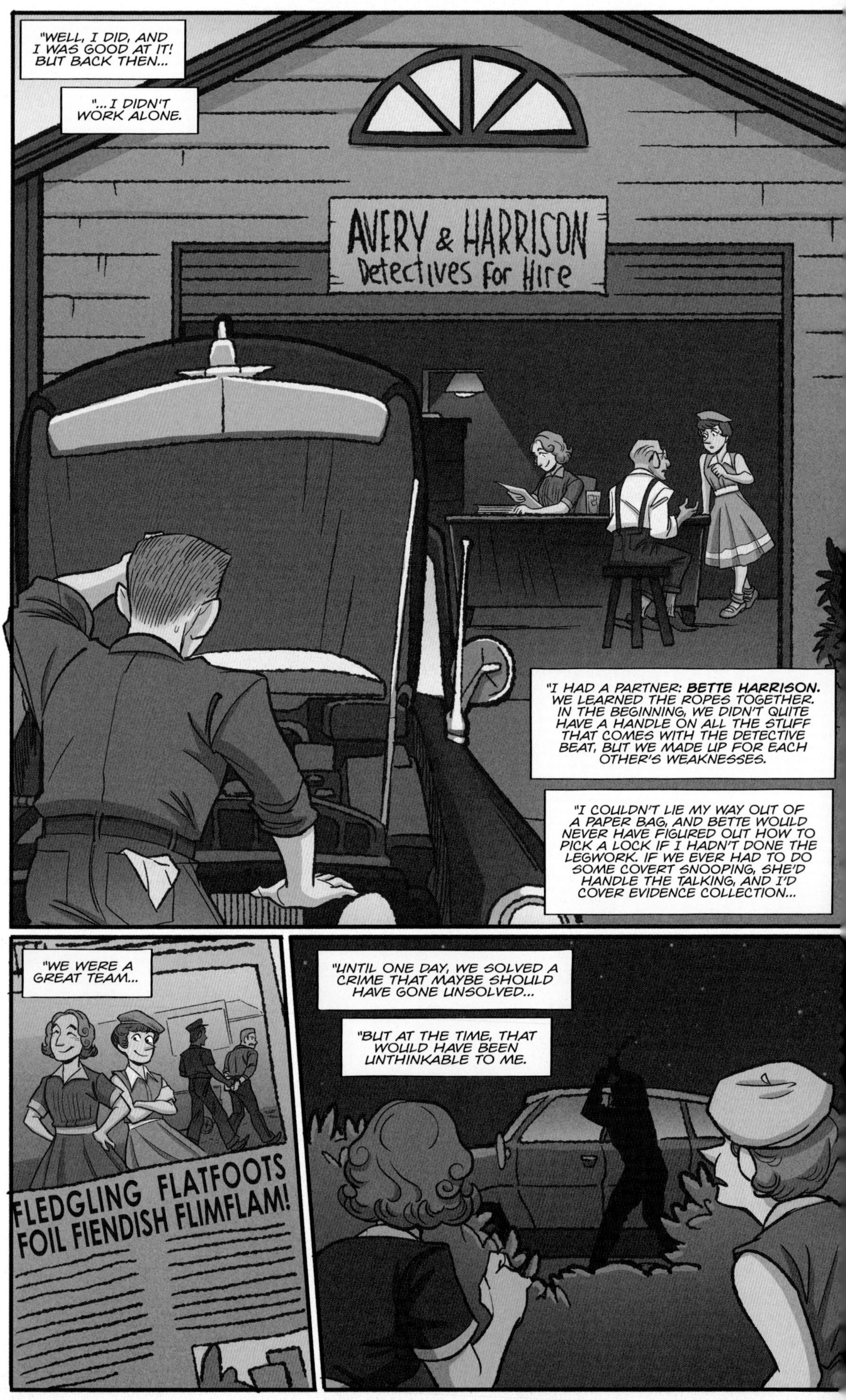
"WELL, I DID, AND I WAS GOOD AT IT! BUT BACK THEN...
"...I DIDN'T WORK ALONE.
AVERY & HARRISON
Detectives For Hire
"I HAD A PARTNER: BETTE HARRISON. WE LEARNED THE ROPES TOGETHER. IN THE BEGINNING, WE DIDN'T QUITE HAVE A HANDLE ON ALL THE STUFF THAT COMES WITH THE DETECTIVE BEAT, BUT WE MADE UP FOR EACH OTHER'S WEAKNESSES.
"I COULDN'T LIE MY WAY OUT OF A PAPER BAG, AND BETTE WOULD NEVER HAVE FIGURED OUT HOW TO PICK A LOCK IF I HADN'T DONE THE LEGWORK. IF WE EVER HAD TO DO SOME COVERT SNOOPING, SHE'D HANDLE THE TALKING, AND I'D COVER EVIDENCE COLLECTION...
"WE WERE A GREAT TEAM...
FLEDGLING FLATFOOTS FOIL FIENDISH FLIMFLAM!
"UNTIL ONE DAY, WE SOLVED A CRIME THAT MAYBE SHOULD HAVE GONE UNSOLVED...
"BUT AT THE TIME, THAT WOULD HAVE BEEN UNTHINKABLE TO ME.

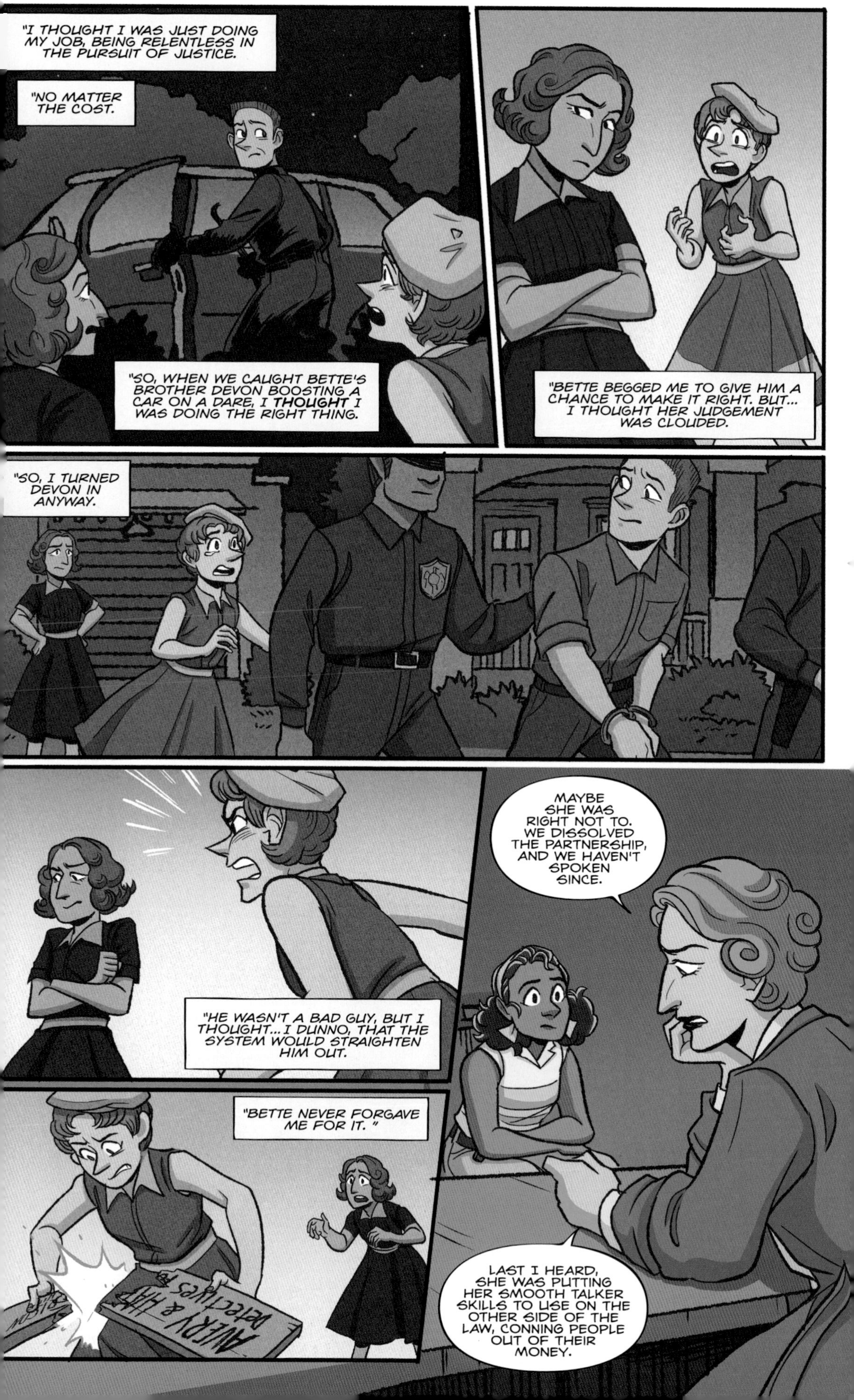
"I THOUGHT I WAS JUST DOING MY JOB, BEING RELENTLESS IN THE PURSUIT OF JUSTICE.
"NO MATTER THE COST.
"SO, WHEN WE CAUGHT BETTE'S BROTHER DEVON BOOSTING A CAR ON A DARE, I THOUGHT I WAS DOING THE RIGHT THING.
"BETTE BEGGED ME TO GIVE HIM A CHANCE TO MAKE IT RIGHT. BUT... I THOUGHT HER JUDGEMENT WAS CLOUDED.
"SO, I TURNED DEVON IN ANYWAY.
"HE WASN'T A BAD GUY, BUT I THOUGHT...I DUNNO, THAT THE SYSTEM WOULD STRAIGHTEN HIM OUT.
"BETTE NEVER FORGAVE ME FOR IT."
MAYBE SHE WAS RIGHT NOT TO. WE DISSOLVED THE PARTNERSHIP, AND WE HAVEN'T SPOKEN SINCE.
LAST I HEARD, SHE WAS PUTTING HER SMOOTH TALKER SKILLS TO USE ON THE OTHER SIDE OF THE LAW, CONNING PEOPLE OUT OF THEIR MONEY.

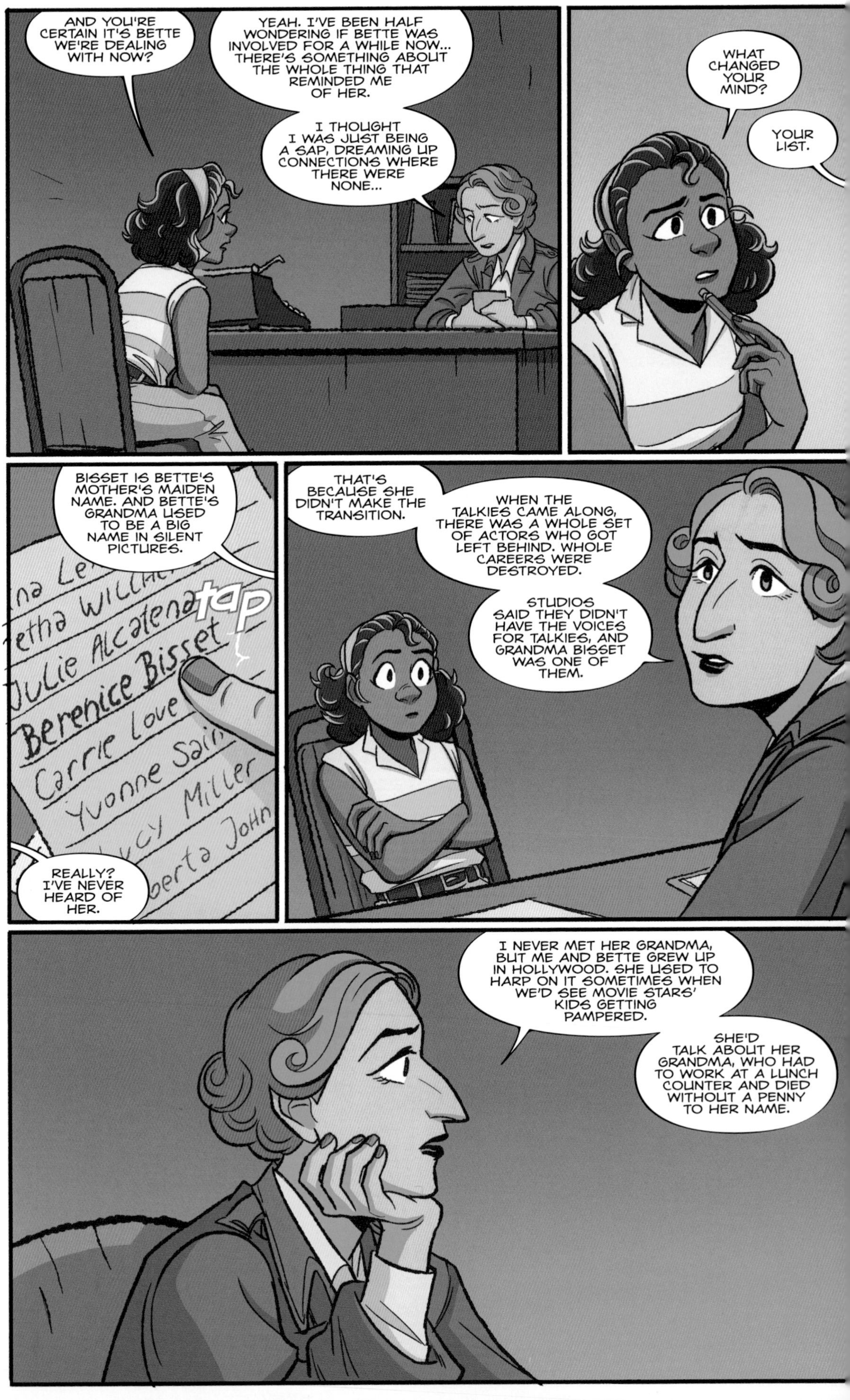
AND YOU'RE CERTAIN IT'S BETTE WE'RE DEALING WITH NOW?
YEAH. I'VE BEEN HALF WONDERING IF BETTE WAS INVOLVED FOR A WHILE NOW... THERE'S SOMETHING ABOUT THE WHOLE THING THAT REMINDED ME OF HER.
I THOUGHT I WAS JUST BEING A SAP, DREAMING UP CONNECTIONS WHERE THERE WERE NONE...
WHAT CHANGED YOUR MIND?
YOUR LIST.
BISSET IS BETTE'S MOTHER'S MAIDEN NAME. AND BETTE'S GRANDMA USED TO BE A BIG NAME IN SILENT PICTURES.
Julie Alcatena
tap
Berenice Bisset
Carrie Love
Yvonne Miller
REALLY? I'VE NEVER HEARD OF HER.
THAT'S BECAUSE SHE DIDN'T MAKE THE TRANSITION.
WHEN THE TALKIES CAME ALONG, THERE WAS A WHOLE SET OF ACTORS WHO GOT LEFT BEHIND. WHOLE CAREERS WERE DESTROYED.
STUDIOS SAID THEY DIDN'T HAVE THE VOICES FOR TALKIES, AND GRANDMA BISSET WAS ONE OF THEM.
I NEVER MET HER GRANDMA, BUT ME AND BETTE GREW UP IN HOLLYWOOD. SHE USED TO HARP ON IT SOMETIMES WHEN WE'D SEE MOVIE STARS' KIDS GETTING PAMPERED.
SHE'D TALK ABOUT HER GRANDMA, WHO HAD TO WORK AT A LUNCH COUNTER AND DIED WITHOUT A PENNY TO HER NAME.

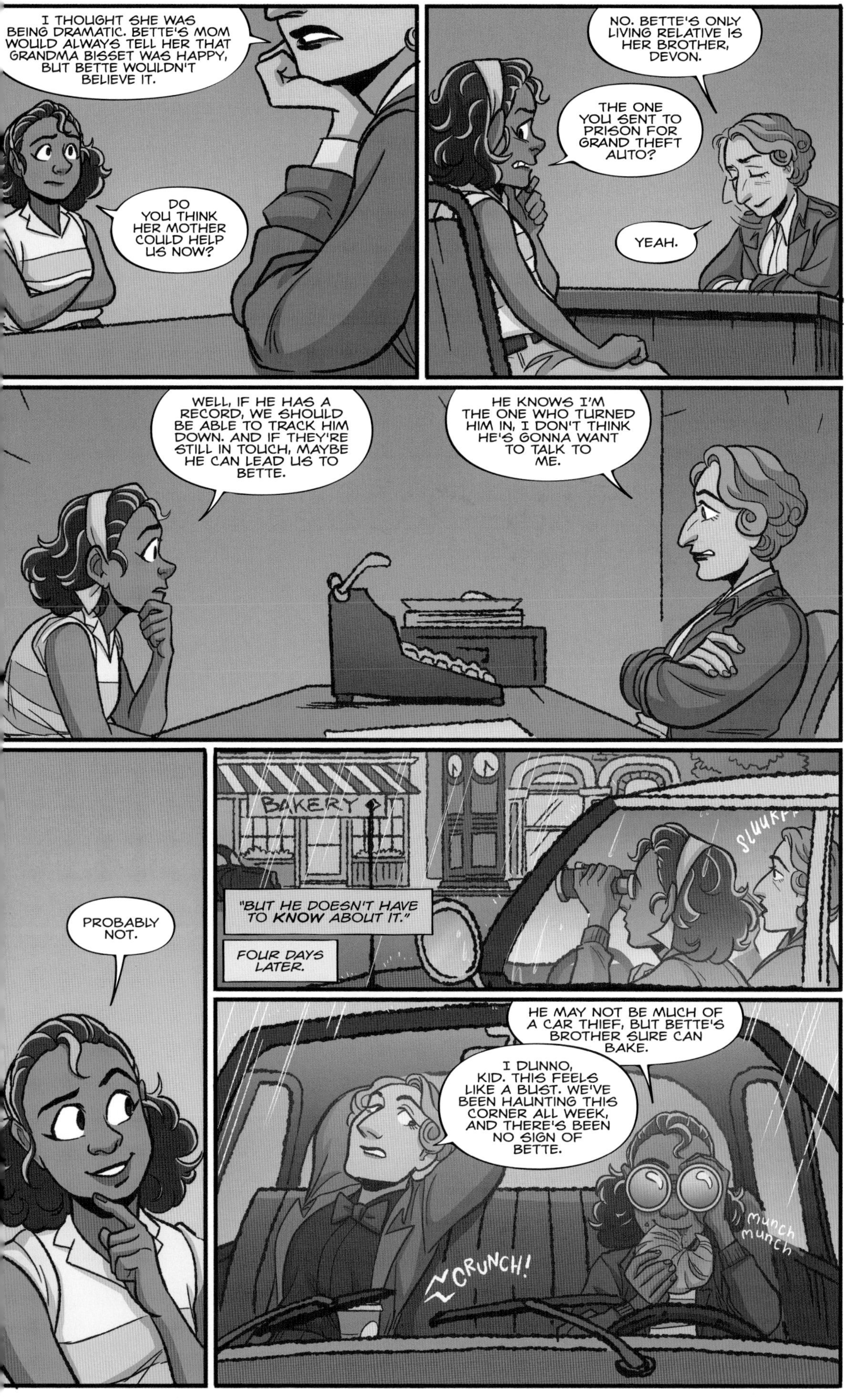

I THOUGHT SHE WAS BEING DRAMATIC. BETTE'S MOM WOULD ALWAYS TELL HER THAT GRANDMA BISSET WAS HAPPY, BUT BETTE WOULDN'T BELIEVE IT.
DO YOU THINK HER MOTHER COULD HELP US NOW?
NO. BETTE'S ONLY LIVING RELATIVE IS HER BROTHER, DEVON.
THE ONE YOU SENT TO PRISON FOR GRAND THEFT AUTO?
YEAH.
WELL, IF HE HAS A RECORD, WE SHOULD BE ABLE TO TRACK HIM DOWN. AND IF THEY'RE STILL IN TOUCH, MAYBE HE CAN LEAD US TO BETTE.
HE KNOWS I'M THE ONE WHO TURNED HIM IN, I DON'T THINK HE'S GONNA WANT TO TALK TO ME.
PROBABLY NOT.
BAKERY
"BUT HE DOESN'T HAVE TO KNOW ABOUT IT."
FOUR DAYS LATER.
HE MAY NOT BE MUCH OF A CAR THIEF, BUT BETTE'S BROTHER SURE CAN BAKE.
I DUNNO, KID. THIS FEELS LIKE A BUST. WE'VE BEEN HAUNTING THIS CORNER ALL WEEK, AND THERE'S BEEN NO SIGN OF BETTE.
CRUNCH!
munch munch

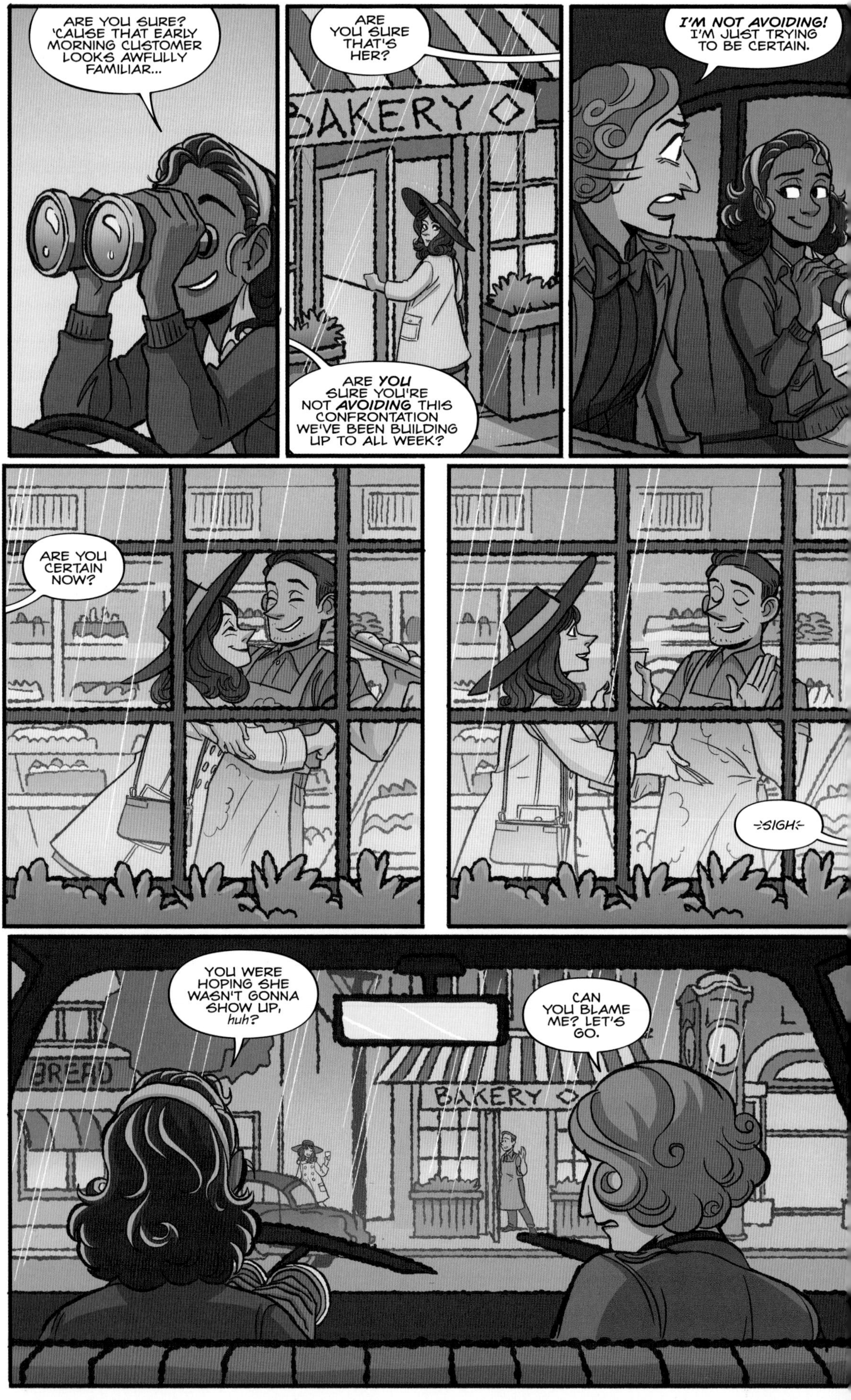

ARE YOU SURE? 'CAUSE THAT EARLY MORNING CUSTOMER LOOKS AWFULLY FAMILIAR...
ARE YOU SURE THAT'S HER?
BAKERY
ARE *YOU* SURE YOU'RE NOT *AVOIDING* THIS CONFRONTATION WE'VE BEEN BUILDING UP TO ALL WEEK?
I'M NOT AVOIDING! I'M JUST TRYING TO BE CERTAIN.
ARE YOU CERTAIN NOW?
SIGH
YOU WERE HOPING SHE WASN'T GONNA SHOW UP, *huh*?
CAN YOU BLAME ME? LET'S GO.
BREAD
BAKERY

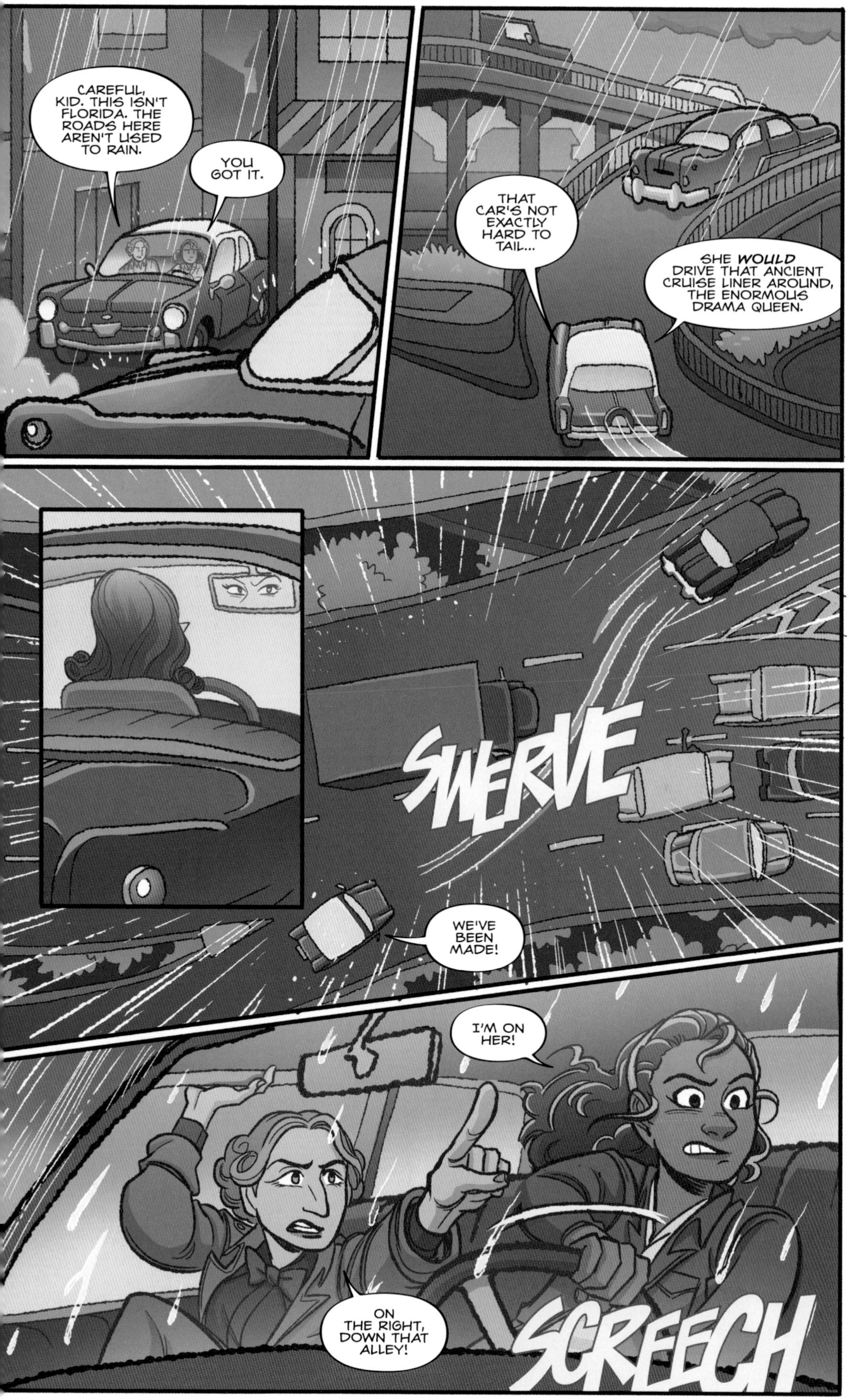
CAREFUL, KID. THIS ISN'T FLORIDA. THE ROADS HERE AREN'T USED TO RAIN.
YOU GOT IT.
THAT CAR'S NOT EXACTLY HARD TO TAIL...
SHE *WOULD* DRIVE THAT ANCIENT CRUISE LINER AROUND, THE ENORMOUS DRAMA QUEEN.
SWERVE
WE'VE BEEN MADE!
I'M ON HER!
ON THE RIGHT, DOWN THAT ALLEY!
SCREECH

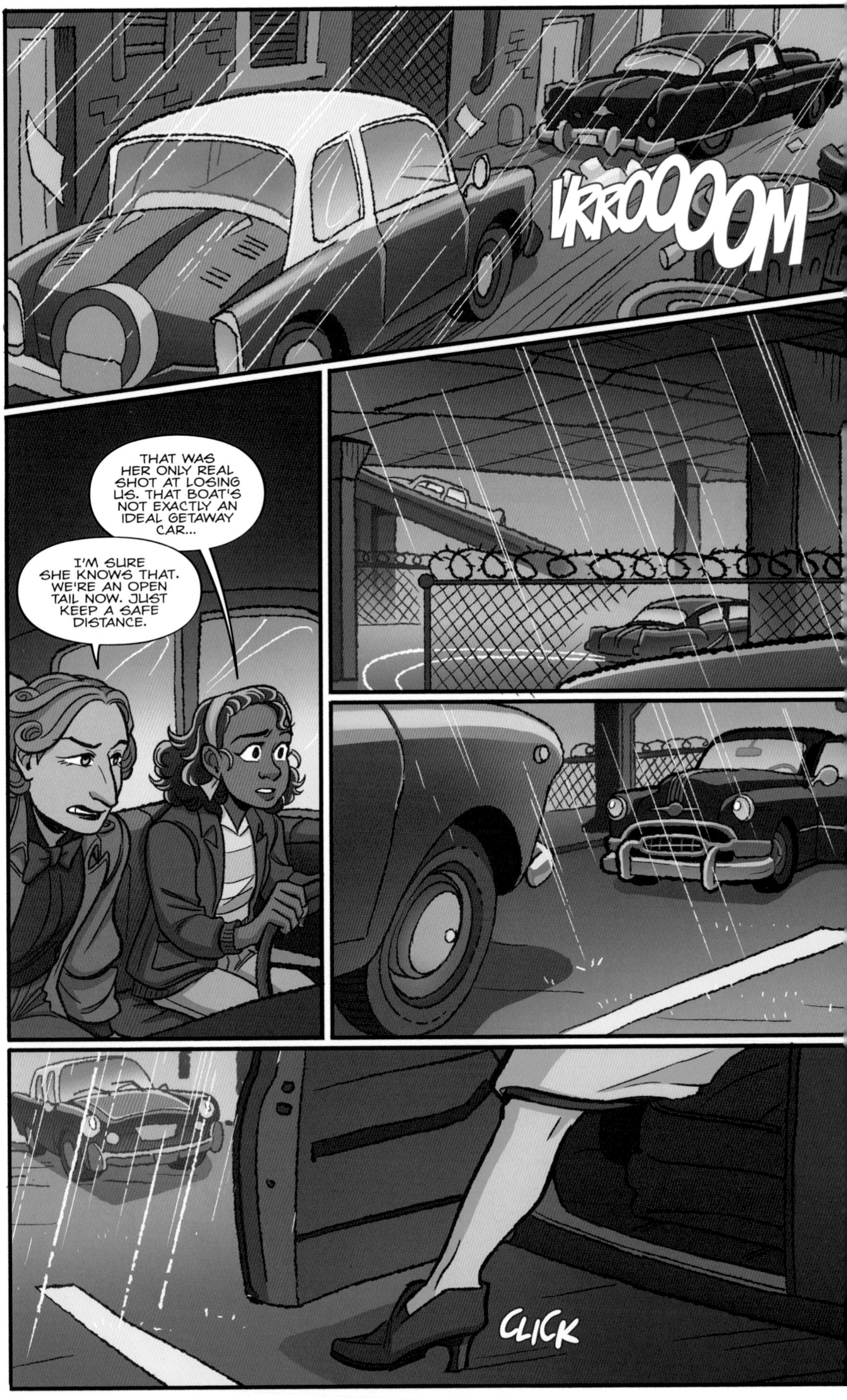
VRROOOOOM
THAT WAS HER ONLY REAL SHOT AT LOSING US. THAT BOAT'S NOT EXACTLY AN IDEAL GETAWAY CAR...
I'M SURE SHE KNOWS THAT. WE'RE AN OPEN TAIL NOW. JUST KEEP A SAFE DISTANCE.
CLICK

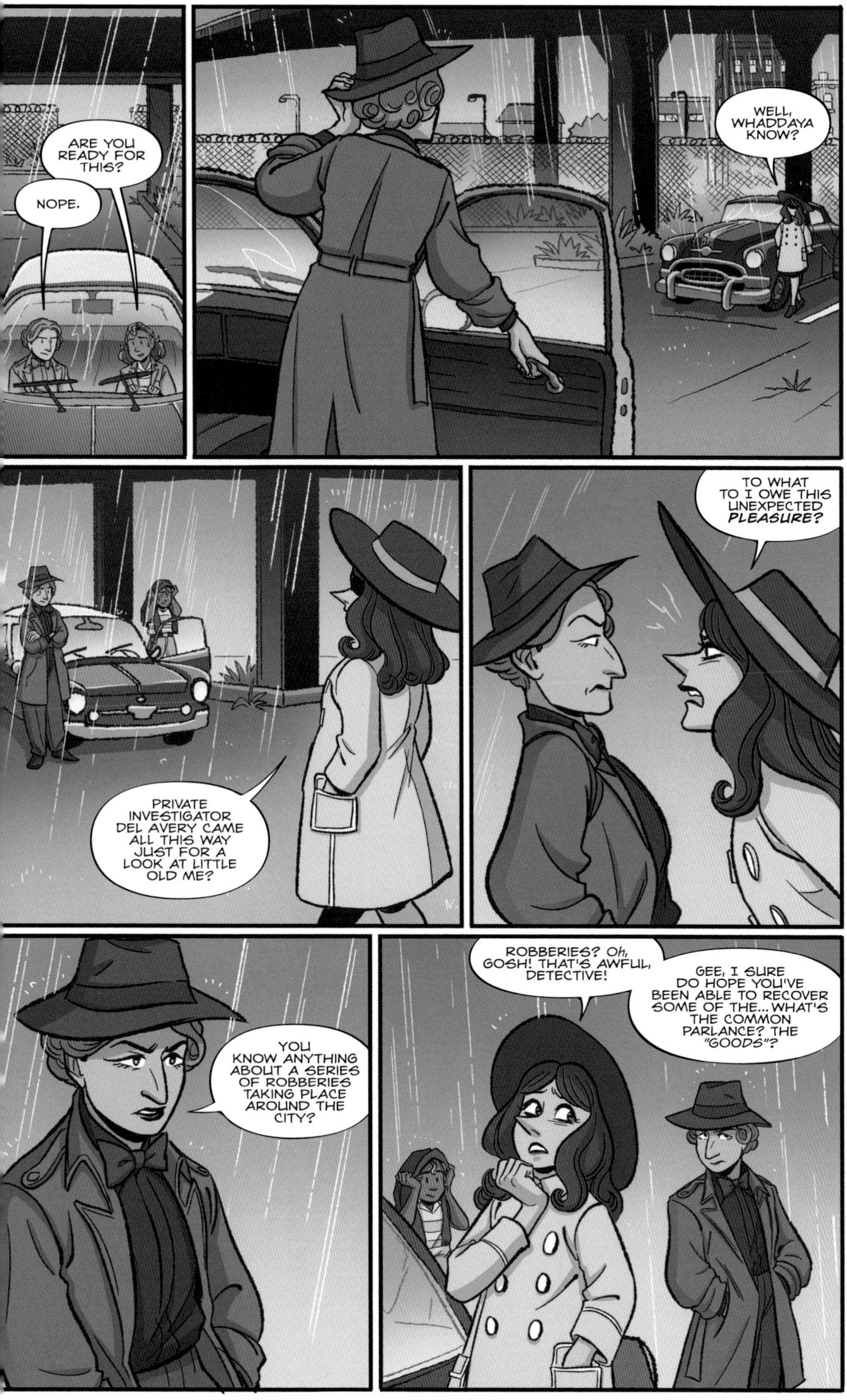
ARE YOU READY FOR THIS?
NOPE.
WELL, WHADDAYA KNOW?
PRIVATE INVESTIGATOR DEL AVERY CAME ALL THIS WAY JUST FOR A LOOK AT LITTLE OLD ME?
TO WHAT TO I OWE THIS UNEXPECTED *PLEASURE?*
YOU KNOW ANYTHING ABOUT A SERIES OF ROBBERIES TAKING PLACE AROUND THE CITY?
ROBBERIES? *Oh,* GOSH! THAT'S AWFUL, DETECTIVE!
GEE, I SURE DO HOPE YOU'VE BEEN ABLE TO RECOVER SOME OF THE... WHAT'S THE COMMON PARLANCE? THE "GOODS"?

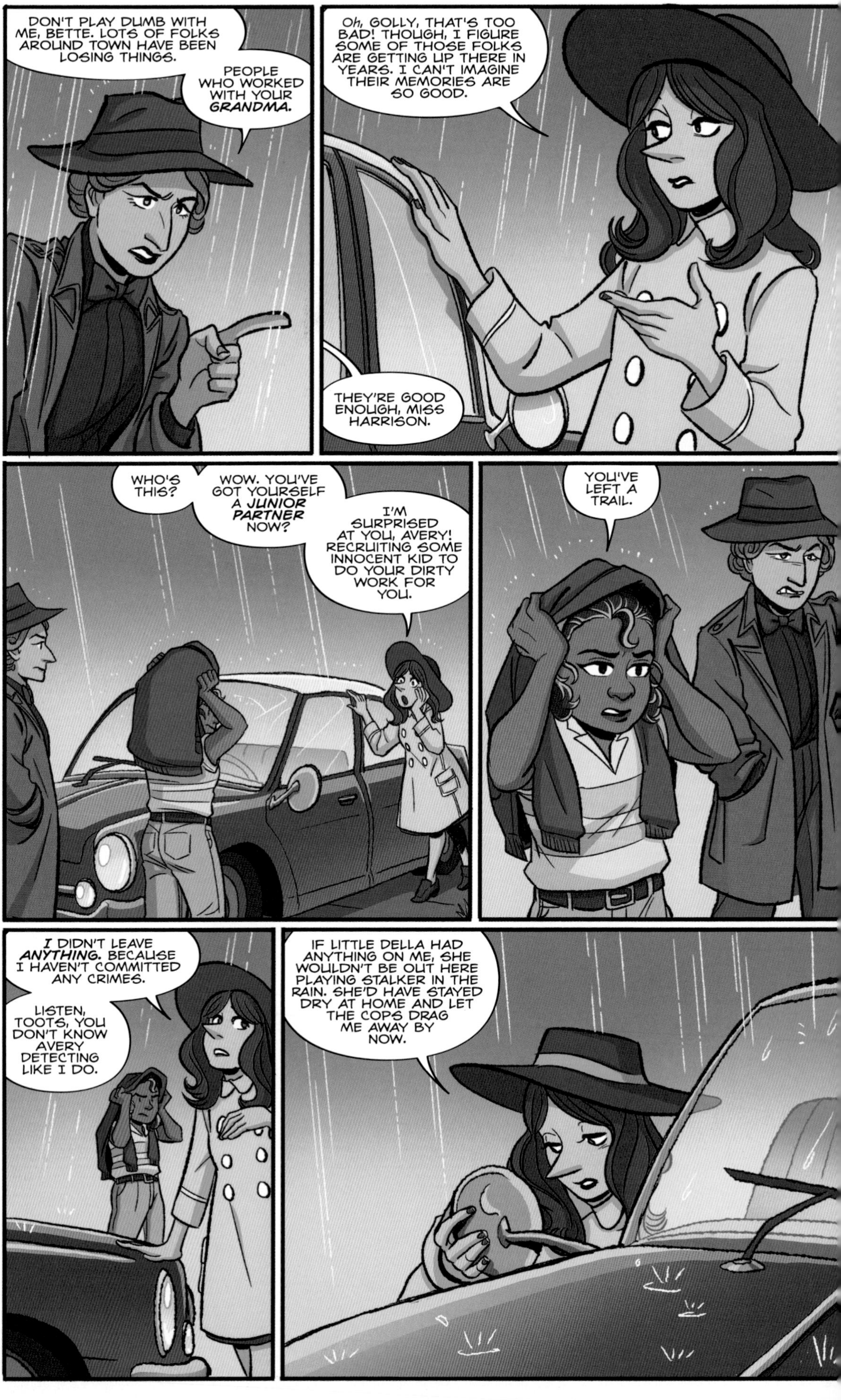

DON'T PLAY DUMB WITH ME, BETTE. LOTS OF FOLKS AROUND TOWN HAVE BEEN LOSING THINGS.
PEOPLE WHO WORKED WITH YOUR *GRANDMA.*
Oh, GOLLY, THAT'S TOO BAD! THOUGH, I FIGURE SOME OF THOSE FOLKS ARE GETTING UP THERE IN YEARS. I CAN'T IMAGINE THEIR MEMORIES ARE SO GOOD.
THEY'RE GOOD ENOUGH, MISS HARRISON.
WHO'S THIS?
WOW. YOU'VE GOT YOURSELF A *JUNIOR PARTNER* NOW?
I'M SURPRISED AT YOU, AVERY! RECRUITING SOME INNOCENT KID TO DO YOUR DIRTY WORK FOR YOU.
YOU'VE LEFT A TRAIL.
I DIDN'T LEAVE *ANYTHING.* BECAUSE I HAVEN'T COMMITTED ANY CRIMES.
LISTEN, TOOTS, YOU DON'T KNOW AVERY DETECTING LIKE I DO.
IF LITTLE DELLA HAD ANYTHING ON ME, SHE WOULDN'T BE OUT HERE PLAYING STALKER IN THE RAIN. SHE'D HAVE STAYED DRY AT HOME AND LET THE COPS DRAG ME AWAY BY NOW.

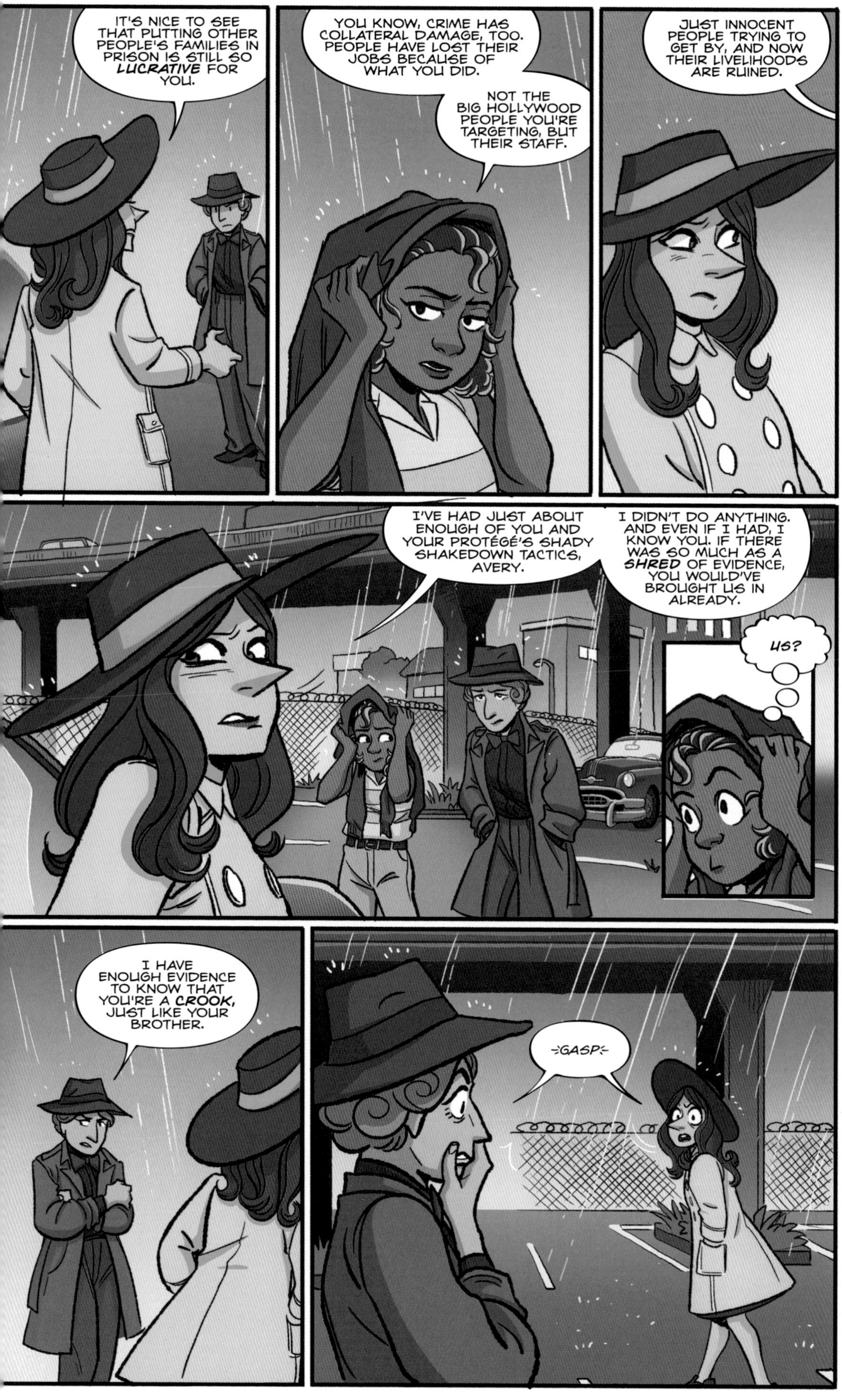
IT'S NICE TO SEE THAT PUTTING OTHER PEOPLE'S FAMILIES IN PRISON IS STILL SO *LUCRATIVE* FOR YOU.
YOU KNOW, CRIME HAS COLLATERAL DAMAGE, TOO. PEOPLE HAVE LOST THEIR JOBS BECAUSE OF WHAT YOU DID.
NOT THE BIG HOLLYWOOD PEOPLE YOU'RE TARGETING, BUT THEIR STAFF.
JUST INNOCENT PEOPLE TRYING TO GET BY, AND NOW THEIR LIVELIHOODS ARE RUINED.
I'VE HAD JUST ABOUT ENOUGH OF YOU AND YOUR PROTÉGÉ'S SHADY SHAKEDOWN TACTICS, AVERY.
I DIDN'T DO ANYTHING. AND EVEN IF I HAD, I KNOW YOU. IF THERE WAS SO MUCH AS A *SHRED* OF EVIDENCE, YOU WOULD'VE BROUGHT US IN ALREADY.
US?
I HAVE ENOUGH EVIDENCE TO KNOW THAT YOU'RE A *CROOK,* JUST LIKE YOUR BROTHER.
GASP

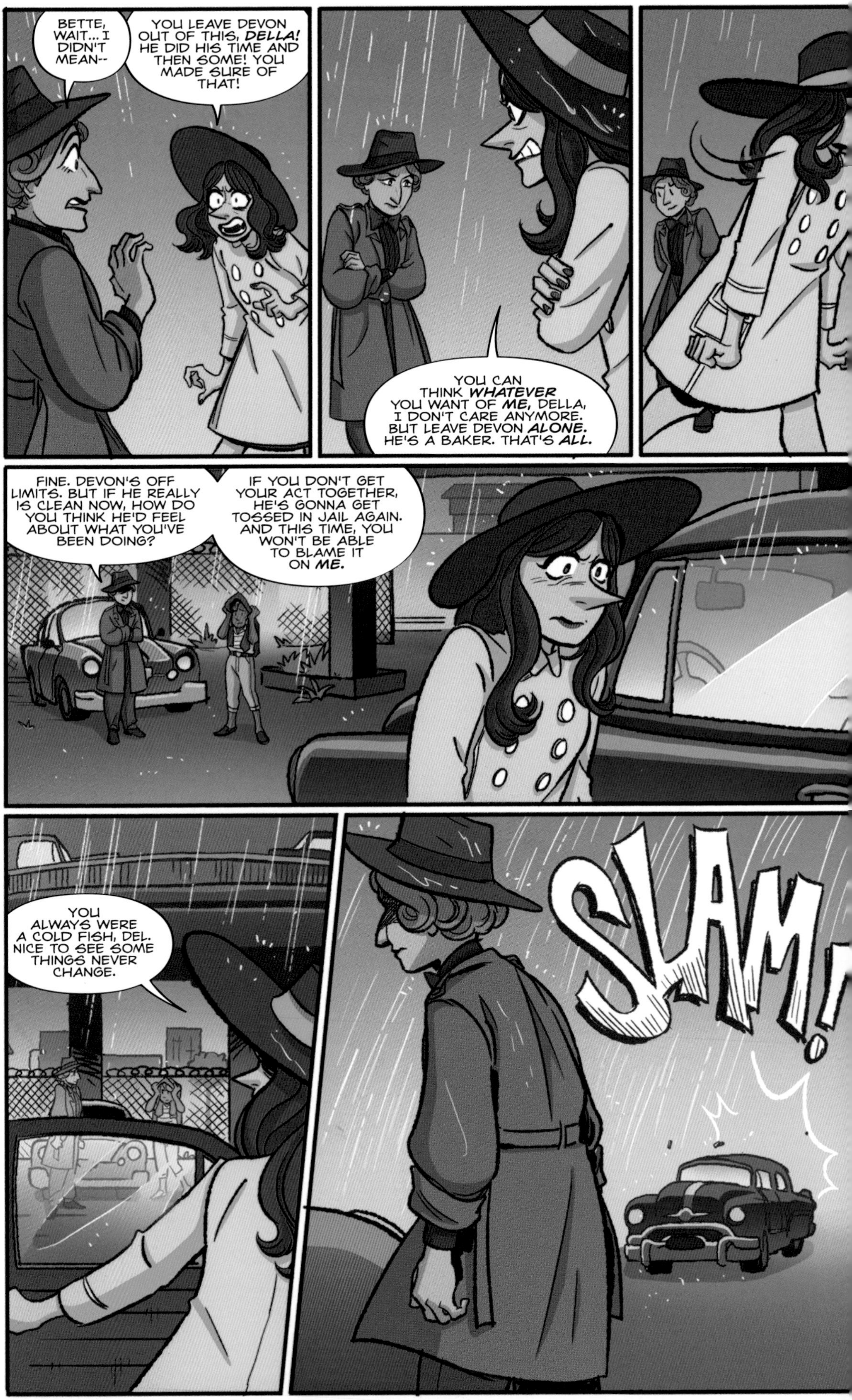
BETTE, WAIT... I DIDN'T MEAN--
YOU LEAVE DEVON OUT OF THIS, DELLA! HE DID HIS TIME AND THEN SOME! YOU MADE SURE OF THAT!
YOU CAN THINK WHATEVER YOU WANT OF ME, DELLA, I DON'T CARE ANYMORE. BUT LEAVE DEVON ALONE. HE'S A BAKER. THAT'S ALL.
FINE. DEVON'S OFF LIMITS. BUT IF HE REALLY IS CLEAN NOW, HOW DO YOU THINK HE'D FEEL ABOUT WHAT YOU'VE BEEN DOING?
IF YOU DON'T GET YOUR ACT TOGETHER, HE'S GONNA GET TOSSED IN JAIL AGAIN. AND THIS TIME, YOU WON'T BE ABLE TO BLAME IT ON ME.
YOU ALWAYS WERE A COLD FISH, DEL. NICE TO SEE SOME THINGS NEVER CHANGE.
SLAM!

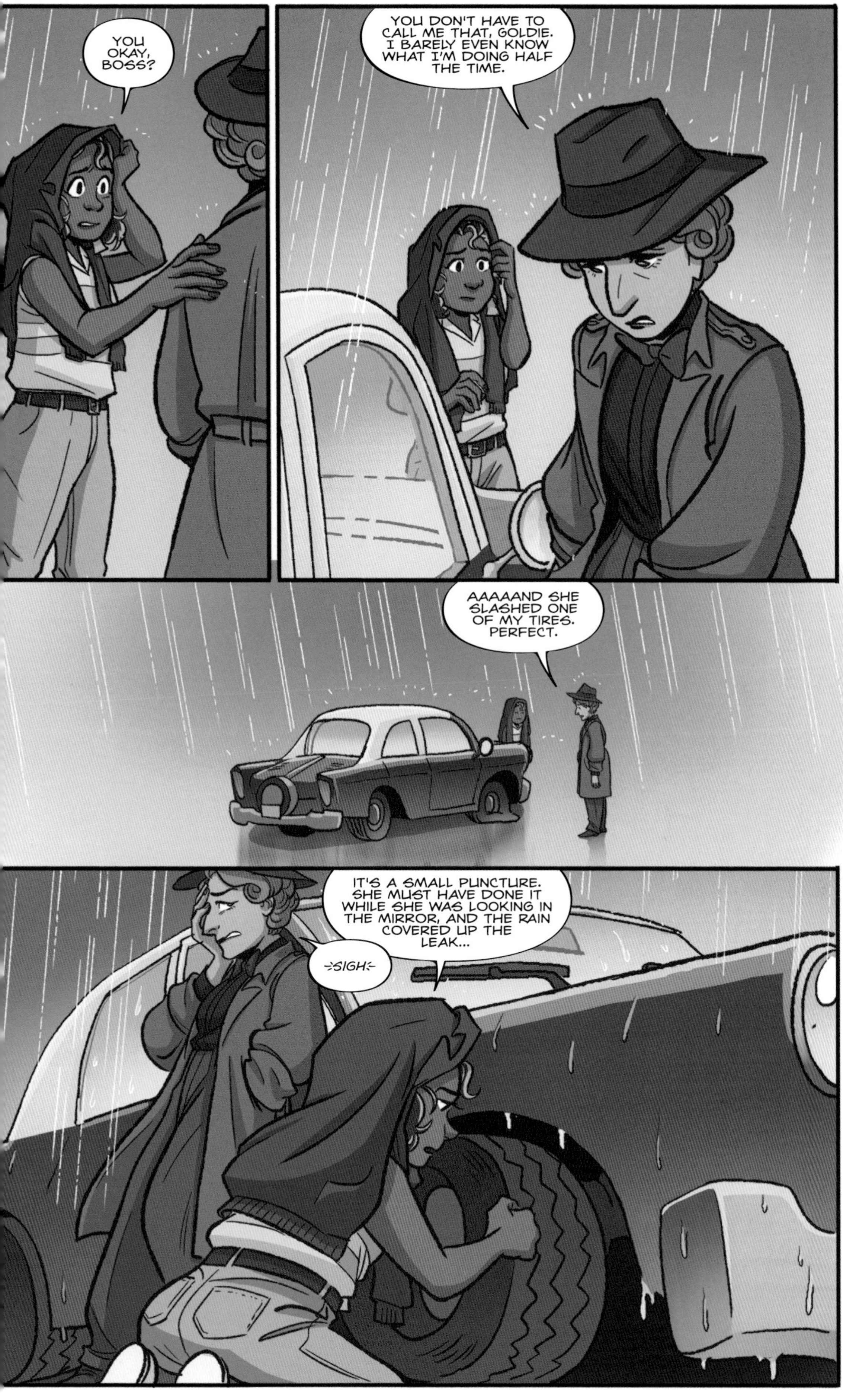
YOU OKAY, BOSS?
YOU DON'T HAVE TO CALL ME THAT, GOLDIE. I BARELY EVEN KNOW WHAT I'M DOING HALF THE TIME.
AAAAAND SHE SLASHED ONE OF MY TIRES. PERFECT.
IT'S A SMALL PUNCTURE. SHE MUST HAVE DONE IT WHILE SHE WAS LOOKING IN THE MIRROR, AND THE RAIN COVERED UP THE LEAK...
SIGH

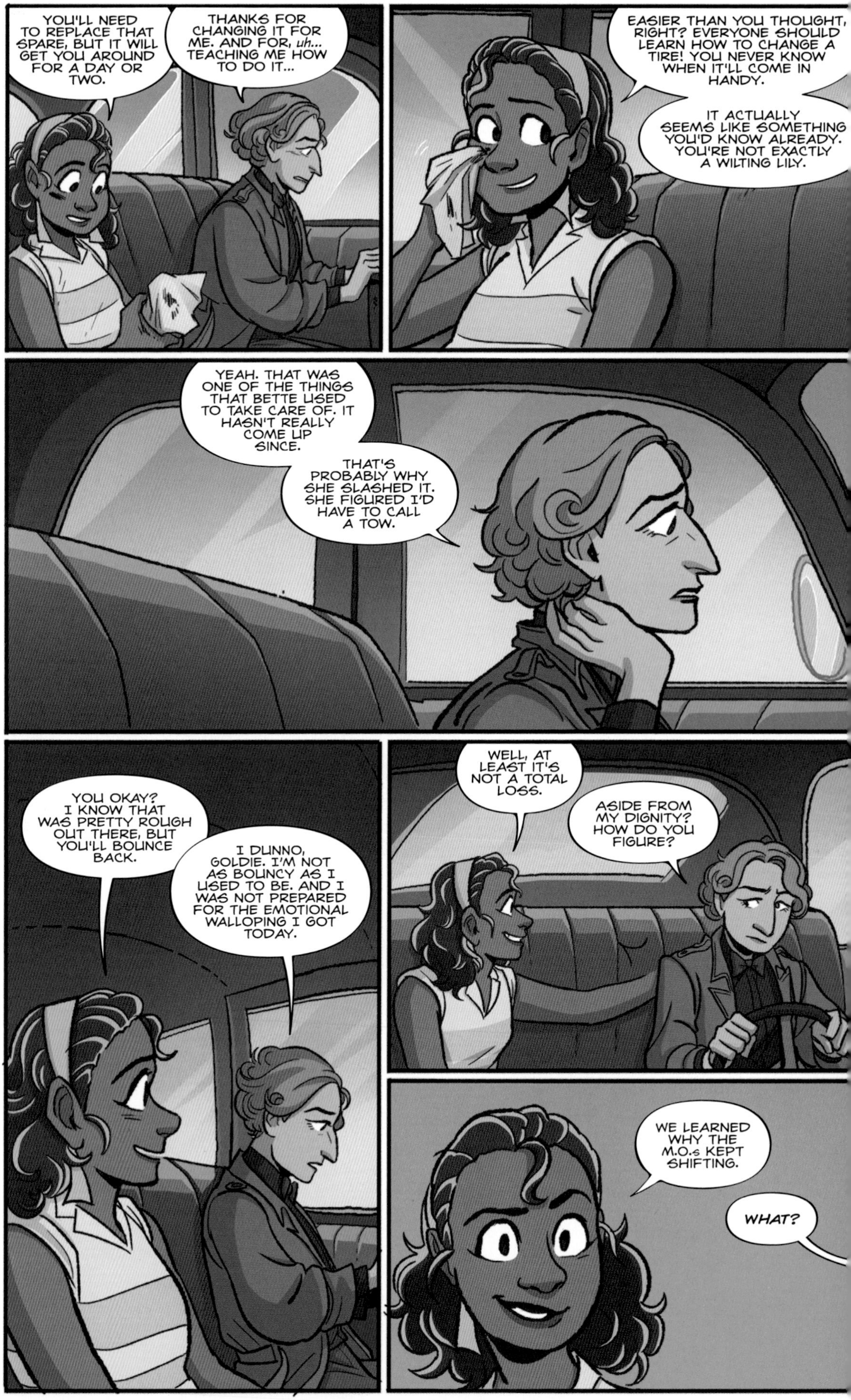
YOU'LL NEED TO REPLACE THAT SPARE, BUT IT WILL GET YOU AROUND FOR A DAY OR TWO.
THANKS FOR CHANGING IT FOR ME. AND FOR, *uh...* TEACHING ME HOW TO DO IT...
EASIER THAN YOU THOUGHT, RIGHT? EVERYONE SHOULD LEARN HOW TO CHANGE A TIRE! YOU NEVER KNOW WHEN IT'LL COME IN HANDY.
IT ACTUALLY SEEMS LIKE SOMETHING YOU'D KNOW ALREADY. YOU'RE NOT EXACTLY A WILTING LILY.
YEAH. THAT WAS ONE OF THE THINGS THAT BETTE USED TO TAKE CARE OF. IT HASN'T REALLY COME UP SINCE.
THAT'S PROBABLY WHY SHE SLASHED IT. SHE FIGURED I'D HAVE TO CALL A TOW.
YOU OKAY? I KNOW THAT WAS PRETTY ROUGH OUT THERE, BUT YOU'LL BOUNCE BACK.
I DUNNO, GOLDIE. I'M NOT AS BOUNCY AS I USED TO BE. AND I WAS NOT PREPARED FOR THE EMOTIONAL WALLOPING I GOT TODAY.
WELL, AT LEAST IT'S NOT A TOTAL LOSS.
ASIDE FROM MY DIGNITY? HOW DO YOU FIGURE?
WE LEARNED WHY THE M.O.s KEPT SHIFTING.
WHAT?

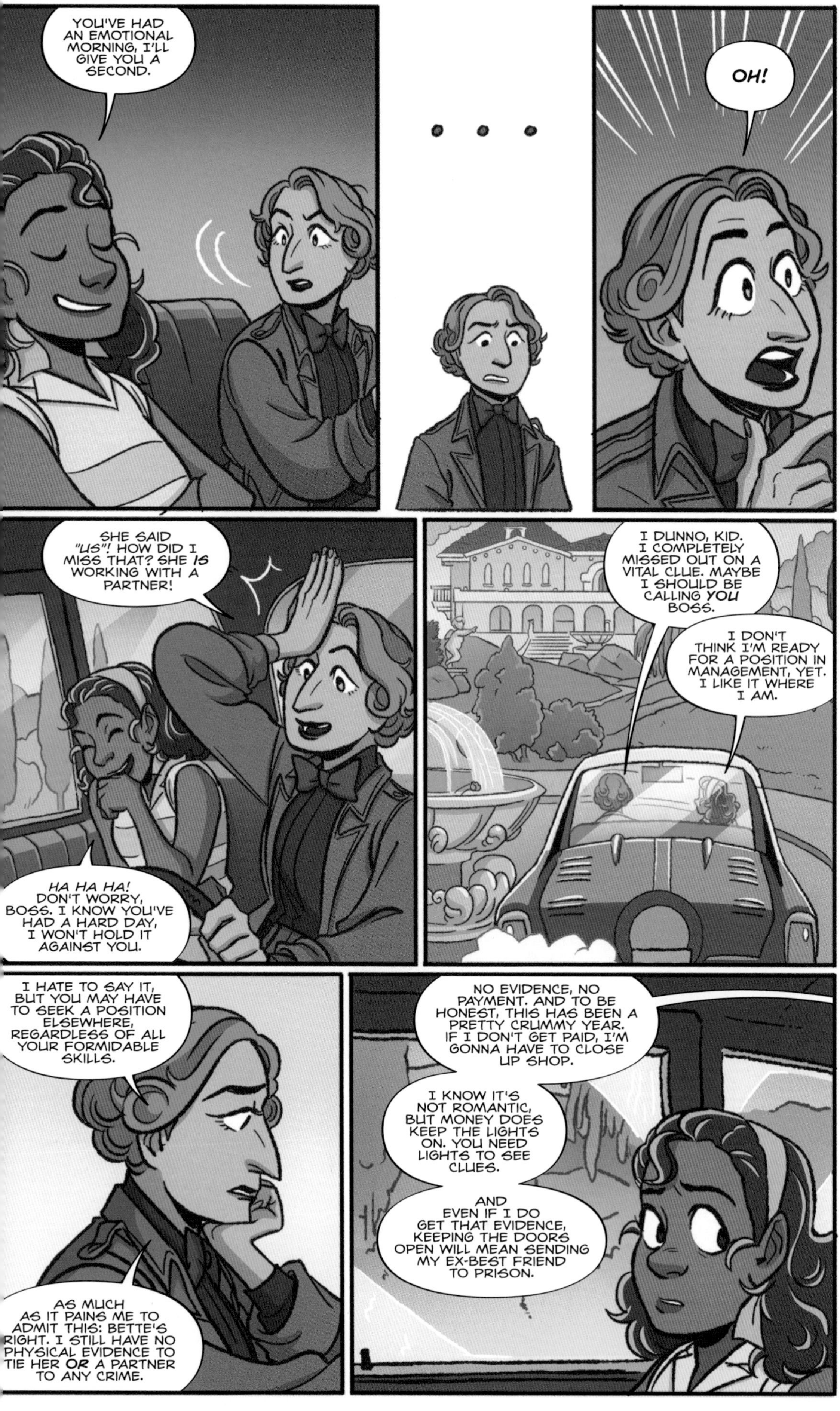
YOU'VE HAD AN EMOTIONAL MORNING, I'LL GIVE YOU A SECOND.
...
OH!
SHE SAID *"US"*! HOW DID I MISS THAT? SHE *IS* WORKING WITH A PARTNER!
HA HA HA! DON'T WORRY, BOSS. I KNOW YOU'VE HAD A HARD DAY, I WON'T HOLD IT AGAINST YOU.
I DUNNO, KID. I COMPLETELY MISSED OUT ON A VITAL CLUE. MAYBE I SHOULD BE CALLING **YOU** BOSS.
I DON'T THINK I'M READY FOR A POSITION IN MANAGEMENT, YET. I LIKE IT WHERE I AM.
I HATE TO SAY IT, BUT YOU MAY HAVE TO SEEK A POSITION ELSEWHERE, REGARDLESS OF ALL YOUR FORMIDABLE SKILLS.
AS MUCH AS IT PAINS ME TO ADMIT THIS: BETTE'S RIGHT. I STILL HAVE NO PHYSICAL EVIDENCE TO TIE HER **OR** A PARTNER TO ANY CRIME.
NO EVIDENCE, NO PAYMENT. AND TO BE HONEST, THIS HAS BEEN A PRETTY CRUMMY YEAR. IF I DON'T GET PAID, I'M GONNA HAVE TO CLOSE UP SHOP.
I KNOW IT'S NOT ROMANTIC, BUT MONEY DOES KEEP THE LIGHTS ON. YOU NEED LIGHTS TO SEE CLUES.
AND EVEN IF I DO GET THAT EVIDENCE, KEEPING THE DOORS OPEN WILL MEAN SENDING MY EX-BEST FRIEND TO PRISON.

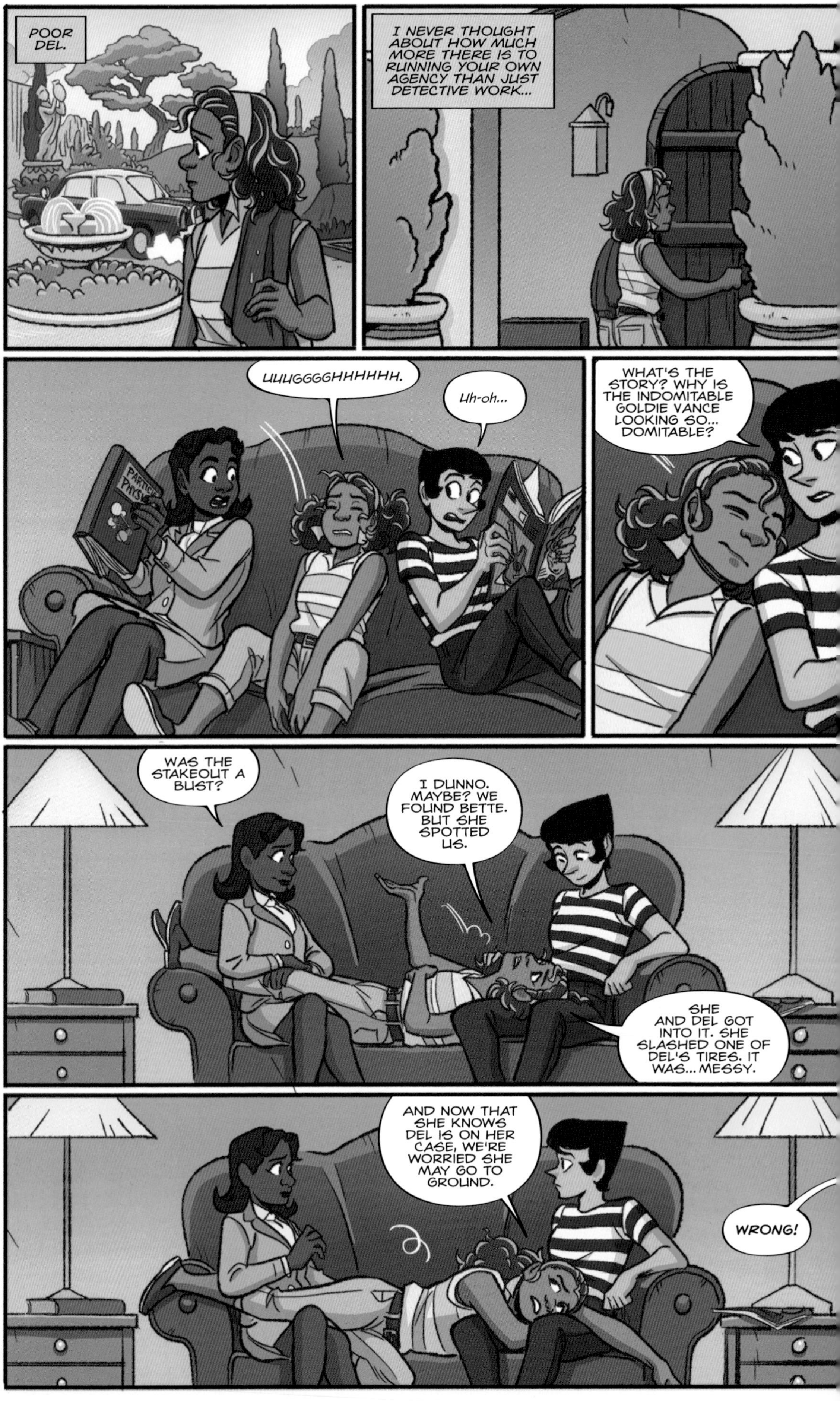
POOR DEL.
I NEVER THOUGHT ABOUT HOW MUCH MORE THERE IS TO RUNNING YOUR OWN AGENCY THAN JUST DETECTIVE WORK...
UUUGGGGHHHHHH.
Uh-oh...
WHAT'S THE STORY? WHY IS THE INDOMITABLE GOLDIE VANCE LOOKING SO... DOMITABLE?
WAS THE STAKEOUT A BUST?
I DUNNO. MAYBE? WE FOUND BETTE. BUT SHE SPOTTED US.
SHE AND DEL GOT INTO IT. SHE SLASHED ONE OF DEL'S TIRES. IT WAS... MESSY.
AND NOW THAT SHE KNOWS DEL IS ON HER CASE, WE'RE WORRIED SHE MAY GO TO GROUND.
WRONG!

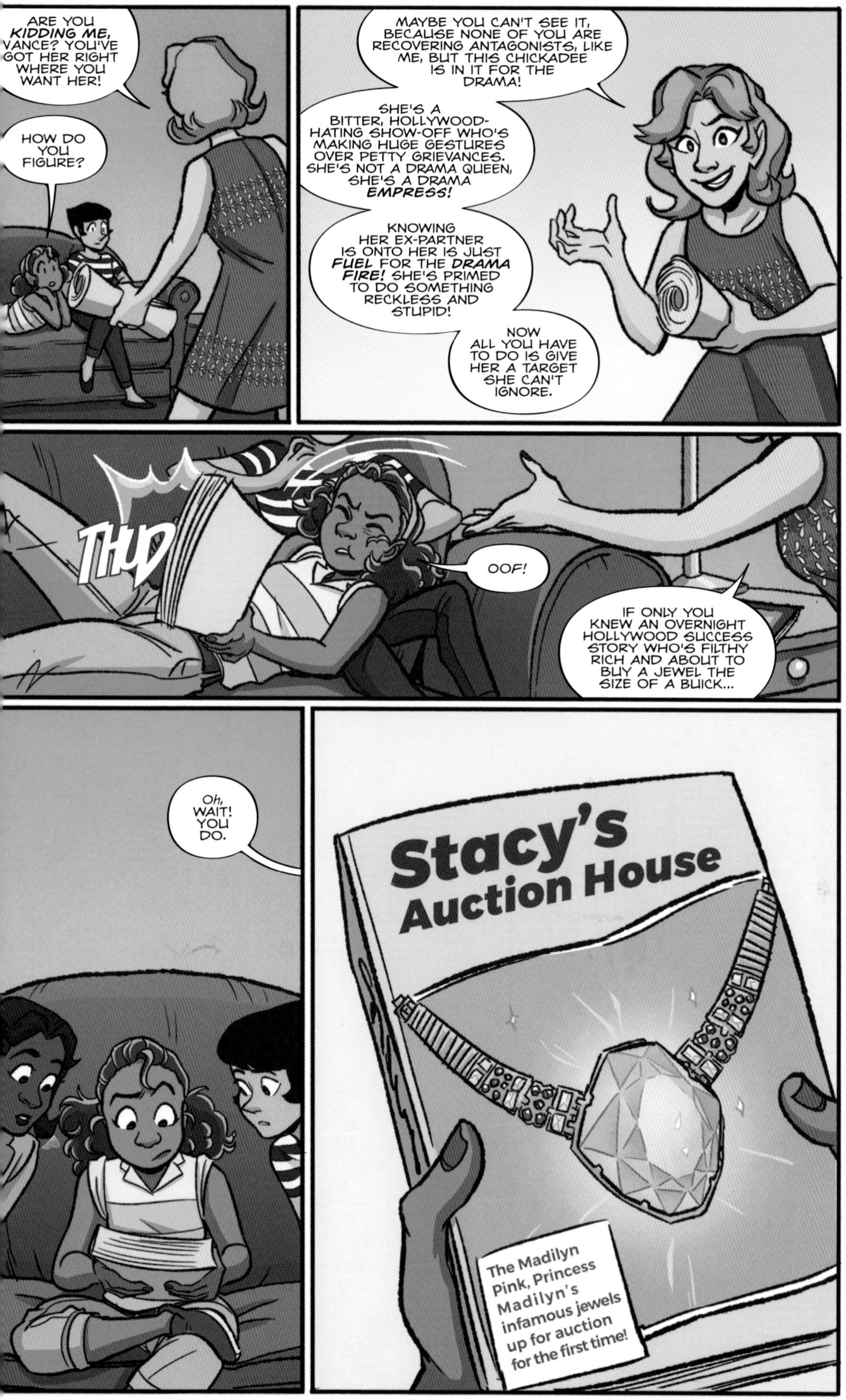

ARE YOU KIDDING ME, VANCE? YOU'VE GOT HER RIGHT WHERE YOU WANT HER!
HOW DO YOU FIGURE?
MAYBE YOU CAN'T SEE IT, BECAUSE NONE OF YOU ARE RECOVERING ANTAGONISTS, LIKE ME, BUT THIS CHICKADEE IS IN IT FOR THE DRAMA!
SHE'S A BITTER, HOLLYWOOD-HATING SHOW-OFF WHO'S MAKING HUGE GESTURES OVER PETTY GRIEVANCES. SHE'S NOT A DRAMA QUEEN, SHE'S A DRAMA EMPRESS!
KNOWING HER EX-PARTNER IS ONTO HER IS JUST FUEL FOR THE DRAMA FIRE! SHE'S PRIMED TO DO SOMETHING RECKLESS AND STUPID!
NOW ALL YOU HAVE TO DO IS GIVE HER A TARGET SHE CAN'T IGNORE.
THUD
OOF!
IF ONLY YOU KNEW AN OVERNIGHT HOLLYWOOD SUCCESS STORY WHO'S FILTHY RICH AND ABOUT TO BUY A JEWEL THE SIZE OF A BUICK...
Oh, WAIT! YOU DO.
Stacy's Auction House
The Madilyn Pink, Princess Madilyn's infamous jewels up for auction for the first time!

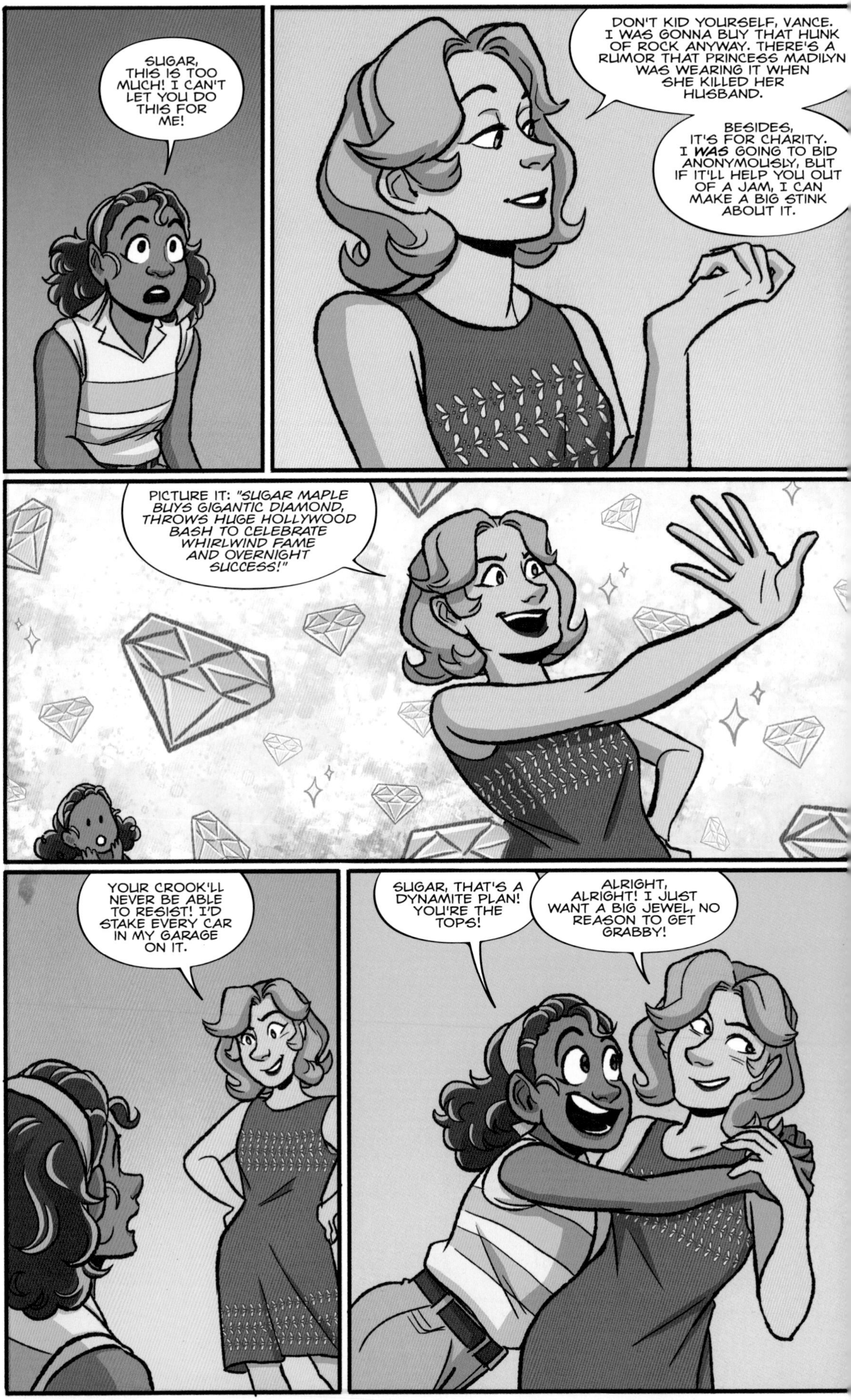
SUGAR, THIS IS TOO MUCH! I CAN'T LET YOU DO THIS FOR ME!
DON'T KID YOURSELF, VANCE. I WAS GONNA BUY THAT HUNK OF ROCK ANYWAY. THERE'S A RUMOR THAT PRINCESS MADILYN WAS WEARING IT WHEN SHE KILLED HER HUSBAND.
BESIDES, IT'S FOR CHARITY. I *WAS* GOING TO BID ANONYMOUSLY, BUT IF IT'LL HELP YOU OUT OF A JAM, I CAN MAKE A BIG STINK ABOUT IT.
PICTURE IT: "SUGAR MAPLE BUYS GIGANTIC DIAMOND, THROWS HUGE HOLLYWOOD BASH TO CELEBRATE WHIRLWIND FAME AND OVERNIGHT SUCCESS!"
YOUR CROOK'LL NEVER BE ABLE TO RESIST! I'D STAKE EVERY CAR IN MY GARAGE ON IT.
SUGAR, THAT'S A DYNAMITE PLAN! YOU'RE THE TOPS!
ALRIGHT, ALRIGHT! I JUST WANT A BIG JEWEL, NO REASON TO GET GRABBY!

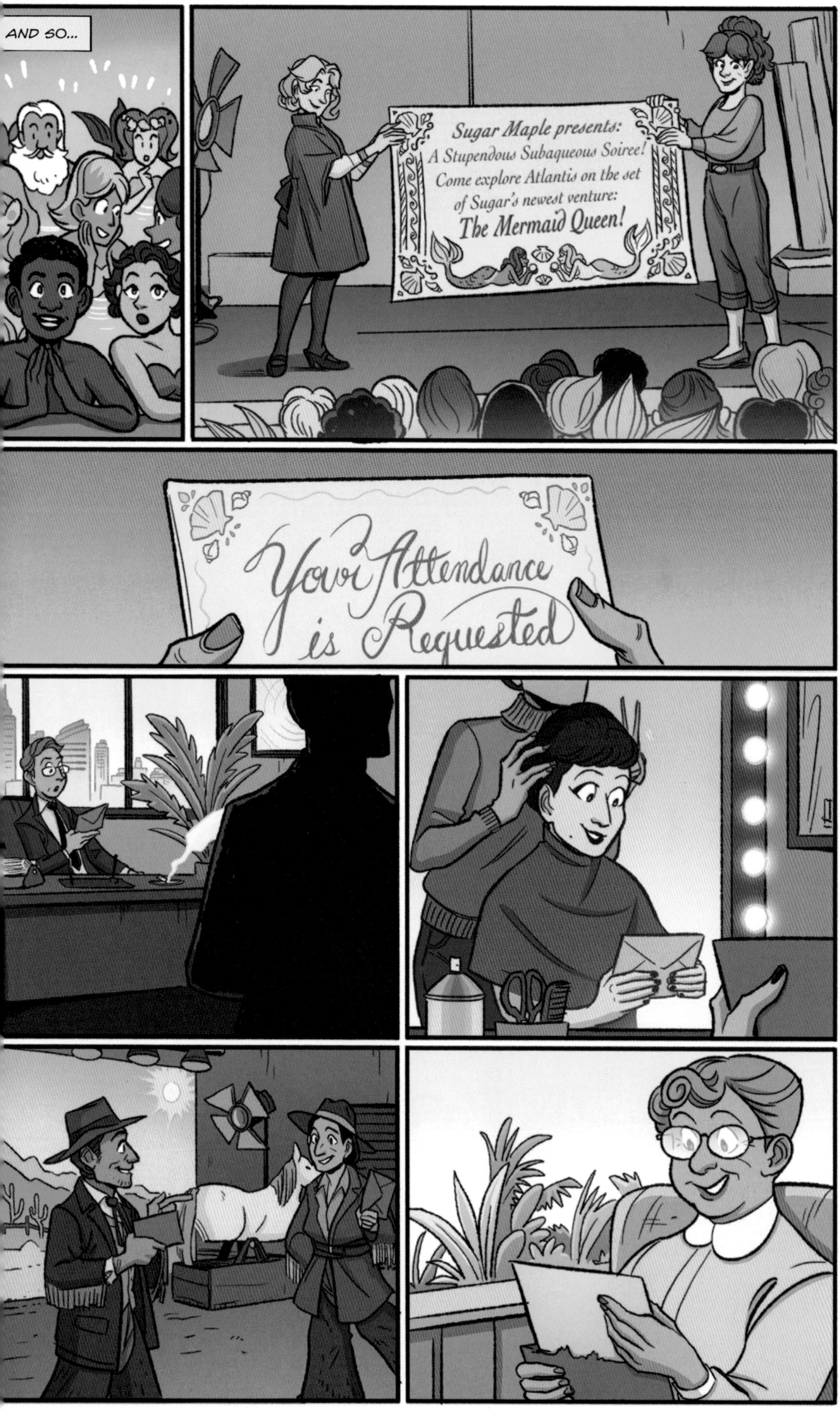
AND SO...
Sugar Maple presents:
A Stupendous Subaqueous Soiree!
Come explore Atlantis on the set
of Sugar's newest venture:
The Mermaid Queen!
Your Attendance
is Requested

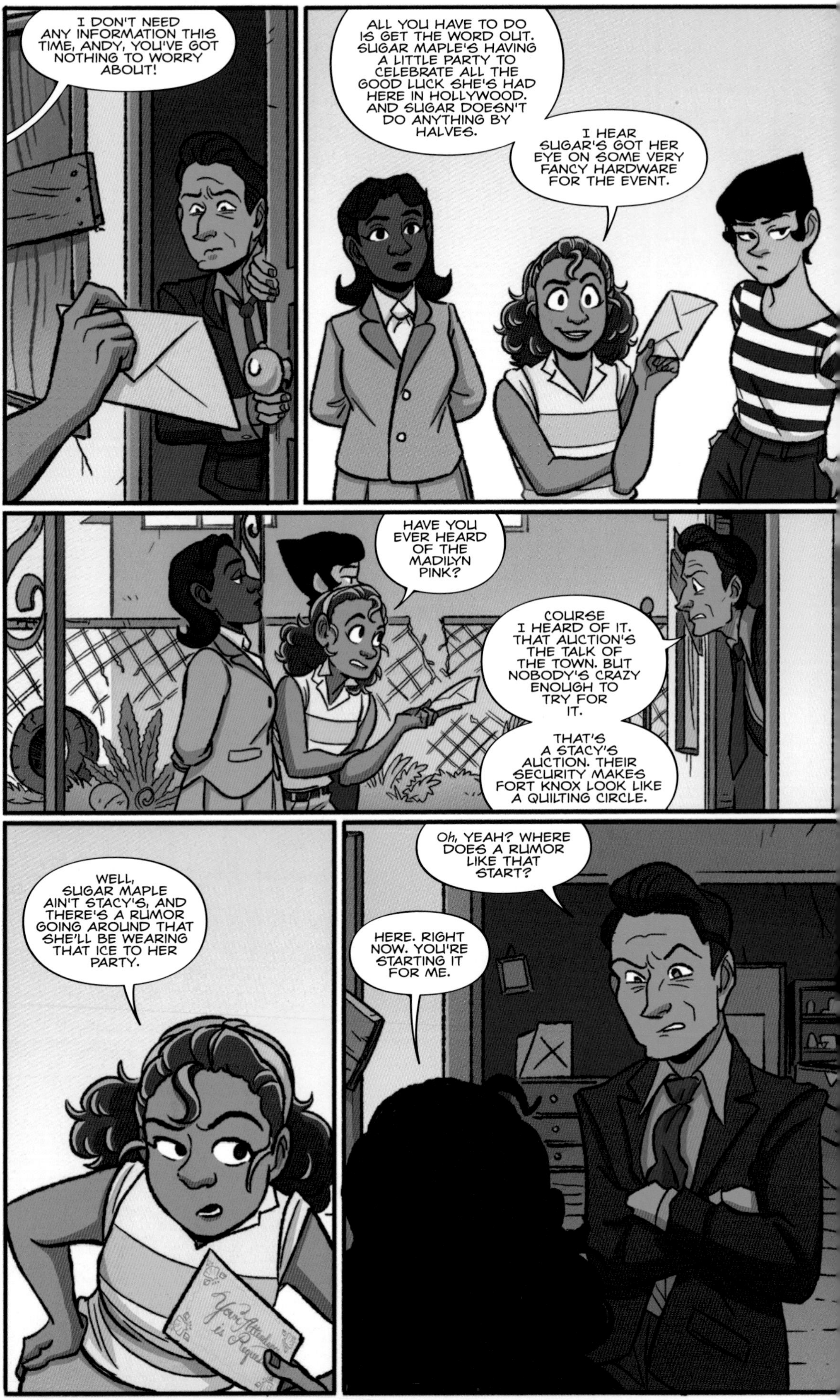
I DON'T NEED ANY INFORMATION THIS TIME, ANDY, YOU'VE GOT NOTHING TO WORRY ABOUT!
ALL YOU HAVE TO DO IS GET THE WORD OUT. SUGAR MAPLE'S HAVING A LITTLE PARTY TO CELEBRATE ALL THE GOOD LUCK SHE'S HAD HERE IN HOLLYWOOD. AND SUGAR DOESN'T DO ANYTHING BY HALVES.
I HEAR SUGAR'S GOT HER EYE ON SOME VERY FANCY HARDWARE FOR THE EVENT.
HAVE YOU EVER HEARD OF THE MADILYN PINK?
COURSE I HEARD OF IT. THAT AUCTION'S THE TALK OF THE TOWN. BUT NOBODY'S CRAZY ENOUGH TO TRY FOR IT.
THAT'S A STACY'S AUCTION. THEIR SECURITY MAKES FORT KNOX LOOK LIKE A QUILTING CIRCLE.
WELL, SUGAR MAPLE AIN'T STACY'S, AND THERE'S A RUMOR GOING AROUND THAT SHE'LL BE WEARING THAT ICE TO HER PARTY.
Oh, YEAH? WHERE DOES A RUMOR LIKE THAT START?
HERE. RIGHT NOW. YOU'RE STARTING IT FOR ME.

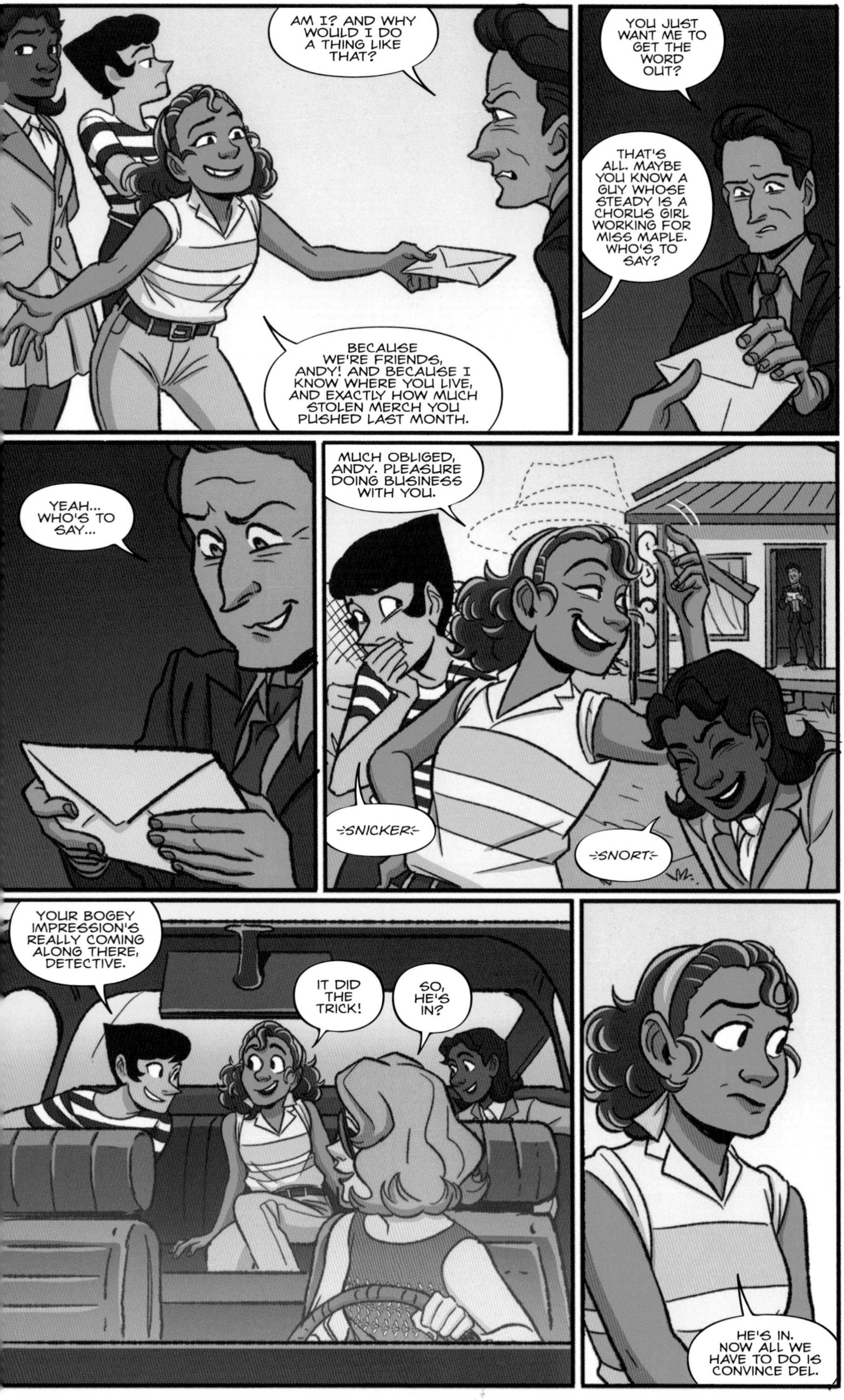

AM I? AND WHY WOULD I DO A THING LIKE THAT?
BECAUSE WE'RE FRIENDS, ANDY! AND BECAUSE I KNOW WHERE YOU LIVE, AND EXACTLY HOW MUCH STOLEN MERCH YOU PUSHED LAST MONTH.
YOU JUST WANT ME TO GET THE WORD OUT?
THAT'S ALL. MAYBE YOU KNOW A GUY WHOSE STEADY IS A CHORUS GIRL WORKING FOR MISS MAPLE. WHO'S TO SAY?
YEAH... WHO'S TO SAY...
MUCH OBLIGED, ANDY. PLEASURE DOING BUSINESS WITH YOU.
SNICKER
SNORT
YOUR BOGEY IMPRESSION'S REALLY COMING ALONG THERE, DETECTIVE.
IT DID THE TRICK!
SO, HE'S IN?
HE'S IN. NOW ALL WE HAVE TO DO IS CONVINCE DEL.

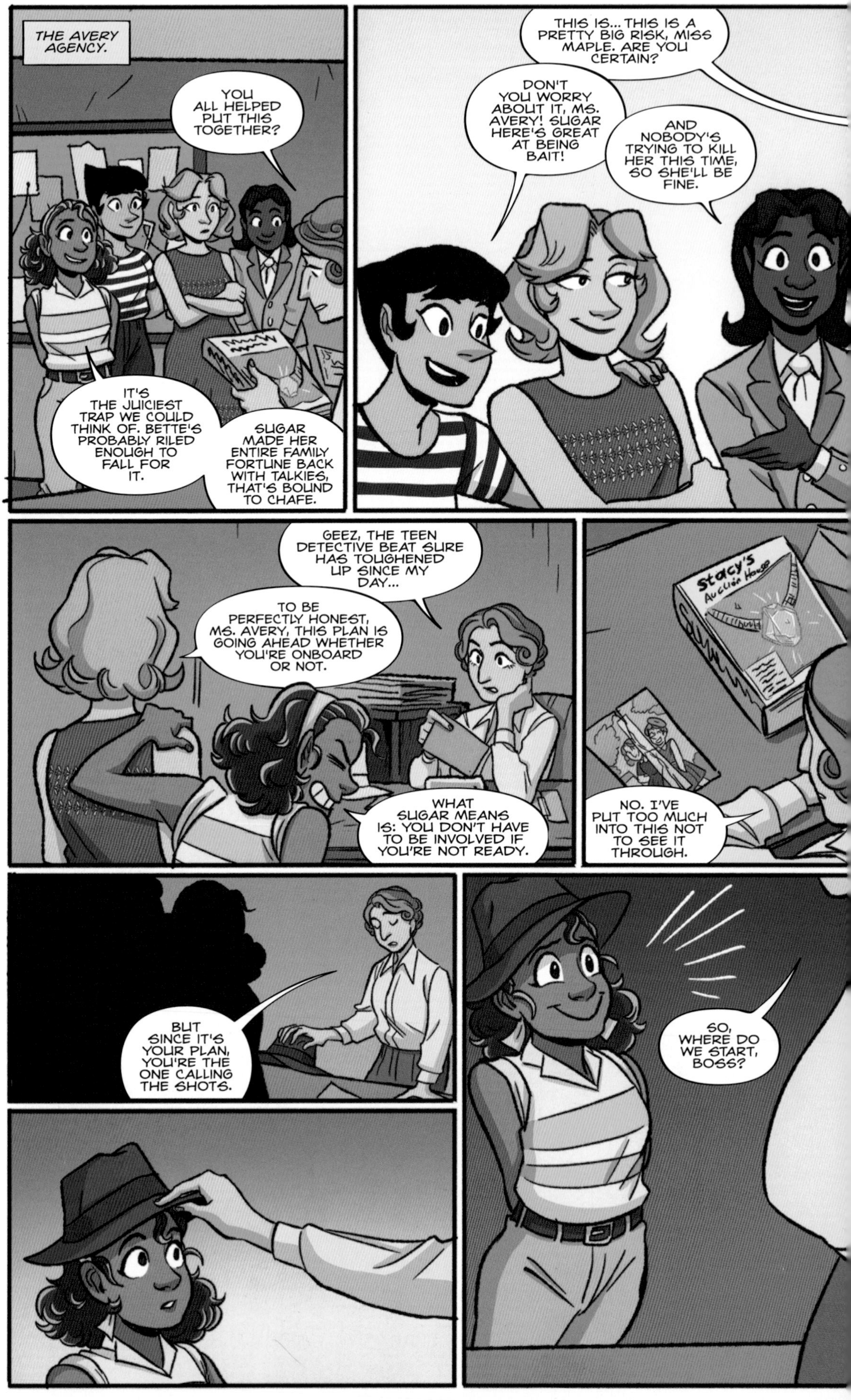
THE AVERY AGENCY.
YOU ALL HELPED PUT THIS TOGETHER?
IT'S THE JUICIEST TRAP WE COULD THINK OF. BETTE'S PROBABLY RILED ENOUGH TO FALL FOR IT.
SUGAR MADE HER ENTIRE FAMILY FORTUNE BACK WITH TALKIES, THAT'S BOUND TO CHAFE.
THIS IS... THIS IS A PRETTY BIG RISK, MISS MAPLE. ARE YOU CERTAIN?
DON'T YOU WORRY ABOUT IT, MS. AVERY! SUGAR HERE'S GREAT AT BEING BAIT!
AND NOBODY'S TRYING TO KILL HER THIS TIME, SO SHE'LL BE FINE.
GEEZ, THE TEEN DETECTIVE BEAT SURE HAS TOUGHENED UP SINCE MY DAY...
TO BE PERFECTLY HONEST, MS. AVERY, THIS PLAN IS GOING AHEAD WHETHER YOU'RE ONBOARD OR NOT.
WHAT SUGAR MEANS IS: YOU DON'T HAVE TO BE INVOLVED IF YOU'RE NOT READY.
Stacy's Auction House
NO. I'VE PUT TOO MUCH INTO THIS NOT TO SEE IT THROUGH.
BUT SINCE IT'S YOUR PLAN, YOU'RE THE ONE CALLING THE SHOTS.
SO, WHERE DO WE START, BOSS?

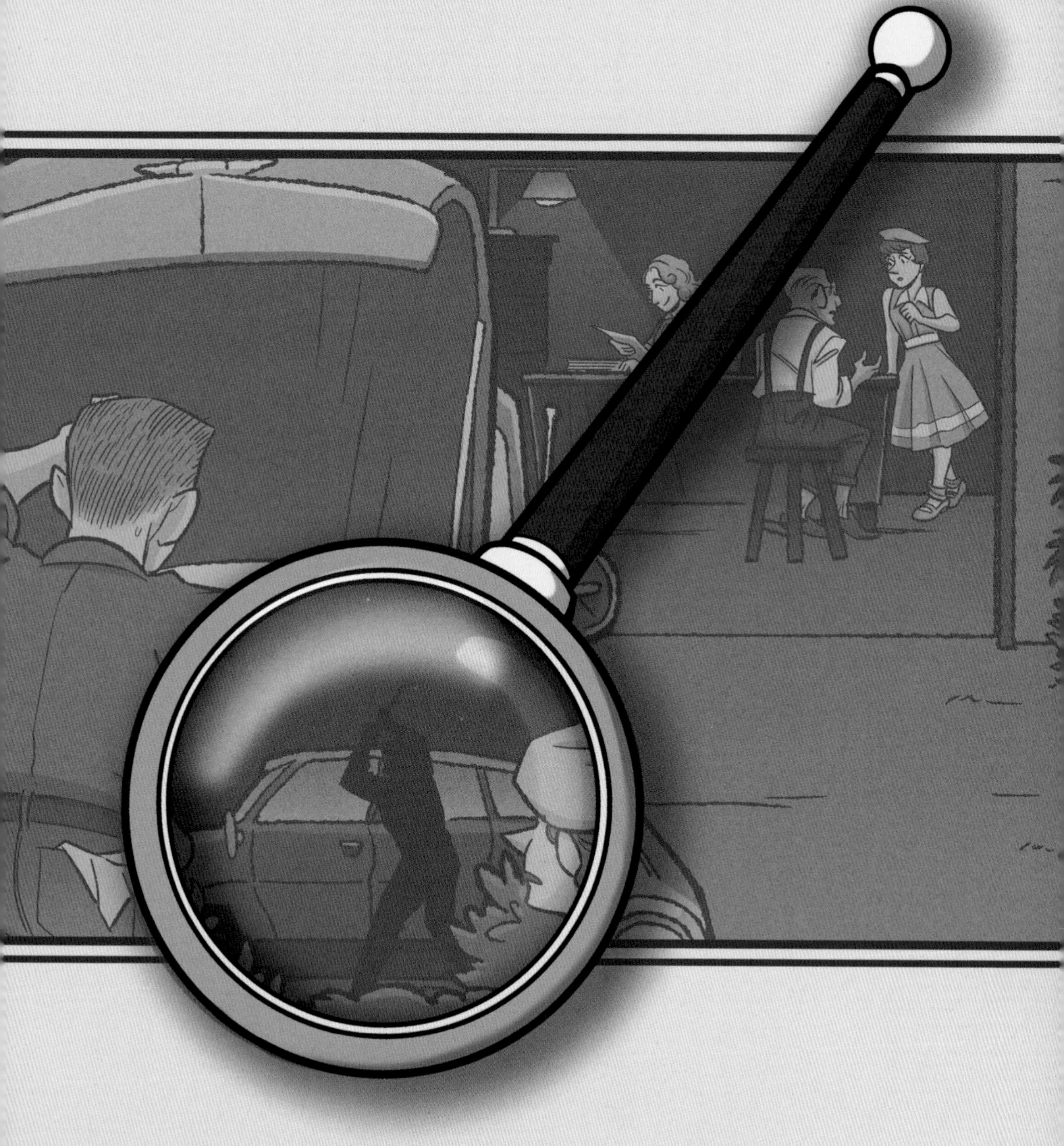

chapter
TWENTY

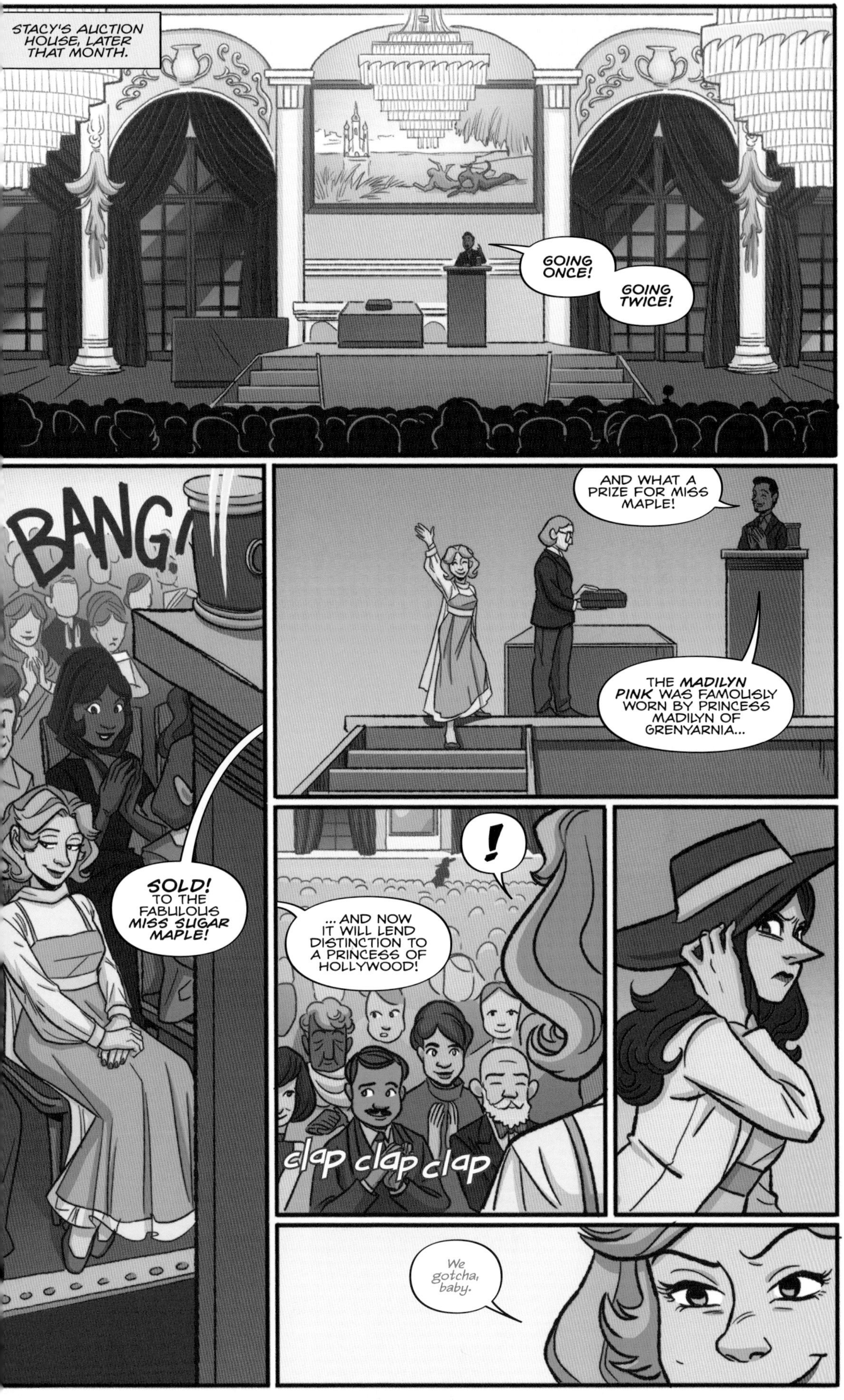
STACY'S AUCTION HOUSE, LATER THAT MONTH.
GOING ONCE!
GOING TWICE!
BANG!
SOLD! TO THE FABULOUS MISS SUGAR MAPLE!
AND WHAT A PRIZE FOR MISS MAPLE!
THE MADILYN PINK WAS FAMOUSLY WORN BY PRINCESS MADILYN OF GRENYARNIA...
...AND NOW IT WILL LEND DISTINCTION TO A PRINCESS OF HOLLYWOOD!
!
clap clap clap
We gotcha, baby.

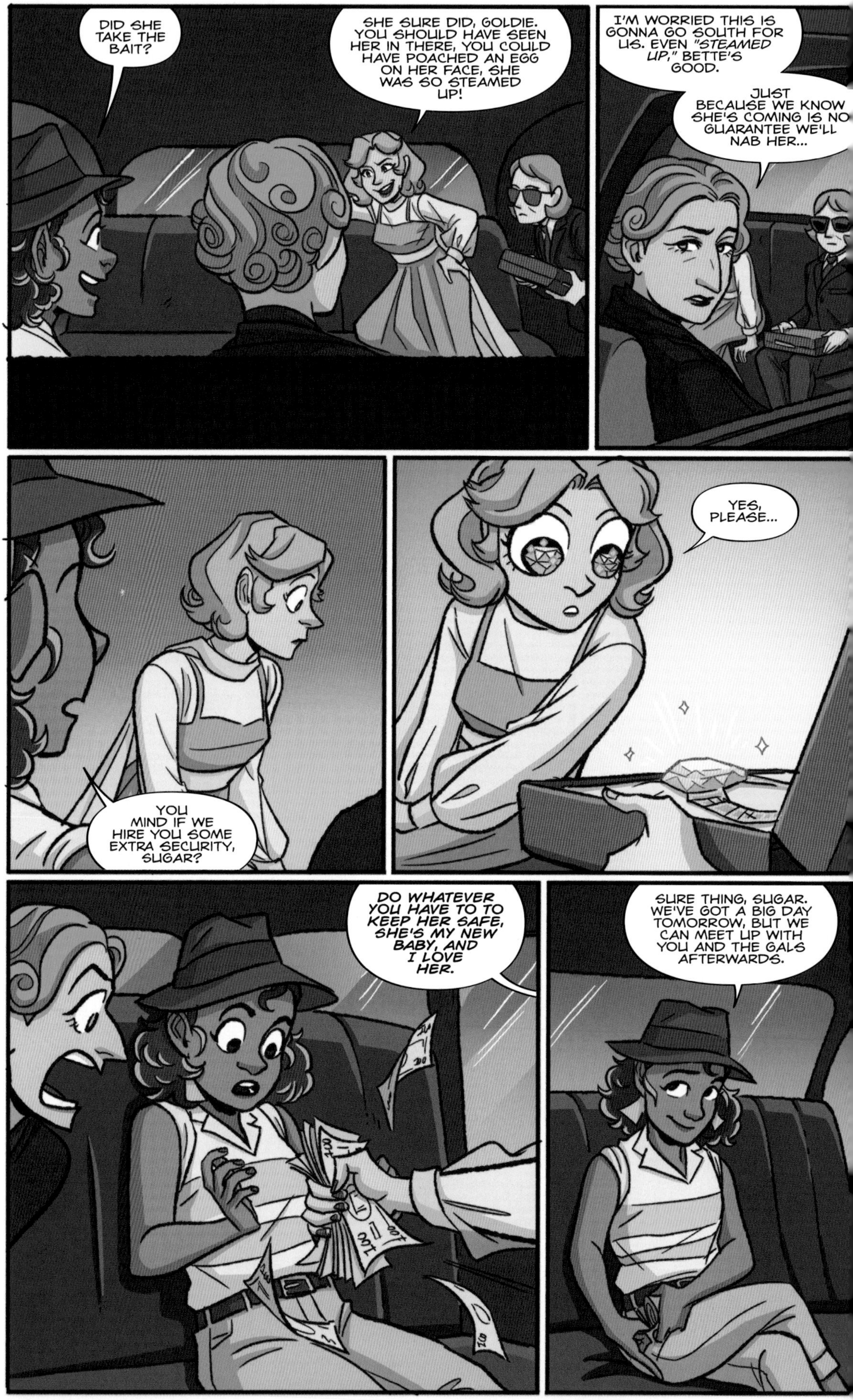
DID SHE TAKE THE BAIT?
SHE SURE DID, GOLDIE. YOU SHOULD HAVE SEEN HER IN THERE, YOU COULD HAVE POACHED AN EGG ON HER FACE, SHE WAS SO STEAMED UP!
I'M WORRIED THIS IS GONNA GO SOUTH FOR US. EVEN "STEAMED UP," BETTE'S GOOD.
JUST BECAUSE WE KNOW SHE'S COMING IS NO GUARANTEE WE'LL NAB HER...
YOU MIND IF WE HIRE YOU SOME EXTRA SECURITY, SUGAR?
YES, PLEASE...
DO WHATEVER YOU HAVE TO TO KEEP HER SAFE, SHE'S MY NEW BABY, AND I LOVE HER.
SURE THING, SUGAR. WE'VE GOT A BIG DAY TOMORROW, BUT WE CAN MEET UP WITH YOU AND THE GALS AFTERWARDS.

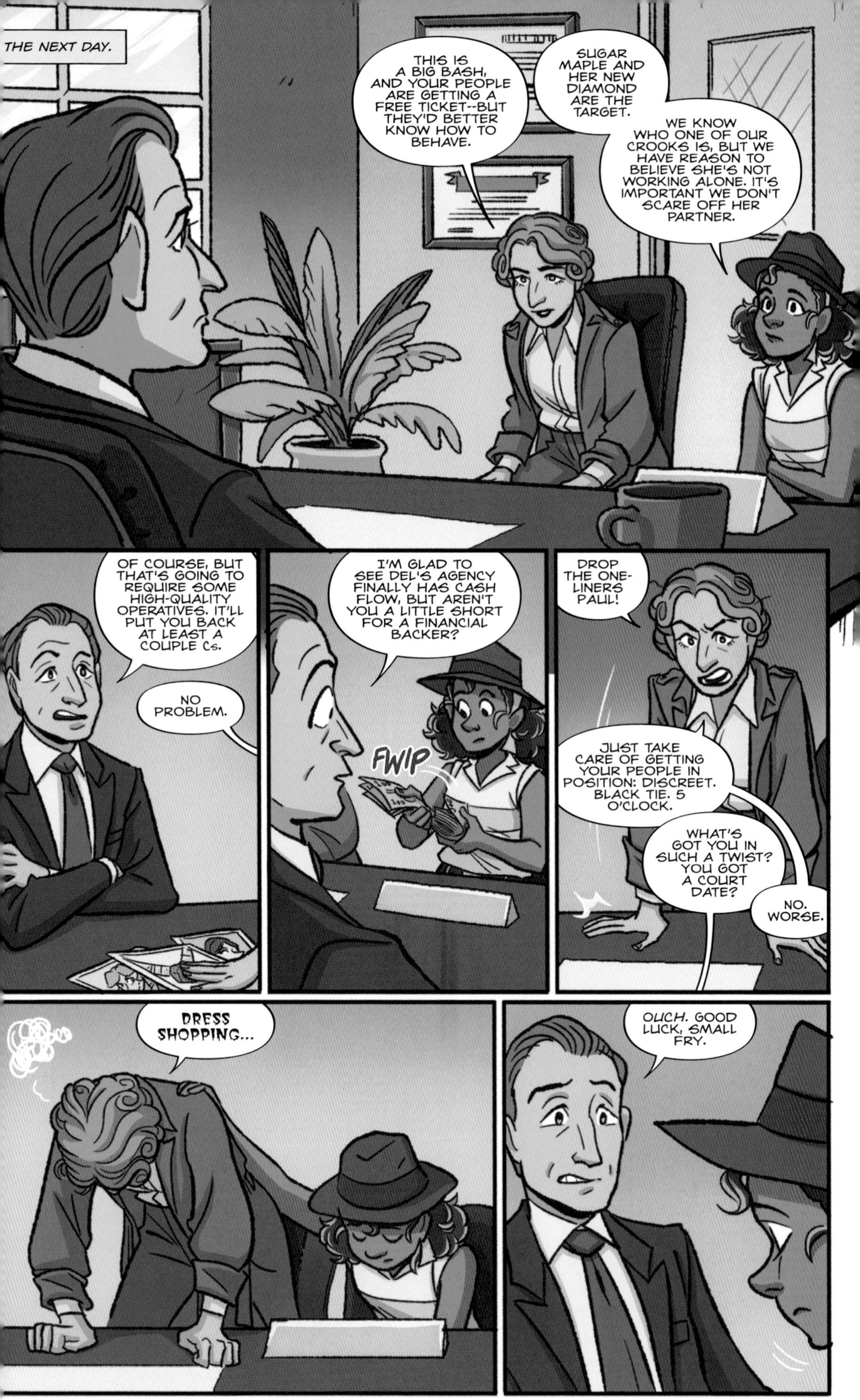
THE NEXT DAY.
THIS IS A BIG BASH, AND YOUR PEOPLE ARE GETTING A FREE TICKET--BUT THEY'D BETTER KNOW HOW TO BEHAVE.
SUGAR MAPLE AND HER NEW DIAMOND ARE THE TARGET.
WE KNOW WHO ONE OF OUR CROOKS IS, BUT WE HAVE REASON TO BELIEVE SHE'S NOT WORKING ALONE. IT'S IMPORTANT WE DON'T SCARE OFF HER PARTNER.
OF COURSE, BUT THAT'S GOING TO REQUIRE SOME HIGH-QUALITY OPERATIVES. IT'LL PUT YOU BACK AT LEAST A COUPLE Cs.
NO PROBLEM.
I'M GLAD TO SEE DEL'S AGENCY FINALLY HAS CASH FLOW, BUT AREN'T YOU A LITTLE SHORT FOR A FINANCIAL BACKER?
FWIP
DROP THE ONE-LINERS PAUL!
JUST TAKE CARE OF GETTING YOUR PEOPLE IN POSITION: DISCREET. BLACK TIE. 5 O'CLOCK.
WHAT'S GOT YOU IN SUCH A TWIST? YOU GOT A COURT DATE?
NO. WORSE.
DRESS SHOPPING...
OUCH. GOOD LUCK, SMALL FRY.

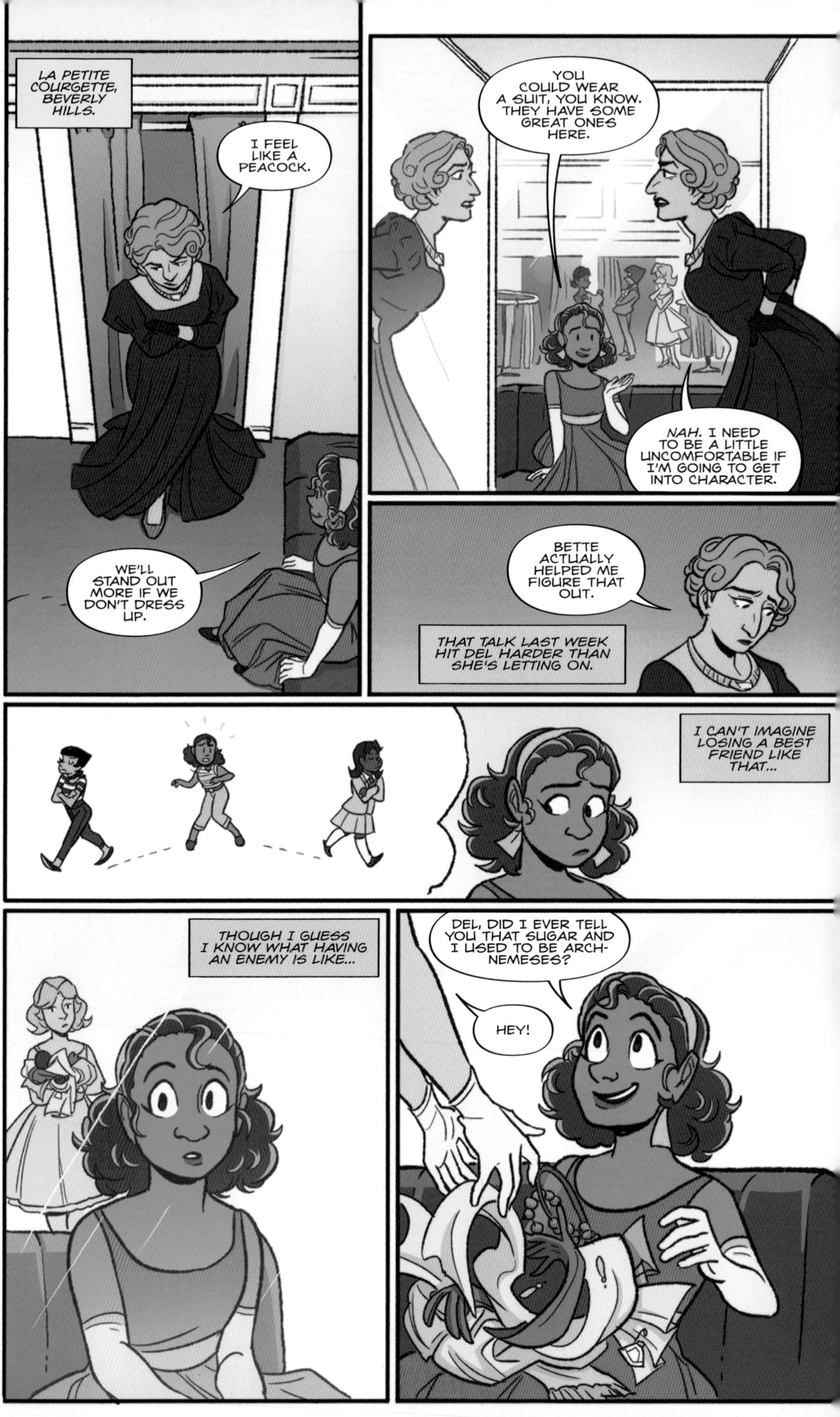
LA PETITE COURGETTE, BEVERLY HILLS.
I FEEL LIKE A PEACOCK.
WE'LL STAND OUT MORE IF WE DON'T DRESS UP.
YOU COULD WEAR A SUIT, YOU KNOW. THEY HAVE SOME GREAT ONES HERE.
NAH. I NEED TO BE A LITTLE UNCOMFORTABLE IF I'M GOING TO GET INTO CHARACTER.
BETTE ACTUALLY HELPED ME FIGURE THAT OUT.
THAT TALK LAST WEEK HIT DEL HARDER THAN SHE'S LETTING ON.
I CAN'T IMAGINE LOSING A BEST FRIEND LIKE THAT...
THOUGH I GUESS I KNOW WHAT HAVING AN ENEMY IS LIKE...
DEL, DID I EVER TELL YOU THAT SUGAR AND I USED TO BE ARCH-NEMESES?
HEY!

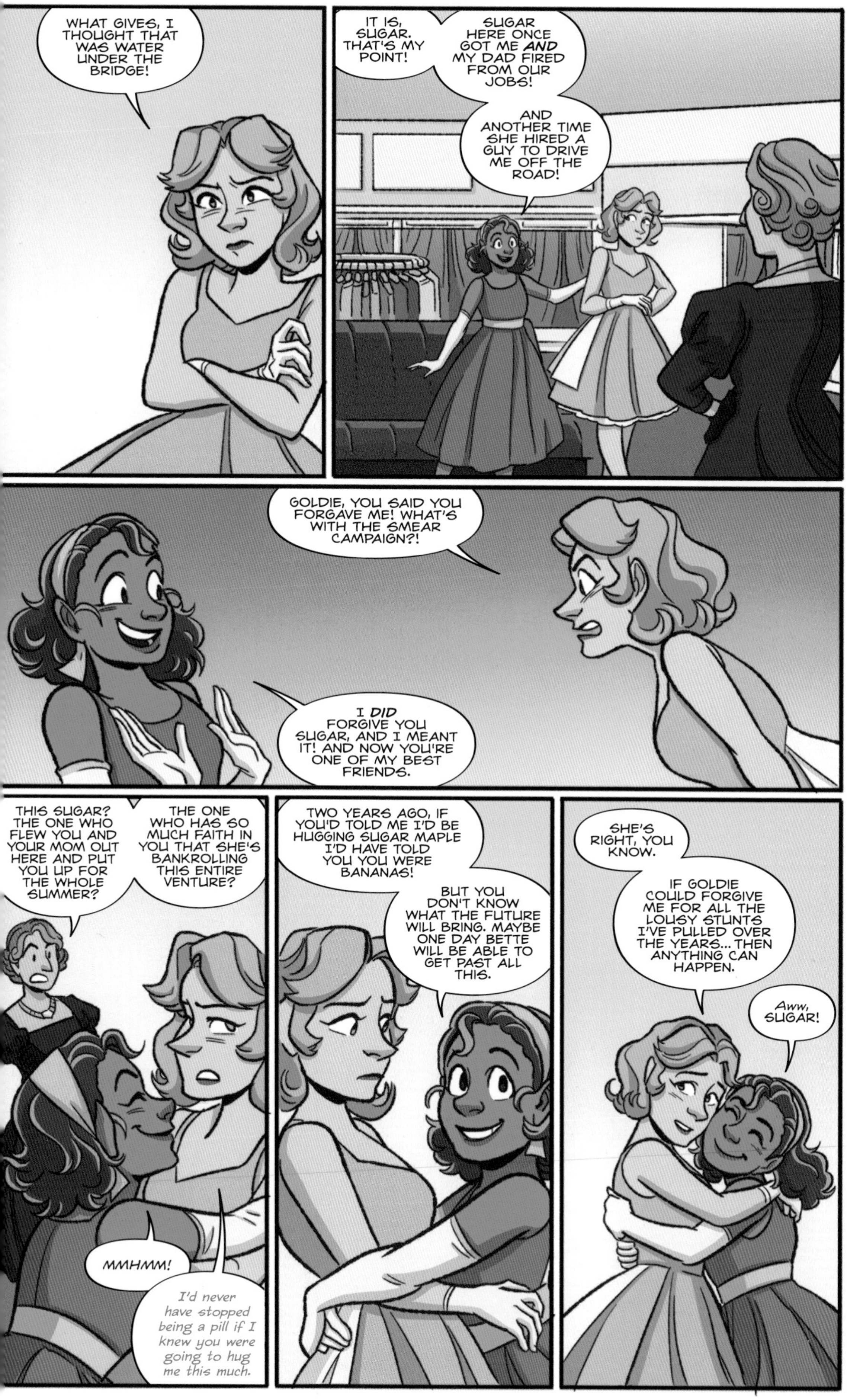

WHAT GIVES, I THOUGHT THAT WAS WATER UNDER THE BRIDGE!
IT IS, SUGAR. THAT'S MY POINT!
SUGAR HERE ONCE GOT ME *AND* MY DAD FIRED FROM OUR JOBS!
AND ANOTHER TIME SHE HIRED A GUY TO DRIVE ME OFF THE ROAD!
GOLDIE, YOU SAID YOU FORGAVE ME! WHAT'S WITH THE SMEAR CAMPAIGN?!
I *DID* FORGIVE YOU SUGAR, AND I MEANT IT! AND NOW YOU'RE ONE OF MY BEST FRIENDS.
THIS SUGAR? THE ONE WHO FLEW YOU AND YOUR MOM OUT HERE AND PUT YOU UP FOR THE WHOLE SUMMER?
THE ONE WHO HAS SO MUCH FAITH IN YOU THAT SHE'S BANKROLLING THIS ENTIRE VENTURE?
MMHMM!
I'd never have stopped being a pill if I knew you were going to hug me this much.
TWO YEARS AGO, IF YOU'D TOLD ME I'D BE HUGGING SUGAR MAPLE I'D HAVE TOLD YOU YOU WERE BANANAS!
BUT YOU DON'T KNOW WHAT THE FUTURE WILL BRING. MAYBE ONE DAY BETTE WILL BE ABLE TO GET PAST ALL THIS.
SHE'S RIGHT, YOU KNOW.
IF GOLDIE COULD FORGIVE ME FOR ALL THE LOUSY STUNTS I'VE PULLED OVER THE YEARS... THEN ANYTHING CAN HAPPEN.
Aww, SUGAR!

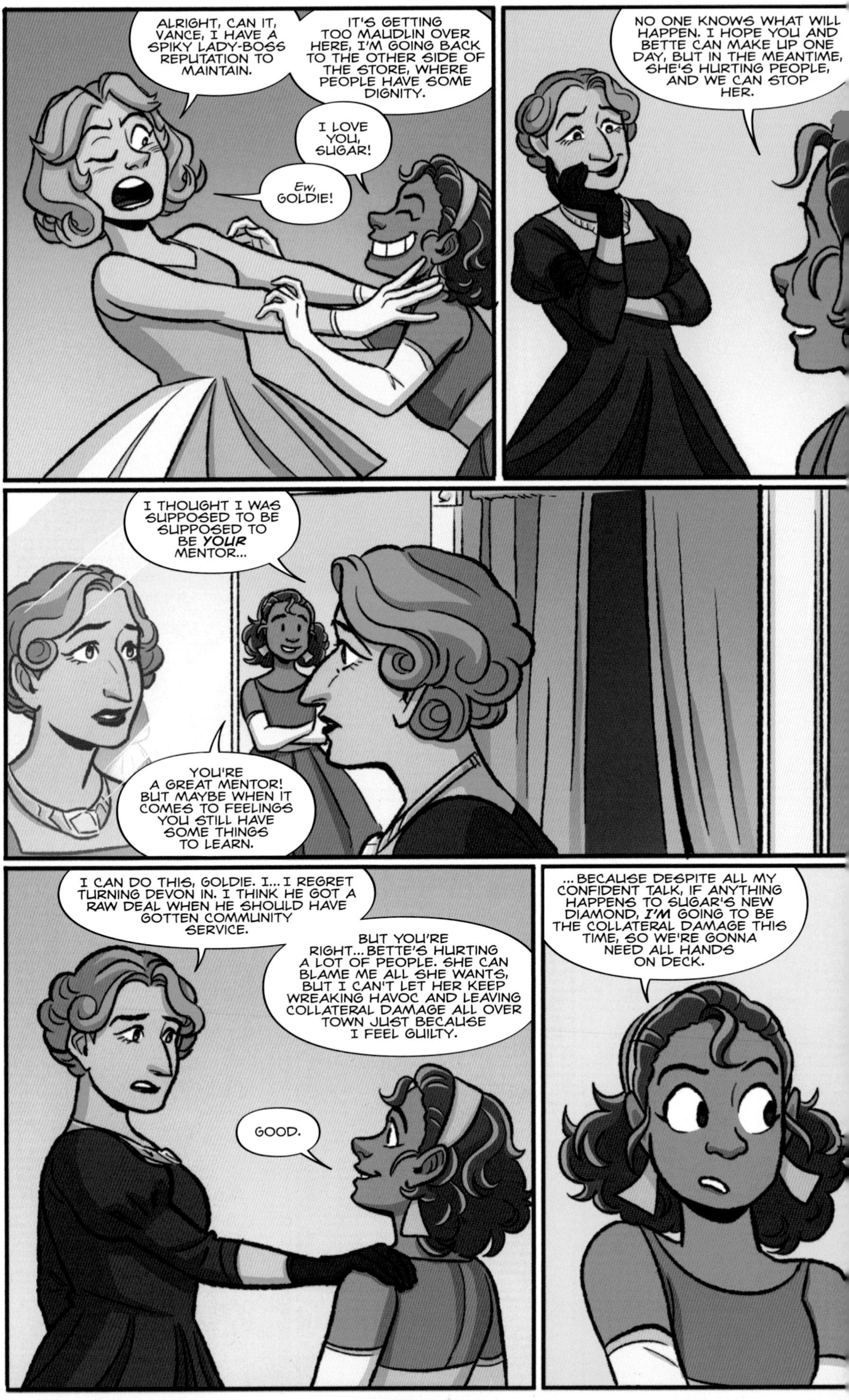

ALRIGHT, CAN IT, VANCE, I HAVE A SPIKY LADY-BOSS REPUTATION TO MAINTAIN.
IT'S GETTING TOO MAUDLIN OVER HERE, I'M GOING BACK TO THE OTHER SIDE OF THE STORE, WHERE PEOPLE HAVE SOME DIGNITY.
I LOVE YOU, SUGAR!
Ew, GOLDIE!
NO ONE KNOWS WHAT WILL HAPPEN. I HOPE YOU AND BETTE CAN MAKE UP ONE DAY, BUT IN THE MEANTIME, SHE'S HURTING PEOPLE, AND WE CAN STOP HER.
I THOUGHT I WAS SUPPOSED TO BE SUPPOSED TO BE ***YOUR*** MENTOR...
YOU'RE A GREAT MENTOR! BUT MAYBE WHEN IT COMES TO FEELINGS YOU STILL HAVE SOME THINGS TO LEARN.
I CAN DO THIS, GOLDIE. I... I REGRET TURNING DEVON IN. I THINK HE GOT A RAW DEAL WHEN HE SHOULD HAVE GOTTEN COMMUNITY SERVICE.
BUT YOU'RE RIGHT... BETTE'S HURTING A LOT OF PEOPLE. SHE CAN BLAME ME ALL SHE WANTS, BUT I CAN'T LET HER KEEP WREAKING HAVOC AND LEAVING COLLATERAL DAMAGE ALL OVER TOWN JUST BECAUSE I FEEL GUILTY.
GOOD.
...BECAUSE DESPITE ALL MY CONFIDENT TALK, IF ANYTHING HAPPENS TO SUGAR'S NEW DIAMOND, ***I'M*** GOING TO BE THE COLLATERAL DAMAGE THIS TIME, SO WE'RE GONNA NEED ALL HANDS ON DECK.

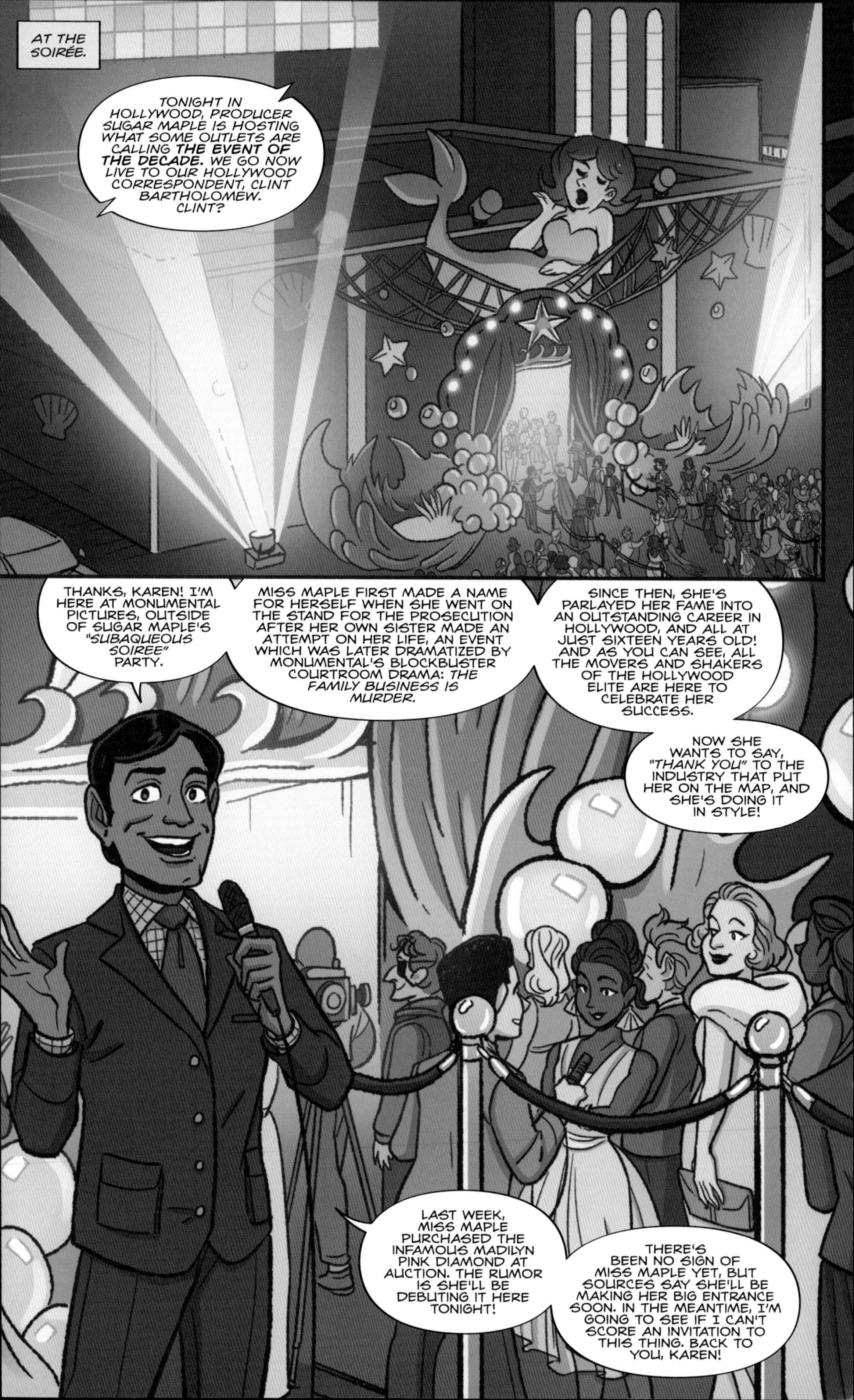
AT THE SOIRÉE.
TONIGHT IN HOLLYWOOD, PRODUCER SUGAR MAPLE IS HOSTING WHAT SOME OUTLETS ARE CALLING **THE EVENT OF THE DECADE.** WE GO NOW LIVE TO OUR HOLLYWOOD CORRESPONDENT, CLINT BARTHOLOMEW. CLINT?
THANKS, KAREN! I'M HERE AT MONUMENTAL PICTURES, OUTSIDE OF SUGAR MAPLE'S *"SUBAQUEOUS SOIREE"* PARTY.
MISS MAPLE FIRST MADE A NAME FOR HERSELF WHEN SHE WENT ON THE STAND FOR THE PROSECUTION AFTER HER OWN SISTER MADE AN ATTEMPT ON HER LIFE, AN EVENT WHICH WAS LATER DRAMATIZED BY MONUMENTAL'S BLOCKBUSTER COURTROOM DRAMA: *THE FAMILY BUSINESS IS MURDER.*
SINCE THEN, SHE'S PARLAYED HER FAME INTO AN OUTSTANDING CAREER IN HOLLYWOOD, AND ALL AT JUST SIXTEEN YEARS OLD! AND AS YOU CAN SEE, ALL THE MOVERS AND SHAKERS OF THE HOLLYWOOD ELITE ARE HERE TO CELEBRATE HER SUCCESS.
NOW SHE WANTS TO SAY, *"THANK YOU"* TO THE INDUSTRY THAT PUT HER ON THE MAP, AND SHE'S DOING IT IN STYLE!
LAST WEEK, MISS MAPLE PURCHASED THE INFAMOUS MADILYN PINK DIAMOND AT AUCTION. THE RUMOR IS SHE'LL BE DEBUTING IT HERE TONIGHT!
THERE'S BEEN NO SIGN OF MISS MAPLE YET, BUT SOURCES SAY SHE'LL BE MAKING HER BIG ENTRANCE SOON. IN THE MEANTIME, I'M GOING TO SEE IF I CAN'T SCORE AN INVITATION TO THIS THING. BACK TO YOU, KAREN!

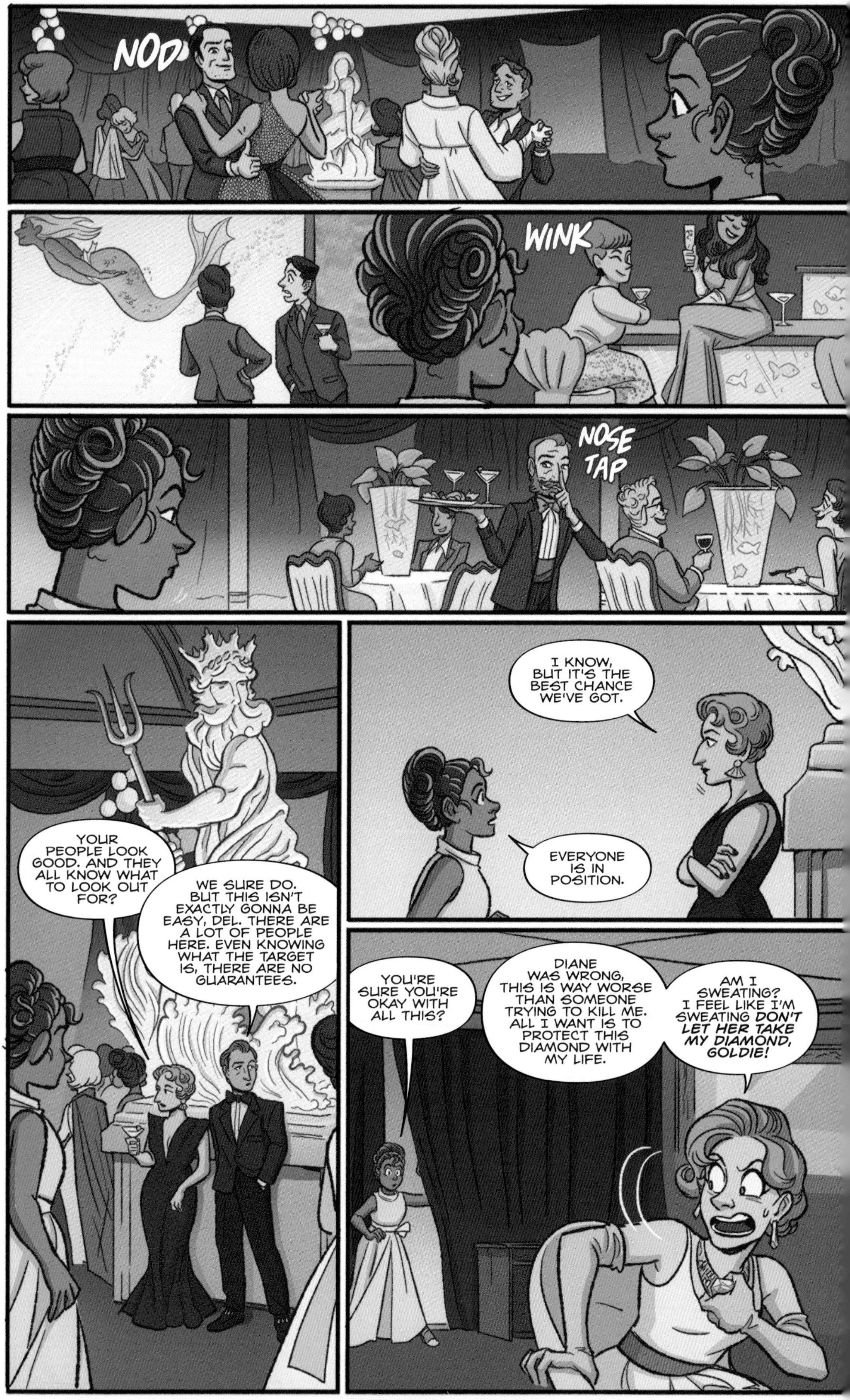
NOD
WINK
NOSE TAP
YOUR PEOPLE LOOK GOOD. AND THEY ALL KNOW WHAT TO LOOK OUT FOR?
WE SURE DO. BUT THIS ISN'T EXACTLY GONNA BE EASY, DEL. THERE ARE A LOT OF PEOPLE HERE. EVEN KNOWING WHAT THE TARGET IS, THERE ARE NO GUARANTEES.
EVERYONE IS IN POSITION.
I KNOW, BUT IT'S THE BEST CHANCE WE'VE GOT.
YOU'RE SURE YOU'RE OKAY WITH ALL THIS?
DIANE WAS WRONG, THIS IS WAY WORSE THAN SOMEONE TRYING TO KILL ME. ALL I WANT IS TO PROTECT THIS DIAMOND WITH MY LIFE.
AM I SWEATING? I FEEL LIKE I'M SWEATING *DON'T LET HER TAKE MY DIAMOND, GOLDIE!*

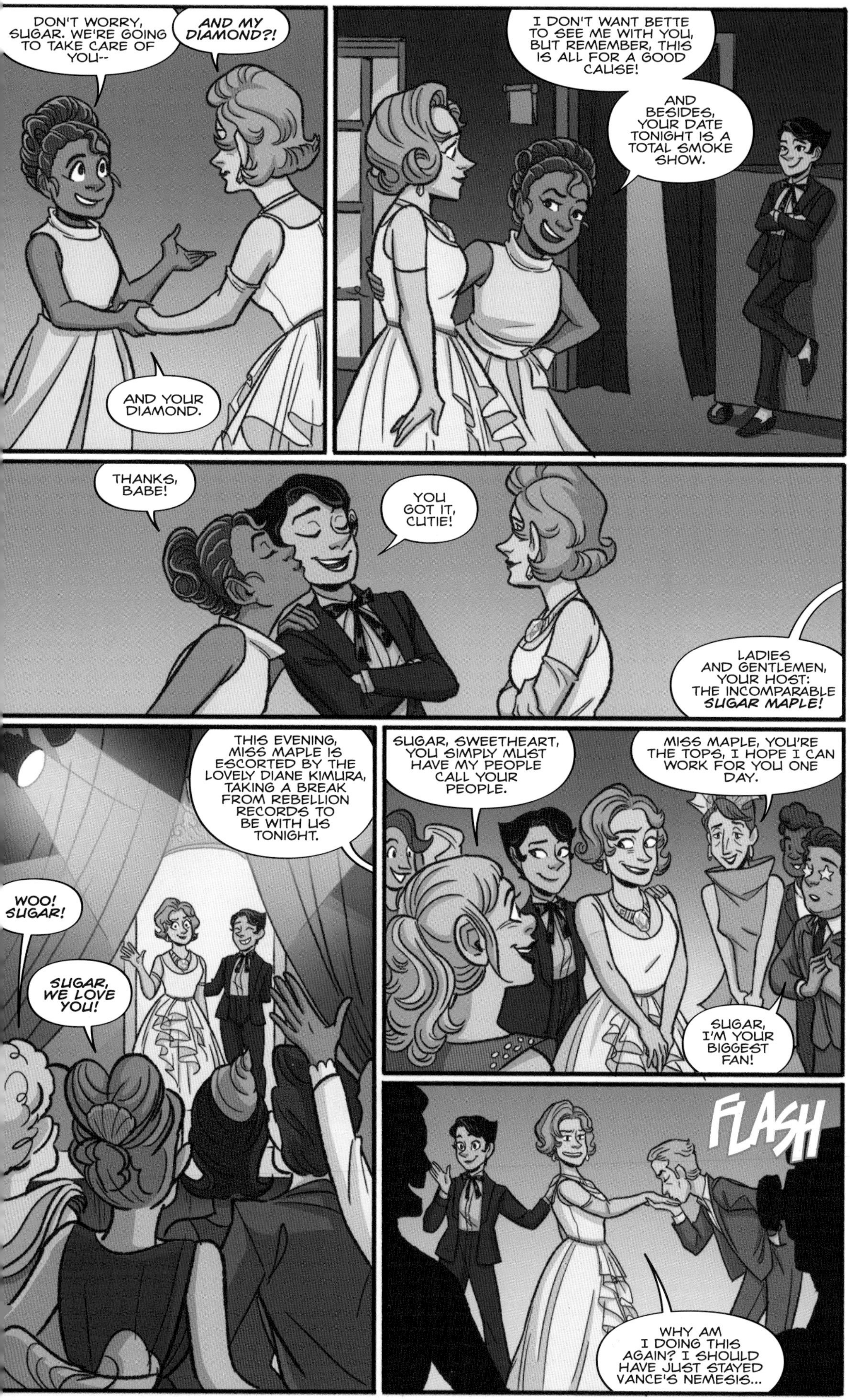

DON'T WORRY, SUGAR. WE'RE GOING TO TAKE CARE OF YOU--
AND MY DIAMOND?!
AND YOUR DIAMOND.
I DON'T WANT BETTE TO SEE ME WITH YOU, BUT REMEMBER, THIS IS ALL FOR A GOOD CAUSE!
AND BESIDES, YOUR DATE TONIGHT IS A TOTAL SMOKE SHOW.
THANKS, BABE!
YOU GOT IT, CUTIE!
LADIES AND GENTLEMEN, YOUR HOST: THE INCOMPARABLE SUGAR MAPLE!
THIS EVENING, MISS MAPLE IS ESCORTED BY THE LOVELY DIANE KIMURA, TAKING A BREAK FROM REBELLION RECORDS TO BE WITH US TONIGHT.
WOO! SUGAR!
SUGAR, WE LOVE YOU!
SUGAR, SWEETHEART, YOU SIMPLY MUST HAVE MY PEOPLE CALL YOUR PEOPLE.
MISS MAPLE, YOU'RE THE TOPS, I HOPE I CAN WORK FOR YOU ONE DAY.
SUGAR, I'M YOUR BIGGEST FAN!
FLASH
WHY AM I DOING THIS AGAIN? I SHOULD HAVE JUST STAYED VANCE'S NEMESIS...

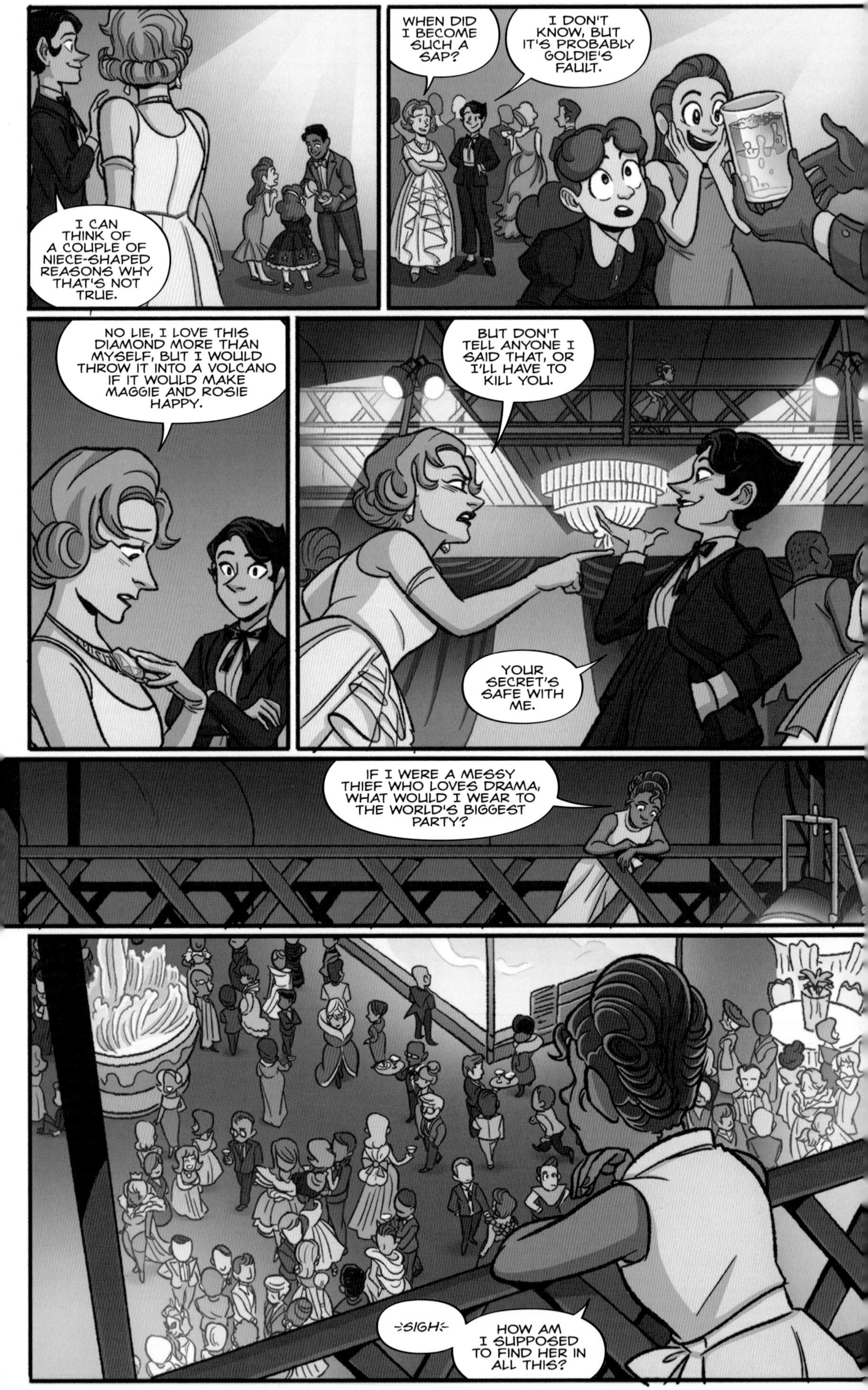
I CAN THINK OF A COUPLE OF NIECE-SHAPED REASONS WHY THAT'S NOT TRUE.
WHEN DID I BECOME SUCH A SAP?
I DON'T KNOW, BUT IT'S PROBABLY GOLDIE'S FAULT.
NO LIE, I LOVE THIS DIAMOND MORE THAN MYSELF, BUT I WOULD THROW IT INTO A VOLCANO IF IT WOULD MAKE MAGGIE AND ROSIE HAPPY.
BUT DON'T TELL ANYONE I SAID THAT, OR I'LL HAVE TO KILL YOU.
YOUR SECRET'S SAFE WITH ME.
IF I WERE A MESSY THIEF WHO LOVES DRAMA, WHAT WOULD I WEAR TO THE WORLD'S BIGGEST PARTY?
-SIGH-
HOW AM I SUPPOSED TO FIND HER IN ALL THIS?

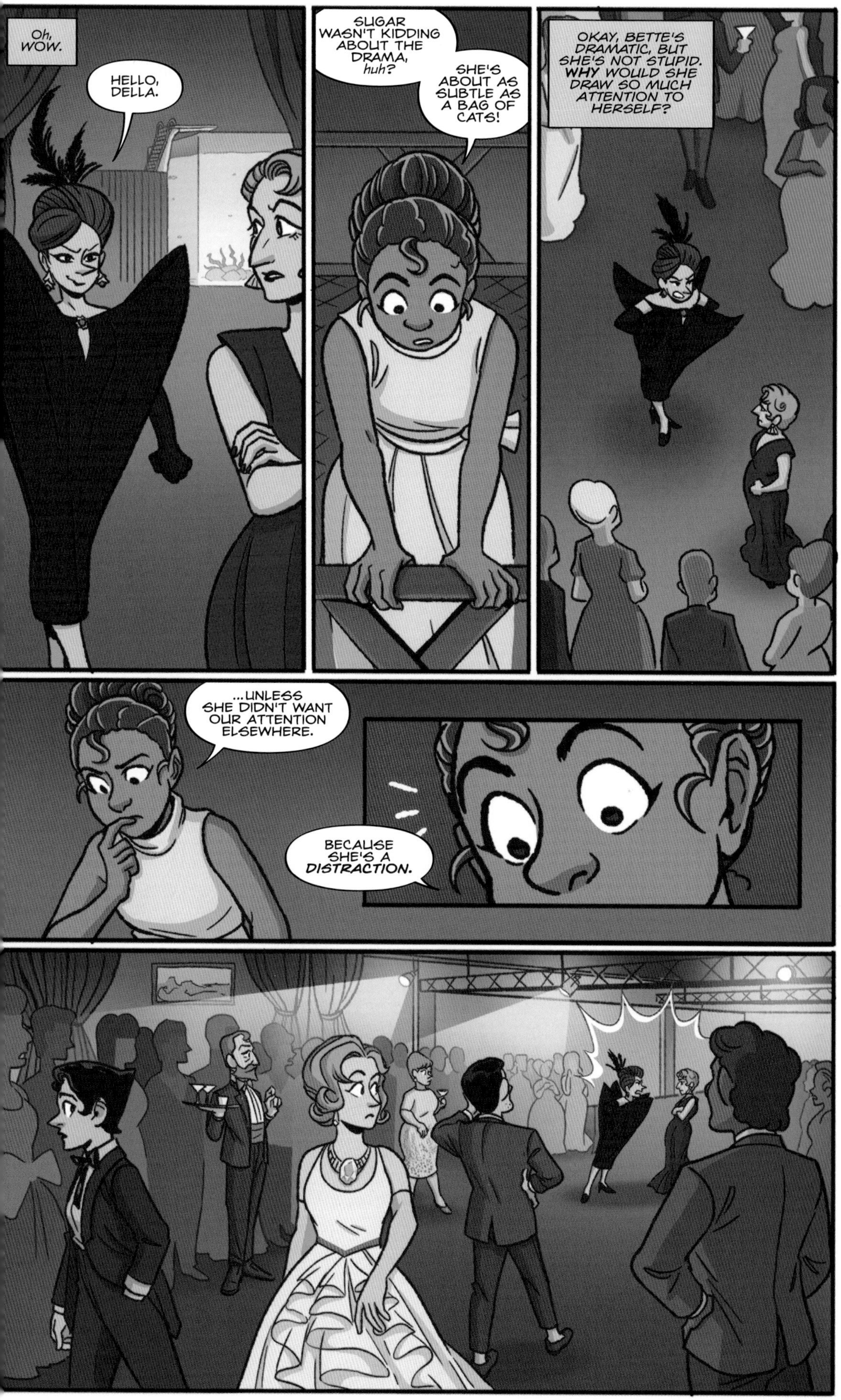
Oh, WOW.
HELLO, DELLA.
SUGAR WASN'T KIDDING ABOUT THE DRAMA, *huh?*
SHE'S ABOUT AS SUBTLE AS A BAG OF CATS!
OKAY, BETTE'S DRAMATIC, BUT SHE'S NOT STUPID. **WHY** WOULD SHE DRAW SO MUCH ATTENTION TO HERSELF?
...UNLESS SHE DIDN'T WANT OUR ATTENTION ELSEWHERE.
BECAUSE SHE'S A *DISTRACTION.*

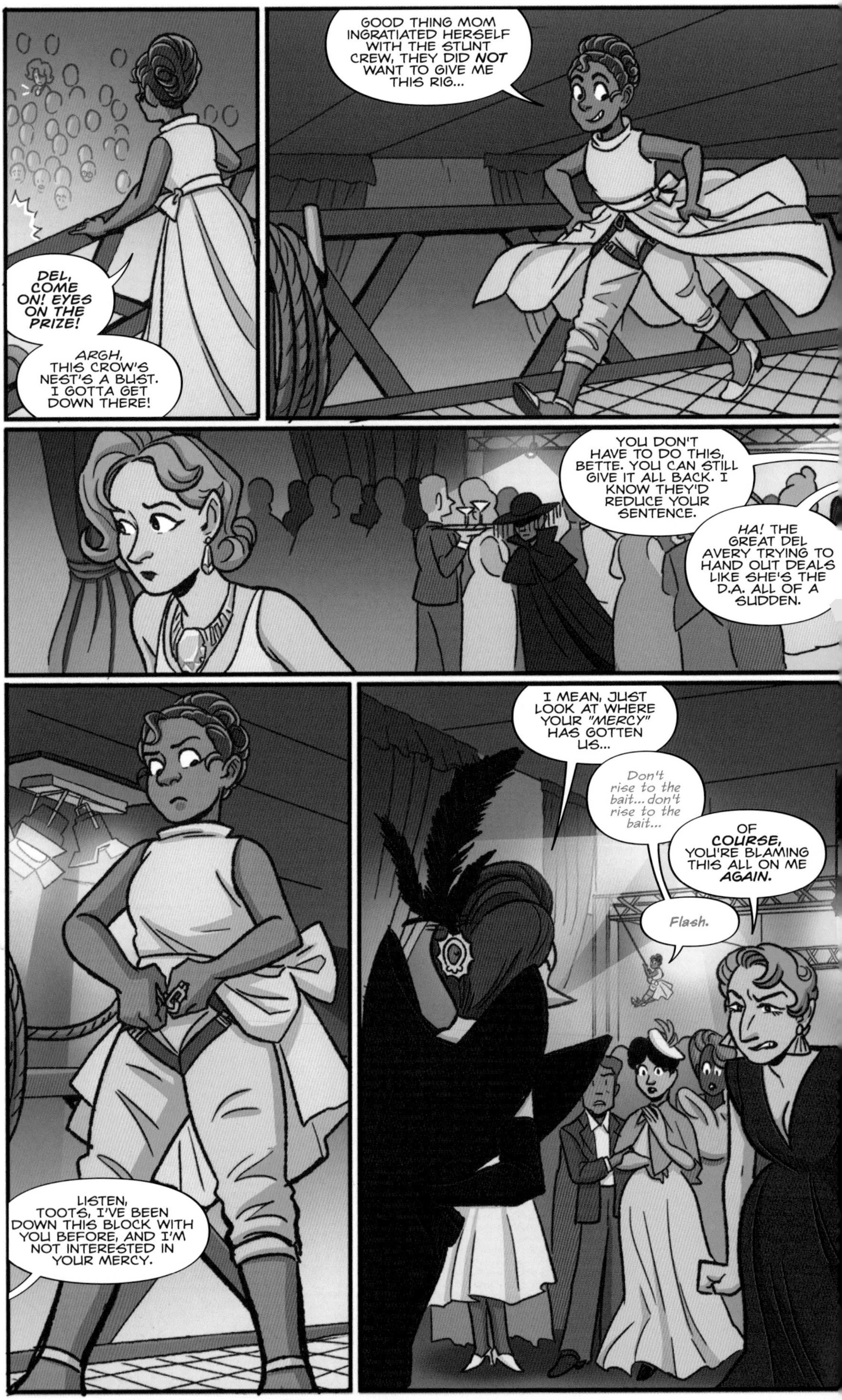
DEL, COME ON! EYES ON THE PRIZE!
ARGH, THIS CROW'S NEST'S A BUST. I GOTTA GET DOWN THERE!
GOOD THING MOM INGRATIATED HERSELF WITH THE STUNT CREW, THEY DID NOT WANT TO GIVE ME THIS RIG...
YOU DON'T HAVE TO DO THIS, BETTE. YOU CAN STILL GIVE IT ALL BACK. I KNOW THEY'D REDUCE YOUR SENTENCE.
HA! THE GREAT DEL AVERY TRYING TO HAND OUT DEALS LIKE SHE'S THE D.A. ALL OF A SUDDEN.
LISTEN, TOOTS, I'VE BEEN DOWN THIS BLOCK WITH YOU BEFORE, AND I'M NOT INTERESTED IN YOUR MERCY.
I MEAN, JUST LOOK AT WHERE YOUR "MERCY" HAS GOTTEN US...
Don't rise to the bait... don't rise to the bait...
OF COURSE, YOU'RE BLAMING THIS ALL ON ME AGAIN.
Flash.

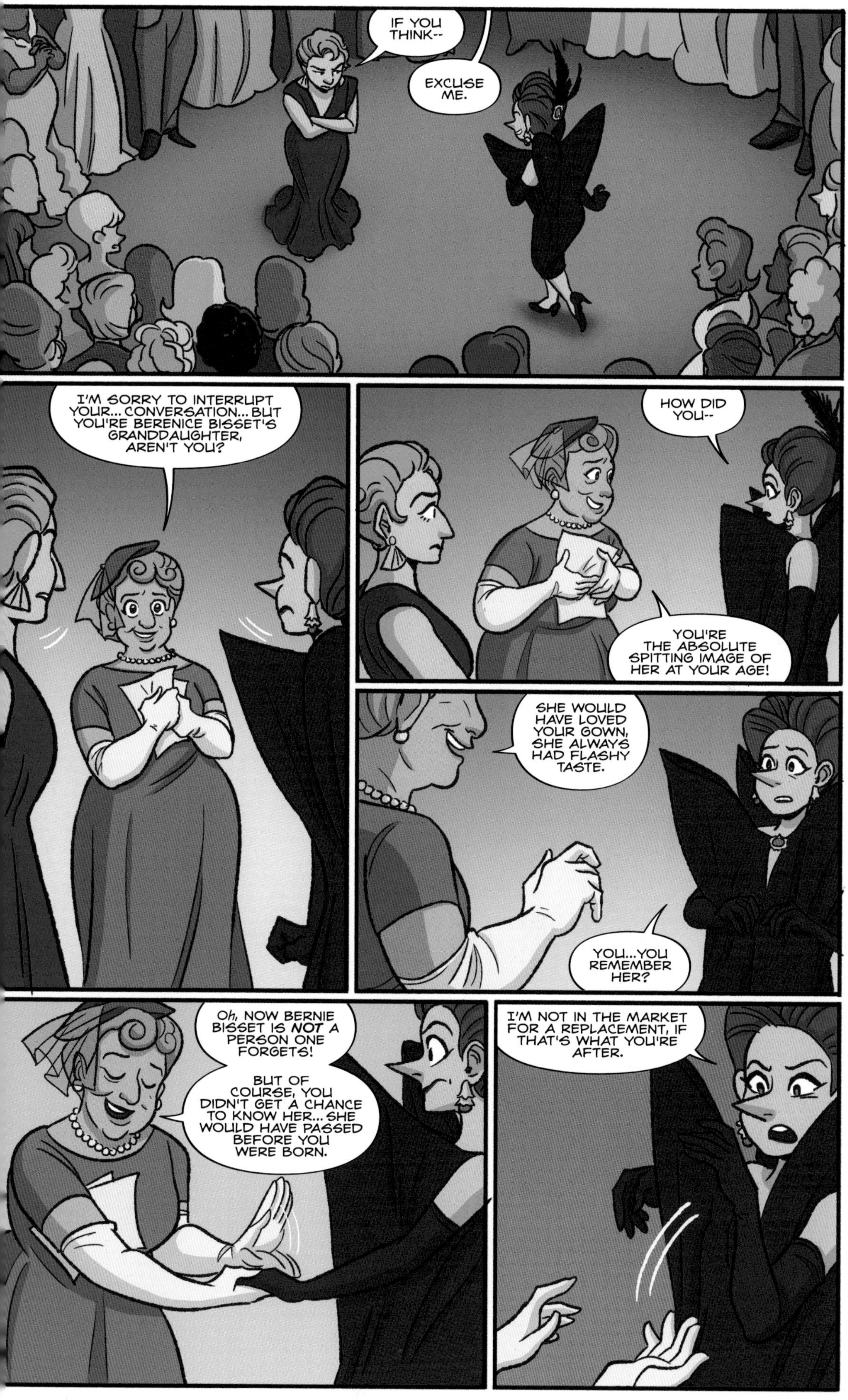
IF YOU THINK--
EXCUSE ME.
I'M SORRY TO INTERRUPT YOUR... CONVERSATION... BUT YOU'RE BERENICE BISSET'S GRANDDAUGHTER, AREN'T YOU?
HOW DID YOU--
YOU'RE THE ABSOLUTE SPITTING IMAGE OF HER AT YOUR AGE!
SHE WOULD HAVE LOVED YOUR GOWN, SHE ALWAYS HAD FLASHY TASTE.
YOU...YOU REMEMBER HER?
Oh, NOW BERNIE BISSET IS ***NOT*** A PERSON ONE FORGETS!
BUT OF COURSE, YOU DIDN'T GET A CHANCE TO KNOW HER... SHE WOULD HAVE PASSED BEFORE YOU WERE BORN.
I'M NOT IN THE MARKET FOR A REPLACEMENT, IF THAT'S WHAT YOU'RE AFTER.

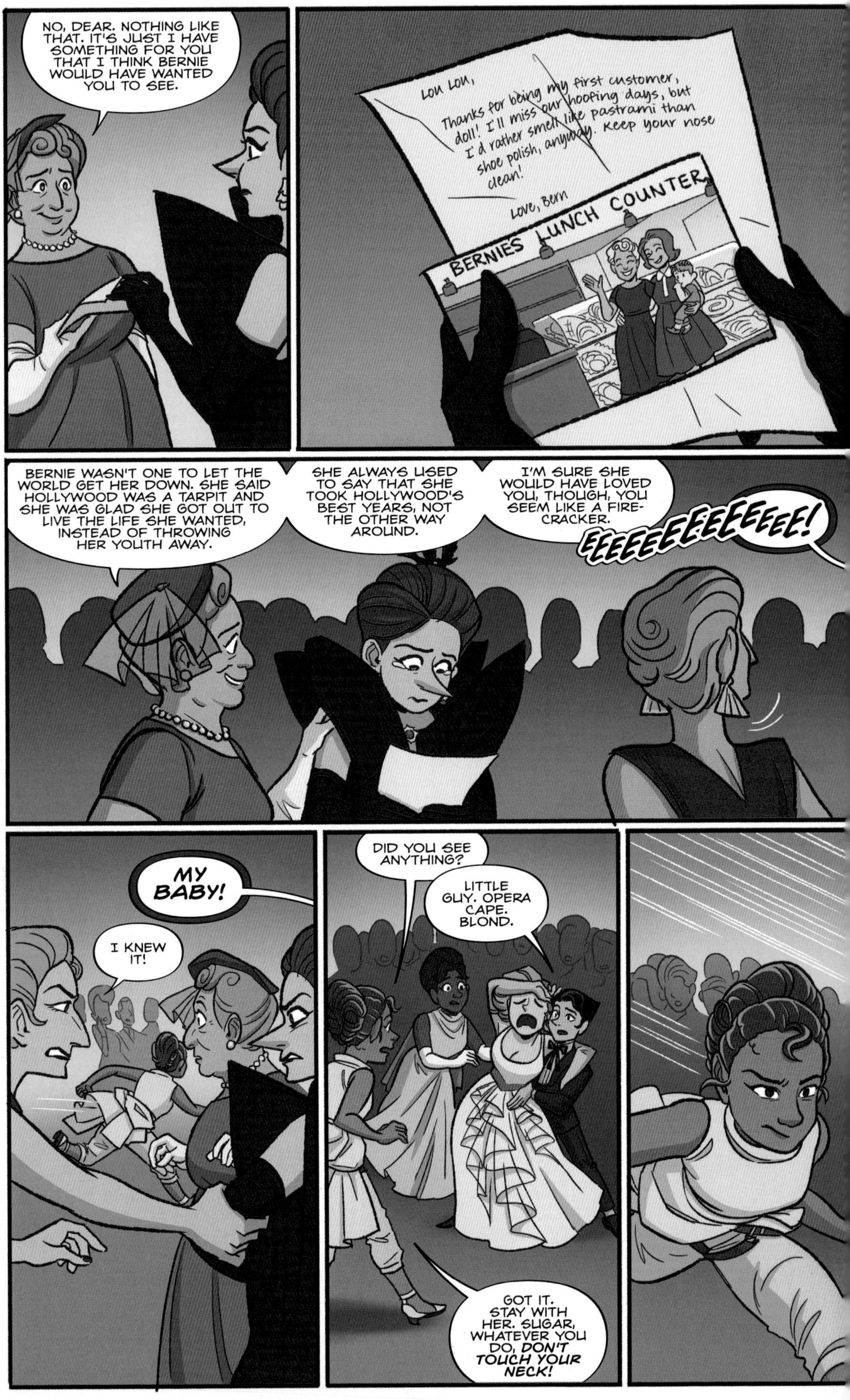
NO, DEAR. NOTHING LIKE THAT. IT'S JUST I HAVE SOMETHING FOR YOU THAT I THINK BERNIE WOULD HAVE WANTED YOU TO SEE.
Lou Lou,
Thanks for being my first customer, doll! I'll miss our hoofing days, but I'd rather smell like pastrami than shoe polish, anyway. Keep your nose clean!
Love, Bern
BERNIES LUNCH COUNTER
BERNIE WASN'T ONE TO LET THE WORLD GET HER DOWN. SHE SAID HOLLYWOOD WAS A TARPIT AND SHE WAS GLAD SHE GOT OUT TO LIVE THE LIFE SHE WANTED, INSTEAD OF THROWING HER YOUTH AWAY.
SHE ALWAYS USED TO SAY THAT SHE TOOK HOLLYWOOD'S BEST YEARS, NOT THE OTHER WAY AROUND.
I'M SURE SHE WOULD HAVE LOVED YOU, THOUGH. YOU SEEM LIKE A FIRE-CRACKER.
EEEEEEEEEEEEEEE!
MY BABY!
I KNEW IT!
DID YOU SEE ANYTHING?
LITTLE GUY. OPERA CAPE. BLOND.
GOT IT. STAY WITH HER. SUGAR, WHATEVER YOU DO, DON'T TOUCH YOUR NECK!

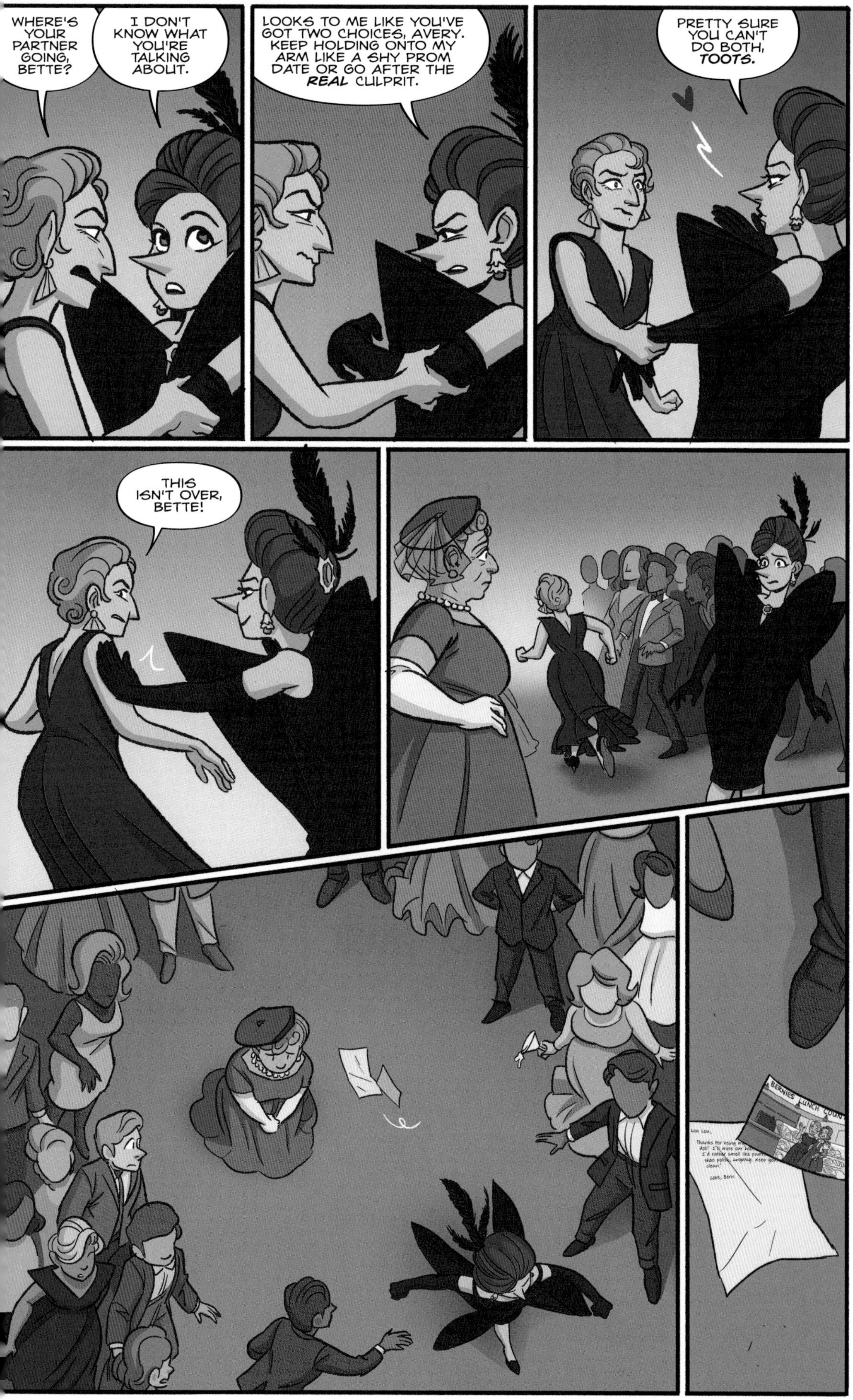
WHERE'S YOUR PARTNER GOING, BETTE?
I DON'T KNOW WHAT YOU'RE TALKING ABOUT.
LOOKS TO ME LIKE YOU'VE GOT TWO CHOICES, AVERY. KEEP HOLDING ONTO MY ARM LIKE A SHY PROM DATE OR GO AFTER THE *REAL* CULPRIT.
PRETTY SURE YOU CAN'T DO BOTH, *TOOTS.*
THIS ISN'T OVER, BETTE!
BERNIES LUNCH COUN
Lou Lou,
Thanks for being w
doll! I'll miss our ho
I'd rather smell like pas
shoe polish, anyway. Keep you
clean!
Love, Bern

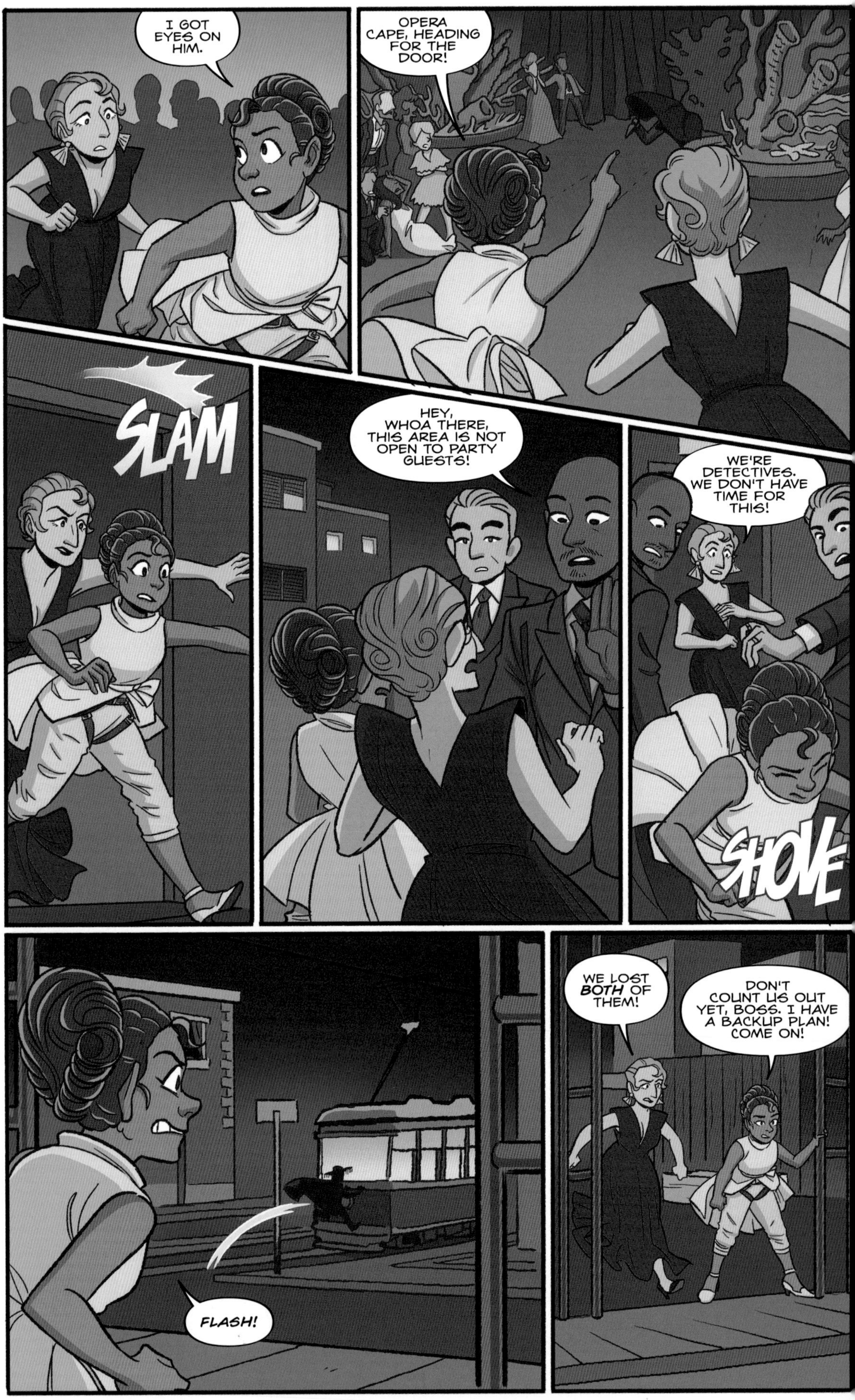
I GOT EYES ON HIM.
OPERA CAPE, HEADING FOR THE DOOR!
SLAM
HEY, WHOA THERE, THIS AREA IS NOT OPEN TO PARTY GUESTS!
WE'RE DETECTIVES. WE DON'T HAVE TIME FOR THIS!
SHOVE
FLASH!
WE LOST *BOTH* OF THEM!
DON'T COUNT US OUT YET, BOSS. I HAVE A BACKUP PLAN! COME ON!

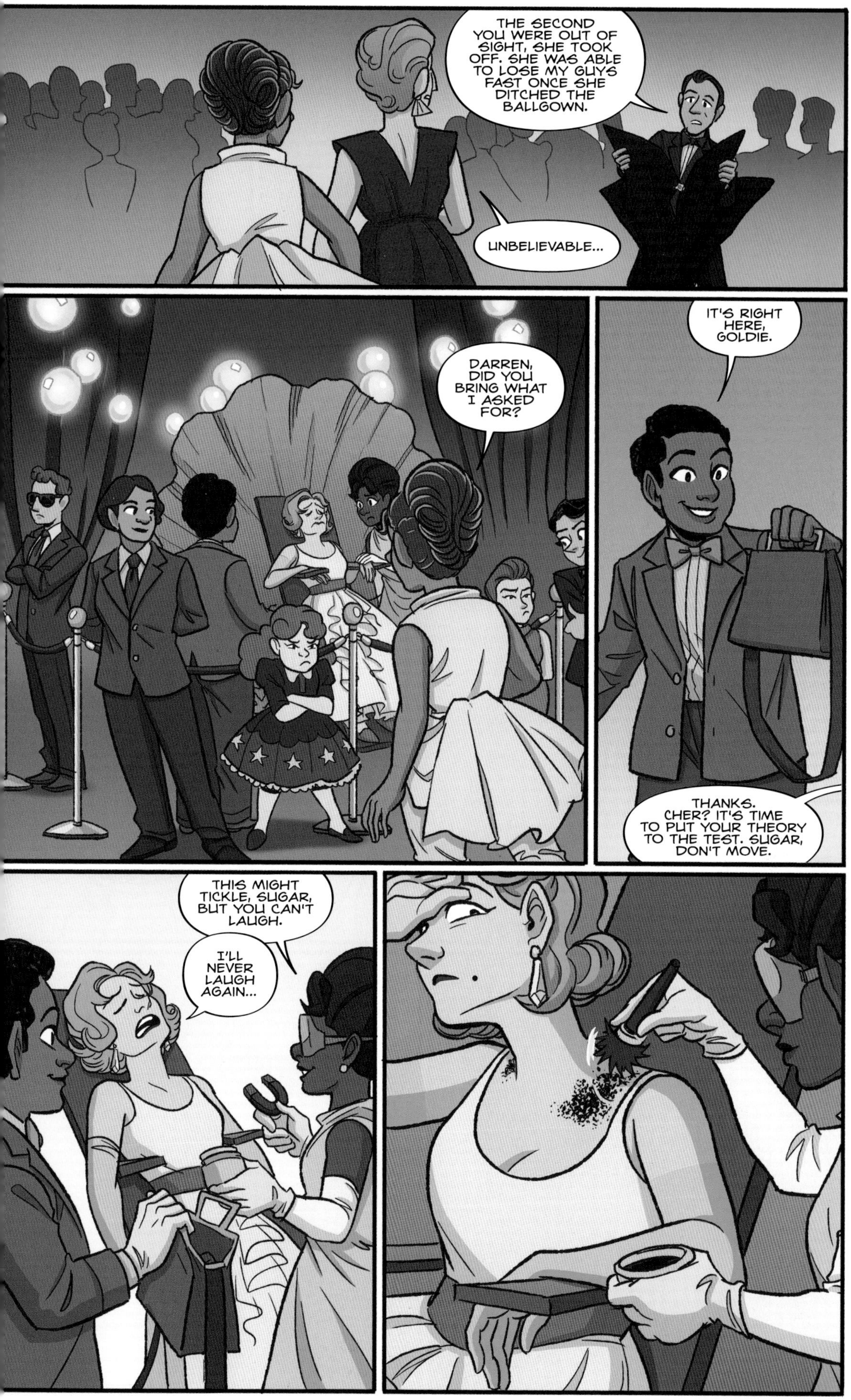
THE SECOND YOU WERE OUT OF SIGHT, SHE TOOK OFF. SHE WAS ABLE TO LOSE MY GUYS FAST ONCE SHE DITCHED THE BALLGOWN.
UNBELIEVABLE...
DARREN, DID YOU BRING WHAT I ASKED FOR?
IT'S RIGHT HERE, GOLDIE.
THANKS. CHER? IT'S TIME TO PUT YOUR THEORY TO THE TEST. SUGAR, DON'T MOVE.
THIS MIGHT TICKLE, SUGAR, BUT YOU CAN'T LAUGH.
I'LL NEVER LAUGH AGAIN...

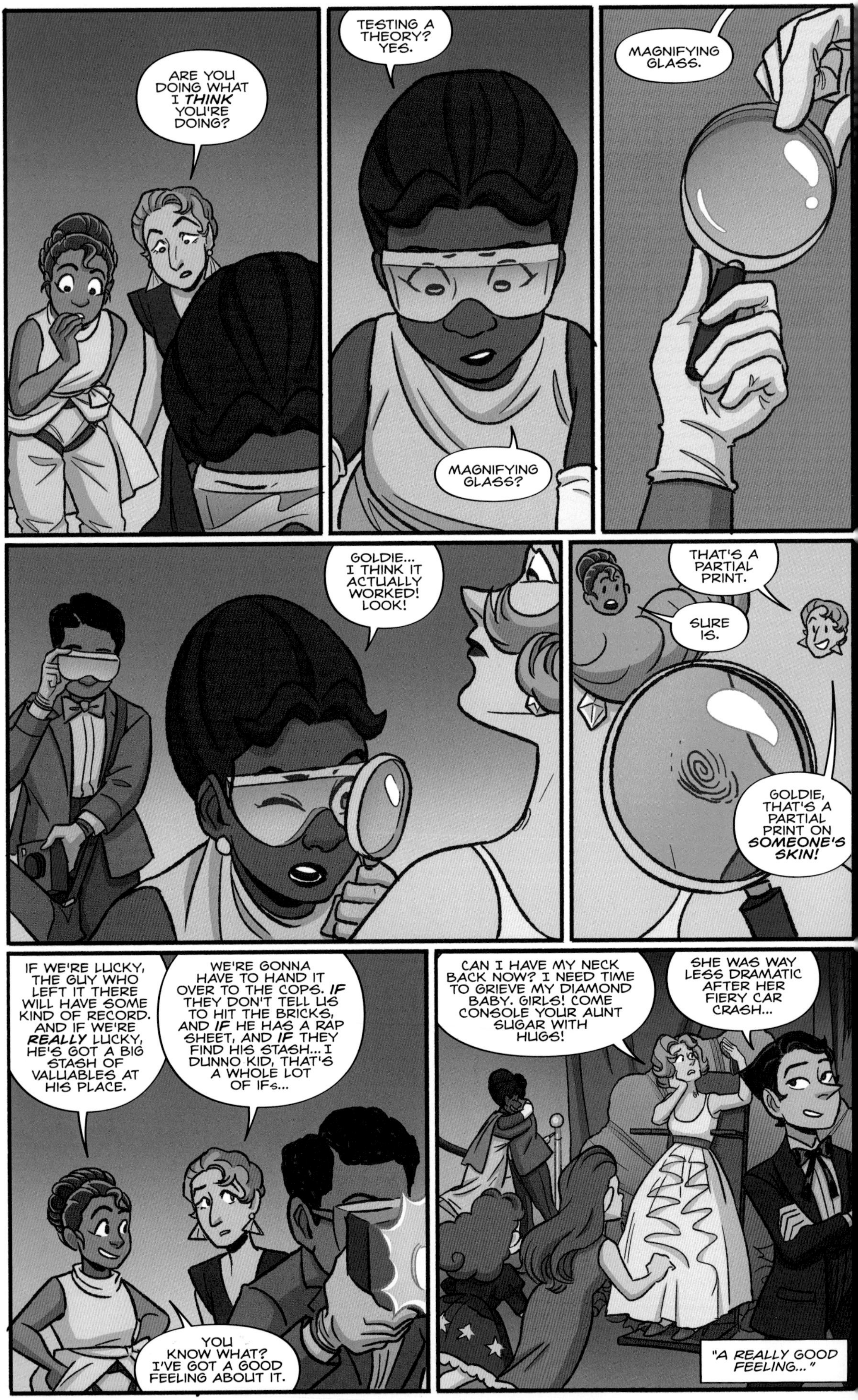
ARE YOU DOING WHAT I THINK YOU'RE DOING?
TESTING A THEORY? YES.
MAGNIFYING GLASS?
MAGNIFYING GLASS.
GOLDIE... I THINK IT ACTUALLY WORKED! LOOK!
THAT'S A PARTIAL PRINT.
SURE IS.
GOLDIE, THAT'S A PARTIAL PRINT ON SOMEONE'S SKIN!
IF WE'RE LUCKY, THE GUY WHO LEFT IT THERE WILL HAVE SOME KIND OF RECORD. AND IF WE'RE REALLY LUCKY, HE'S GOT A BIG STASH OF VALUABLES AT HIS PLACE.
WE'RE GONNA HAVE TO HAND IT OVER TO THE COPS. IF THEY DON'T TELL US TO HIT THE BRICKS, AND IF HE HAS A RAP SHEET, AND IF THEY FIND HIS STASH... I DUNNO KID, THAT'S A WHOLE LOT OF IFs...
YOU KNOW WHAT? I'VE GOT A GOOD FEELING ABOUT IT.
CAN I HAVE MY NECK BACK NOW? I NEED TIME TO GRIEVE MY DIAMOND BABY. GIRLS! COME CONSOLE YOUR AUNT SUGAR WITH HUGS!
SHE WAS WAY LESS DRAMATIC AFTER HER FIERY CAR CRASH...
"A REALLY GOOD FEELING..."

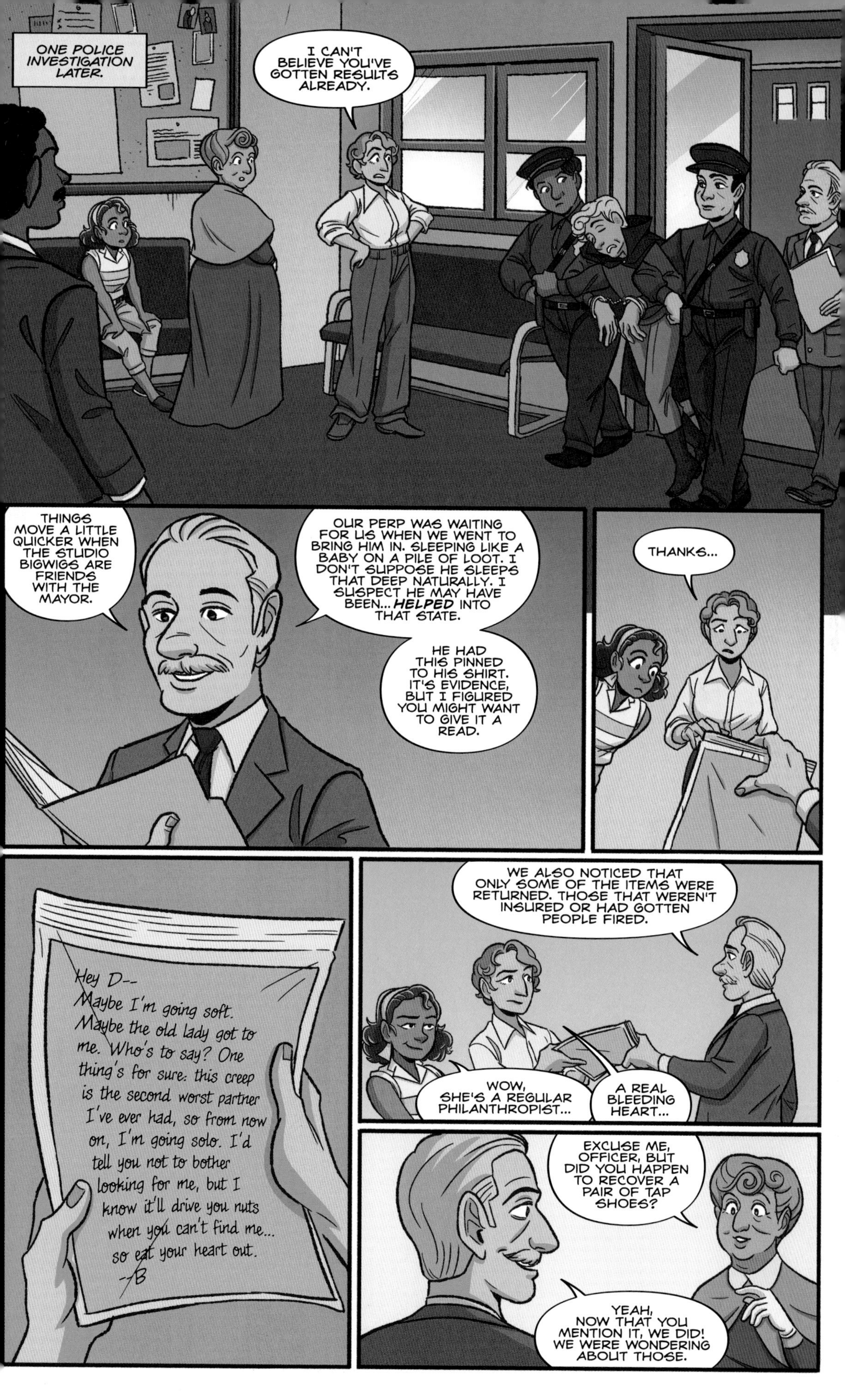
ONE POLICE INVESTIGATION LATER.
I CAN'T BELIEVE YOU'VE GOTTEN RESULTS ALREADY.
THINGS MOVE A LITTLE QUICKER WHEN THE STUDIO BIGWIGS ARE FRIENDS WITH THE MAYOR.
OUR PERP WAS WAITING FOR US WHEN WE WENT TO BRING HIM IN. SLEEPING LIKE A BABY ON A PILE OF LOOT. I DON'T SUPPOSE HE SLEEPS THAT DEEP NATURALLY. I SUSPECT HE MAY HAVE BEEN... HELPED INTO THAT STATE.
HE HAD THIS PINNED TO HIS SHIRT. IT'S EVIDENCE, BUT I FIGURED YOU MIGHT WANT TO GIVE IT A READ.
THANKS...
Hey D--
Maybe I'm going soft. Maybe the old lady got to me. Who's to say? One thing's for sure: this creep is the second worst partner I've ever had, so from now on, I'm going solo. I'd tell you not to bother looking for me, but I know it'll drive you nuts when you can't find me... so eat your heart out.
--B
WE ALSO NOTICED THAT ONLY SOME OF THE ITEMS WERE RETURNED. THOSE THAT WEREN'T INSURED OR HAD GOTTEN PEOPLE FIRED.
WOW, SHE'S A REGULAR PHILANTHROPIST...
A REAL BLEEDING HEART...
EXCUSE ME, OFFICER, BUT DID YOU HAPPEN TO RECOVER A PAIR OF TAP SHOES?
YEAH, NOW THAT YOU MENTION IT, WE DID! WE WERE WONDERING ABOUT THOSE.

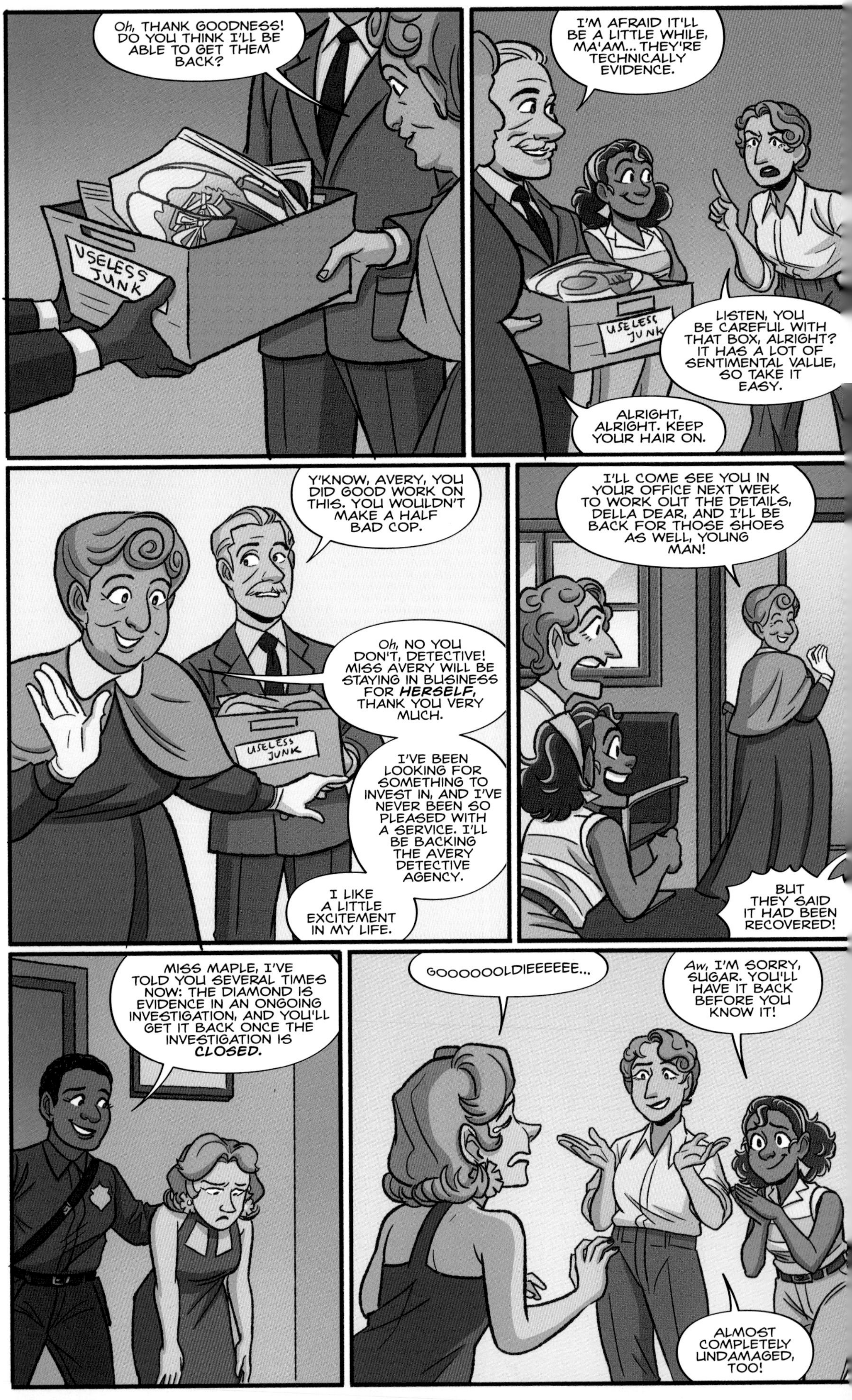

Oh, THANK GOODNESS! DO YOU THINK I'LL BE ABLE TO GET THEM BACK?
USELESS JUNK
I'M AFRAID IT'LL BE A LITTLE WHILE, MA'AM... THEY'RE TECHNICALLY EVIDENCE.
USELESS JUNK
LISTEN, YOU BE CAREFUL WITH THAT BOX, ALRIGHT? IT HAS A LOT OF SENTIMENTAL VALUE, SO TAKE IT EASY.
ALRIGHT, ALRIGHT. KEEP YOUR HAIR ON.
Y'KNOW, AVERY, YOU DID GOOD WORK ON THIS. YOU WOULDN'T MAKE A HALF BAD COP.
Oh, NO YOU DON'T, DETECTIVE! MISS AVERY WILL BE STAYING IN BUSINESS FOR ***HERSELF***, THANK YOU VERY MUCH.
USELESS JUNK
I'VE BEEN LOOKING FOR SOMETHING TO INVEST IN, AND I'VE NEVER BEEN SO PLEASED WITH A SERVICE. I'LL BE BACKING THE AVERY DETECTIVE AGENCY.
I LIKE A LITTLE EXCITEMENT IN MY LIFE.
I'LL COME SEE YOU IN YOUR OFFICE NEXT WEEK TO WORK OUT THE DETAILS, DELLA DEAR, AND I'LL BE BACK FOR THOSE SHOES AS WELL, YOUNG MAN!
BUT THEY SAID IT HAD BEEN RECOVERED!
MISS MAPLE, I'VE TOLD YOU SEVERAL TIMES NOW: THE DIAMOND IS EVIDENCE IN AN ONGOING INVESTIGATION, AND YOU'LL GET IT BACK ONCE THE INVESTIGATION IS ***CLOSED.***
GOOOOOOLDIEEEEEE...
Aw, I'M SORRY, SUGAR. YOU'LL HAVE IT BACK BEFORE YOU KNOW IT!
ALMOST COMPLETELY UNDAMAGED, TOO!

SNIFF

HOW'RE YOU FEELING ABOUT THAT LETTER, DEL?

HONESTLY? KIND OF RELIEVED.

IF SHE'S BUSY ANTAGONIZING ME, MAYBE SHE'LL STAY OFF THE COPS' RADAR...

PLUS, SHE DOESN'T KNOW MY OPERATION'S JUST BEEN FULLY BACKED, SO...

I'll go get the car...

WHO KNOWS? MAYBE ONE DAY I'LL HAVE MY VERY OWN REFORMED FORMER NEMESIS.

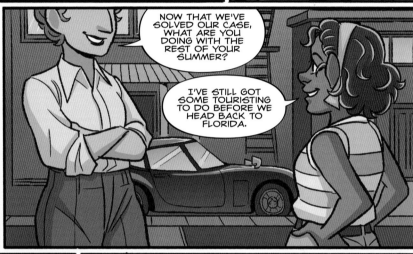

NOW THAT WE'VE SOLVED OUR CASE, WHAT ARE YOU DOING WITH THE REST OF YOUR SUMMER?

I'VE STILL GOT SOME TOURISTING TO DO BEFORE WE HEAD BACK TO FLORIDA.

WELL. YOU'RE A GREAT DETECTIVE, GOLDIE VANCE. AND YOU'VE GOT A JOB AT THE AVERY DETECTIVE AGENCY ANY TIME YOU WANT ONE.

BUT, IN THE MEANTIME, YOU COULD KEEP UP YOUR APPRENTICESHIP VIA CORRESPONDENCE. IF YOU WANTED TO.

REALLY?

WELL, I'M GONNA NEED A GOOD SOUNDING BOARD AS I GET MY FEET UNDER ME. WHAT DO YOU SAY?

I CAN'T WAIT! I'LL WRITE YOU AS SOON AS I GET HOME!

I WOULDN'T HAVE EXPECTED ANY LESS, KID.

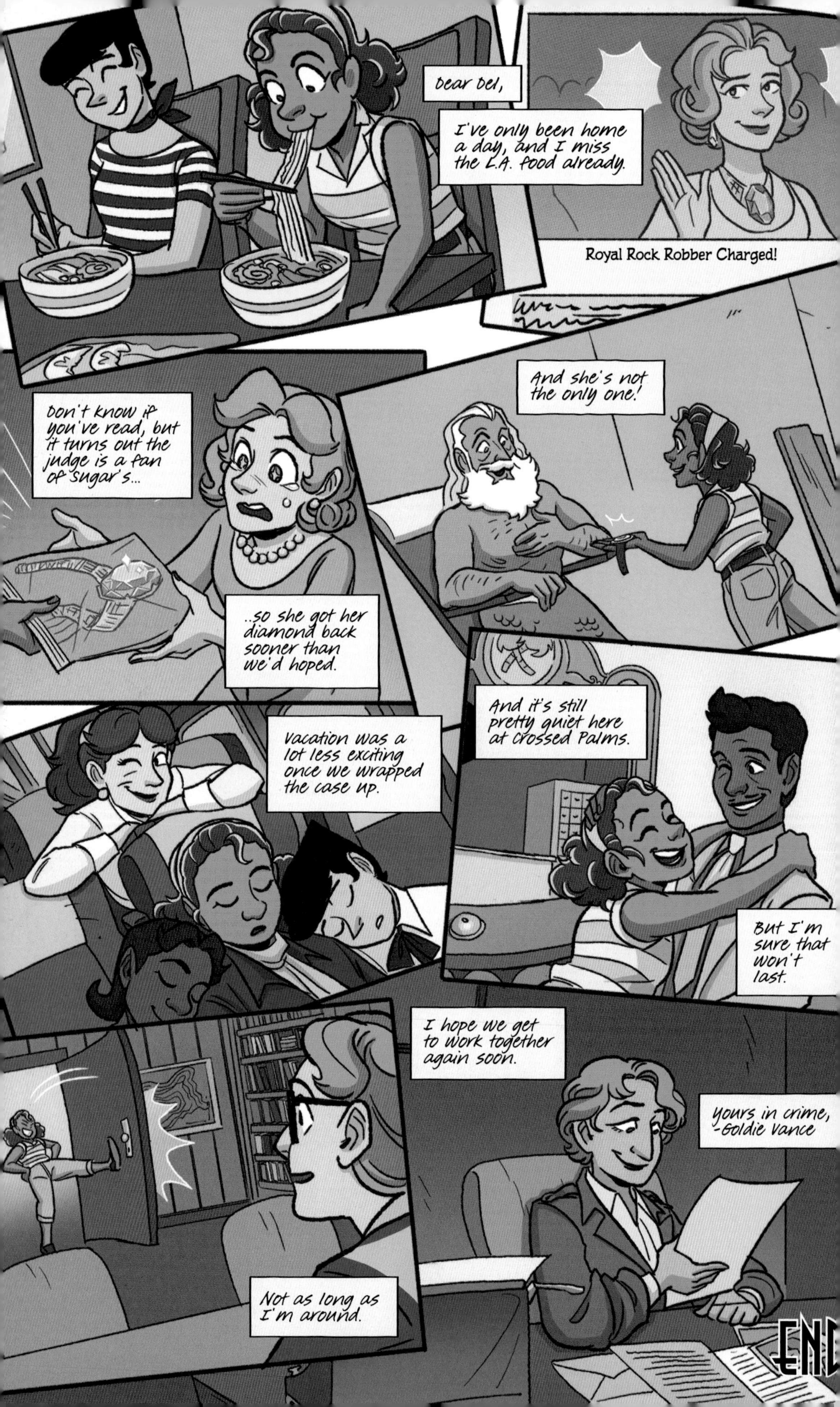
Dear Del,
I've only been home a day, and I miss the L.A. food already.
Royal Rock Robber Charged!
Don't know if you've read, but it turns out the judge is a fan of Sugar's...
..so she got her diamond back sooner than we'd hoped.
And she's not the only one!
Vacation was a lot less exciting once we wrapped the case up.
And it's still pretty quiet here at Crossed Palms.
But I'm sure that won't last.
I hope we get to work together again soon.
Yours in crime,
-Goldie Vance
Not as long as I'm around.
END

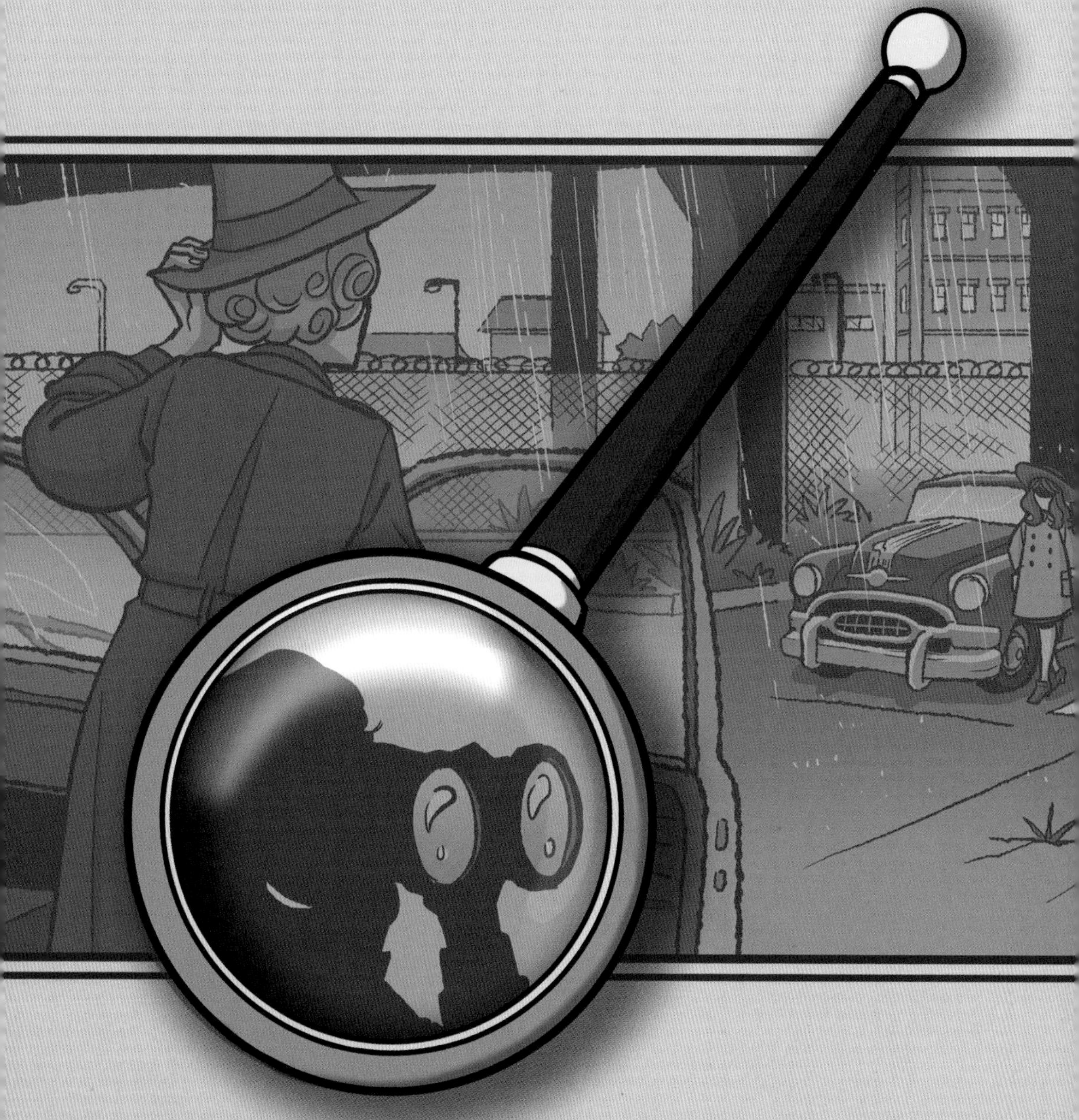

CASE STUDY

from script to page

CHAPTER SEVENTEEN: PAGE FOUR

PANEL ONE: Exterior - Goldie is sitting out on the beach, melting in the heat, and looking like a sad, melting Jell-o mold of a girl. Diane and Cheryl call to her opposite sides of the panel

    GOLDIE (THOUGHT BUBBLE): Maybe...maybe being a hotel detective isn't my destiny after all?

    GOLDIE (THOUGHT BUBBLE): At least I still have Cher and Diane to keep me company this summer...

    CHERYL (OS): GOLDIE!!

    DIANE (OS): GOLDIE!!

PANEL TWO: Full shot as both Cheryl and Diane appear from either side of the panel and shout in unison. Goldie, still sitting on the ground, whips her head back and forth, trying to look at both of them at once.

    CHERYL AND DIANE (IN UNISON): You'll never guess what just happened!

    CHERYL AND DIANE (IN UNISON): I JUST GOT A JOB IN LOS ANGELES!

PANEL THREE: Tighter on Cheryl and Diane as they see each other with shocked grins. The top of Goldie's little face is just barely in frame, still trying to track the conversation.

CHERYL: *GASP*
DIANE: You too!

PANEL FOUR: Tighter on Cheryl and Diane. Goldie is out of frame. They grab each other's arms as Cheryl nods intensely. Diane jumps up and down.

CHERYL: I got an internship at the Jet Propulsion Lab! That's NASA! Actual NASA!
DIANE: Chris got me a summer gig shadowing DARYL BELCHERA!

PANEL FIVE: Cheryl grabs Diane in a bear hug. Goldie is still out of frame.

CHERYL: I don't know who that is, but I'm so happy for you!

PANEL SIX: They are startled as Goldie wriggles up into the center of their hug from the bottom of frame.

CHERYL: Oof.
DIANE: Huh?

PANEL SEVEN: Goldie holds them both, looking comically happy tearful.

GOLDIE: I'm so happy for both of you!

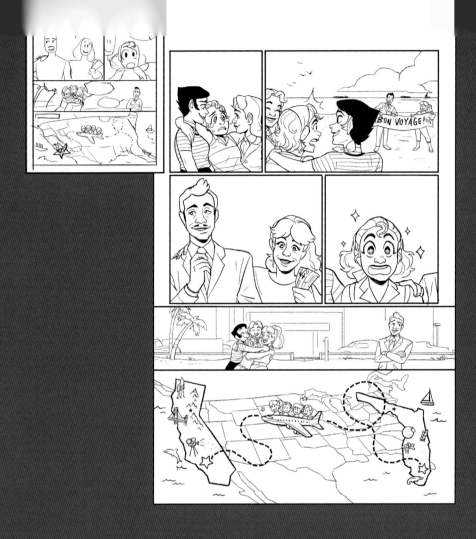

CHAPTER SEVENTEEN: PAGE FIVE

PANEL ONE: They both squeeze her tightly, chuckling, but she suddenly gets sad and tearful. Still comical.

> GOLDIE (TEARFULLY): What am I going to do?
>
> GOLDIE (TEARFULLY, JOINED): This summer is going to be so boring I may as well bury myself in this sand and sleep until it's over….
>
> SYLVIE (OS): Well, we can't have that!

PANEL TWO: Still hugged on either side by Cheryl and Diane, who are smiling knowingly over her head, Goldie looks up, surprised to see Sylvie and Art on the beach nearby with a hand drawn Bon Voyage banner.

> ART: I guess we'll just have to send you to Los Angeles with them!
>
> SYLVIE: Surprise!
>
> GOLDIE: What? But...how?

PANEL THREE: On Sylvie and Art, smiling indulgently at Goldie, and holding out a set of plane tickets.

> ART: It turns out your old friend Sugar Maple has really taken Hollywood by storm.
>
> SYLVIE: She's practically running the place, and these days she's telling some producers what to do on a new beach musical.

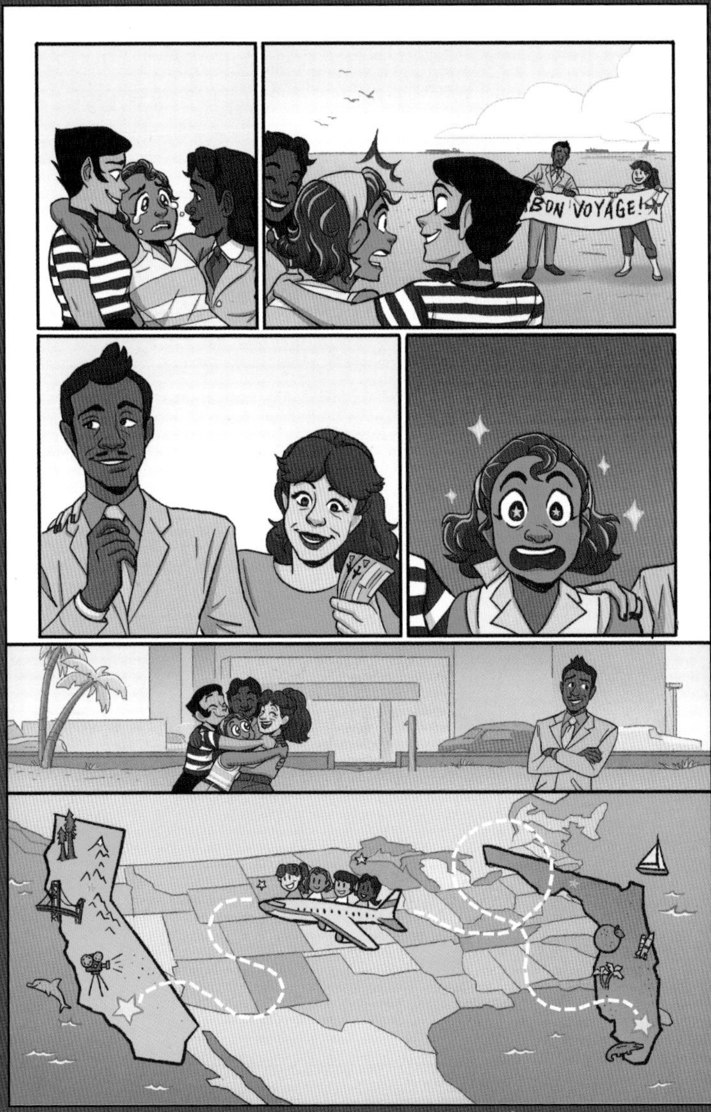
BON VOYAGE!

PANEL FOUR: On Goldie, still in Cheryl and Diane's arms, eyes wide.

ART: She heard about the movie they shot at the Mermaid Club, so she's flying your mother out as a consultant.

SYLVIE: And you know I won't be leaving my favorite mer-baby behind!

PANEL FIVE: Sylvie gathers all the girls up in her arms, and Art pretends to pout in the background in good-natured Dad-fashion.

SYLVIE: WE'RE ALL GOING TO LOS ANGELES!

ART: Well, I'm not. I've gotta stay here and run this hotel. And I'm the one who's always stuck in a three piece suit...but does Art get a vacation? No...

PANEL SIX: Adorable smiling little plane illustration following the dotted line from Florida to California, with smiling heads of Diane, Cheryl, Goldie, and Sylvie flying to LA!

CAPTION

AND SO...

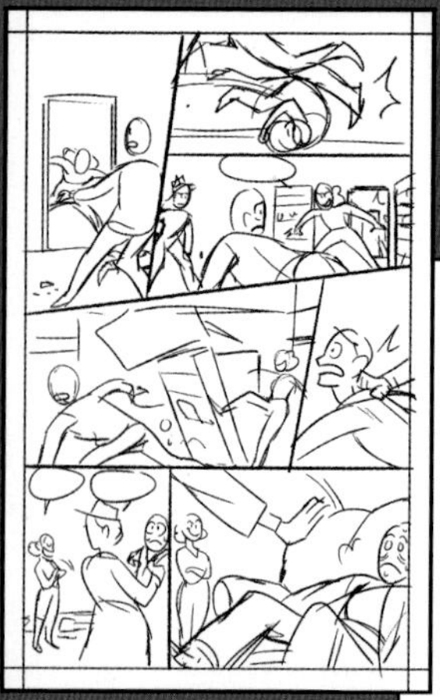

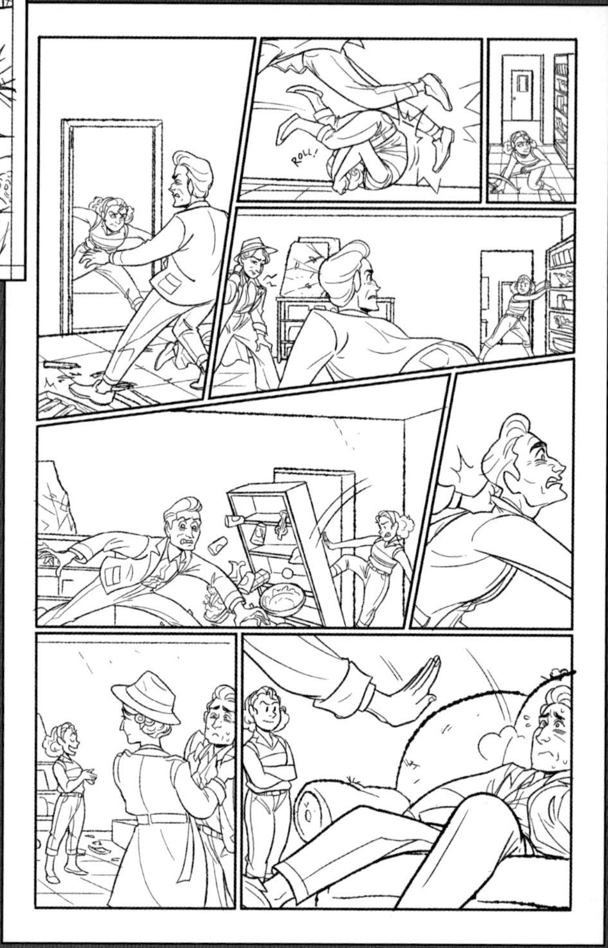
ROLL!

CHAPTER EIGHTEEN: PAGE THREE

PANEL ONE: As Del crashes to the ground, the fence makes for the open door, but Goldie is diving through it, arms out for a tackle.

GOLDIE: Hold it, mister!

PANEL TWO: Goldie does a barrel roll, taking the fence's legs out from under him.

SFX (GOLDIE): roll!

FENCE : OOF!

PANEL THREE: Goldie hops up as the fence tries to scramble toward the back door of the room. Del gets to her feet, bits of chair falling off her back as she rises.

GOLDIE: Sorry to invite myself in!

PANEL FOUR: Goldie kicks a shelf of stolen items over, blocking the fence's exit to the back of the room, he tries to change direction fast to make for the front door again.

GOLDIE: But the scouts are really serious about making our cookie quotas these days...

PANEL FIVE: Del catches him by the collar as he tries to sprint past her.

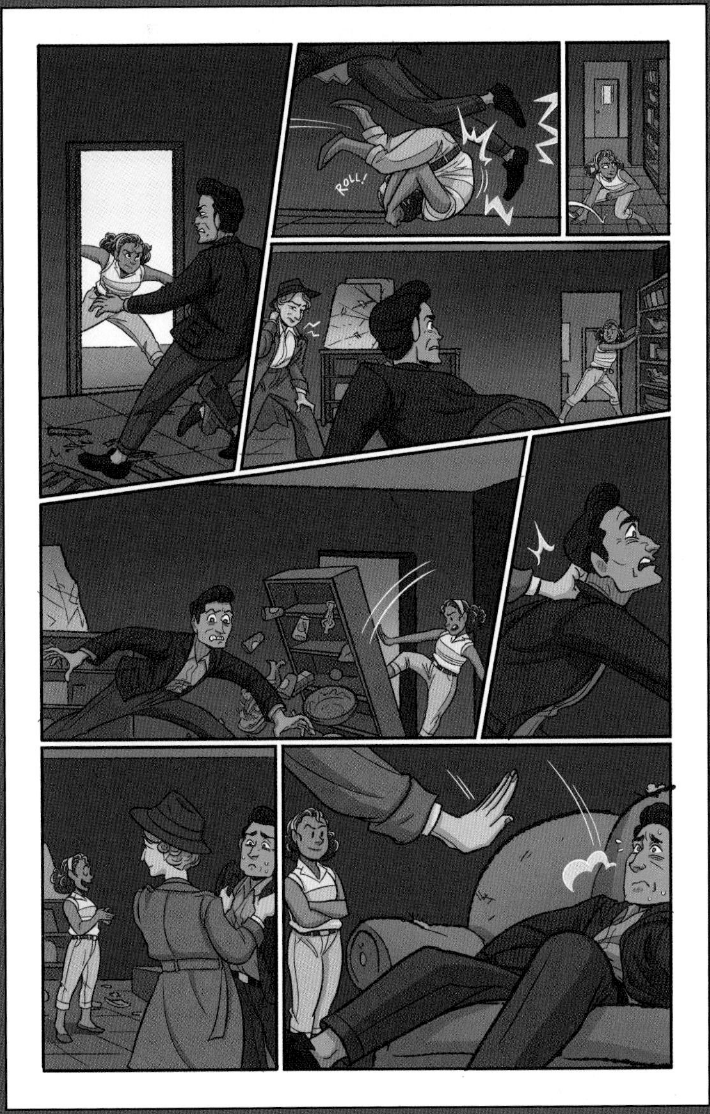
ROLL!

PANEL SIX: The fence squirms, and Del grins appreciatively at the destruction in the room. Goldie dusts off her hands, looking proud.

GOLDIE: How's that for tenacious?

DEL (GOOD NATURED): Don't look so smug, kid, the shelf did all the work.

PANEL SEVEN: Goldie chuckles and Del roughly shoves the man down onto the couch.

DEL: Look, Andy. I know you're scared, but if you don't give me some answers, I'm gonna let my little assistant here knock over a couple more shelves.

CHAPTER EIGHTEEN: PAGE FOUR

PANEL ONE: Del shows him a photo of one of the missing items.
> DEL: What do you know about this vase? I know for a fact you fenced it. Saw it leave your store.

PANEL TWO: Andy doesn't look directly at the photo, but side eyes it, hesitating.
> FENCE: I don't know what you're talking about, Avery.

PANEL THREE: Del gives Goldie a nod, and she gleefully reaches for another shelf of stolen goods.

PANEL FOUR: Andy holds his hands up placatingly, and Goldie stops, looking mildly disappointed.
> ANDY: Call her off! Look--if I did sell anything like that, it was before it was stolen. A piece like that's too hot for me. Big ticket items like that, I'm strictly above board! Whoever you're looking for stole it from the guy I'd already sold it to.

STEVENSON · ELLIS · WATTERS · ALLEN
LUMBERJANES
BEWARE THE KITTEN HOLY
NEW YORK TIMES BESTSELLING SERIES

Allison + Treiman + Cogar
GIANT DAYS
VOLUME ONE

From a writer of Disney's Moana
RIBON · FISH · PEER
SLAM!
VOLUME ONE

Hope Larson · Brittney Williams · Sarah Stern
GOLDIE VANCE
"Scoot over Nancy Drew..." —Los Angeles Times
Volume One

JAMES TYNION IV · RIAN SYGH · WALTER BAIAMONTE
THE BACKSTAGERS

TYSON HESSE'S
DIESEL
IGNITION

Noelle Stevenson, Shannon Watters,
Grace Ellis, Brooklyn Allen, and Others
Volume 1: Beware the Kitten Holy
ISBN: 978-1-60886-687-8 | $14.99 US
Volume 2: Friendship to the Max
ISBN: 978-1-60886-737-0 | $14.99 US
Volume 3: A Terrible Plan
ISBN: 978-1-60886-803-2 | $14.99 US
Volume 4: Out of Time
ISBN: 978-1-60886-860-5 | $14.99 US
Volume 5: Band Together
ISBN: 978-1-60886-919-0 | $14.99 US

Giant Days
John Allison, Lissa Treiman, Max Sarin
Volume 1
ISBN: 978-1-60886-789-9 | $9.99 US
Volume 2
ISBN: 978-1-60886-804-9 | $14.99 US
Volume 3
ISBN: 978-1-60886-851-3 | $14.99 US

Jonesy
Sam Humphries, Caitlin Rose Boyle
Volume 1
ISBN: 978-1-60886-883-4 | $9.99 US
Volume 2
ISBN: 978-1-60886-999-2 | $14.99 US

Slam!
Pamela Ribon, Veronica Fish,
Brittany Peer
Volume 1
ISBN: 978-1-68415-004-5 | $14.99 US

Goldie Vance
Hope Larson, Brittney Williams
Volume 1
ISBN: 978-1-60886-898-8 | $9.99 US
Volume 2
ISBN: 978-1-60886-974-9 | $14.99 US

The Backstagers
James Tynion IV, Rian Sygh
Volume 1
ISBN: 978-1-60886-993-0 | $14.99 US

Tyson Hesse's Diesel: Ignition
Tyson Hesse
ISBN: 978-1-60886-907-7 | $14.99 US

Coady & The Creepies
Liz Prince, Amanda Kirk,
Hannah Fisher
ISBN: 978-1-68415-029-8 | $14.99 US

BOOM! BOX™

AVAILABLE AT YOUR LOCAL COMICS SHOP AND BOOKSTORE

To find a comics shop in your area, visit www.comicshoplocator.com

WWW.**BOOM-STUDIOS**.COM

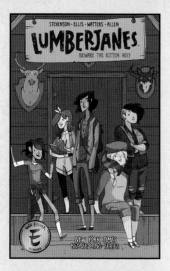

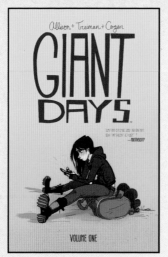

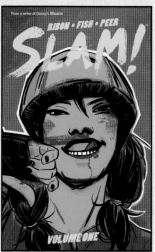

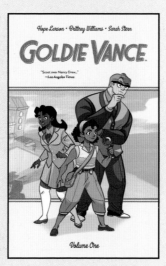

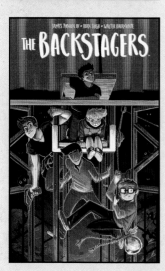

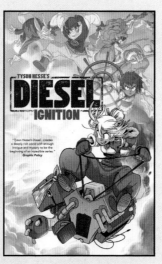

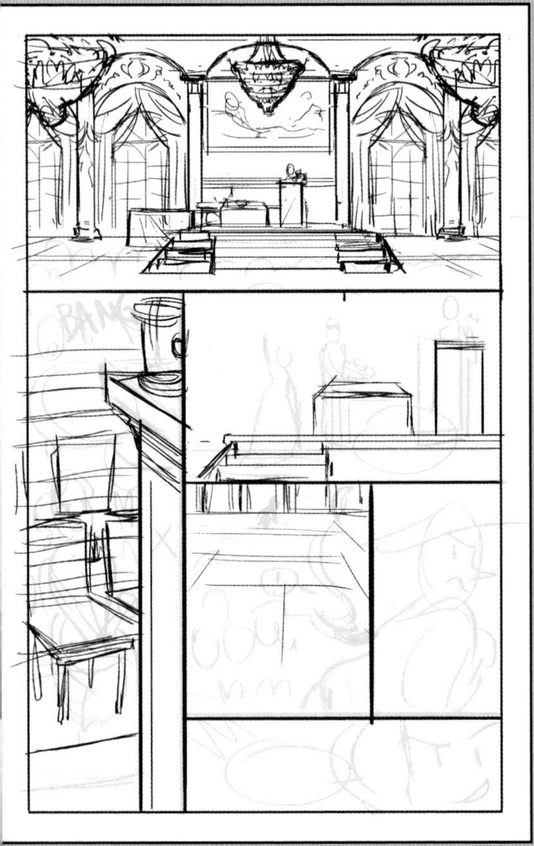
BANG

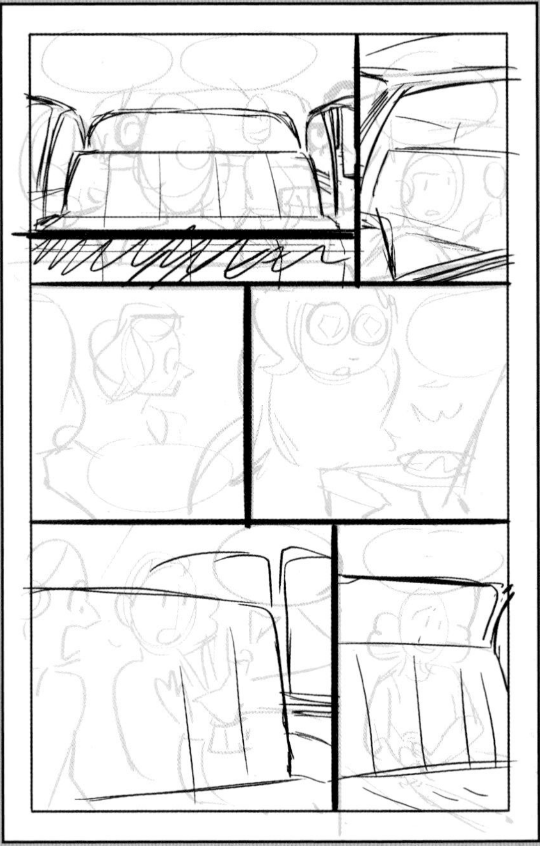

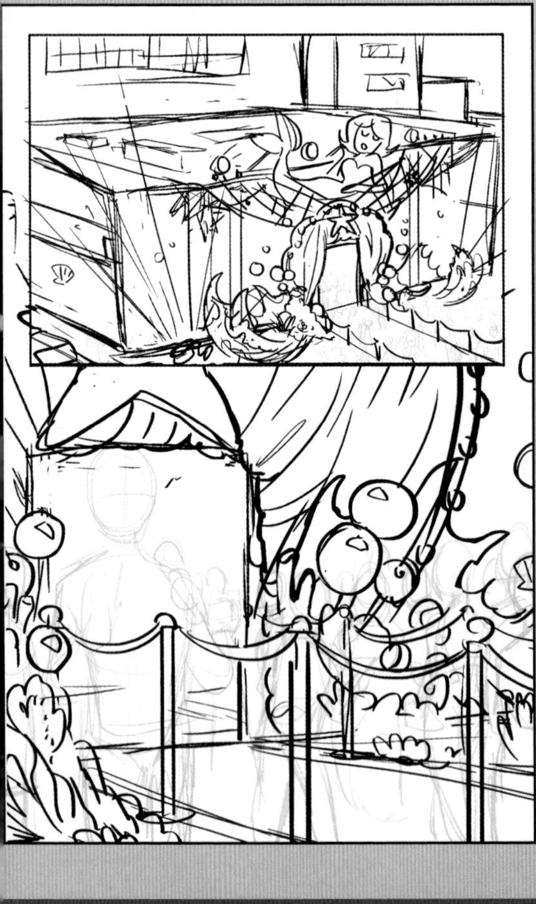

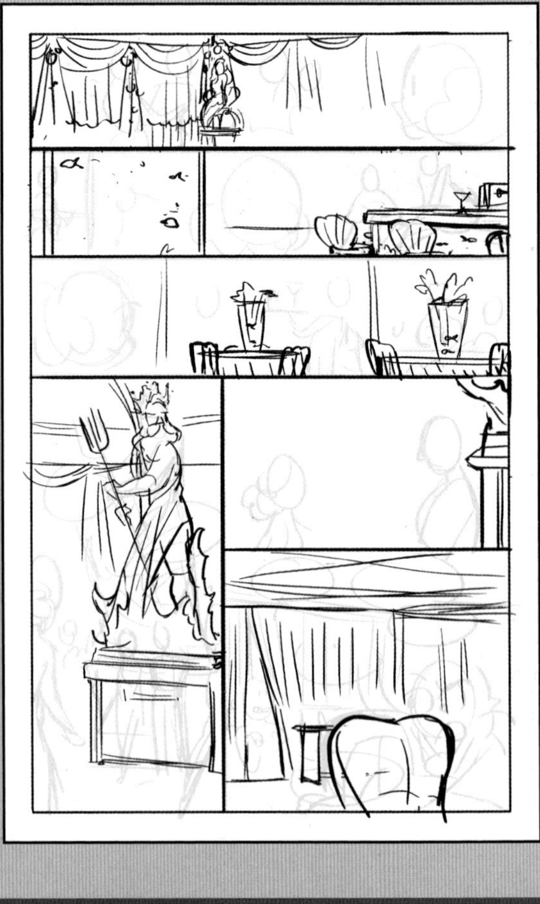

CHAPTER TWENTY PENCILS BY **MOLLIE ROSE**

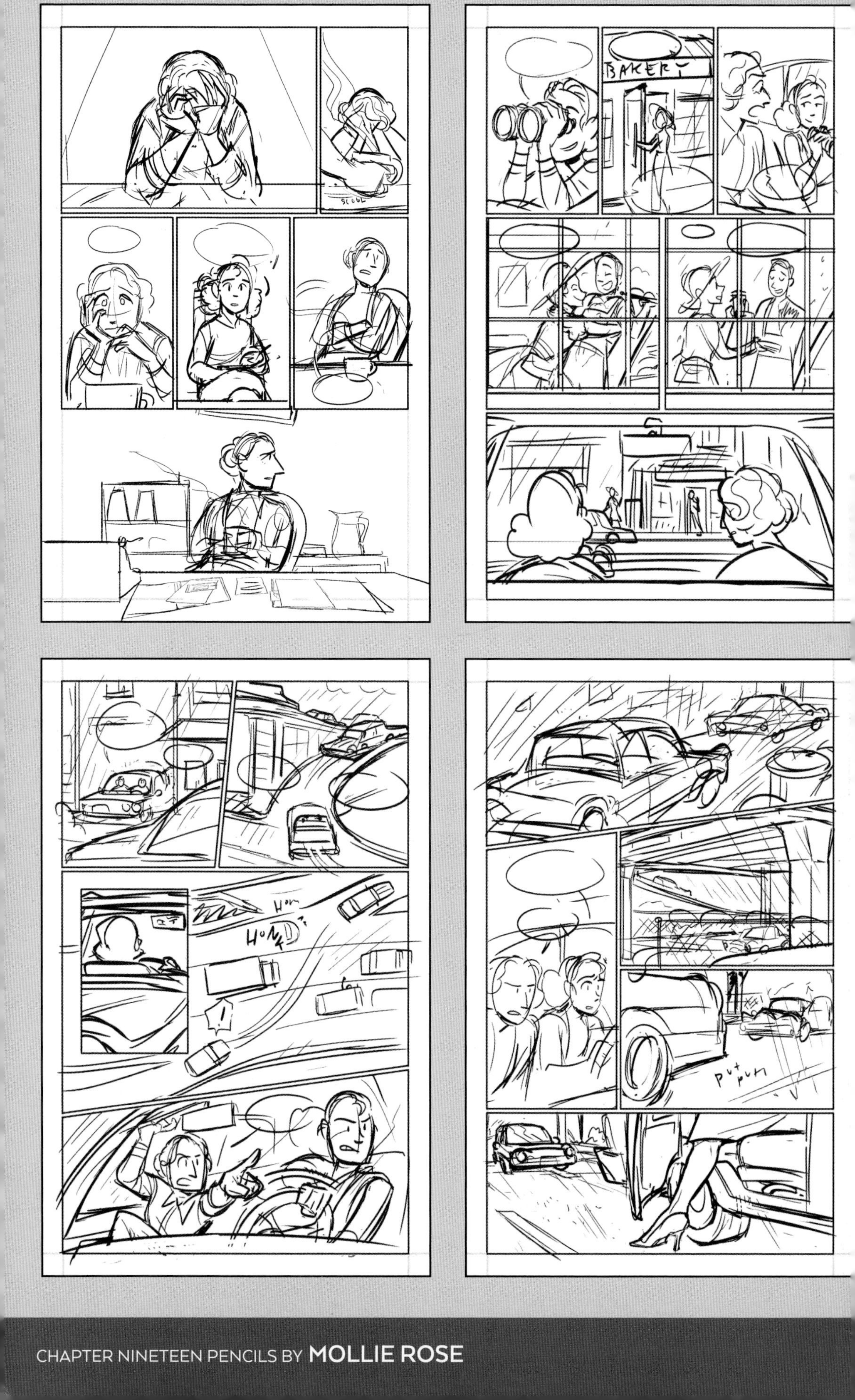
BAKERY
HONK
put put

CHAPTER NINETEEN PENCILS BY **MOLLIE ROSE**

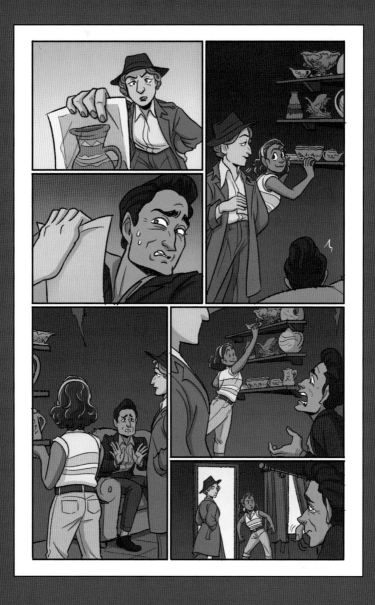

PANEL FIVE: Del gives him a suspicious side-eye and he quails. Goldie starts to reach for the shelf again.

    ANDY: No, no, I swear I don't know anything else about it. I promise, having you sniffin' around my shop is bad for business. And I don't need your new sidekick wreckin' up my place.

    DEL: Fine. But if you hear anything, you get in touch with me. Otherwise, me and the kid might set up shop at your store.

PANEL SIX: Andy wipes his nose poutily, Del heads for the front door, and Goldie turns to give him an intimidating flex.